GW00738743

# Sunny Spells & Scattered Showers

ELLIE PHILPOTT

# DEDICATION

This one's for Brian.
I'd never have got this far without him.

# DISCLAIMER

This is a work of fiction. The characters and dialogues are products of the author's imagination and are not to be construed as real. Any resemblance to actual persons, living or dead, is entirely coincidental.

# 1

# NOAH TAKES HIS EYE OFF THE BALL

### Noah's Diary:
*Saturday 15 November*

**Quote of the day:** *"There never was a cloud, that did not have sunshine coming after." Author unknown (quote courtesy of Isaac).*

*Okay, so you get the award for super sleuth - you've spotted it. No diary entries from me for quite a while. In fact, no diary entries for 3 months, 15 days, 5 hours. Well, give or take an hour or so. So much for my writerly ambitions. But, inspired by Isaac's encouraging quote he once told me, I am taking up my pen and the tattered shreds of my once promising life. Okay, I can't be bothered to write all the painful details and I'm in a rush, so you'll have to make do with this summary:*

***2 lifetimes ago:*** *Got my A-Level results. Didn't get the grades for uni. 'Really?' I query. 'Me a straight A-grade prediction?' Huge rigmarole of regrade and 'Oh yes, young master Noah Foster, we made an error and actually you did get an A for English.' 'Oh great,' quoth me, 'Now I can go to university'. 'Alas,' came the reply, 'that's not possible,' (throat clearing and embarrassed coughing here), 'We took so long to sort out your regrade, you're now too late to apply this year. We're sure you'll get the university of your choice next year, with your (now) excellent grades blah, blah, blah...' (stunned silence from master Foster).*

*2 months ago: Séamus, Luke, Steve aka my best mates went off to Vet college/Brighton Uni/LSE. Good for them I say. Couldn't be more proud of me old pals etc etc. Yeah, I'll be fine on my own here. I can laze around for a whole year before I have to study again (pathetically obvious false joviality).*

*2 weeks ago: Catherine and Arnaud broke the news they are leaving for Wales. I think the word they were looking for is 'defecting'. Abandoning their mates here. Great.*

*2 days ago: After hundreds of job applications (well loads anyway), I finally had an Interview and (drum roll here) got the job. Just in time - Dad announced he was withdrawing all funding and I would have to pay for my own clothes from now on, and for running costs for Catherine's car that she's just given - yes, given - to me, the one nice event in an otherwise bog of doom. So, it is with huge relief I can announce to you that I am now officially Henry VI's court jester. Couldn't have happened to a more worthy bloke I say. 'When do you start?' I hear you say. Actually, today and*

"Noah, you're late!"

Toby's voice ricocheted up the stairwell.

"Cripes," muttered the slight, curly-haired diarist. He pushed his chair away from the desk, knocking a half-full mug of tea over in the process. A muddy brown river flowed across the white Formica. Before Noah could react, the tea streamed onto his notebook, blurring, then obliterating the text he had just written.

*Oh well, who cares*, thought Noah and continued his progress towards the door, grabbing his faded denim rucksack en route. *It's not like anyone's ever going to read my diary, anyway.*

As he emerged from the passage towards the front of the house, with its huge windows overlooking the beach, Noah glanced down over the balustrade. A slim, dark-haired man wearing a thunderous expression on his face was standing at the stairwell on the floor below. Behind him lay the open plan first floor of the enormous Art Deco house. Noah trotted down the curved staircase that hugged the front of the building, deftly hooked a bunch of keys from the man's outstretched hand and walked swiftly on to the next flight of stairs leading down to the ground floor.

"Thanks Dad, saved my bacon," he threw over his shoulder in passing.

Toby sighed heavily and grimaced over the banister at the younger image of himself scudding across the hallway.

"Coat...!" His words chased after the boy, failing to reach him. He winced as the oak door crashed shut, rattling the metal catch.

Outside, Noah kept on running, his feet crunching on the shell path which skirted around the edge of the square building.

"Darn it, coat," he muttered, spinning round and heading back towards the white house. He hauled open the heavy door, seized a black jacket from a wooden coat hook on the far wall and sprinted out again.

Upstairs, Toby blinked as the door banged a second time.

Noah's chestnut-coloured eyes narrowed as he allowed himself a quick glance at his watch. Half an hour. He might just make it. With a following wind.

The old pale blue Citroën 2CV was parked at the end of the garden wall. As Noah approached it, a winter breeze whipped out of nowhere, rocking the car slightly. He eased the key into the lock and carefully opened the flimsy door, making sure it didn't swing back in the wind. A smile played on his lips as he slid into the driver's seat, pushing his rucksack beside him. *My own space. My own car.* The thought was still a novel one. Then, a renewed sense of urgency hit him. He slotted the key into the ignition and pumped the accelerator. The car obligingly whined into life at first go and jolted along the uneven shingle track through the marshes towards the coast road.

By the time he arrived at the castle, Noah had made up some time and he was beginning to feel a sense of anticipation.

"New day, new job, Noah my lad," he told himself, swinging the car around a hairpin bend and underneath the portcullis. A startled seagull fluttered off the roadway and landed on the grassy verge a few yards away, giving him a filthy look.

From the black wooden sentry box, the elderly gatekeeper recognised the distinctive 2CV and its eighteen-year-old driver, with his dark hair and cheeky grin. Noah screeched to a standstill beside him.

"Hi there. Remember me? I'm the new juggler," he announced jauntily.

"As it happens, I do," came the reply. "You're just in time, they're still setting up. You can park up at the top, outside the keep." He waved Noah through with a final, "Good luck, mate."

The 2CV whined up the steep hillside towards the staff car park, struggling with the gradient. Noah pumped the accelerator for the final stretch, swung into a parking bay and pulled on the handbrake. He snatched his rucksack from the passenger seat and ran up the pathway to the keep, where the medieval market was located. The sea wind was chilly, slicing across the cliff tops and tousling Noah's hair. Fortunately, no rain was forecast and a golden winter sun sparkled on the enormous flint walls of the vast castle complex.

Noah jogged past emerald green grassy banks, through the narrow, enclosed tunnel of the barbican and across the wooden gatehouse drawbridge. He emerged into the inner courtyard, skidding to a standstill in front of the great tower. Spinning around, he looked at the scene, taking in the blur of movement and colour. Jaunty stalls and people in medieval costume spilled over the clipped grass lawns which wrapped around the square tower. Noah headed to the right, almost colliding with a man in full armour carrying a wicked-looking mace. He sidestepped quickly and dived into a small open doorway in the outer wall of the courtyard.

Maggie, the events manager, was sitting at a desk in the poky little office, shuffling through pieces of paper. She looked up, a tense expression on her face.

"It's Noah, the juggler," he prompted, sensing her hesitation.

"Oh yes, sorry. There are so many new people at this time of year. It's always a bit chaotic for the first weekend market. We'll get into the swing of it by the time the school holidays start properly." Maggie ran her hand distractedly through her short greying hair. She spoke quickly in clipped tones.

"If you go next door, there's a selection of costumes on a rack. Have a look through and find one that fits you. The weather forecast is good for today, so you'll be outside. I'd like you to start off next to the fire eater so that he can show you the ropes. His name is Clive. And you'll need to be quick. We'll be opening in fifteen minutes." She looked back down at her papers. Noah was dismissed.

He left the room and cautiously opened a heavy black wooden door further along the castle wall. Daylight filtered feebly through narrow slits high up in the wall. In the gloom, Noah could make out two long metal racks

5

containing an assortment of medieval costumes. He rummaged through them, releasing a sharp odour of mothballs laced with stale sweat. Noah wrinkled his nose and continued along one rail, dismissing some bits and pieces of armour, a series of ladies' gowns and a long red cloak, edged in white fur.

Then, he hit upon a turquoise and red harlequin tunic and matching leggings. He pulled them off the rack and measured them against his body. The outfit seemed more or less his size. Noah edged behind the rack, took his jeans off and pulled on the leggings. Then he slipped off his jumper and eased the tunic over his head. It was a perfect fit. Around the neck was a star-shaped frill and on the bottom of tunic, little silver bells were attached to each of the pointed edges. On the same hanger was a turquoise and red hat featuring two moon-shaped horns with a matching bell on each end. Noah tried it on. It was a bit tight over his mop of curly hair, but he decided it would do. As he was smoothing down the tunic, he spotted a pair of huge pointed turquoise boots on the floor underneath the rack.

He chuckled, kicked his trainers off and pulled them onto his feet. They were slightly too narrow at the ends, but with a bit of effort, he managed to force his feet into them. Spotting a long mirror on the opposite wall of the room, Noah pushed past the clothes rack and appraised the juggler standing in front of him. He tugged the hat down a little further, winked at the figure in front of him and gave a satisfied smile.

Leaving his normal clothes in an untidy heap in the corner, Noah picked up his rucksack and walked out into the courtyard, suddenly feeling foolish. He stumbled, almost tripping over the pointed boots. It took a certain amount of skill to walk in them. Noah adopted a slightly shuffling gait, which seemed to help. Inside the courtyard walls, the traders were now putting the finishing touches to their market stalls. The Christmas Fayre was coming to life. In front of an old cannon, a hog roast on a spit was slowly rotating, sending a mouth-watering smell wafting around the courtyard. Noah sniffed appreciatively, then looked around for the fire eater, but couldn't see him. He hobbled over to a stall selling fudge, where a freckle-faced woman in a long purple dress and a white headscarf was standing behind the counter. Noah made a mental note to visit the stall after he'd finished his shift.

"Hi, I'm Noah. Do you know where Clive the fire eater is?"

She smiled, green eyes crinkling at the corners. "I'm Shona. Is this your first time here?"

Noah nodded.

"Clive's usually round the other side of the tower, by the trebuchet."

"The what?" Noah's knowledge of ancient siege machinery was non-existent.

"The big wooden sling - you can't miss it."

"Cheers Shona," replied Noah, and shuffled along the path around the edge of the outer wall, past a pottery stall and a plump woman in a plain brown dress who was hand-spinning a mottled brown and white coloured fleece.

"Good luck!" Shona called after him.

He spotted a bare-chested man wearing a light brown leather jerkin further along the path, in front of a large wooden catapult. He was holding a couple of long metal rods with dirty rags wrapped around their ends.

"Clive?"

"That's me."

"I'm Noah. I was told to do my juggling next to you."

"That's right. They like to keep the entertainers near the people queuing to visit the tower. What happened to the last lad?"

Noah shrugged his shoulders. He had no idea.

"It's usually the kids that get to them. Don't last long, you jugglers. No staying power."

Noah ignored the jibe. "What's so bad about the kids?"

"You'll find out," came the reply.

Clive seemed like a man of few (not necessarily positive) words.

The burly fire eater sauntered over to a pile of bits and pieces and pulled out a black jerry can. He unscrewed the lid and sloshed a clear liquid onto the dirty rags at the end of his fire sticks. Noah watched, fascinated. As Clive bent to replace the cap, a gull swooped down at Noah's head, flapping in his face. Clive looked over and grumbled, "Pain in the arse those gulls are. There's signs everywhere not to feed them and what do the punters do?"

"Feed them?" supplied Noah.

Clive had turned away from the jerry can, not noticing the lid was half off. Noah was just about to point it out, when he was distracted by a seagull pooping down his costume. He rummaged around in his rucksack for a tissue to wipe it off.

"Ten minutes to opening, ten minutes to opening," a muffled voice announced over the PA system.

Noah withdrew his squashy seed-filled juggling balls out of the rucksack and began to warm up. He hadn't factored in the costume when he'd been rehearsing at home. The long sleeves got in the way and he kept dropping the juggling balls. Then the hat slipped over his eye. He pushed it back in annoyance.

Piped medieval music began to play from the PA system.

Clive cleared his throat noisily and took a large swig of water from a bottle next to him. He glanced over at Noah. "Bit of a rookie, aren't you?"

"Yeah, I need to earn my keep until I can get to university next year. My dad's pulled the plug on finances. I've been trying to get a job for ages, then this came up."

Clive looked at Noah with a slight sneer on his face. "Just keep your distance from me. It's surprising how far the flames travel."

Noah moved away, nearly tripping over his pointed shoes again. A cold gust flung itself at him, setting the bells on his hat ringing. He shivered. The jester costume was made of thin material. He'd have to keep moving if he wanted to stay warm.

Visitors were now trickling through the main gate and fanning out around the stalls. A queue started to form at the entrance door to the great hall. Inside, costumed actors performed a series of cameos from the past history of the castle. They were good. Noah had watched them rehearsing when he'd visited the previous week for his interview.

Noah set to, warming up slowly, getting used to the confines of his costume. He was annoyed, as he still kept dropping balls more often than he'd have liked. A young boy in the queue commented loudly, "That juggler's crap, he keeps dropping his balls."

"Language Martin," came from his father, who didn't dispute Noah's lousy juggling.

Noah's face reddened and he tried to concentrate harder. Soon he felt more confident and he popped in a few high balls to show young Martin what was what. The boy stuck his tongue out and shuffled behind his father into the castle.

An hour later, Noah's arms were sore and he'd encountered a number of other annoying children. One wiry, fair-haired little boy decided it would be funny to try and put Noah off, by jumping at him and waving his arms just as Noah was trying high tricks. His parents and younger sister sniggered, clearly thinking the boy's actions were hilarious. Noah was tempted to offer him the juggling balls and ask if he could do any better, but just then his new boss, Maggie, walked past. Noah immediately focused, Zen-like, on his task and hoped Maggie hadn't noticed the filthy look he had flung at the boy. He attempted a three ball flash with pirouette and it came off nicely.

"Good work Noah," commented Maggie loudly, and then more softly as she approached him, "Cheerful face please, you're here to entertain, not judge the kids." She moved on, her heels rapping on the tarmac path.

Noah had been so engrossed in his juggling, he'd not paid much attention to Clive's act. He paused for a breather and looked over. The fire eater was impressive all right. He knew how to please the crowds, puffing out his well-muscled bare chest and engaging in banter. Actually, it seemed to Noah that most of Clive's act was talk and posturing. There wasn't a huge amount of fire eating going on. He guessed you could only eat so much fire in one day. Clive was right, the fire was pretty spectacular when he breathed it out. That must be why there was a cordon well in front of him - to stop the audience from getting too close.

Noah became conscious of the fact that he'd been standing around doing nothing a bit too long and started to juggle again. His fingers were getting cramped from the cold.

Behind his back, a group of skinny girls were giggling at him. As he turned, a little boy dashed out of the queue and snatched one of Noah's juggling balls that had been lying on the ground. He started throwing it up in the air. "Look, I can do it better than that stupid juggler," he shouted in a high-pitched voice. The girls giggled all the more.

"Hey, give that back!" Noah shouted at the boy. Heads turned towards him.

"How about please?" the boy sneered, and threw the ball hard at Noah, slamming it into his cheek. Noah winced from the pain. He started to move towards the boy, then realised where he was. He gave himself a talking to. He needed to focus on the juggling and ignore the kids.

Half an hour later, a large group of people walked past, just as Noah was attempting a fancy trick. He was making up new moves now, getting into his stride. He'd started to draw a small crowd, so he made the most of it, twisting his head to jingle the bells on his hat while he was juggling. As it happened, it was pride and not lack of skill that was his undoing.

Looking back, Noah decided it was unfair to penalise him for what was quite clearly an unfortunate sequence of events. It started innocently enough. He'd begun a series of high throws, tossing each ball further up, almost making himself dizzy as he tracked them against the backdrop of the castle walls. The audience pressed in, and Noah was unaware that he'd unconsciously begun to back away from them, towards the pile of belongings behind Clive.

One last step saw him trip over the black jerry can of paraffin and land heavily on the cobbles. A stream of paraffin trickled out of the mouth of the can downhill towards Clive, who was in the middle of juggling with his fire sticks. Noah's cry of pain put Clive off his stride and he dropped a burning stick into the spilled paraffin. A line of flame shot along the paraffin stream towards Noah, licking up the sleeve of his costume. Noah bashed at the burning garment just as the jerry can caught alight with a whoosh. Without thinking, he raced towards the crowd, away from the fire. Terrified children fled from the flames, screaming as they ran.

Noah flung himself onto the grass, rolling over to extinguish his burning clothes. He lay panting, as people ran past him, some running towards the fire to help put it out, others fleeing. Sitting up, he examined his arm. It hurt, but fortunately he'd managed to put the flames out before they'd done him any real damage. Behind him, he could hear the hiss of escaping foam as the castle safety team tackled the blaze.

He turned to look. Clive had a face like thunder, but nobody seemed injured, thank goodness. Noah put his head in his hands. He was pretty sure his juggling days had just come to an abrupt end.

Maggie was swift to act. As soon as the visitors had been reassured and she'd ascertained that no-one had been hurt, she didn't hesitate to pronounce judgment. Clive was out of a job - no second chance for a fire eater who didn't secure jerry cans of paraffin properly. Noah was out too. As well as the fire incident, there had been one or two comments about his attitude towards the children.

"I didn't say anything to them," Noah protested.

"No, but according to several parents, you did stop and try to stare the kids out and hand gestures are definitely not acceptable. Pack up your things and go please."

*Oh well*, Noah reasoned, *at least she gave me twenty quid for the morning's work.* Then he remembered he'd borrowed fifteen pounds from Toby for petrol money. *I need another job soon or I won't be able to afford the car*, Noah thought grimly.

## 2

## WHAT WE LEAVE BEHIND

*Noah's Diary:*
*Wednesday 30 November*
**Quote of the day:** *"It is not death that man should fear, but he should fear never beginning to live." Marcus Aurelius.*

*Nice cheery quote from Catherine today. So, we meet again dear reader. Sorry I've been neglecting you again. I've been putting all my energy and cunning into trying to find another job. And, ta-da, I now have two interviews lined up. One for a 'picker and packer' (wish I could say in a chocolate factory, but boring old clothes company I'm afraid) and another for a supermarket shelf stacker. Not so keen on this as it's night work. On the other hand, good experience for me as a writer to enter nether regions of the nocturnal world. After all, Charles Dickens did a lot of strolling around London at night and look what he came up with. Just about to go for a last ride with Catherine before she and Arnaud head off so, once more into the breeches... (nearly fell off my chair laughing at my own wit). More later.*

In the kitchen, the Radio 4 weather forecaster was broadcasting to an empty room: *And now the outlook for London and the South East. A largely sunny day, with the occasional patch of cloud towards late afternoon. Top temperatures will be around 11 degrees, warm for this time of year...*

Three storeys up on the flat roof of the enormous Art Deco house, Noah hung upside down, his knees hooked over a thick rope line attached to two wooden struts. He shifted his balance slightly and swung round to survey the beach in front of his home. The water had receded, leaving a series of shallow pools scattered across the mud flats; puddles of liquid amber reflecting the early morning sunshine. Beyond the distant grey-green stripe of sea, wisps of cloud endlessly formed and reformed in the pale blue sky. From his inverted universe, Noah imagined what it would be like if he could swim in the sky; soft strokes, pulling him through the clouds, mist droplets spattering his face as he floated among patches of swirling vapour.

After a few moments, he twisted his head and contemplated the marshes that wrapped around the back of the house. Tufts of thick green grass, tall elegant rushes and prickly clumps of gorse bushes stabbed at the sky. His gaze roamed across the bleak winter landscape and came to focus on a woman hanging from a brown and white horse - the same way up - or rather down - as he was.

"Huh?" muttered Noah, and flicked his legs off the rope line, flopping onto the roof of the house. A sudden dizziness made him blink. When he looked out at the marshes again, over the top of the low crenelated walls bordering the edges of the roof, the horse was standing sniffing at a body lying on the ground. Noah cupped his hands round his mouth and shouted, "Catherine - are you okay?"

She was too far away to hear Noah's voice, but even as he called out, the woman sat up sluggishly and looked around her. She climbed stiffly to her feet and tried to

14

reach for the horse's reins. The tall skewbald stepped back, startled at the sudden movement, dragging the reins out of reach. The two engaged in a jerky dance for a while, the horse retreating as Catherine stepped forwards, pulling away from her grasp, before finally giving in, dropping its head and allowing itself to be caught. Noah scanned the landscape and spotted a second horse standing a few metres away near a gorse bush, delicately nibbling at a clump of grass. The stocky, white Camargue horse was preoccupied with eating and barely moved when the woman took hold of its trailing lead rope.

Noah stood with his arms hooked over the rope line, his body gently swaying. He gazed across the sweeping marshland, which filled the view as far as his eye could see. As a young child, he used to stand on this roof, feeling like a king in a great castle, lord of all he surveyed. A seagull landed clumsily beside him, disturbing his thoughts with its chattering. It eyeballed Noah for a while, then flapped off, wheeling around the house before heading out beyond the shoreline. Noah snapped himself out of his reverie. Catherine had remounted and was riding across the marshes on the skewbald horse, one hand on the reins, the other holding the leading rope of the white horse, which followed behind her. She would be at the house soon.

He walked smartly across the roof, towards the rusting flight of metal steps that led down to the third storey of the house. At the foot of the steps, he picked his way through a jumble of terracotta pots that filled a tiny garden in front of the huge glazed windows. Most of them contained ornamental grasses, leaves whispering to Noah as the sea breeze played with them. Opening a glass-panelled door, he stepped into the art studios that

15

spanned the third floor of the house. A series of white sheets, hung from pieces of string tied across the ceiling, separated the space into rough cubicles. Noah could hear a scraping sound from the far end of the room.

"Hi Sarah!" he called out in passing, as he swished past a sheet and over to the staircase.

"Noah, hi," Sarah called back. She was always the first in. Most of the other people who rented the studios were sluggish in the mornings, barely appearing before ten or so.

"Gotta dash. Catherine's nearly here."

"Have a nice ride!" Sarah called out to his retreating back.

Noah slunk down the stairs, taking in the view from the front of the house. A miniature container ship was slowly making its way across the horizon, the distance masking its vast bulk.

Noah always felt like he was travelling down the layers of an enormous square wedding cake when he came from the roof to the ground floor of the house. Each of the four tiers was successively larger as you descended. A wedding cake with no frills though, he decided. The smooth, white painted walls of the house were forbiddingly plain and square, embellished only by the curving semi-circular walls at the front, with their huge windows, designed to maximise the sea views.

He left the staircase at the second floor, and ran down a corridor to his bedroom, on the right of the passageway. His eyes darted round the room, which was filled with disorderly piles of clothes, pieces of driftwood and stacks of books. He spotted a faded black riding hat lying discarded in a corner and swooped on it, grabbing the chin strap. Noah squashed the hat down over his hair, and ran back out of the room, towards the front staircase again.

The next floor down was the main hub of the house. The vast, open plan space housed a kitchen to one side, with lime washed wooden units running along the edge of the wall. Black and white chequered tiles formed the flooring, delineating the space. In the middle of the kitchen area stood an enormous oak table, around which were randomly scattered chairs and stools made from driftwood.

On the other side of the room, in the far right-hand wall, a huge fireplace had been built out into the space with a semi-circular pit made of slate. An old brown leather armchair and matching sofa faced the fireplace. To one side was a wicker dog basket with a moth-eaten red tartan blanket escaping over the edge. A half-gnawed bone lay abandoned a few feet away. In the basket, a black dog, peppered with grey, lifted its head and thumped its tail.

"Are you coming too?" Noah asked Oscar.

Oscar eased himself up, stepped delicately over the edge of the basket and stretched. He shook himself and then trotted over to Noah, eyes shining, ears pricked at the prospect of a walk.

Outside, Catherine was just approaching the enormous garden that stretched out from the back of the property. It was hidden from view by the vast white wall that surrounded it, protecting the plants inside from the vicious winds that whipped across the marshes in winter. Only a green-painted wooden door punctuated the long stretch of white, that blended into the house at the far end. The horses' feet crunched on the path of tiny white shells.

A sudden movement from the marshland to her left caught Catherine's eye and she spotted a female sparrowhawk, with its distinctive brown striped chest, plunging out of the sky. A startled thrush flapped out of the gorse bush where it had been perching. Expertly, the sparrowhawk speared the thrush with its talons and swooped over Catherine's head towards the beach, its prey hanging from its claws, just as two figures emerged from the front of the building.

She squeezed her heels on the skewbald's flanks, and it quickened its pace. The horse behind moved forward, sniffing at Catherine's hand as they approached Noah. The two people intersected at the edge of the shingle, where the patchy scrub had been worn down into a long, sinuous track that ran parallel with the beach.

"Hi Catherine, are you okay?"

She flicked a wisp of mouse-coloured hair out of her face and grimaced. "You saw me fall? I'm fine thanks Noah, just a few bruises. My own stupid fault. I didn't check Kimba's girth properly and his saddle slipped. What an idiot."

Oscar barked a welcome at Catherine, and walked up to Kimba. The horse lowered its head and gently touched noses with the little mongrel. They were old friends.

Noah walked around the skewbald and took the leading rein from Catherine.

"You can ride Baloo today," she told him.

Noah grinned. He loved the white Camargue horse, with its dark grey nose and flowing cream mane.

He knotted the lead rope around Baloo's neck, pulled the stirrups down to the bottom of the leathers, and checked the girth, smiling cheekily at Catherine. "Don't want the same thing happening to me."

Then he swung himself neatly into the saddle, gently pulling Baloo's head up and nudging him into a walk. Kimba tracked alongside Baloo, not needing any encouragement from Catherine. Behind them, Oscar ran in and out of the clumps of gorse at the edge of the marshland, following an unseen looping trail of fox and rabbit scents.

They rode in companionable silence for a while. The wind was light and a pale November sun bathed the landscape. The path wound along the bottom edge of the marshes, just touching the shingle. To their right, the sea had exposed the wide expanse of mudflats. In her mind's eye, Catherine could see an image of Noah as a skinny-limbed young boy, digging for cockles in the exposed beach.

Noah broke the silence.

"I can't believe it's your last day here Catherine."

She sighed and glanced over at him, "Neither can I, Noah."

"But you're happy to go, aren't you? It sounds so cool, running a trekking farm in Wales. I'm dead jealous of you and Arnaud."

She smiled and wrinkled her nose. "I bet you'd love it there Noah. The Black Mountains are amazing - there's just so much space. And the horses and ponies at the farm are beautiful - not your usual dumpy trekking mounts at all. Arnaud can't wait. He's always dreamed of running something much bigger than our smallholding."

Noah gave her a sharp glance. "And you? Really Catherine, tell me the truth."

She paused for an instant. "Okay Noah, but please don't say anything to Arnaud."

"Promise."

19

"If it wasn't for him, I wouldn't be going. I feel ungrateful. It's such a beautiful place to live and work, but I hadn't realised how hard I would find it to leave here."

Noah thought for a moment, then said, "I can understand that. Gull Cove is a pretty special place." He sighed in turn. "We've had some cool times here eh, Catherine?"

"You can say that again."

"Did you know, it's nine years since you turned up at the white house. It feels like forever."

Catherine cast her mind back to the first day she had driven her blue 2CV along the coast track to the house. She had never expected to inherit the property from her aunt Ozzie. In fact, she hadn't even known the house, built by her great-grandfather in the 1930s, even existed. Her mother had refused all contact with her sister for years, and rarely spoke about her family. Catherine's father wasn't around to fill her in with any details either - he had died in a climbing accident before she was born.

"It was such a surprise. And then to find the house was full of tenants - you, Toby, Milly, Isaac, Oscar…"

"I bet you never thought you'd end up living with us," Noah said, grinning.

"There's no way I would have joined you if my house hadn't caught fire. I was happy living in Canterbury on my own - well I thought I was."

Noah looked at Catherine. Her fine shoulder length hair was blowing across her face in the sea breeze. A face that Noah had always loved. Gentle, with soft grey-green eyes and an expressive mouth that infallibly gave away what its owner was thinking.

"Hah, do you remember when we thought you were the enemy?" He laughed at the absurdity of the idea.

Catherine was the most non-confrontational, reasonable, naturally kind person he'd ever met.

She grinned back, her eyes twinkling. "That's understandable. You were all in shock after Ozzie's death and you thought her niece was going to throw you all out of the house. In your place, I would have been suspicious of me. Do you think Ozzie would be surprised at all that's happened since she left me the property? If only we could tell her…"

"I'm sure she would have been glad to see you married and happy," Noah pronounced. "If you hadn't been forced to live with us in the white house, you might never have met Arnaud.

Catherine smiled inwardly at the thought of her tall, gentle-natured French husband. "Not just Arnaud - all of you Noah. You all became my family - I'm closer to you guys than I ever was to my mother. As you're aware, I never really knew anything of my family. Even though they're all dead, the white house lives and breathes who they were. It's my only connection to them. I feel as if I'm leaving so much of my identity behind."

Noah felt for Catherine. His own mother had left both Noah and his father when he was just a small toddler. The other occupants of the white house had been his family too. Although it was a sadly diminished family now. He thought about the task in hand, casting his gaze towards the tiny sailors' chapel at the end of the bay.

Catherine tried to be more positive, for Noah's sake. "There is one thing Noah. I'd completely forgotten about it, until a couple of days ago when something jogged my memory. Did you know, my mother met my father when she was staying in the Black Mountains - near to where we're going I think. She told me once. I guess there will be one connection for me there."

"That's funny. Maybe it was meant to be - you and Arnaud off to Wales."

"Maybe," she was ambivalent. Catherine wasn't a great believer in fate. She changed the subject. "We agreed that today wouldn't be a sad day Noah. We've got so many amazing memories. And we're bound to have loads more."

Noah wasn't sure, but a pact was a pact.

He kicked his heels into Baloo's sides, "Come on, race you to the chapel!"

Catherine took up the challenge and both horses cantered along the track, nostrils flared, enjoying the run. Behind them, Oscar followed at a lope.

They slowed as they approached the chapel, giving the horses a breather. Baloo snorted and shied at something rustling in a gorse bush. Noah slid forwards, unbalanced. He grabbed a handful of mane to steady himself, and pushed himself back into the saddle.

They reached the crumbling flint wall that ran lopsidedly around the little chapel and dismounted. Catherine eased open the ancient wooden gate and walked through, leading Kimba. Noah followed behind with Baloo. He glanced back and saw Oscar, covering the final stretch to them, panting. "Poor old boy, you're not as speedy as you used to be," he commented.

Oscar's eyes were sparkling, pink tongue hanging out of the side of his mouth. He looked happy enough. The little dog followed Baloo through the gate, and disappeared into some undergrowth near the flint wall. Noah closed the gate, ran his stirrup irons up the leathers and slipped Baloo's bridle off, turning the horse loose to graze. Beyond him, Catherine had done the same with her horse, Kimba.

In the centre of the graveyard stood a small dark stone building, with a rusting iron cross jutting lopsidedly from the front tip of its high-pitched slate roof. Just beyond Catherine, the sun glistened on a clump of faded sea holly flowers nodding in the breeze. Wordlessly, the pair walked through the grass, heading towards the left of the chapel building, where a group of gravestones stood slightly apart. The sight of two fresh white headstones at the far end of the row still made Catherine's throat catch. She forced herself forward, sensing Noah behind her, close on her heels. Her eyes came to rest on the first of the new gravestones The lettering on it read, "Here lives Milly. The best actress that ever was."

Catherine put her hand in the pocket of her jacket and drew out a handful of faded red rose petals she had collected in the summer. She sprinkled them on the grave. The breeze caught them, and they swirled in the eddies, falling like confetti at a wedding.

Noah moved slowly to the front of the second headstone. He tugged a lock of his dark curly hair out of respect for Isaac, his mentor and the wisest person he had ever known. An inscription, crudely cut into the stone stated, "Isaac. Known unto God."

Noah had once heard the phrase was carved onto the gravestones of all the unidentified soldiers in the war cemeteries in France. He decided it was also a fitting tribute for somebody who had owned a well-read leather-bound Bible and a living faith for over eighty years. He had painstakingly chiselled the words on Isaac and Milly's gravestones himself.

Catherine spoke, a catch in her voice. "Do you want to go first?"

Noah nodded and drew himself upright. He pulled a crumpled piece of paper out of his back pocket, glanced at it for a few seconds, then pushed it back. He cleared his throat and spoke, "Isaac, it's been almost a year since you left our earthly shores for the great fishing fleet in heaven. I remember all the things you showed me. How to get winkles off the breakwaters and dig for cockles in the sand. I remember when I found Oscar, dumped in this graveyard when he was a puppy. You helped me look after him and persuaded Dad to let me keep him. You taught me how to make bread. You jumped into the sea from the breakwater to save me when my raft capsized, even though you couldn't swim. You would have died trying to save me. You always had wise words for us. Because of you, I'm a bigger, stronger and better person. I'll miss you every day of my life."

They stood in silence for a while, the sea breeze ruffling their hair.

Then Catherine shifted slightly and said, "Milly. I wish I'd known you longer. I wish I'd known you when you were a young girl in the Land Army. I wish I could have been there for you when your parents were killed by a bomb and you thought your brother was dead. I'm so grateful for the time I did spend with you. I loved your courage and determination. It was you who often steadied me and understood my feelings when I first came to live with you all. You gave me a shoulder to cry on and filled my life with so many stories of the family I never knew. You were my grandmother's best and dearest friend, and you became my friend too. I am so privileged to have met you."

Catherine and Noah stood quietly for a few moments, paying tribute to the two former inhabitants of the white house. Noah had loved Isaac and Milly fiercely. They had lent colour, wisdom and love to his childhood. Once upon a time, Isaac had been a fisherman, working off the coast around Whitstable. His rough ways belied a gentle nature and deep faith in God that had given the house stability in difficult times. Milly had started out as an actress in London and Noah had loved to listen to her stories of the theatre, and her exploits during the early years of the war as a land girl, before the dementia had taken away even those memories. Their stories and voices still echoed in his mind.

Noah broke the silence. "It's odd you know. In some ways, it was a relief when Milly died. She seemed so frustrated and unhappy at the end. Is it wrong to feel like that?"

"Why should it be wrong, Noah? Sometimes people die before they're dead. I think Milly slipped away from us a good few years ago really."

Noah nodded, feeling better. But then he remembered the reason for their visit to the graveyard. Catherine and Arnaud were leaving and she'd wanted to say a final farewell to her friends and family who lay buried here. He felt as if everything was slipping away from him.

Catherine put her hand on his arm. "Noah, Arnaud and I are not dead yet and you've got Christmas in Wales with us and about eighty horses to look forward to. And before that, breakfast. I'm starving!"

Noah, temporarily cheered out of his gloom by the prospect of a fry up, and the novelty of spending a week over Christmas in the heart of the Black Mountains, walked over to Kimba and began putting the horse's bridle back on.

Catherine followed behind, with a final glance over her

shoulder at her family's graves which lay further along the row. She nodded a silent farewell to the grandparents and aunt she'd never met and turned away from the past, forcing herself on towards the future.

# 3

## A HEARTY BREAKFAST

Arnaud surveyed the boxes and bulging carrier bags stacked across the ground floor of the cottage with amazement. He'd arrived in England nine years ago with a bare minimum of possessions, proud of his ability to live lightly and simply. It was also something that he had found attractive in Catherine - the lack of regard she had for tangible things. He wondered how they had managed to accumulate so much between them in just five years of marriage. There was barely enough room to walk from the stairs to the front door.

He looked around the pale terracotta walls, now bereft of the hangings and paintings that had once brightened up the room. He'd woven a series of tapestries from his sheep and llama fleeces, abstract designs echoing the wildness of the marshes, that looked perfect hung around the small living space of the old cottage. They'd been complemented by a couple of Toby's paintings; one of a storm far out to sea, the other of the cove where they all lived, showing the sweep of the beach with the chapel at one end and the white house at the other.

It felt like the end of an era. He had found refuge in this ancient marsh dwelling when he had arrived in

England eight years ago. Cocooned in its shell, he had mourned the tragic death of his little baby son, and the subsequent break up of his first marriage. He never expected to be given a second chance in life, and still wondered how he had found the courage to begin again and allow Catherine to get close to him. Perhaps it was her very reserve that had enabled him to do so. Theirs had been a slow courtship. A friendship born out of respect that had slowly seeped its way deeper into their souls.

The squat, timber-framed cottage was low built, with thick plaster walls, hugging the marshland in an effort to stop the winter winds from sweeping it away. The single low-ceilinged room downstairs was simply furnished, with a wood burning range and small kitchen space at one end. The range provided all the heat they needed and made the space wonderfully cosy in winter. Upstairs a little attic bedroom and adjoining bathroom jostled for space under the eaves of the slate tiled roof.

The cottage and their lifestyle had suited Arnaud and Catherine perfectly. Arnaud loved to spend time outside or in the outbuilding next door, caring for their herd of sheep and llamas and working on craft projects. The outbuilding housed a rudimentary milking parlour at one end and provided shelter for the tiny black Ouessant sheep at lambing time. The llamas were perfectly happy to live all year round out in the rough paddocks that Arnaud had created on the marshland. The grazing was poor, but mostly good enough for their livestock.

A loft platform above the milking station was full of bundles of llama and sheep fleeces. When the weather closed in, Arnaud spent his time in a workspace at the far end of the outbuilding; spinning, weaving and knitting the wool from the llamas and sheep, or working with wood. Once or twice a week, he took his handcrafted goods to local markets, where they sold well. Now his two spinning wheels, looms and woodworking tools were already packed into the trailer, ready for the move to Wales the next day.

As a writer, Catherine required the bare minimum of work space. She preferred to sit at a tiny desk in a corner of the bedroom, in front of the dormer window with its view across the marshland. There was barely enough room for her laptop and a notebook on the desk, but Catherine found the view across the marshes inspirational. She earned a good living writing novels and Arnaud admired her discipline, which led her to spend a large portion of her day cooped up under the eaves. He would have found it suffocating, but he knew Catherine retreated into her imagination, enjoying the freedom to roam anywhere she chose in her thoughts.

He cast a final glance around the ground floor room and walked over to the newly painted front door. He had redecorated the house in preparation for its next owners and it still smelled of fresh paint. Arnaud stepped out into the fresh air. A gentle breeze carried the smell of gorse and a faint tang of sea. He pulled the door to, not bothering to lock it, and headed towards the paddock a few yards in front of the house. The llamas were over the far side, clustered around a bale of hay that he'd scattered for them earlier, to supplement the winter grazing. The sheep were nowhere to be seen.

Arnaud ducked under the fence and strode across the field towards the white house, a fifteen-minute walk away. Rather than taking the coastal road, which ran past his little cottage towards the sea, ending just before the white house, he chose one of the tracks worn by the white Romney sheep that roamed free across the marshes. It meandered through grassy hillocks, gorse bushes and small shrubs. The peaty ground was soft and springy underneath his feet, smelling of earthy dampness in the pale autumn sunshine.

Arnaud's long legs covered the ground quickly. For somebody so tall, he moved with an innate, almost animal grace. There was a peace to the rhythm of his stride. His grey hair was tied back in a ponytail, which reached down to his shoulder blades. His worn brown leather jacket kept the autumn chill at bay.

As he drew nearer, the huge white house loomed in front of Arnaud, like a vast modern-day castle, brooding over the place where land met sea. Arnaud could see flickers of movement through the windows of the top floor art studios, where the resident painters were busy working. The light was perfect for them and there was always a waiting list for the spaces there. Arnaud could understand why Catherine's great-grandfather had chosen to build his house in this stunning, if bleak, location, but the scale of the construction was truly impressive.

He walked around the side of the square, whitewashed Art Deco house and sprang lightly up the shallow concrete steps that ran alongside the semi-circular front window. Then, Arnaud turned the wrought iron handle, eased open the front door and stepped into the building.

He paused. It was impossible not to stop to take in the lofty beauty of the immense round entrance hall which encircled him. The plain white painted walls provided the perfect backdrop for a series of oil paintings hanging around the room. Shards of light, streaming in from the front window, flickered on the seascapes, bringing them to life. Arnaud could almost hear the roar and slap of the painted waves.

He drew himself out of the tableaux and called out, "*Salut* Toby!" Twisting around, he walked towards the concrete staircase which wrapped itself around the semi-circular front wall. His footsteps slapped across the oiled wooden floor, echoing in the cavernous space.

This morning, as Arnaud prepared to say goodbye, the house whispered to him, unwilling to let him go. Each step upwards released a burst of memories that flooded his mind. Not all of them belonged to him. Fleeting images of social gatherings from the building's Art Deco heydays insinuated themselves in between his own experiences of the house. Bob-haired skinny women in tiny-waisted silk dresses flirted with white-suited young men, wide-brimmed glasses of champagne in their hands.

The shadows of two young boys, Noah and his friend Séamus, slipped past him and ran across the hallway, intent on mischief. An elegant elderly lady in a long flowing evening dress, with pinned up snow-white hair glided down the steps, one hand loosely resting on the metal banisters. Milly - but Milly before Arnaud ever knew her, before the ravages of dementia had taken their hold. And Catherine, of course. Catherine, standing at the top of the staircase, a bemused expression on her face, wondering how on earth she had lowered her reserve enough to accept a tall, lanky Frenchman's proposal of marriage.

"Arnaud, come on up." Toby's voice echoed down the stairwell, pulling him out of his thoughts.

Arnaud batted the memories away and strode upwards into the enormous open plan space. Light flooded in through the huge windows, illuminating the slim, dark-haired man standing at the wooden worktop in the kitchen area.

Arnaud clasped Toby's proffered hand, and sat down at a huge oak table, leaning back in one of the chairs that had been crafted from driftwood, scavenged on the beach by Toby and Noah.

It was an unlikely friendship. The usually prickly Toby, burdened with an artist's hyper-sensibility, had warmed to the Frenchman from their first encounter on the marshes. Arnaud had just moved to the little cottage with his llamas and sheep when Toby had bumped into him in the middle of a particularly difficult day. Arnaud's calm, reassuring presence, was balm to a harassed Toby, fraught with the challenges of recovering from a nervous breakdown and raising a young, sensitive boy on his own.

"So, are you all packed?"

"Yes, almost. Well, pretty much everything but the animals. We'll catch them just before we leave tomorrow."

"And Catherine, how is she feeling about the move?"

Arnaud shifted slightly in the chair. "You know, Toby, she doesn't really say, but I can see it's hard for her to leave this place. She's pleased for me, of course. She knows I have always wanted to do something like this. But for her, I'm not so sure. Her only connection to the family she never really knew is here - and you know what that means to Catherine. Between you and me, I am asking myself if we are doing the right thing."

"I can understand that. It's a big step." A pause, and then he added, "The farm, what's it like? I haven't had a chance to catch up with you properly since you visited Wales and agreed to take the job."

"Well…" Arnaud was unusually hesitant. Toby glanced

over at him, concerned.

"It's like this. You know, normally I have a real sense of what direction is the good one. When the owners of our cottage here told us they were planning to sell it, I had a feeling something would come up. So, I wasn't really surprised when my friend Sebastian asked us if were interested in managing his trekking centre. But, I don't know. I feel a bit unsure. I hope it *is* the right thing."

"As I understand it, Sebastian's wife managed the centre, but she's recently left him? That's why he wants your help isn't it?" asked Toby.

"Yes, it is. I can see why Emily, had had enough of the situation. I've known Sebastian for many years - he's one of my closest friends and a good man - but rather lacking in perception where people are concerned. How he thought he could leave running the pony trekking centre to his wife while he spent the weekdays in London working in the City - it's beyond me. To be honest, I'm surprised Emily stayed as long as she did. It's a pretty remote location - right at the foothills of the Black Mountains. I think she must have been quite lonely - certainly in the winter when business is pretty quiet."

Arnaud watched Toby methodically measuring coffee grounds into the percolator. He continued, "What's also bothering me, Toby, is the condition of the place. I understand that Emily did her best, but it's clear she wasn't really focused for the last few months. To say the centre is in a bit of a mess is an understatement."

"What was Catherine's impression when you visited?"

"You know Catherine, she takes challenges head on, but I'm not sure the implications of leaving here had really registered with her."

Toby looked intently at Arnaud, meeting his gaze.

"Arnaud, it feels presumptuous of me to say this - this is Catherine's house after all - but you know you two can always live here. There's plenty of room, especially now Milly and Isaac are…gone. I mean, if you prefer your own space, Noah and I can easily afford to move out nowadays. It's not as if I'm strapped for cash any longer."

Arnaud smiled, pleased at his friend's growing recognition in the art world and commercial success. Then he shook his head. "Thank you, Toby, but this house belongs to artists - it always has done. I know it was Catherine who renovated the old studio on the top floor and welcomed painters back into the house, but I guess at heart, both of us prefer a simple, more rustic life. Although it gives her enormous pleasure to see this house living again."

Toby nodded, acknowledging the truth of this. He knew that, as a writer, Catherine preferred to work in solitude. Forced to reopen the art studios to afford to keep the house running, and to meet the huge repair bills that she had inherited along with the property, she had retreated more and more into herself as the artists had established themselves in the upper floor space. Arnaud's offer of marriage and her subsequent move to the little cottage in the marshes, provided an ideal solution for her.

A thump from the hall below was followed by a draft of cold sea air that came skittering up the stairs.

"Yo Dad, we're back. When's breakfast? I'm starving!" Noah's voice echoed around the lobby. Toby glanced at Arnaud and raised his eyebrows.

"I don't think I've ever known that boy not to be hungry," Toby muttered.

A mop of unruly black hair appeared at the top of the stairs. Noah's face lit up when he saw the visitor.

"Arnaud, *bonjour. Ça va?*"

"*Oui, merci. Et toi?*"

"*Ah ou*i." Noah's French petered out. He reverted to English. "Three beauties from the girls this morning."

He held out his hands, which cocooned two enormous pale brown eggs and one darker speckled one.

"Just in time," Toby commented. "You can add them into the bowl for me Noah. There weren't many eggs left in the larder this morning."

A bowl of whisked eggs was standing by the sink. Noah cracked his three eggs into the mixture and began beating it. Toby opened the fridge and pulled out two greaseproof paper packages. He placed them on the oak table and opened them. One contained a stack of bacon rashers and the other gleaming fat, pink sausages.

Noah sniffed. "I love the smell of raw sausages when the packet's just been opened," he enthused.

"Me, I prefer the smell of them cooking," Arnaud commented, adding, "What can I do boys?"

"If you could lay the table, Noah can make the scrambled egg and cut bread. Where's Catherine, Noah?" Toby suddenly noticed her absence.

"Oh, I left her in the garden. I think she wanted to have one last look. You know, say goodbye to the house and all that…" Noah's voice petered out as he looked at Arnaud, thinking back to what Catherine had told him in confidence. He hastily added, "I mean, just so she can remember how it is. Not in a bad way. I don't think she's sad or anything…"

Arnaud glanced at Toby.

In the garden, Catherine stood looking at the gnarled old apple tree. She guessed it must have been planted by her great-grandfather just after the house had been built. It certainly looked old enough. Toby had made a seat in the well of the branches at the base of the tree and Catherine sat down on it, warm in the sunshine and the shelter of the walled garden. She looked at the neat vegetable beds, dark chocolate soil freshly dug over for winter, apart from a patch where the winter greens stood in rows like ranks of soldiers. The currant bushes were bare now, but the old apple tree still had a few knobbly green cooking apples that hadn't yet been picked. Noah used to shin up the tree and pick the apples when he was younger and lighter, but in the past couple of years, Toby had resorted to shaking the branches and leaving the few remaining stubborn, clinging on apples for the birds.

The garden was Toby's domain. It always had been, even before Catherine had joined them in the house. In those days, the residents eked out a spartan living and Toby's home-grown fruit and vegetables had made a vital contribution to the household. Even when the finances improved, Toby had continued to grow vegetables and trap rabbits on the marshes.

Catherine spotted a flash of brown on the far side of the vegetable garden. One of Noah's chickens had escaped the run and was enjoying a furtive snack of kale leaves, stabbing at the plants with its beak.

She stood up and shooed the chicken towards the run. Fortunately, Noah had thrown down a few handfuls of corn when he had collected the eggs a few moments earlier and the chicken was happy to join the rest of the flock inside, pecking up the little yellow grains with relish. Catherine closed the door to the coop, and walked back towards the house.

As she crossed the lawn, she could just make out the

hazy shapes of people playing croquet. The thud of a mallet against a croquet ball broke the stillness of the morning. The shadowed people, visitors from another time, were oblivious of her as she slipped between them. She sighed heavily, aware that she would miss this precious connection with her family's past.

Inside the hallway, the smell of frying bacon drifted down the stairwell. She could hear the mumble of voices and clatter as breakfast was prepared. Aware that time was running out, Catherine hurried her pace, heading towards a small door to the side of the passageway. She opened it into darkness, and reached for the light switch. A pale glow from a naked light bulb above her head illuminated a steep passageway heading downstairs into the cellars.

Upstairs, Noah was cutting thick doorstep slices of homemade bread.

"How is your castle job coming along Noah?" Arnaud asked.

"I am," said Noah, his voice muffled by a mouthful of bread, "no longer a jester."

"No? What happened?"

Toby, who knew all the gory details, busied himself with frying sausages and biting his tongue to refrain from commenting.

"Suffice to say," said Noah loftily, "no kids were killed or burned or punched in the face. Although it was a close thing." He launched into a narrative of his first and last day as a paid entertainer.

Catherine let her feet lead her down the worn steps into the mustiness of the basement's interconnecting rooms, housing jars of homemade preserves, Toby's canvases, an old wooden saw horse and a bench littered with woodworking tools. Wood chips and shavings lay scattered across the floor of the far room, faintly scenting the air. She looked at the jars of jams - some of them dating back a few years, showing their age by Noah's once childish scrawl on the labels. A faint waft of sea air drifted into the room, coming from the underground smuggler's passage that connected the basement to a cave further up the beach. Catherine closed her eyes and breathed in.

Here, her great-grandfather and her grandfather had sawn up logs for the fire and mended the gardening tools that were still stored in the shed behind the house. Perhaps her grandmother had asked him to build the shelves that held the jars of preserves and pickles. There was still so much she didn't know about her family. She guessed she would never know.

A wet nose poked her leg. Catherine jumped and looked down into the liquid eyes of the little black dog.

"Oscar, you startled me!" She bent to pat him, and then unusually for her, picked the dog up and held him. Oscar, sensing her sadness, pushed his head into her shoulder and lay still in her arms. Catherine stood for a while, blinking back tears.

Noah poured the deep yellow egg mixture into the frying pan. Arnaud pushed back his chair and stood up.

"I'll go and find Catherine."

He walked to the far side of the room, peering out over the garden to see if he could locate her there.

On the floor below, Catherine crept softly across the hall and opened the door to what had once been Milly's room. An ebony dressing table was still cluttered with a handful of Milly's belongings - a silver-backed hairbrush, a cut-glass pot for a ladies' powder puff, an almost empty bottle of Chanel No 5 and piled up in the corner of the room, a stack of old scrapbooks. Her clothes and other possessions were gone, but the room still smelled of face powder and perfume. Oscar was waiting at the door. He sat on his haunches and looked intently at Catherine. Try as she might, Catherine couldn't conjure up an image of Milly in her mind. It seemed as if all the shadow people were receding, drawing away from her. Oscar gave a faint whine, pulling Catherine back into the present. She responded to his tug.

"Come on then, let's go up and join the others."

Suddenly, the smell of frying bacon was too much for him and he leapt ahead, bounding up the stairs, ears flapping.

Catherine followed the little dog, bumping into Arnaud on the stairs.

"Catherine, just in time. How was your ride?"

"Great thank you darling. Well apart from the fact I forgot to check Kimba's girth and the saddle slipped. I haven't fallen off in ages." She gave a forced, rueful grin, determined to be cheerful.

Noah pulled Catherine to an empty seat and playfully pushed her into the chair.

"Grub's up," he was impatient to eat.

Catherine looked at the food, filling the table; scrambled eggs, sausages, bacon, baked beans, grilled tomatoes, huge field mushrooms. She knew from experience that Noah, Arnaud and Toby were all capable of demolishing enormous quantities of food when they were hungry. She forced herself to fill her plate and began to eat.

"So, Toby, how is the painting coming along?" Arnaud never ceased to be impressed by his friend's talent.

"Actually, not bad at all," responded Toby with uncharacteristic positivity. "I've got a couple of nice commissions on the go. The annoying thing is finding the time to work on them at the moment. There always seems to be some business meeting or art gallery event or something."

"Ah, the price of fame," Arnaud grinned.

Toby shrugged his shoulders, "As you know, I'd rather just shut myself away and paint. At least you've got that one sorted Catherine. You've got your publishers well and truly in order."

Catherine smiled in agreement. "Yes, they know better than to force me to attend publicity events. Thankfully, as long as the books sell okay, they're reasonably happy. I know I'm lucky. By the way, before I forget to mention it, did Noah let you know that you're both invited to Wales for Christmas?"

"I meant to tell you dad," Noah interjected quickly, "Sorry. We're invited to Christmas on the farm. You, me, Oscar, Catherine, Arnaud, Arnaud's mate Sebastian, the llamas and sheep, oh and about eighty horses. How cool is that?"

Arnaud filled Toby in, "Sebastian phoned a couple of days ago and very kindly asked us if there was anybody we wanted to have over for the Christmas holidays. I think he's keen to help us settle in and there's plenty of accommodation for guests at the farm. As you know, it's a residential centre that takes in school groups. You can stay in the teacher's ranch house - it's really quite luxurious."

Toby paused, considering the idea. "How does

Sebastian feel about being descended on? Will he be around?"

"Yes, and really, Toby, the more the merrier as far as Sebastian is concerned. He is quite a people person and he's hoping a houseful of guests will banish the memories of the past."

"Well in that case, I have to admit, it would be good to get away. I've not got anything on around Christmas. Yes, why not?"

For Toby, this passed as serious enthusiasm. Catherine glanced at Arnaud and smiled, relieved. At least they would have familiar faces with them for the festive season.

# 4

## ARRIVAL

Catherine swung the Land Rover to the right, off the country lane and onto a gravel track. She slowed down, as first the car, then the trailer she was towing, rattled violently over a cattle grid. Her eyes were caught by a wooden sign, half-buried in the long grass at the edge of the track.

*Kestrel Farm*
*Trekking & Accommodation*

In her rear-view mirror, she could see Arnaud turning the large horsebox onto the farm track behind her. She eased forwards down the slope towards the farmhouse. On her right, she could see the accommodation block. To her left, a paddock, enclosed by a dry stone wall, was bordered by a stand of trees on the far side. Beyond, Catherine could see the top of the mountains. She breathed in a sigh of relief. They'd made the journey with no problems.

Behind her, the horsebox headlights flashed and Arnaud climbed out of the cab. Catherine drew to a halt and waited for him, winding the window down.

"*Chérie*, we might as well stop here and offload the sheep immediately. This is the paddock Sebastian wanted to us to put them in."

"Makes sense to me." She flexed her hands, stiff from gripping the steering wheel, and realised how tense she must have been during the journey from Kent.

As she climbed out of the Land Rover and stretched her legs, Arnaud was already unhitching the trailer and swinging it round to face the paddock entrance. He unlatched the gate, opening it wide, then turned back and pulled down the loading ramp of the trailer. A rustling of straw, as six dark brown woolly faces peered out curiously, blinking in the daylight. Catherine helped Arnaud to push out the wooden side panels to form a barrier on either side. When they were happy it was secure, she unlatched the metal barred gate. Hesitant at first, the sheep sniffed the air, then skittered down the ramp and into the field. They seemed reluctant to explore their new surroundings, staying close to the field entrance and looking around nervously.

Arnaud closed the trailer and hitched it back onto the Land Rover.

"If you ease forward a bit, I'll bring the horsebox up and we can offload the llamas and horses too."

Catherine climbed back into the Land Rover and turned the ignition. It coughed into life and she drove a few metres further down the track. The she slipped out of the car and walked back up to the horsebox. She was glad of her fleece jacket. The winter sunshine held little warmth and the breeze was icy. At least it wasn't raining.

A deep voice boomed out from beyond the Land Rover, "Catherine, Arnaud, *bore da*. It's good to see you both!"

Catherine turned back to look as a portly, balding man appeared into view. She forced her face into a smile, replying, "Sebastian, good to see you too. We were just letting the animals out before we came down to the parking space."

"Good thinking. Let me give you a hand." The collar of Sebastian's green waxed jacket was turned up against the cold. He walked with Catherine to the rear of the horsebox and smiled broadly when he caught sight of Arnaud, moving forward to clasp the taller, thinner man in a bear hug.

"So, you didn't change your minds?"

"Of course not," Arnaud smiled, but the smile didn't reach his eyes.

"I'm curious to meet these llamas," Sebastian was already walking up the ramp.

Arnaud looked back at Catherine, concerned. "Are you okay? Not too tired?"

"No, the journey was much better than I thought. We made good time."

He peered into the horsebox. "Oh, hang on Sebastian. You have to be a little careful with llamas. They're not quite as straightforward as horses. If you help Catherine with Baloo and Kimba, I'll start bringing them out. They're a bit wary of strangers."

"Okay." Sebastian walked around the grey Camargue horse, talking softly, one hand on its rump. He stroked Baloo's dark grey muzzle, then gently unhitched the halter rope and drew the horse round towards the ramp. Baloo was cautious, sniffing the air.

Catherine undid Kimba's halter and began moving forwards with him. The skewbald was placid, and followed her easily down the ramp. Baloo took courage and came on behind. Catherine opened the field gate and swung it in front of her, leading Kimba through the gap and then holding it for Sebastian and Baloo. The white horse was restless, eager to stretch his legs.

"Go on then," Sebastian unhitched the head collar and patted Baloo on the shoulder. The horse moved forward a few paces, then stood, nodding its head, eyes sweeping around the paddock. Suddenly he took off, cantering across the field, followed by the newly-released Kimba. The little brown sheep, which had been clustered next to the dry stone wall, lifted their heads to watch, as the horses skittered around the field, tossing their heads and whinnying.

Behind them, Arnaud appeared leading two of the six llamas. Catherine disappeared into the horsebox to retrieve two more, while Arnaud introduced Sebastian to the pair.

"This dark brown one is Filou. He's the big boy. All the rest are female."

"Lucky guy," Sebastian raised his eyebrows.

"And this is Milly. She's quite young - she's named after a good friend of ours. She's got a beautiful temperament. You can stroke her like this - here on her neck. They don't like you touching their faces so much."

Sebastian reached out towards the cream-coloured, much slighter llama. She stood still, not resisting his touch, but not responding either.

"They'll soon settle here," Arnaud was confident. He led the llamas into the field and undid their halters. Catherine did the same behind him, with her two ginger-haired females.

"These are Dilly and Dally - mother and daughter," she told Sebastian.

When the final pair - both cream, speckled with dark brown dots - were released, Sebastian shut the gate and watched the animals settle in for a few moments.

"I still can't get over the view," Arnaud gestured towards the mountain range in the distance beyond the paddock.

"It's pretty spectacular," Sebastian agreed. He glanced at Catherine. Noticing her pale face and dark patches under her eyes, Sebastian put his arm around her shoulders.

"Come on, you must be hungry. Let's have some lunch and then we can get your stuff unpacked."

Food was a generous spread of local produce. Arnaud's eyes lit up in anticipation.

"I think the Welsh have much in common with the French," was his remark. "Certainly, their appreciation of gastronomy." Sebastian's girth spoke for itself.

They were sitting around a pale blue wooden table in the kitchen. A white, old-fashioned iron cooking range was providing the heat, but even so, Catherine was aware of a cold draught hitting her neck from the window behind her. She glanced over at the entrance to the house. The main door led into the kitchen. A little porch provided a buffer against the worst of the cold, and was useful for muddy boots and wet coats. Life in the Welsh mountains was all about minimising the onslaught of the weather, Catherine decided.

Her attention went back to the table. It was groaning with food.

"You've got to try my cider. This one's just about ready for drinking." Sebastian poured the cloudy liquid into chunky green-hued glasses, and sat down on the other side of the table.

"Let's see if your Breton farmers can beat this," he challenged Arnaud, as he pointed to a range of cheeses laid out on a slate slab. "Tefi cheese made from unpasteurised milk, Perl Las, a beautiful organic blue - much stronger than your Stilton - and a local Red Leicester with chillies and pepper."

Arnaud smiled appreciatively.

"Come on, eat up, eat up. I could wax lyrical about our local food all day. Taste for yourselves."

Catherine filled her plate with salad leaves, giant stalks of leafy celery and two home-made rolls, one with poppy seeds, the other with fennel. The sharp hit of aniseed caught her palate as she bit into it. She added slices of delicately smoked chicken, generous chunks of air dried ham and a beef carpaccio with what looked like coriander. At least six jars of different chutneys graced the far end of the table.

They ate in silence, savouring each mouthful reverently.

It was Sebastian who broke into the stillness. "Having softened you up, I'm afraid I have a confession to make."

Catherine looked up quickly. She had a sinking feeling that she knew what was coming. She wasn't wrong.

"I don't know how to break this to you easily, but I'm going to have to head back to London after the weekend, and I might not make it over here until just before Christmas. I'm so sorry guys - we've got a huge deal on with a company in Hong Kong and it's hit a bit of a rocky patch. My company have asked me to fly out there to try and sort things out. It's not the kind of thing I can refuse - not if I value my job."

Catherine was all too aware of the importance of Sebastian's job. As it stood, the trekking centre would have made a substantial loss without his income. When he had inherited the farm from his parents, Sebastian had invested considerable sums of money upgrading the accommodation and facilities. As Sebastian had explained to them on their first visit - it was his income that was paying off this loan. Still, three days instead of the anticipated two week handover was a challenge.

Without thinking, Catherine sighed heavily. She realised both men were looking at her. For Arnaud's sake, she tried to make light of the situation.

"Well, that leaves us three days to pick your brains Sebastian. I guess we're going to have to learn the ropes super quickly."

"Great, honestly I don't think there's a huge amount for you guys to have to take on board. It's pretty intuitive really and you got a reasonable idea of how things work when you came up last time."

Catherine didn't agree, but she chose not to make a retort.

Sebastian looked relieved, misinterpreting her silence for calm acquiescence. Arnaud knew better.

"Perhaps tomorrow, you can give us a detailed tour of the whole centre and fill us in on anything we might have missed on our last visit." His mind was already working methodically, finding a way forward.

Catherine's gaze flicked around the kitchen. Last time they visited, it had seemed a pretty, airy room. Now, the sparse December light was already beginning to fade outside and the grey slate flooring gave the room a gloomy atmosphere, which wasn't helped by the low, dark-beamed ceiling. The blue wooden kitchen cupboards were grimy and the walls badly in need of repainting. Catherine could see patches of mould in the corner by the front door. She had to give Emily some credit - the kitchen was pretty, with its matching table and chairs, white butler sink and cheerful rag rugs on the floor. Sebastian had told them on their last visit that he'd given Emily free rein with the interiors of the farmhouse. Dried herbs hung from a rack on the ceiling, and a pine dresser in the corner boasted an array of cheerful spotted tableware. But nothing could hide the general air of disuse and neglect. It was as if the house itself felt discontented and abandoned, Catherine decided.

She looked through the open doorway to the sitting room beyond - the only other room on the ground floor, apart from a cupboard under the stairs and a little tiny scullery, home to the washing machine and fridge.

A huge slate fireplace dominated one wall of the sitting room. In the middle of the hearth was a small log burning stove. Catherine dimly recalled that the house didn't have central heating. It hadn't seemed important at the time, but now she realised that would mean chilly mornings and smoky evenings. Again, she had to admire Emily for her taste. Cheerful cream and red check curtains matched the dark burgundy of the leather sofas that took up most of the rest of the space in the room. The uneven, lumpy thick stone walls of the cottage had been painted in a pale cream - to make the most of the light, Catherine assumed.

A large dark burgundy rag rug covered most of the wooden flooring. In its centre, was a low pine table with a pale cream jug. Catherine decided to buy some flowers as soon as possible, to give the room - and herself - a bit of life.

Sebastian caught her gaze, thinking she was looking at the view from the sitting room window. He commented, "I love the fact that you can see the mountains from all of the windows at the back of the farmhouse."

Catherine nodded silently, wondering why Sebastian spent so much time in London if he was so fond of the scenery in Wales.

"Is that snow on the mountain tops?" Arnaud asked.

"Yes, we had a light dusting last night. There's not much forecast for a while though at least," Sebastian told him.

Grudgingly, Catherine had to admit that the low, white-capped mountain range, glistening red-gold in the setting sun, did look stunning.

"Let's get at least some of our stuff unpacked while there's still a bit of light," Arnaud commented.

"Good idea. You forget how short the days are in December," Sebastian remarked. "I've cleared all of my gear - and some bits and pieces that Emily left - out of the bedrooms upstairs."

"Where will you sleep? When you're here." Catherine couldn't resist the second comment. It came out more sharply than she intended, but Sebastian didn't notice the barb.

"For the time being, I've dumped my stuff in a couple of the rooms in the teacher's ranch. My uncle died last year, leaving my cousin his cottage just over the way. My cousin doesn't want to live there at the moment, and he's happy for me to stay there and keep an eye on the place for him. It will need a bit of a clear out before I can move in though."

Catherine was relieved. They hadn't thought to discuss where Sebastian would stay when he had offered them the farmhouse accommodation with the job. She was glad to think they wouldn't have to share it with him, even occasionally. Catherine guarded her privacy jealously, and was already struggling with the thought of the school groups that would be populating the centre from the spring onwards. The farmhouse, she decided, and its little garden at the back, would be definitely out of bounds for visitors.

After lunch, while Arnaud was making coffee, Catherine excused herself and headed up the narrow wooden staircase to the bathroom. As she passed by the master bedroom, a final burst of sunshine was sending golden shards of light through the window, illuminating the wooden floorboards. Sebastian had made up the bed, with crisp white cotton sheets and had even put out two fluffy white guest towels on the rocking chair that sat next to the window. She was grateful for his thoughtful touch.

The room, with its white painted stone walls and low roof struts reminded Catherine of their little cottage on the marshes. She moved over to the window and gazed out towards the mountains, imagining herself sitting at her desk in this spot, writing. She glanced down at the little cottage garden, surrounded by its low stone wall. The grass was overgrown and all she could pick out were a few straggly bushes, but it could be made to look beautiful with a little effort.

She felt a little more positive. Perhaps the venture would work out. She hoped so, for everybody's sake.

# 5

## IN THE BLEAK MIDWINTER

Noah was amazed. Toby hadn't complained once about his driving, even after the second near miss, when he had almost clipped the side of the car as he was pulling out to overtake a lorry. Negotiating heavy traffic on a motorway was quite a challenge in the flimsy little 2CV. There weren't an awful lot of revs to get them out of trouble, Noah discovered. Perhaps Toby's lack of reaction was due to the fact that Oscar was sitting on his knee, restricting his forward field of vision. They had tried to encourage the little black dog to stay on the rear seat, but Oscar had whined non-stop until Toby's patience was exhausted.

Regrettably, Toby's *sang froid* over Noah's driving was offset by a frosty interrogation about his job prospects. Noah had suspected a lecture was in the offing. He'd been trying to avoid his father for the last week or so, but there was nowhere to run in the cramped confines of the little car.

Toby stared gloomily ahead, pushing Oscar's woolly fur out of his face for the umpteenth time. Noah could tell a slow burn was coming on.

"What did you say happened with the animal park job?

I thought that sounded perfect for you. You love animals," Toby snapped.

"I was doing fine at first. I thought I might even get taken on permanently. I was dead good with the wolves. They seemed to like me."

"So what went wrong?"

Noah winced, then remembered to glance over his right shoulder before he pulled out this time. "I managed to let the wild boars out by accident."

"How did you do that?"

"Heaven only knows. I thought I checked the gate, but maybe not. As luck would have it, two of them somehow found their way out of the park entrance. Don't ask me how."

"Have they recaptured them?"

Noah wriggled in his seat. "No, not yet. It's in all the local papers - they're asking people to look out for them. At least it's media exposure for the animal park - you know what they say, any publicity is good."

"I'm not so sure," Toby muttered.

"Neither was the man who sacked me," Noah acknowledged.

Oscar shifted, digging his claws into Toby's legs. It didn't help his mood. "And what about the job at the gallery?" He fired off a second salvo.

"Yeah, I felt bad about that as Sarah from our studios helped me to get that work. She didn't seem to think it was such a deal though. She said she might have done the same."

Toby growled, "Done the same? What did you do?"

"Well you know her friend Matt was doing this project about sleep with a couple of other guys in the entrance lobby at the Matchstick Gallery and she very kindly got me the job of being a sleeper?"

"Yes, I'd gathered that."

"It sounded a cool thing to do, but believe you me, it's quite boring when all you're meant to do is lie in a bed and pretend you're asleep for hours on end. Did my head in," was Noah's jaded comment.

"Go on…" Toby persisted.

"I managed it for a morning. And they let me have lunch in the restaurant for free - good grub - so I was doing quite well out of it. But the afternoon was killing me so I decided to liven it up a bit. I tried to lie as still as I could, so it looked as if I was a dummy or something, then I'd wait until some old biddy was right up close, sit up and point my finger at them, whispering 'you're next on the grim reaper's list'. Got some quite good reactions. Apart from the 90-year-old bloke who had to be sat down and given a cup of tea. Shame really. It was good money for doing nothing."

Toby sighed. He had tried to be fair to Noah - it wasn't the boy's fault about the exam grading error. Noah had taken it very hard when all his schoolfriends had headed off to university and he'd been stuck at home, waiting out another year. But Toby was concerned that Noah needed to learn some life skills - and soon. The boy was too dreamy by far. Maybe it was a good thing after all that the university place had been deferred. Though how Noah was ever going to be able to stick at a job was beyond Toby's imagination.

Noah tried to lighten the atmosphere. "You know dad, I haven't even had to ask you for money to pay for petrol or anything yet. I have managed to earn a bit."

Toby had to admit that. Catherine had generously offered her old 2CV to Noah when she and Arnaud had made the decision to leave for Wales. Toby had allowed Noah to accept on the condition that the boy paid for the running costs. He'd wanted him to take responsibility.

"And, Arnaud's going to pay me for the work I do at the farm."

Toby had received a call from Arnaud the week before, asking if he and Noah would be able to come up a few days earlier to give him a hand with some of the heavier building repairs. Toby had been only too happy to comply. He enjoyed working with his hands and with little to do in the garden over winter, he'd been feeling cooped up for a while.

"That's good Noah. At least that should get you through Christmas."

"Yeah, and I've applied for that job as a supermarket shelf stacker. I reckon I'm in with a chance there. Not many people like night work, I'm guessing. Actually..." Noah hesitated, "Catherine and Arnaud did ask me if I wanted to come and be a trek leader at the farm when the school groups start in April."

"Sounds like a plan."

"Ye-es," Noah wasn't so sure. He didn't want to think Catherine and Arnaud were offering him the job out of charity. He had his pride to consider. And he wasn't quite convinced his riding skills were up to taking groups of schoolchildren out all day on the mountains. "I'll take a rain check on it dad, I think. Case the joint when we get there."

Toby picked up the piece of paper with Catherine's directions, and peered at them through Oscar's ears. Then he shouted, waving at a motorway sign, "Junction 15, junction 15, this is where we turn off!"

Noah did a last-minute swerve, managing to avoid a

coach. The 2CV leaned over wildly as it turned sharply onto the exit road and continued along the A419 towards Wales.

Catherine collected an armful of sheets from the laundry store and staggered along the verandah to the teacher's accommodation. She pushed open the sitting room door with her elbow and deposited the sheets on the sideboard, before bending down to take her dirty boots off. It was either that or trample mud over the newly washed floor. It was amazing how much mud she could accrue simply from walking across the track from the farmhouse. *This is going to be a constant cleaning job when it rains*, she thought. *Why on earth isn't the road tarmacked or concreted or something?* She and Arnaud had been at the farm for just three weeks and Catherine was feeling worn down by the constant irritations that were facing them at every turn.

Grudgingly, she had to admit that Sebastian had made a superb job of renovating the accommodation. He explained to Catherine and Arnaud how he had started with the existing single storey barn on the lower, south side and added three wings in the same local stone to form a square courtyard. The roofs were tiled in dark slate and inside, the walls were bare stone, except for the teachers' wing, which was clad in pine.

The original section had been turned into a dining room, with an open plan catering kitchen at the far end. Two round arches on the opposite wall to the kitchen led into a games room, fitted with low wooden benches, a pool table, dart board and wood burning stove. Two of the new wings housed the children's accommodation, and the wing nearest the farm track formed the laundry and teachers' accommodation. The result was simple, but charming, and blended in perfectly with its rural setting.

The teachers' accommodation was more luxurious than the bunkhouses. Sebastian had explained the key was to keep the teachers onside. They were the ones who made the decision about whether to rebook the school group for the next year, and much of his efforts had gone into giving them a good experience. Each teacher had an individual room with a matching pine bed, chest of drawers and bedside table. One corner of each bedroom had been walled off to create a small, neat en suite toilet and shower room. The rooms had a prime view of the top paddock, where Arnaud's llamas, sheep and horses were now grazing, and the mountain ridge beyond.

Catherine scanned the large sitting room where she was now standing. Similar burgundy sofas to the one in the main farmhouse were grouped around a stone fireplace containing a wood burning stove. Again, there were matching rag rugs on the polished wooden floorboards and brightly coloured fleece blankets had been strewn on the arms of the furniture, for additional warmth in the spring and autumn evenings. Tea and coffee making facilities were neatly stored on a tray on the wooden pine sideboard, and a small fridge had been built into one of its cupboards. The final touch was a huge wicker log basket full of firewood next to the fire.

Sebastian had been a little coy as to how much the conversion had cost, but Catherine and Arnaud suspected he would be paying off the loan for some time to come.

Catherine sighed, as she picked up a pile of bed linen and walked out onto the enclosed verandah that ran along the inside edge of the teachers' wing. She began with the bedroom nearest to the lounge. The plop, plop, plop of a dripping tap caught her ear and grated on her. It wasn't the only thing that needed attention. The entire accommodation block was desperate for a new coat of paint and a plethora of other jobs. The rooms had obviously seen a few years of high intensity use with little attempt at repairs. In the teachers' wing, many of the showers were mouldy, some of the toilets didn't flush properly and several dripping taps had left ugly deposits of limescale in the bathroom sinks. The childrens' bunkhouses were in a similar state of disrepair. She hated to think of the time - and cost - involved in redecorating before the next season. Even the view of the mountains failed to cheer her. A low cloud hung over the top peaks, and the chilly air was damp, threatening rain.

She bent over the bed and started to stretch a fitted sheet over the mattress, then fought with the duvet to get its cover on before finally slipping two crisp, white pillowcases on the pillows.

Catherine straightened up from making the bed and suddenly reeled as a wave of dizziness and nausea hit her. For a moment, she thought she was going to be sick. A sheen of sweat covered her face and back. She licked her lips and swallowed, tasting salt. She sat down on the bed and gradually the feeling left her. Suddenly, she felt claustrophobic, trapped in a life she wasn't particularly enjoying. All she had done for the last few weeks was round up horses, feed horses, clean up after horses, exercise horses, inventory bed linen and a thousand other tasks besides.

Her hands were red raw from the cold, her nails torn to shreds and her entire body felt constantly stiff and exhausted. She'd not been able to find any free time for her own writing. She needed to get away, even if it was just for a couple of snatched hours, before Toby and Noah arrived and she was submerged in more activity. She stood up and strode out of the bunkhouse.

Arnaud studied her as she entered the farmhouse kitchen, a worried expression on his face. "You're pale, Catherine. Are you okay?"

"Not brilliant. I've been feeling a bit under par all week. Hope I'm not going down with a bug just before Christmas," she grimaced.

"Why don't you take a rest? There's nothing much more to do until the guys get here. I can make the soup for lunch." In front of him on the kitchen table lay a list of that day's jobs that needed doing. Most of them now had little ticks alongside them.

"I was thinking of quickly popping into Hay. We seem to have run out of tea bags and a few other things."

"Fine, you go and I'll sort out lunch."

"See you later," Catherine bent over to kiss Arnaud and headed off to the Land Rover. As she drove through the forest, down the steep winding lane to the village beyond, she felt an unaccustomed sense of freedom. She tried to work out why. Arnaud lived life lightly and was one of the most undemanding people she had ever met. It was that which had attracted her to him in the first place. Much of her life had been solitary and she recoiled at any sense of pressure from people, easily feeling trapped and suffocated. She loved Arnaud with an intensity that surprised her, but sometimes Catherine missed her own company more than she cared to admit. She shuddered. Maybe she wasn't cut out for marriage after all.

In the kitchen, Arnaud opened the pantry door in search of a stock cube for the soup. In front of him, was a large, unopened box of tea bags. He gazed at it for a few seconds, frowning.

The drive into Hay distracted Catherine. On either side of the country lane, high hedgerows were dotted with crimson berries and white wisps of old man's beard, as if somebody had been decorating them for Christmas. Every now and then, a gap in the hedge revealed pale green fields filled with lazy, mud-slapped cows, flicking their tails and dozing.

Catherine hesitated as she drove through the outskirts of the town, looking for somewhere to park in the unfamiliar streets. It was only the second time she had visited the little border town. She found a space in front of a grocery store, and manoeuvred the Land Rover into it, struggling with the steep gradient of the sloping road. The dark stone buildings on either side of the street would have looked gloomy, but light from the sparkling shop windows spilled out into the grey day, creating patches of golden shimmer on the pavement.

For a short while, she allowed herself the luxury of a wander around the maze of hilly, winding streets. Turning up a back lane, she found herself in a small market square, surrounded by gift shops. A second hand bookshop right on the corner, called *The Well-Thumbed Page*, drew her in, and she gazed in delight at the shelves crammed full of books featuring every conceivable subject under the sun. She browsed randomly, greedily devouring the snippets of information their pages revealed. As she did so, her equilibrium gradually returned. She picked up a book of recipes illustrated with drawings in coloured pencil. The randomness of the author's selection of exotic recipes - the wife of a diplomat who had spent most of her life travelling the world and collecting recipes as she did so - delighted her and she went to purchase the book, as a Christmas present for Sebastian.

"I'm going to have to watch myself," she commented to the elegant, grey-haired lady behind the till, "or I'm going to end up buying half the books in Hay."

"Impossible," came a brisk response, "there are millions of them. Visiting, are you?"

"No, we've just moved to the area - a couple of weeks ago."

"Well take one of these then. And welcome to Hay." She handed Catherine a printed leaflet with a hand-drawn map of the town on it.

"Perfect," said Catherine with satisfaction. "That will save me from driving round in circles again." She turned to leave the shop when she caught sight of the book. *Of course, this was bound to happen sooner or later*, she thought to herself. She picked it up and looked at the familiar name on the front.

"We get a lot of Amelia Dewar books coming in," the lady at the till commented. "She's quite popular with our customers. We've got some more of her novels in the back if you're interested. She visited the area once or twice you know. I think I'm right in saying she met her husband here."

"Er no, no thanks. Actually, I've got them all," Catherine stuttered a response.

"Are you a fan of hers?" The elegant woman behind the counter seemed genuinely interested and it was her warmth that broke through Catherine's normal reserve.

"She was my mother," Catherine replied, and burst into tears.

"Goodness…" was the lady's response, before she

came around the other side of the counter and drew Catherine to a big armchair at the back of the shop. "Wait here," the command was soft-spoken, but impossible not to obey.

Catherine fumbled in her pockets and retrieved a tattered tissue just in time to wipe her nose. The woman made her way to the front of the shop and turned the 'open' sign around to 'closed'.

"How about a cup of tea? I was just going to make myself one. Business is rather slack this morning and I was thinking of taking a little break. I'm Eve, by the way."

"That's very kind, thank you. I'm Catherine." Catherine's voice was faint and her throat felt dry.

The woman threw a concerned glance at her and slipped through a beaded curtain into the cubbyhole that served as a kitchen. She emerged a couple of minutes later with two large mugs and handed one of them to Catherine.

"How are you feeling?"

"Better thanks." Catherine took a sip of tea. "What a stupid thing to do. I don't normally burst into tears in public."

"Don't be embarrassed," Eve was sympathetic. "Sometimes these things catch us out." She frowned. "Your mother died quite a while ago, didn't she? Were you close to her?"

"Yes. Well no. Not really. She was a very distant person. It was impossible to know her. She wrote more about feelings in her books than she ever demonstrated in real life."

"Why don't you tell me a bit about her. I'm curious."

To her surprise, Catherine found the words spilling out of herself.

Eve sat in silence as Catherine talked. She was a good listener and Catherine felt as if she talked for hours. Finally, the words dried up, and she sat back, feeling a curious kind of relief.

"What a sad - and yet fascinating story," was Eve's comment. "I can't believe you simply finished off the manuscript she was writing just before she died and the publishers didn't realise. And you were only eighteen at the time."

"It's amazing what you think you can do when you're young," Catherine smiled.

"And now you write under your own name? You said you continued to write."

"Yes, the publishers were kind to me. Gave me a chance. They were a bit annoyed when I didn't want to use my mother's surname though. I wanted to distance myself from her - to make my own way. So, I took my grandfather's name - Croft."

"You're Catherine Croft? I love your books!" Eve paused, "I can see the similarities now. There's something in the style of writing that's reminiscent of her. But of course, your genre is different."

"My mother wrote romantic novels - if I'm honest, I find them a little shallow. However, they paid the bills for a single woman bringing up a child, so I can understand how she kept on going when she found a formula that worked. I prefer something a little deeper - perhaps more unusual."

"And you're working on a new book now?" Eve was enthusiastic.

Catherine grimaced. "I'm meant to be, but I've not found any time to write since we got to Wales. I'm getting more and more frustrated."

Eve wrinkled her nose in sympathy. "That's not good."

A knock at the door interrupted them. The older woman jumped up, smoothing her skirt.

"Here's Graham, with a delivery. I'm sorry, I'm going to have to sort this out."

Catherine looked at her watch. "I need to go; our visitors will be due any minute."

Eve looked genuinely sorry. "Please do call by any time Catherine. I've really enjoyed meeting you."

"Thank you, yes I will." Catherine picked up her bag and headed for the door. It felt good to have an ally in this new, hostile world.


Noah was having fun with the Welsh signposts.

"Welcome to Wales. *Croeso I Gymru*." He massacred the Welsh pronunciation. "Cyclists dismount. *Llid y bledren dymchwelyd*."

"Mind that sheep," Toby commented loudly.

"Oops." Noah breathed a sigh of relief as the stray sheep turned and ran back towards its field, rather than in front of the car.

"*Ysgol* - school," Noah spotted another sign. "Maybe Arnaud's friend Sebastian can teach us some Welsh." He was enthusiastic. He loved anything to do with words.

Half an hour later, the 2CV drew into a little village at the foot of the mountains.

"Llaneilar," Toby read the black-bordered sign. "That's it, we're here."

Oscar pricked up his ears and lifted his head.

"*Araf* - slow." Toby pointed at the writing on the road, just before a tight bend, which Noah took at speed.

"More important - pub," added Noah, whose sharp

eyes had spotted a signpost marked 'Wily Wolf' swaying in the breeze. Underneath the words was a black and white image of a wolf's head, its fangs bared in a snarl.

"Nothing like a nice warm welcoming sign," Toby retorted. "You want to turn left just after the pub according to Arnaud's directions."

Noah swung the 2CV sharply around the corner, narrowly missing a girl with frizzy dark brown hair who was stepping out of a side door. She looked at the car's occupants with a scowl on her face.

Noah mouthed 'sorry' at her and carried on along the road leading them up through the village. It twisted to the right and then split in two. The main road ran steeply uphill, a sprinkling of houses on either side of it.

"Left hand fork," read Toby. Noah turned onto a small side road that wound up the hillside through the middle of a pine forest.

Oscar peered out of the window, taking stock of the new surroundings.

As they cleared the pine woods, the landscape opened up before them. A series of lush green paddocks, running down the valley to their right were overshadowed by the mountain range behind. On their left, fields of young winter wheat stretched into the distance, an undulating carpet of green in the breeze.

"It's quite a view," commented Toby. "I can see what Arnaud and Catherine were talking about now." He refocused on the directions. "Past the cottage on the right and turn immediately right onto the farm track, over the cattle grid. There it is now, there's the farmhouse," he pointed to the red brick building further along the track with its dark grey-green slate roof.

"And there's Arnaud's llamas, looking like pigs in…"

The Citroën juddered over the cattle grid, drowning out Noah's final comment, passed the llama field and came to a halt next the farmhouse. On the opposite side of the track was a huge corral, lined with post and rail fences.

"Wow, it's like High Noon," said Noah, excitedly. His gaze slipped further down the valley, to a large paddock. "Look, horses, loads of them!"

"There's Catherine," Toby commented.

Noah's gaze swung round and spotted a slim figure emerging from the farmhouse door, waving an enthusiastic greeting. Lower down the hill below the corral, Arnaud appeared out of a tall barn and walked up a flight of steep steps to join them.

Noah parked the car. Toby opened the passenger door and Oscar sprung out, jumping and barking at Catherine and Arnaud. When he judged the greeting sufficient, he began to sniff around, luxuriating in a whole new range of intoxicating farmyard scents.

Catherine's eyes were shining. "It's so good to see you boys!" Toby and Noah both received an unusually fierce hug.

Arnaud slapped their shoulders. "Come into the farmhouse and I'll put the kettle on. We can take your stuff over to the lodge later."

Noah was desperate to explore. Arnaud noticed. "Feel free to take a snoop around if you like Noah."

He immediately headed for the huge paddock that lay below the farm buildings, intent on checking out the horses, with Oscar hot on his heels. Arnaud drew Toby into the red brick farmhouse. They walked through the large entrance porch, full of boots and waterproofs, into the stone-flagged kitchen. Warmth from the Aga radiated through the room. In the far corner, a large tabby cat was lying curled on a chair.

"I see you've got yourself a new animal," Toby commented to Catherine.

"It turned up a couple of days ago and made itself straight at home. I hope it's a good ratter, Arnaud says the barn is infested."

"We're going to have to restrain Oscar from chasing it," Toby was concerned.

"I think you'll find that cat can hold its own," Catherine laughed. "The sheepdog from the farm across the way is terrified of it."

After tea, Toby and Arnaud went to inspect the barns together while it was still light enough to see the buildings properly.

"I'm so glad you've come," Arnaud commented, "there's even more work to do than I realised. We keep finding things that need fixing."

"Glad to be of use Arnaud," replied Toby, relishing the challenge.

Catherine was clearing up the tea things, when Noah finally arrived at the kitchen, hungry. She cut him a slice of cherry cake. Oscar caught sight of the cat and ran towards it. The tabby raised its head and looked at him contemptuously.

"I wouldn't, Oscar…" Catherine cautioned.

As the black dog approached the cat, slightly puzzled by its lack of fear, the tabby reached down and batted Oscar across the face with its paw. The little dog retreated behind Noah's legs.

"That'll teach you," Noah laughed and choked on a crumb of cake.

After Noah had finished eating, he and Catherine took

the luggage to the teachers' accommodation, a few hundred metres back up the track on the other side to the farmhouse. Catherine led the way up to a side entrance. She opened the door, releasing a smell of pine wood, laced with a hint of furniture polish and newly laundered linen.

"This is your room Noah. Your dad's got the one next door. Sebastian will be staying in one of the other rooms when he gets back."

Noah whistled at the size of the accommodation blocks. "Wow, it's quite a set up here."

"Yes, it's really well built. It's just a shame it's so run down. And I'm not sure why Sebastian hasn't sorted out the bare earth in the middle of the courtyard. It's turning into a quagmire with all this rain. I dread to think what it's going to be like when an entire group of kids starts running around here…" she trailed off.

Noah caught the catch in her voice. "What's up Catherine? You don't look very happy."

"I don't know. Everything and nothing. There so much to do here, I feel completely overwhelmed. As you know, Sebastian hightailed it off to Hong Kong just after we arrived here, and he barely had time to explain how things work. We're still trying to identify all the different horses, and to be honest, he was a bit vague on details. Emily did most of the running of the centre, and I think it's been quite a while since Sebastian was really involved. It's hard Noah. I don't want to criticise him to Arnaud – their friendship goes back a long way – but I'm pretty frustrated."

Noah probed, "And Arnaud, how is he feeling about the move here?"

Catherine sighed deeply, "He absolutely loves it here.

From the moment we arrived, he's been so enthusiastic. He seems to feel totally in his element, with all the horses and the wildness of the place. As far as I'm concerned, it's bleak and lonely."

Noah studied her face. There were dark smudges beneath her eyes, her skin looked pale and taut and she'd clearly lost weight. This was a Catherine he had never seen before. He moved over to the woman and wrapped his arms around her. She was the closest thing he had to a mother and it unnerved him to see her so upset.

Catherine allowed the hug for a few moments, then pulled away. "Come on. Arnaud and your dad will be wanting lunch soon. Let's just enjoy the Christmas break for now." Then, she smiled at Noah, adding, "It's so good to have you both around."

# 6

## CHRISTMAS

The black Subaru wove in and out of the heavy traffic on the M4. A light sleet was falling and Sebastian was aware the road was becoming slippery, but he was anxious to get to Wales before the driving conditions worsened. He stamped on the brake, then accelerated sharply and pulled out, just as a BMW came up behind him in the fast lane. The BMW flashed him, but Sebastian was oblivious, focusing on the next gap. It was a relief to head off the busy motorway half an hour later, and take the A417 up to Birdlip. Sebastian put his foot down hard on the accelerator and the Subaru powered forward.

An hour later, he slid the car into second gear and headed up the steep forest road to Kestrel Farm. The sleet was falling more heavily now, slushy snowflakes fighting for territory with the windscreen wipers.

Inside the kitchen, Catherine heard the crunch of tyres on the farm track. She placed a freshly-washed mug on the draining board and wiped her hands on the kitchen towel, turning towards the entrance door. A car door banged and a few seconds later, Sebastian appeared, bringing with him a light dusting of snow which drifted off his coat.

"Sebastian, hi. How was your journey? Not too much snow I hope."

"A little bit, but I've had worse up here. Where are the others?"

"They're all in the indoor school with a bunch of horses. I opted to stay in the kitchen. It's a bit warmer in here."

Sebastian lightly kissed Catherine on the cheek and shed his coat onto one of the kitchen chairs. He sat down heavily, rubbing his eyes. "I'd forgotten just how bad the traffic gets just before Christmas. It was nose to tail all the way from London to the Swindon turn off." He stood up again, restless, stretching his stiff legs.

"Would you like a tea or coffee?" Catherine asked him.

"I think I'll pour myself a whisky. I've been looking forward to it for the last half hour. Would you like one too?"

"No thanks, not just yet."

Sebastian took a tumbler out of the cupboard and walked into the sitting room. Then he came back into the kitchen. "I'm sorry, this isn't my place any more. I'm rude to just help myself."

Catherine glanced over her shoulder, "Not at all, there's a bottle of Glenlivet left in the drinks cabinet from when you were last here. Please, feel free."

Sebastian returned, the glass holding a generous measure, and took a sip. He sat down at the kitchen table again, visibly relaxing. "So how are things Catherine? Sorry, I literally arrived off the plane from Hong Kong last night, slept over at the flat and picked up a few bits and pieces before I drove on over. I've not had a chance to look at any emails for a few days. I hope things have been okay."

Catherine hesitated, unsure. Then she plunged in. "Well, I know Arnaud wanted to talk to you. He was waiting until you got back to the UK. I don't want to spoil your Christmas, but we're going to have to talk about the finances pretty quickly. There's not much money in the farm bank account and we've got a few urgent bills that need paying."

Sebastian was puzzled. "I don't understand. There should be plenty in the account. I checked it before I left for Hong Kong."

Catherine gritted her teeth. "It looks like Emily ran up several large bills on a credit card linked to the account. They've only just come in."

"How much?" Sebastian was curious.

Catherine told him and he winced. "That's not good. I'm sorry Catherine, you and Arnaud don't deserve this. I'll sort something out as soon as possible and get Emily's card cancelled. I can't believe she's done that." He paused, angrily gripping his glass. "Is there any Internet connection? It usually gets a bit hit and miss in this kind of weather. "

"You're right, it's down at the moment."

"No worries, if it's not back up in a couple of days, I'll go into Hay and log on there to transfer some money. How are things otherwise?"

Catherine tried to keep a measured tone to her voice. "We-ell, let's just say we've got our work cut out to get the farm up and running for the early spring. We're coping fine with the customers who are booking up for casual rides at the moment. To be honest, there aren't many of them, as it's not exactly riding weather right now, but there's a huge amount to do before the residential school groups start arriving in April."

Sebastian looked sheepish. "I'm sorry Catherine. Things are obviously worse than I realised. I guess I should have done a more thorough inspection before you both arrived."

Catherine wanted to say it didn't take more than a cursory glance to see the place was completely run down, but, it was Christmas Eve. Time enough to tackle Sebastian in a few days' time when the festivities were over. She made an effort to be gracious.

"Well, there's nothing that can't be fixed, but realistically we're going to have to redecorate a large part of the accommodation - some of it's quite mouldy and you can't expect people to sleep there. We're compiling a list of urgent and long-term work, and trying to tackle what we can."

Sebastian put his hands on the table. "I don't know what to say Catherine. I'll do whatever I can to help. I'll ask around to see if anyone local can help with the decorating if you like."

Catherine was relieved. "That would be fantastic if you could. That would mean we could concentrate on trying to find staff for the season and checking through the horses' tack and other bits and pieces."

Then, she noticed the haggard expression on his face. Judging by the emails they had received from Sebastian while he'd been in Hong Kong, he'd done little but dash from meeting to meeting. He looked exhausted. She took pity on him.

"Don't worry for now, we'll sort something out. Let's just enjoy Christmas. Why don't you pop over to the indoor school? I know Noah and Toby are looking forward to meeting you."

Sebastian looked relieved. "If you don't mind being

abandoned, I do feel like stretching my legs a bit."

"No not at all. There's not much more to do here. Tell them food will be ready in an hour."

"Will do," Sebastian grabbed his coat, rummaged amongst the jumble of clothes in the porch for more suitable footwear and disappeared out into the swirling snow.

In the indoor school next to the barn, Toby was sprawled out on a sagging, faded red sofa, his feet resting on a wooden post and rail fence that ran around the manege. Oscar was curled up beside him. He eased himself up to greet Sebastian, shaking his hand formally. Oscar crawled lazily off the sofa, sniffed Sebastian's leg and climbed back up again, settling down with a sigh.

"Toby, I presume? In fact, *the* Toby Foster?" Sebastian asked.

Toby looked at him slightly quizzically.

"Arnaud mentioned that you were an artist," Sebastian explained. "The penny only just dropped this morning when I popped by the office. As chance would have it, we've got one of your paintings in our boardroom. I love it."

"Thank you," Toby said awkwardly and changed the subject. "Glad you made it here okay. It looks like the weather's closing in. I gather you've only just got back from Hong Kong. I hope your trip was successful."

"It was good. Definitely worth going. I think we managed to salvage a tricky situation, but it's a shame I had to abandon Catherine and Arnaud so quickly. I gather you and Noah have been helping out for a few days."

"Yes, actually I've quite enjoyed it. It's been a good break, and the scenery here is quite stunning. I'll have to come up with my painting gear in the summer."

Sebastian noticed a section of new wood panelling high up in the indoor school. A series of pale planks had been nailed over gaps where the old wooden boards had rotted. He pointed to the upper wall of the school. "My goodness, how did you get up there to do that?" he commented, impressed.

"Noah's quite nimble and he's not afraid of heights."

Sebastian's eyes dropped down to where Arnaud and Noah were riding two horses around the huge school, each weaving their own pattern, intent. Arnaud's horse flicked up sprays of sawdust with its hooves as it came around the corner towards Toby and Sebastian. Arnaud waved at them, and eased his mount, a large grey cob, to a walk, then halted. The horse was sweating and panting heavily. Arnaud slipped out of the saddle and came over to the barrier, out of breath himself.

"*Salut* Sebastian! Hope your journey wasn't too bad. I'm so glad you made it here for Christmas."

Noah rode up to the barrier, greeting Sebastian from his saddle. Sebastian stroked the cream-coloured nose of the little palomino that Noah was riding and asked, "Enjoying the horses Noah?"

"They're amazing. Cripes, where did you get them all from, Sebastian? I mean there are masses of them."

"And most of them pretty out of condition, I'm afraid. I really appreciate your help, Noah, and your dad's. I'm sure Arnaud's been grateful to you too. I've rather left him and Catherine in the lurch."

"We've had a right laugh. What an amazing place," Noah enthused.

"Are you going to come and have a ride Sebastian?" Arnaud pointed to a group of horses that had been tied up behind the barrier on the opposite side of the school. "There's plenty of choice."

Sebastian was tempted. It would be good to loosen his muscles after sitting cramped in the car for five hours.

"Yes, why not." He quickly scanned the group of waiting horses. "Have you exercised Prezel yet?" He pointed at a stocky chestnut horse at the end of the row, its chin resting on the gate.

"Not yet," Arnaud responded.

On the opposite end of the line, a tall bay horse was tied up at a distance from the others. Every now and then it shook its head nervously. The action caught Sebastian's eye as he walked across the school to the horses. Arnaud strode beside him, leading the grey cob.

"You've brought Jester inside, Arnaud? And he's standing tied up without any fuss. I am impressed."

"Yes, I've been doing some work with him. It bothers me to have an unhappy horse in the herd."

"I'm not sure what possessed Emily when she bought him. He's not exactly riding school material," Sebastian said. "I think I told you he was only purchased a few months ago. She said she felt sorry for the horse. Apparently, he'd been badly bullied by a stallion. Don't know why the previous owner kept them together, but there you go, some people don't think - or don't care."

"He's a beautiful animal. I'm pretty sure we can overcome his fear of the other horses." Arnaud added more quietly, "Sebastian, I have an idea. Bear with me my friend…"

He called over to Noah. "Hey Noah, do you fancy a bit more of a challenge?"

Noah did. Calico, the gold-coloured palomino horse he had been riding, was fine, did everything she asked him to and was...well, rather boring. He trotted her over to where Arnaud and Sebastian were standing by the group of horses.

"You see Jester here?"

The boy nodded, appraising the dark bay horse. Arnaud had explained earlier why he'd wanted it tethered away from the group.

"Are you up for having a ride on him? It would do him good to have someone else onboard for a change, not just me."

"Absolutely," replied Noah.

"Just be gentle when you get on him, and watch the other horses in the school," Arnaud instructed. "Make sure you keep him a bit apart from them. If you get too close, he'll shy away and they might also try to kick him."

The soft-hearted Noah was all sympathy for Jester. He tied up Calico and walked towards the big horse cautiously. At Noah's approach, the bay snorted and backed away slightly, tugging at the rope that held him to the wall. Arnaud breathed in. If Noah was too abrupt, Jester could well panic and pull away, breaking his tether and scaring himself.

Noah stopped in his tracks and spoke quietly to Jester. Cautiously, he held out a hand. After a few moments, the horse shifted his weight towards Noah and extended his neck. Tentatively, he sniffed the boy's outstretched palm. Noah eased forward with slow, steady movements, and began to stroke Jester's neck, hardly touching the horse. Then, Jester put his head down and nosed at Noah's riding boots, calm now.

Arnaud smiled to himself. His hunch had paid off.

"I see you haven't lost your touch with people either," commented Sebastian.

Noah woke once in the night and remembered the ride on Jester. He felt a deep satisfaction in his soul at having reached out to the damaged horse and connected with it.

He shifted in bed and something rustled by his feet. In the moonlight, he spotted a lumpy sock, full of things. Santa must have left it. He hadn't even noticed it when he'd crawled into bed earlier. It wasn't difficult to work out his - or rather her - identity. Toby had never really done the Father Christmas thing, but Catherine had always left him a stocking, right from her first Christmas with them at the white house. Even after she'd married and moved to the cottage with Arnaud, she'd still made sure Noah had his Christmas stocking. He reached for the tatty old fisherman's sock, then made the adult decision of leaving it until the morning. The truth was, he had a thumping headache after trying out Sebastian's selection of homemade berry wines and wasn't up for unwrapping just yet.

In the farmhouse, Catherine too was awake. The alarm clock next to her showed three am. She eased herself out of bed, trying not to disturb Arnaud, and padded over to the window. Behind the farmhouse, the moon had risen above the mountain range, throwing a blue light onto the dusting of snow that sat there.

"Catherine, I'm worried about you."

She turned around in surprise. She didn't think she'd woken Arnaud.

He spoke softly into the night. "I thought this would be a fun thing for us to do, but every day your shoulders seem to droop a little more. And you look really run down. It's not a problem for us to leave here you know. We can find someone else to replace us and go back to

Kent. We can always rent a field somewhere for the llamas and move to the white house until we decide what to do."

For a second or two, Catherine was tempted to lie, but she had never been comfortable with falsehood.

"It's true, I'm feeling a bit…overwhelmed. I'm not totally sure why, I knew what I was getting into. It's odd Arnaud, somehow I just don't see myself here. I'm not sure how to explain it. I thought I'd love living in these mountains, but it feels…foreboding, heavy." She realised what had been eating into her, "I don't feel I can write here. I used to find it easy to write, and if I was struggling occasionally, I could just take a walk on the marshes and whoosh, my head was full of new ideas. You know that. But all I feel here is a kind of deadness."

Arnaud was concerned. He'd never heard Catherine talk like this. There was a heaviness, a lethargy about her that he hadn't seen before and she was getting painfully thin.

He swallowed and said, "Then we leave. We tell Sebastian as soon as Christmas is over. We should stay until he finds somebody else I think. Could you manage that much?"

Catherine walked over to the bed and slumped next to Arnaud, grasping his hand. "That doesn't feel right either. I've never run away from anything in my life. And you're so happy here. You've…you've found your dream place it seems."

"Catherine, there is no point in me being happy here if you are dead inside. You know how guilty Toby feels - he's always thinking he drove you out of the white house. We can always stay - or even live - there. It would make him feel better."

Something inside Catherine leapt at the chance to leave the farm. She paused, sifting the idea. And then decided it felt wrong. "I don't think that's the answer. Somebody once said that it's a dangerous thing to go backwards." She seized her courage in both hands. "You know Arnaud, it's early days and it's the middle of winter. I suggest we at least give this place a chance. What if we review the situation in a couple of months? At worst, we will have sorted things out somewhat for Sebastian - make it easier for him to find another manager. At best - I'll feel differently."

Arnaud desperately hoped time would change things. It was true, he felt happier than he had ever done in his life in these Welsh mountains. The remoteness called to his spirit and he responded with joy. He hesitated. Then, "Okay Catherine, it's a deal. But we put a date in the diary. I won't let this drag on if you are still unhappy."

Catherine agreed reluctantly. It was a compromise, but not one that filled either with satisfaction.

The next morning, Toby, Sebastian and Noah walked over to the farmhouse for breakfast, crunching through the powdery new snow that had settled the night before. Oscar padded behind them, scenting the smells wafting from the kitchen.

"It's good of you to give up the farmhouse to Arnaud and Catherine," remarked Toby, treading carefully on the slippery track.

"I'd love to think I was that generous, but the truth is Toby, the house has got history for me and I'm happier out of it."

Toby sympathised. He knew all about being abandoned by a wife.

They rolled into the big kitchen, with cries of "Happy Christmas!" Arnaud was cooking on the big range. Noah sniffed appreciatively at the smell of the fry up being prepared for them.

"I'm in heaven," he announced as he sat down at the table and began buttering a large slice of bread.

A few seconds later, Catherine appeared from the stairway at the back of the room with a cheery greeting.

Noah looked up at her face. He wasn't fooled. Tight lines still showed at the corners of Catherine's mouth and her eyes had dark circles underneath them. She was putting on a very good show, but the unhappiness was still there.

Over breakfast, Catherine got everybody organised. "Arnaud and I have done most of the preparation for lunch already. If I finish off some bits and pieces, are you all happy to sort out the animals? If you're quick, I reckon you could fit in a trip to the pub before lunch is served. Does that work for everybody?" She looked around at them.

"It doesn't seem very fair to be leaving you in the kitchen," was Sebastian's comment.

"No, no I'm quite happy. There's honestly not much to do." Catherine was craving a little time to herself and was adamant.

"Okay. As far as the animals go," Arnaud commented, "we just need to give the sheep and llamas a bit of hay, make sure the water hasn't frozen over in the troughs and quickly check the horses over. Shouldn't take too long."

Outside, the wind was biting and Noah was glad of the extra fleece he'd put on under his coat. He agreed to help Arnaud take a look at the horses to make sure there had been no incidents overnight, while Toby and Sebastian fed the llamas and sheep in the top paddock.

Sebastian hitched the utility trailer to the old farm Land Rover and backed it down to the barn, while Toby opened the small barn entrance door and stepped inside. He walked over to the left-hand wall where the hay bales were stored.

They tossed a few of the hay bales into the trailer and drove them up to the top paddock. The air was icy, and Toby was glad of the thick lined gloves he'd discovered in the porch. A good inch of snow lay on top of the hard, frosty ground. They eased open the frost-kissed gate and hauled the bales of hay out of the trailer and into the field. Oscar's head appeared, peering over the top of the dry stone wall a few metres further down. A few seconds later, he'd jumped the fence and was walking towards the llamas. They lowered their heads to greet him.

"They seem to have settled down well," Sebastian observed, stroked the neck of a large, ginger coloured llama that had walked over to him.

The six tiny, dark brown Ouessant sheep were soon busy pulling strands of hay from one of the bales. One of them climbed on top of the bay and began headbutting another one.

"Hey stop that," Toby called. The sheep raised its head to look, before resuming its head butting.

Sebastian pulled out a penknife and began cutting the orange twine from around one of the bales. When he'd finished, Toby began to scatter the hay while Sebastian started on the next bale.

"I gather you've known Arnaud for quite a while," Toby was curious. Arnaud had never spoken about how he had met Sebastian.

"Yes, funnily enough it was through our wives - or

rather our ex-wives should I say," Sebastian explained. "Estelle and Emily were studying together in Paris. Emily was doing a year abroad for her business course. She came over from the States, but never went back - well not to live or finish her studies. I happened to be working for a Parisian bank at the time and met them both at some café or other. Estelle was already engaged to Arnaud by then. I think so anyway - it seems so long ago. The two women kept in touch over the years, and Arnaud and I have always got on well - I guess we both had a farming background in common." He ripped at the last piece of baling twine and looked up at Toby. "It's curious, our friendship seems to have outlasted both of our marriages."

They both broke up the last hay bale and walked back to the Land Rover.

"I need to make a short social call, so I'll join you in the pub in about half an hour," Sebastian told Toby as he parked the Land Rover back in front of the barn. "Emrys is a family friend. He's a crusty old bugger who lives on his own a few miles east of here. He wouldn't accept an invitation to lunch with us, so I'll just take him round a bottle of whisky and check he's okay. He's got no family to speak of."

He walked over to his black Subaru, while Toby grabbed Oscar's collar and marched him over to the farmhouse to stay with Catherine. The pub would probably be crowded, and Oscar was notorious for getting underfoot. The dog had no objections to being left behind when there was a kitchen full of titbits on offer. As Toby came out of the farmhouse, Noah and Arnaud were walking up from the bottom paddock. They climbed into the Land Rover, and headed down the hill.

Inside the Wily Wolf, a satisfying smell of beer, hot bodies and wood smoke greeted them. Toby made his way to the crowded bar with Noah alongside to give him a hand with the glasses, whilst Arnaud managed to bag a free table near the fire from a group who were just leaving. As Noah gazed dreamily at the rack of bottles behind the bar, relishing the warmth of the pub after the chilly winter morning, a pale face surrounded by a frizz of brown hair came into focus. It was the girl he had almost run over a few days ago when they arrived in the village.

"What can I get you?" she was cheery, not recognising Noah from the incident.

"Actually, I think I owe you an apology first. I almost mowed you down the other day. In my blue Citroën. The funny looking one." Noah looked embarrassed.

"Oh, that was you, was it? Don't feel bad, I should have been looking out. Everyone hares round that corner. Are you new round here?"

Her accent was pure Welsh. Melodic. Noah quite liked it. Then he realised the girl was expecting an answer. "Oh, er yes, well no. I mean we're staying for Christmas up at Kestrel Farm. With Catherine and Arnaud."

"The couple helping Sebastian out?"

"Yeah, that's it."

"They've got their work cut out for them, I expect."

"You can say that again," Noah commented. "Dad and I have been giving Arnaud a hand with some of the repairs to the outbuildings."

There was a lull at the bar, and after Toby had paid for the drinks, Noah stayed chatting.

"I'm Noah, and that was my dad Toby."

"My name's Min. This is my brother Joseph's pub. I'm doing a stint here while his wife recovers from a broken ankle. I'm usually in the kitchen, but we're not serving food today."

"I bet you're enjoying the break from washing up."

"Actually, I'm the chef," she told him.

"I'm sorry, I thought…"

Min laughed at Noah's discomfiture, "Don't worry. I know I'm short and I look much younger than I am. Everyone thinks that when they meet me."

"What sort of stuff do you cook?" Noah was anxious to redeem himself.

"I like to forage. When Joseph lets me, I do a special foraged food tasting menu. Goes down well with the customers on the whole."

"Oh wow, we do a lot of foraging where we come from. Well, dad's specialty is catching rabbits, I'm not sure if that counts as foraging, but he makes a mean nettle soup."

At the table in the corner, Arnaud and Toby glanced at the bar and raised their eyebrows. Noah and Min chatted on, oblivious.

In the steam-filled farmhouse kitchen, Catherine, with help from Oscar, was finishing off preparations for the Christmas dinner. A huge stock pot containing Toby's homemade tomato and tarragon soup was simmering on the Aga. Red gloopy bubbles formed and burst on the surface of the liquid, spattering on the pale kitchen range. Inside the oven, a huge goose was sitting in state, surrounded by a circle of crispy roast potatoes. Pans of vegetables stood on top of the oven, ready to start cooking. Catherine looked up in relief as the door opened, sending a welcome wave of cool air into the overheated room.

"Just in time." Then she noticed there were only three men, "What have you done with Sebastian?"

Arnaud's brow furrowed. "We assumed he'd come back up here when he didn't turn up at the pub. He went to check on an old family friend ages ago. I'll just call his mobile again."

He tried a couple of times, with no success.

Catherine checked the contents of the oven. "If we don't start on the soup now, the goose will be overcooked. Why don't we carry on - he's sure to be back soon - he'll just have to miss out on soup if he's too late. It's not like he's going to starve. There's plenty of main course and dessert."

Her suggestion was greeted with enthusiasm by the others who had worked up an appetite with the morning's work. Soon Catherine was ladling the steaming soup into bowls and passing them around the table, accompanied by hunks of freshly baked bread. They tucked into the food with relish, but Arnaud was uneasy. Catherine looked at him inquiringly.

"It's unlike Sebastian not to let us know if he was going to be delayed," he commented. "I'm just hoping there isn't a problem. I don't even know where Emrys lives so we can't go to check on them."

Twenty minutes later, as they had just started on the roast goose, a face appeared at the kitchen window, followed by a sharp rap on the front door. Toby, sitting nearest to the entrance, swung out of his chair and opened it. In the porch stood a uniformed policeman, his face wooden. At Toby's invitation, the man stepped into the room, pulling the door closed to keep out the cold. He eyed the gathering apprehensively, clearing his throat awkwardly.

"I'm sorry to break into your Christmas lunch. I'm afraid I'm the bearer of bad news. Sebastian has been involved in a serious car accident."

"Is he….?" Catherine couldn't continue.

"He's still alive, but he's in quite a bad condition, in a coma. I'm Dai the local policeman - I live just down in the village so I know Sebastian quite well. I understand that two of you are running the farm for him. Do either of you happen to have a contact number for Emily? I'm assuming she's still his next of kin…?"

Arnaud's face had drained of colour. His legs felt like jelly and wouldn't let him stand on them. He stammered a reply, "I'm not sure I have an up to date number for Emily. Perhaps in Sebastian's phone…?"

"We've tried to get into his mobile, but we can't unlock it. You wouldn't happen to know his passkey would you?"

"Yes, I do. It's the same as the lock to the barn here – 4422," Arnaud stuttered.

Dai made a swift call to update somebody and stayed just long enough to take Arnaud's contact details, promising to keep him updated. His description of the accident was sketchy; Sebastian's black Subaru had been found in a ditch. From appearances, he had swerved to avoid something in the road - another car, an animal. He may even have skidded on a patch of black ice. It wasn't clear. There was nothing else at the scene when he was found.

"His chances of pulling through?" Catherine could hardly hear herself speaking.

"I honestly don't know." Dai's voice sounded hollow. "The car was upside down and the driver's side took the impact. Sebastian has sustained head injuries and a few broken bones, but they're still doing a full examination at the hospital, so we won't know if there are any more injuries for a while. I'll keep you posted and I'm sorry to bring you such bad news at Christmas." He left, refusing the offer of food.

There was a shocked silence. Nobody in the room felt like eating any more.

A thought occurred to Noah. If it hadn't have been for the two pints in the pub and a large glass of homemade wine back at the farmhouse, he might not have spoken it aloud. But he did.

"What happens if Sebastian dies? What happens to the farm? Will you and Catherine have to move out?"

Arnaud answered, "I have no idea Noah. I don't even know if Sebastian has changed his will since Emily left him. Let's not go there just now."

Catherine sat, tight-lipped. She was feeling dreadful about the fleeting thought that crossed her mind. If Sebastian died, they might have to leave the farm. She had to admit, she wouldn't be too upset at that.

# 7

## MARSHES & MOUNTAINS

### Noah's Diary:

Tuesday 16 January

New year, new diary. And, this year come what may, I am going to write. Catherine says if you want to be a good writer, you have to get something down on paper every day, so voilà. And while I'm at it, here's a summary of my Unusual Job Programme (UJP) to date:

<u>Jobs tried so far</u>: juggler, animal keeper, snail breeder, performance artist. Results - less than perfect.

<u>Jobs to try</u>: crisp tester, golf ball diver, London Dungeon actor, waterslide tester.

The reason for these unusual jobs dear reader? To give me life experience. I am young and inexperienced and need something to write about. And, frankly, my own life at this moment in time is about as boring as watching The Sphinx. More boring actually. I saw quite an interesting programme on The Sphinx the other day. Unfortunately, my UJP seems to have taken a nosedive, as I am currently a supermarket shelf packer (part time) (nights). My expectations of seeing the seedier side of life via a night job have not been met. Who knows, I may yet come across some interesting crime being committed on my way home from work. I live in hope.

Aha, do I hear you asking? You want to hear some details of

*my life all the same? Thank you so much, dear reader, for your encouragement. So (dramatic pause) the story so far in a plot that has taken more twists and turns than yarn on Arnaud's spinning wheel. Well, Sebastian is still in hospital in a coma and who knows if he is going to come out of it or not. Of course, this leaves Arnaud and Catherine somewhat in the lurch with the trekking centre. I confess, I am sorely tempted to take up Arnaud's generous offer and work for them. But, on the other hand, I feel I need to make my own way in the*

Noah put down his pen and massaged his cramped fingers. Arnaud's parting gift to him had been a beautiful leather-bound notebook, which, he decided, gave his diary entries and writing notes more gravitas than a computer page. He looked up at the white sheets hanging from the ceiling which divided the artists' work spaces in the top floor studio, remembering how he had helped Catherine and Sarah install them when the studio was re-opened eight years ago. Sarah had painted huge flower designs on the sheets in sweeping brush strokes. The colours were fading now, Noah noticed.

The sheet hanging in front of his work space had been designed with calligraphy instead of flowers. It was where Catherine used to sit at her laptop and write when she lived with them in the white house. Its current occupant was on holiday, so Noah had installed himself there, hoping Catherine's writing muse might transfer itself to him, but no inspiration was forthcoming. He stared out of the window, over the marshes at the now vacant cottage where Arnaud and Catherine used to live. The new owners were due to move in soon. Noah wondered if they might provide him with some material for a book.

Catherine was sitting at her keyboard, trying to focus on the screen. She'd written precisely nothing all morning. She tried to stem the panic that was rising in her throat and swallowed. This never used to happen to her. Usually her head was brimming with ideas and her biggest challenge was to bring them into order and draw out the most useful strands to weave into her writing.

She tried not to think of the fact she was due to deliver a plot synopsis to her publisher by the end of the month. Pressure was the one thing that didn't work for her at all. She looked out at the meadows behind the farmhouse, her gaze following the slope up towards the mountains beyond. The tops of them were still covered with a dusting of snow, like a lace mantle. It was beautiful, she had to admit, but she ached after the background rumble of waves and the cry of seagulls. The mountains felt so silent, so still in comparison.

A rustling from the far corner pulled Noah out of his daydream.

"Sarah?"

"Ye-es…"

"D'you fancy a coffee?"

"I was just thinking of taking a break. Sounds perfect."

The sound of footsteps crossing the room was followed by the sight of an impish face peering round the sheet. This week, Sarah's hair was back to its normal shade of bright red. She'd been trialling turquoise for a while, but her boyfriend had told her it clashed with her green eyes. A bit harsh, but true, Noah had thought.

He stood up, towering above the elfish figure. Sarah was in her mid-thirties now, but still as skinny and waif-like as ever. She undid the lime green scarf that had been holding her long hair back and shook her head. It looked like a sea urchin when the tide floods in and the tentacles spring to life, turning it from a blob of purple jelly into a mass of wispy floating strands, Noah decided.

"Hang on, just got to write something down," he turned back to his notebook and scribbled the description. It was good.

The two of them tramped down the stairs, past the second-floor landing, where Toby and Noah's bedrooms lay, and on down to the first floor. Out of habit, Sarah lit the gas stove and put a battered kettle on to heat, while Noah rummaged in the pantry for something to eat.

"Blast, I told dad I'd go shopping today. Totally forgot. There's no food around. Hang on - a bit of dry bread. That'll do for toast. Want anything Sarah?"

"I'm fine thanks, I had breakfast before I left home."

Noah was ravenous. As usual.

A bundle of shapeless fur on a blanket in the far side of the room morphed into a black dog which stood up, stretched its front legs and yawned loudly. Oscar padded over to the kitchen, deciding it was worth getting out of his sunny bed for food. He rubbed his face on Sarah's leg. She stroked him, absent-mindedly, still concentrating on the kettle.

"I'm just gonna quickly check the chickens for eggs."

"Okay."

Noah ran down to the ground floor, two steps at a time, and strode along the dark passageway to the garden door, Oscar hot on his heels. The light bulb needed replacing - he had promised to do that too. It was amazing how little time there was when you had nothing to do, he mused.

Outside, the sunshine of a few minutes ago had

disappeared and an annoying drizzle tickled Noah's ears. He turned his collar up and headed left across the lawn to the chicken run. He'd forgotten to let them out this morning and they were all bunched up at the door, squawking at him. All except one, that was. A fluffy brown Pekin bantam was floating on the little pond. Two Indian Runner ducks, looking very put out, stood at the edge of the plastic container, quacking loudly.

Noah sighed heavily. The bantam had been a good egg layer and well behaved, on the whole.

"Okay, everybody out. I need to assess the crime scene." He hunched his shoulders, half Colombo, half Poirot, and opened the door. Four chickens scrambled out, pushing past him, while the ducks looked over at Noah, still quacking. He slipped on a pair of blue plastic gloves from a tin trunk on top of the chicken coop and went to fish the corpse out of pond. Oscar crept into the run behind him and began sniffing around.

"Estimated time of death – 05:00 hours," Noah guessed wildly. "Cause of death...ducks - did you see anything? Hello, ducks?"

The ducks looked at him mutely, and as Noah lifted the chicken out of the water by its feet, they swished onto the pond and began swimming around.

He held up the dripping corpse and examined it. No obvious injuries.

"Hmm, death by misadventure. Case closed. Bugger."

Oscar was scrabbling and sniffing by the chicken run fence.

"Oscar, don't start digging or..." Noah paused. He spotted a little hole the other side of the run and freshly turned earth just in front of it.

"Darn it, rats again. Well done Oscar, treat for you my

lad. The dog detective solves the crime."

The last time the local rat population had breached the chicken run fencing, one of the birds had been bitten. Noah had treated its infected leg with wound powder but it died a few days later. He suspected that this time around, the bantam had taken fright at the rat and backed into the pond. Or perhaps she'd died defending her fellow poultry. Anyhow, her fate was sealed, her final destination, the cooking pot.

He opened the nesting box with one hand, the other still holding the dead chicken by its feet. Three pale brown eggs lay on the straw. Noah bent down and held the lid open with his nose, while he picked up the eggs with one hand and put them into the pocket of his combat trousers. Then he exited the chicken run and walked back to the house, swinging the chicken carcass as he went.

In the kitchen area, Sarah had finished making tea and was blowing the steam from her big blue cup. Oscar had beaten Noah upstairs and was crunching on a dog biscuit.

"Not another one," she remarked as he held up the corpse.

"Two in one month. One of old age. This one drowned in the duck pond. Oscar found a rat hole."

"Oh well, at least you don't have to go shopping for supper."

"Every cloud…" Noah acknowledged, slung the carcass on the kitchen counter and picked up his mug of tea, with a nod at Sarah. "Cheers."

Underneath the table, Oscar had finished the biscuit Sarah had thrown to him. He sniffed the air, excited by the scent of the chicken carcass above him. That meant roast chicken for dinner. It was a good day.

After the tea break, Noah stood at the window in the top floor gallery, looking out at the back garden. The chickens had spread out, stabbing the grass lawn for worms and bugs. An idea came to him. He mulled it over. Yes, yes it might work rather well. He dashed back to his booth, scribbled a few words into his journal and underlined them with a flourish: _Oscar, The Dog Detective_. Then, his fingers flew over the page, writing madly to keep up with his train of thought. It was going to be a best seller, he knew it.

Catherine's screen now held the beginnings of a shopping list. She'd given up on her synopsis and allowed the thoughts which she had been keeping at bay, to intrude. A thud from the front door downstairs announced Arnaud's arrival. She closed the document and powered down her laptop.

In the kitchen, Arnaud was standing at the Aga, kettle in one hand. The stray cat, which seemed to have taken up permanent residence with them, had threaded itself around his legs and was purring.

"How was Sebastian?" Catherine asked him.

"Nothing. No response to anything I said. It's so horrible seeing him lying there. He's lost more weight and his skin's a funny greyish colour," Arnaud sounded uncharacteristically depressed.

"What did the hospital staff say?"

"They were pretty non-committal. Apparently, his life signs are good. Steady pulse and so on. All we can do is wait."

It was the third time Arnaud had made the trip to the hospital in Hereford. Catherine walked up to Arnaud and wrapped her arms around him. He hugged her back, letting the tension drain away.

"Coffee?" asked Arnaud.

Catherine pulled away. "No thanks. I've been fuelling myself on caffeine all morning. If you don't mind, I think I'll just drive up to the mountains and get a bit of fresh air. I'm feeling cooped in and fuzzy."

"That's fine. I've going to check the llamas and milk the sheep."

"Okay. I'll be back for lunch. It's too cold to stay out long."

Catherine pulled on an oversized waterproof, checked in the pocket for the car key, and left the house, her walking boots clumping on the drive. She opened the door of the battered old farm Land Rover and climbed in. At the end of the farm track, she turned the vehicle right, towards the mountains. The thin layer of snow from the evening before had melted off the road in the midday sunshine, leaving it wet and glistening. The Land Rover twisted and turned along its serpentine bends for a few hundred yards until she rounded the final corner and slowed down, gritting her teeth as the vehicle juddered over the cattle grid onto the mountain.

She exhaled, enjoying the freedom. In front of her, the winter grass was still green and spongy, flowing and undulating over folds of earth. Small gnarled trees and gorse bushes dotted the lower pastures, which gradually rose to the foot of the mountains half a mile further away. Here and there, clumps of dead bracken and grubby off-white sheep speckled the hillside. The lower part of the mountain was covered in a faint haze of purple heather, which gradually gave way to thin, yellowing grass, interspersed with outcrops of rock higher up. Flickering silver streams slashed the sides of the long ridge that stretched in front of Catherine. At the left end, the mountain range slid down in a curved slope towards Hay Common. To the right, the ridge continued as far as she could see, eventually becoming the Brecon Beacons and Fforest Fawr beyond that. The low mountains were easily climbed in summer, but in this icy weather, she guessed they could become dangerous.

As she drove towards Hay Bluff, the lane took her in and out of clumps of trees, every now and again twisting back to the cropped grassland of the mountain slopes. Eventually she came to a sharp bend in the road, where a stream crossed in front of her, spilling over the steep edge to her left, wending its way to the valley below. She had to stop. The place was magical. She pulled over on a patch of grass at the side of the road and killed the engine. Silence. She opened the car door and climbed out. New sounds gradually penetrated her consciousness, one by one; the faraway bleating of sheep; a tractor in the valley below; the splash of the water as it crossed over the road and danced off the rock face below.

Locking the car, she hesitated briefly, unsure of which direction to take, then struck out towards the mountain. She followed the lane, walking upwards until the trees to her right died out, exposing the mountain range beyond. In front of her, the road dipped and reappeared over the windswept, open expanse of Hay Common. She struck off the road and onto a track that ran parallel to the mountains, rippling over the contours of the land. There were old hoofprints in the mud – indicating it was one of the many riding trails that crisscrossed the lower section of the mountains.

She filled her lungs with the cold, pure air until the muzziness in her head dissipated. Up in the sky, a large black crow wheeled overhead, cawing into the stillness. Unaware of doing so, Catherine closed her eyes. When she opened them, she wasn't alone.

She gasped.

"I'm so sorry, I've startled you."

Catherine peered more closely at the dumpy lady in front of her. Her long grey hair ran amok in curls, blown round her face by the wind. Wrapped up in an assortment of old waterproofs, it was impossible to tell the size of her.

"No...well, yes...but it's my fault for standing around with my eyes closed," Catherine stammered.

The lady smiled and her face changed instantly, revealing laughter lines at the edge of her eyes. "Forgive me, but, I noticed you walking along the road and you seemed familiar somehow. Have we met before? I'm shocking with names and faces and I'm always dreading being rude to people." Her articulation was crystal clear and her voice one of the most melodious that Catherine had ever heard.

"No, no not that I recall." Catherine was convinced they had never made their acquaintance before now. She would have remembered her for sure.

"I'm probably getting old and muddled," the woman confided. "No, delete that, I *am* old and muddled."

Catherine allowed herself a hesitant smile. "Do you live around here? We - my husband and I - have just moved to the area. We're working at the trekking centre just above Llaneilis."

"Kestrel Farm? You must be the new managers. Have you heard any news of Sebastian?"

"Arnaud - my husband - has just come back from

visiting him this morning. He's still in a coma. No change yet, I'm afraid."

The woman's mouth pursed. "Is there anything I can do? For Sebastian? For you?"

Catherine was touched by the spontaneous willingness to help. "I don't think there's much anyone can do for him just now. We can only hope - and if you're the praying sort, pray…" her voice trailed off.

Surprisingly a smile twitched at the corners of the woman's mouth. Then, "And you? How are you managing at the farm? I gather it's in a bit of a muddle. I'm afraid it's a small world around here and the local grapevine is pretty fruitful," she grimaced apologetically.

"Well, it's not the easiest situation at all," Catherine acknowledged. "We'll try and hold things together until Sebastian comes round and see what's what then. We can manage with looking after the horses and sorting out the centre, but Sebastian hadn't got around to telling us anything about the school bookings for this season and how that all works. That's a bit of a worry, for sure."

"Have you always worked with horses?" The woman seemed to see deeper than Catherine's answers.

"No, actually not at all. My husband, Arnaud, keeps llamas and sheep and has a couple of horses of his own. He's brilliant with animals, but we've neither of us done anything like this before. I'm a writer by profession and until recently, spent most of my time locked away scribbling books."

The woman opened her mouth in a wide 'O' of surprise. She put her hand on Catherine's arm.

"I have a feeling I do know who you are after all. Was your mother a writer too, by any chance?"

"Yes, yes she was," Catherine was taken aback.

You must be Catherine then. You're the spitting image of Amelia at that age."

"You knew my mother?"

"Yes, and your father too."

The mountains seemed to be spinning around Catherine. She breathed in sharply and they righted themselves. She was glad of the woman's hand on her arm, now holding her steady.

"I'm sorry, now I've shocked you. Why don't you come back to my house for a cup of tea? It's just around the corner. I'm sure you will be interested in what I can tell you. And I would love the chance to get to know you better. You were a very young child the last time I met you."

# 8

# JOHANNA

From the exterior, the house looked virtually uninhabitable. At the far end of the old farm cottage, the moss-covered slate roof had collapsed, leaving the beams partially exposed. A few tiles clung on precariously to the wooden trusses; others lay stacked up on the ground in neat piles. The roof over the nearest part of the stone building was sagging, but intact. Catherine could see the timber around the windows was rotting, paint peeling and some of the stonework looked in desperate need of repair. Johanna pushed open a rickety wooden gate and trod carefully along an uneven brick pathway to a door in the side of the building.

"We'll have to go in this way. I had to board up the front door to stop it falling apart." She seemed completely unperturbed by the state of her dwelling.

The side door led directly into a large sitting room. Pale cream walls reflected the late morning sunshine streaming in through windows on two sides, creating a surprisingly light space. Catherine was struck by its simplicity. The only furniture was a rocking chair, an old sofa, and a small foldaway table with a couple of dining chairs. The walls were almost bare, apart from a faded watercolour of the Black Mountains that hung at the far end and a small wooden cross on the opposite side. There were no ornaments, no knick-knacks.

"Sit here, that sheep fleece is definitely the luxury item I would take to my desert island," the silver-haired woman directed Catherine to the rocking chair which was draped with a dark brown fluffy sheepskin.

Catherine sunk down into it. The fleece was beautifully warm and incredibly relaxing. Johanna, disappeared through a doorway and returned a few minutes later, handing Catherine a glass.

"Elderflower cordial. I've just defrosted a container from last year. I hope you enjoy it."

Catherine took a sip. The silky, slightly tart drink tasted delicious.

Her hostess took off her layers of outer clothing, hung her coat on a rusty nail that was sticking out of the wall, and eased herself onto the sofa, a glass of the golden cordial in her hand. She sniffed it and sipped, appreciatively, commenting, "I'll be sad when this is all gone. I'll have to wait until June to pick more flowers."

Divested of her coat and fleece, the older woman was much slimmer than she'd first appeared. She'd tied her long silver curly hair into a ponytail, revealing a nut-brown, weather-beaten face, with the creases of laughter lines around her eyes and wide, generous mouth. Catherine guessed that she spent a considerable amount of time outside on the mountains.

"I'm so sorry my dear, it's just occurred to me that you don't even know my name. I'm Johanna. I can't imagine your mother ever spoke of me. She wasn't the kind of person to talk much about anyone else in her life."

"No, you're right. She never did."

Johanna sighed. "You must have had quite a lonely childhood, I'm guessing."

Catherine felt uncomfortable. She was unhappy at a total stranger passing judgment on her life.

Johanna picked up the shift in atmosphere immediately. "What if I told you a bit about myself and how I came to know your mother? I hesitate to ramble, I don't even know how busy you are or how much time you've got. People always seem so rushed nowadays..."

Catherine loosened up slightly, still on edge. "Yes, yes, if you could, I would like that. I'm in no particular hurry." Her tone had become distant and polite.

"If you'll bear with me, I'll try and make a long story short."

Johanna was a born storyteller, with a way of weaving words together in her melodious voice that created vivid images in Catherine's mind. After a few sentences, she was totally engaged. The walls of the room disappeared and Catherine stepped into Johanna's tale, an onlooker in the wings of a stage set, watching a play unfolding...

"I was born on the Isle of Wight. Such a *normal* childhood you know. Running around on beaches, shrimping, catching the ferry over to the mainland. It's quite an unremarkable kind of place really. Nothing much happened there. And then we moved here, to the Black Mountains. My father decided he wanted to give up his job as a solicitor and become a farmer. In those days, you could actually make money farming. And he did too. He was surprisingly successful. I think my mother could never quite believe it. Once in a while, I was taken to London to be clothed properly. We always went to Harvey Nichols - it was quite something after the little provincial shops near us. My father used to tag along too. He used the opportunity to catch up with his accountant and other business acquaintances.

"That's when I first met your grandfather. Once, I don't remember when, I was taken to tea at Claridge's. I stuffed my face and felt as sick as a dog afterwards, but it was worth it. I was introduced to a tall, white-haired man and his two daughters. I don't even know whether my parents had arranged to meet them or if they'd just bumped into them by chance, the memories are a bit hazy now. I was told that the man was an old family friend and - in a hushed tone - that the girls' mother had died some time before.

"I thought I ought to feel sorry for them, but you couldn't really, they looked so alive, so vital. Particularly the younger one. Of course, I'm talking about your aunt Ozzie. Funnily enough, it was your mother I was drawn to. More reserved, very self-possessed. But very much her own person. That appealed to me. I don't like people who grab at you and want to own you. Never have done.

"I did all the usual school stuff and I think I got the kind of results I was expected to get. I don't think I really distinguished myself in any particular field. I had a happy childhood, but I always felt a little bored with my uneventful life. I wanted to get away. I guess most young people do. I'd just finished school the year that Hugh - your father came to Wales. Your mother had come over to stay with us - I think your grandfather thought it would be helpful for her to see something else of the world, get away from home for a bit. There was a subtext somewhere in the arrangement - I think her relationship with him wasn't good at all. We hung around with a group of my friends, mostly other farming children. I guess it was inevitable that somebody would fall for Hugh. He was glamorous - slim, muscled with a long fringe falling over his eyes. A bit older than the rest of us, he'd already lived abroad in France, working as a ski instructor. He'd come to help with the lambing on one of the local farms, and stayed on into the summer. But his big passion was rock climbing. Of course, there's no real climbing to speak of in these mountains, but Hugh loved to be outside walking, in all weathers."

Catherine was hesitant to interrupt the lyrical flow of Johanna's story, but the question was burning in her head. "What was he like? My father, I mean. My mother never really talked about him much."

"He was very kind, Catherine. That is what I remember about him most. He was good with the sheep - always went the extra mile in caring for them, and he was the same with people. Perhaps that was what attracted your mother to him. I think she was probably a little starved of love in her life. He treated her much as he would one of the orphan lambs. Looking out for her comfort - but not in a claustrophobic way. He was natural, intuitive. We all envied your mother really. Hugh was quite a catch."

"Did you go to the wedding? What was it like?"

"No, I'm sorry to say I wasn't able to. I was out of the country when your parents married. I'd already left for Africa by then, to teach English, and didn't come back until after your father had died. I got a letter from your mother, telling me of the tragedy just before I was due to come back on leave. I arranged for her to come and stay with us at the family farm near here. She decided that she wanted to scatter your father's ashes on the Black Mountains. I couldn't tell you exactly where. She insisted on going out alone. It was a horrible time. I've never seen anybody look so devastated. Hugh was her whole world. She seemed to withdraw from everything - and everybody. It was as if her voice became a whisper and her imprint on the world a shadow of what it once was."

Catherine shuddered. She knew her mother had never recovered from the tragedy. All through Catherine's childhood, her mother had remained distant. Caring but not demonstrative. Barely affectionate. She had been killed in a traffic accident just after Catherine's eighteenth birthday, but it seemed to Catherine as if something in her had died all those years ago with Hugh's climbing accident. She came to. Johanna was still talking.

"It wasn't until I was back in Africa that your mother discovered she was pregnant - with you. The sad thing was, most people would have been pleased to have had something to remind them of their dead husband, something to give them hope. But Amelia resented her pregnancy - she felt somehow God had done a deal with her. Taken Hugh away and left her with you. I'm sorry. Am I being blunt?"

Catherine shook her head. It was all making sense.

"We corresponded fairly regularly during the first years of your life. Amelia wrote about you dispassionately - observing your childhood, but somehow not really engaging with you in an emotional way. I even met you once. She brought you to Wales when I next came back on leave. By then I had become a Christian and turned into a missionary. You were a pretty little thing, with huge big eyes and so many questions! But very solemn. It was not long after that we lost touch. My parents sold the farm and I moved around a bit in Africa. Perhaps letters went astray. I don't know. I regret not trying harder to contact your mother again. I was abroad for over twenty years and Britain felt so remote from my life, so *thin* compared with Africa, where my life was full of colour, singing, heat, life and death, miracles and the struggles of everyday living in sheer and utter poverty."

"So why did you come back here?"

"I caught malaria for the third time and had to return. I was quite a physical wreck. I'd planned to head on back to Africa as soon as I'd recovered, but after a few months the mission station where I had been working was closed down due to lack of staff, and I didn't have the energy to look for a new position. My next step was the craziest thing. I often wonder why I did it."

"Did what?"

"I went into a convent. Became a nun. Looking back, I think it was actually due to culture shock. Britain had moved on so much during the time I was abroad. People seemed so materialistic. I'd become used to a simple, basic existence. I couldn't be happy with the way everyone lived. Nowadays, they call it reverse culture shock. At the time, there was no definition for what I was feeling. And I loved God so much. With an intense passion. I still do - that's never changed."

"I can't place you as a nun," Catherine spoke the words before she'd realised. She bit her lip. "I mean, you just look too vibrant. A bit like Maria from *The Sound of Music.*"

Johanna laughed, a rich, melodic sound. "You've got it in one. I didn't last long in the convent. Although I think Maria was probably a far nicer person than me. I hadn't appreciated how tough I'd become, living in Africa. There I'd had to be virtually self-sufficient, dealing with all sorts of crises. I got asked to leave the convent after I'd called the Mother Superior a bitch. That was actually one of the most satisfying things I've ever done. I had to repent afterwards, but even so, it was the truth. She was a real cow."

Catherine raised her eyebrows. She warmed to Johanna's honesty.

"What did you do next?"

The older woman answered, "I figured I needed some time to reflect and I came back here to Wales as a sort of self-imposed penance. Funnily enough, I've found my place here and I love it. I suppose you could call me a sort of hermit. The locals call me all sorts of things - 'hermit' is probably one of the more polite terms. That's the thing with God, Catherine. He's always full of surprises. And now look, you're here."

"Yes, I can hardly believe it still. It feels as if so many missing pieces of my life have just fallen into place." She sat, reflecting on Johanna's story. Then she ventured, "And my mother? You obviously heard that she'd died?"

"Yes, one day, I happened to see her obituary in the Times. I guess her editor must have submitted it. By then I was too late to make contact with her."

"I didn't even know her obituary was in the paper. How ironic," was Catherine's response.

"It's one of my biggest regrets Catherine, never making contact with your mother again. And another is that I should, after her death, have made an effort to get in touch with you and I didn't. I'm sorry for that." She paused, eyes sparkling, "Now God has given me a second chance. Or so I believe, anyhow."

# 9

## A FARMING LIFE

Arnaud straightened up and lifted the stainless steel pail to one side. He'd just finished milking the last sheep and the pail was now half-full of warm, frothing creamy milk. He untied the makeshift rope halter and released the tiny chocolate brown ewe. She clattered over to the end of the barn where the other four were nibbling on a bale of hay. Arnaud eased himself upright, his knees stiff from the cold. He hung the halter rope over a peg on the wall, picked up the pail, and strode over to the barn entrance A shaft of daylight sliced into the semi-darkness of the barn as he cracked open the door.

The ewes looked up, sensing freedom. They ran towards Arnaud, head butted their way past his legs and dashed out into the yard. In the top paddock, the ram lifted its head and bleated. The ewes called back and darted up the hill towards the paddock, bleating back. Arnaud shut the barn door and followed them, pail in hand. He left the bucket just outside the entrance to the farmhouse, warm milk steaming in the cold air, and strode up the farm track towards the top paddock.

The ewes were waiting for Arnaud at the field gate, impatient at his slowness. Arnaud pushed the catch and swung the gate just wide enough to let them through. Two of the llamas had come to stand by the gate, aiming to escape.

"No you don't," Arnaud chided Pepper and Chili. The two youngest llamas were still quite flighty. Pepper, creamy-coloured with a scattergun of brown dots, snorted at him and nipped Chili's flank in annoyance. The two skittered off, running along the fence and scattering the ewes as they went.

A large dark-brown llama came strolling over to the gate, ears twitching. Arnaud stroked its neck fondly. The llama made a low, throaty humming noise.

"Are you enjoying yourself here Filou? At least you're warm with your thick coat. Reminds me, I need to do some spinning…"

He thought of the pile of fleeces they'd stored in a corner of the barn, regretting that he hadn't had time to do any spinning or weaving since their arrival in Wales. He enjoyed the challenge of their new life, but a small part of him missed the simplicity of their former existence on the marshes, with few demands or worries.

*Unlike the present*, he found himself thinking.

His attention was caught by the noise of a tractor engine. He turned to see an old red Massey Ferguson pulling a trailer, turn into the farm driveway. It rattled over the cattle grid and came to a halt next to Arnaud. He waved and walked over to the cab door, which opened to reveal a grizzled old man with a thick mop of dark grey hair.

"Rhys, that was good timing!"

The farmer nodded a greeting at the Frenchman, then spoke, "I was just taking some silage to my cows and thought I'd bring you the lot over I'd promised."

"Thank you, that's very kind. Are you okay if we take it straight down to the lower paddock?"

"No problem. You may as well hop on the trailer. Be easier with the gate."

Arnaud leapt lightly onto the trailer and held onto the front bar for balance. The tractor lurched off, nearly destabilising him. They bounced and swayed down the track to the horses' field.

Rhys had turned up at the farmhouse a few days after Christmas. His gruff, surly exterior hid a kind heart, Arnaud discovered. At first, he'd struggled to understand the farmer's broad Welsh accent, as he'd muttered, "I've heard about Sebastian. Just wanted to let you know I'm over the way at the farm on the other side of the road. Let me know if you need any help."

It was only then Arnaud discovered that much of Kestrel Farm's winter hay and silage was bought in from Rhys. Another thing that Sebastian had neglected to tell them. Arnaud had told Rhys they had enough fodder to last a couple of weeks, and they agreed that the farmer would bring some over in due course.

The tractor's brakes squealed as Rhys stopped at the entrance to the field. Arnaud jumped off the trailer and ran to open the gate. Rhys halted as he drew level with Arnaud, shouting, "Usually I just drive along the top of the field and somebody scatters the silage from the trailer. Is that okay by you?"

"Yes fine. Let's go."

Arnaud waited as the tractor drew further into the field, then closed the gate. The horses' heads were up, ears pricked. Several of them had started to move towards the vehicle, nostrils flared, scenting the feed.

Arnaud climbed back onto the trailer and began to tear

at one of the huge rolls of fodder, ripping apart chunks of the sweet-smelling fermented grass. The tractor pulled away, jerking the trailer over a rut and Arnaud had to grab the roll of silage to keep his balance. It wasn't helped by the fact they were driving along the side of a steep hill. He managed to wedge himself against a couple of rolls, then tossed chunks of silage off the side of the trailer, to where the ponies were now jostling each other to snatch at the food. More ponies appeared from the bottom of the field, cantering up towards them, as the trailer rumbled on along the edge of the paddock.

Rhys swung around in a slow circle, just as Arnaud had finished distributing the first roll. He sliced the plastic webbing off a second with his penknife and started to tear portions out of it. Arnaud was just throwing the last bit of the third roll as Rhys turned around in the tractor cab and gave Arnaud a thumbs up. He picked up speed and headed for the top of the field. Arnaud jumped off, checking behind the tractor to make sure none of the ponies was about to escape, but they were all occupied with the fodder, heads down, relishing their feed.

Rhys opened the cab window. "Are you still storing the feed in the barn?"

"Yes, we are."

Arnaud followed the old tractor on foot as it laboured its way up the short section of steep track to the barn on Arnaud's left. On the right, below the farmhouse, was the indoor school. He unbarred the large barn door and swung it open. It caught in the breeze and Arnaud had to use all his strength to prevent it being snatched out of his grasp. He leaned down and twisted the bottom latch, so it slipped neatly into a hole in the ground, securing it.

Then the two men manhandled the huge bales of

silage, rolling them into the left-hand side of the barn. It was exhausting work, and they were both red-faced and sweating, despite the cold.

When they had pushed the final roll into the barn, Arnaud turned to Rhys, "Would you like a tea or coffee? There's some cake as well."

"Wouldn't say no," came Rhys's response.

Arnaud knew the elderly farmer lived alone and guessed he would enjoy the chance of a chat.

In the kitchen, Rhys sat down at the table with the ease of somebody who knew his way around. Arnaud ventured, "You obviously knew Sebastian's parents when they were alive."

"Yes, they were a bit older than me, but we pretty much grew up together, attended the school in the village. It was a quite a tight knit community. Still is."

"So, you've farmed here all your life?"

"Yes," the elderly Welshman leaned back in the chair and cupped his hands around the mug of tea that Arnaud placed in front of him, warming them. "I left school as soon as I could and helped my da with the herd. It was always expected that I would take over. I was an only child and fortunately I enjoyed the lifestyle here. Not like my son. He couldn't wait to be gone. He's living over Hereford way, teaching science. Where he gets that from I've no idea. His ma was a farmer's daughter too - from the other side of the valley."

"She's…dead?"

"Yes, love her. Passed away over ten years ago. A massive heart attack and she was gone, just like that. I suppose it's better than creaking into old age," he made a wry grimace.

"You look in good shape Rhys."

"Mustn't grumble. I'm lucky really. The odd twinge and a bit of arthritis, that's all."

"I understand from what Sebastian told me that you took care of the horses after Emily left - until we came."

"I did as much as I could. I'm not a horse person really, but fortunately this herd is pretty hardy. It was just as well you two arrived when you did. I don't like to think what would have happened if you hadn't baled Sebastian out. There was no way he would have come back to manage the farm here. And then with the accident..." Rhys's voice tailed off. Arnaud could see genuine concern on his face, and knew from the hospital staff that Rhys had paid at least one visit to Sebastian's ward.

Rhys continued, "He's no better I'm assuming?"

"No better, no worse. I guess it's a waiting game. Crazy huh. And the police still don't seem to have been able to get hold of Emily."

Rhys frowned, "I'm not surprised, she's probably flitted off with some man. Between you and me, I didn't take to her really. She never seemed satisfied with her lot. Always looking around at the other men. I should think there's plenty of wives in the village who are glad she's gone."

"It must have been hard for her on her own here," Arnaud felt he owed it to Emily to defend her case.

"It was her choice. Sebastian was happy to sell up. Even had a buyer lined up. But Emily wanted to make a go of the place."

"I didn't know that," Arnaud was surprised.

"I gather you knew Emily. Maybe I'm speaking out of turn," Rhys looked a little abashed.

"Well, she was a friend of my first wife. I suppose we got on okay, but she wasn't really my type of person. Too complicated for me, if you know what I mean."

Rhys nodded, "I gather you come from a farming background yourself Arnaud. You certainly seem to know what you're doing here."

"I only wish I did. I'm fine with taking care of the animals, but getting to grips with the business side of things is proving a challenge, particularly with the current state of affairs."

"Where did your family have a farm?"

"The farm was in Brittany, on the north-west coast of France. We had a herd of Normande cows - the brown and cream ones. My father also liked to rear rare breed animals - to do his bit. And we had a few horses. That's where I learned to ride. I couldn't live without my horses."

"And the llamas?"

"They came later. After my first marriage broke up, a friend of mine took pity on me and gave me some work on his farm. I was in a bit of a state. Our child was a cot death baby. Our marriage never survived the grief of that. I spent a year helping my friend and he had a few llamas. Eventually he sold the farm, and gave me the llamas. I brought them over to the UK. I wanted to start afresh somewhere and I'd heard of a cottage to rent on the marshes, on the Kent coast. It was a good move for me. That's where I met Catherine."

"Good luck to you both," Rhys was philosophical. "You've got your work cut out for you here."

Arnaud smiled, "I don't mind a challenge. Another cup of tea?"

Rhys was reluctant to leave the warm kitchen and agreed readily, commenting, "I'm guessing that's milk from your sheep in the tea. It's surprisingly good."

"Yes, it's not as strong tasting as you might think."

"Are they a French breed?"

"Yes - they're Ouessant sheep. Originally from an island just off the western tip of Brittany. Catherine and I bought this little flock a couple of years ago when we went to France to visit. They reminded me of my childhood. I had a couple of Ouessants when I was growing up."

"And the llamas? Can you milk them?"

"Not really. But I spin their fleece and knit with it. I've got a loom and spinning wheels somewhere in the barn. I've not had a chance to even unpack it all since we arrived. I used to sell my stuff in a local market."

"It would go down well in Hay, if you try there. Just the kind of thing the tourists would love."

"That's a good idea, I hadn't even thought of that."

The two talked comfortably until Rhys glanced up and noticed the wooden clock on the kitchen wall.

"Sorry Arnaud, I need to go. I've got to go and look at a new bull over Brecon way."

After Rhys left, Arnaud sat at the kitchen table musing. Coming to the farm in Wales had brought back memories of his childhood in France. Unlike Catherine's, his had been a happy childhood. Although he too was an only child, their farmhouse had always been full of people and activity. His parents were gregarious, happy for neighbours to pop round at any time, and there were plenty of children in the local village for Arnaud to play with. He had spent the summers running wild on the farm with his friends, once he had finished his daily chore of helping his father with the milking.

It was the summers that he remembered the best; harvesting the hay crop well into the night, with the lights from the tractor spooking foxes, field mice, even the odd badger in their glare. Once a little mouse ran up his leg, it was so disorientated. There were plenty of early mornings, but his mother was always up before him, waiting in the kitchen with a bowl of hot chocolate and warmed baguette. He remembered her homemade berry jam - sharp and sweet at the same time. He felt as if his life had come full circle, once again submerged into a daily routine of a large herd of animals and wild nature. He didn't even mind the cold of the winter - somehow it made him feel alive, vital. He was in his element.

The crunch of tyres pulled him out of his reverie. It was Catherine returning. He glanced down at his phone and noticed he had a missed call and a text. Mobile signal tended to be patchy in the lower paddock. He dialled 121 and listened to the message, a quizzical look spreading across his face. Just as the message ended, Catherine burst through the kitchen door.

"Arnaud! You've never guess what. I've just met somebody who knew my parents! Not just my mother, but my father too. I still can't believe it - she was a friend of my mother's. What are the chances of bumping into somebody like that…"

"That's wonderful news Catherine!"

She threw herself into his arms, in an unusual display of emotion, tears in her eyes.

Arnaud hugged her, delighted. "Before you tell me all, I've got some news for you too. The hospital has just left me a message. Sebastian has come round - this morning in fact. They have done some more scans and spoken to him and it looks as if there isn't too much damage to his brain, thank goodness, but there's just one thing…"

"What's that?"

"He has amnesia. He can't remember a thing."

"He can't remember the accident? That's quite normal, isn't it?"

"Well, it's not just the accident. He can't remember anything at all - he doesn't even know his own name. And apparently, they have no idea of when or how much this could improve. I'm allowed to visit him, but they want to do some more tests first and also brief me on how to approach him."

Another complication. Catherine's heart sank. Not for the first time, she wished they had never set eyes on Kestrel Farm.

# 10

## PROGRESS

Sebastian lay in bed, enjoying the sunshine that streamed through the window and brightened up the hospital room. The thought struck him that this was the first morning he hadn't woken with a splitting headache. His broken leg and arm both still twinged uncomfortably and his back was sore, but it was a relief to be able to gaze around without wincing. It made it easier to collect his shuffled thoughts. Not that there were many of them.

For the past couple of mornings, he'd made a game of trying to see how many things he could work out about himself. He went through his mental list:

*I like dark chocolate, but I don't like milk chocolate. I'm fifty-five and I've been in a car accident. Apparently, I work - worked - in London in the City and I own a pony trekking farm in the Black Mountains - well done me. My parents are dead and my wife has left me - poor me. Hospital food is rubbish and I know there is better fare out there somewhere.*

He glanced over at a table opposite him, where somebody had thoughtfully arranged a group of get well cards.

*All those card senders are 'thinking about me' and one of them - my office - is paying for a room in this private hospital. Nice of them - well nice of their medical insurance company I guess.*

He looked around the room. It was small, but tastefully furnished, with pale green and turquoise striped curtains, a green armchair and dark wooden cabinet. There was a television screen on the wall above the cabinet, and a tray containing a bowl of fruit, a few bottles of water and fruit juices and a sealed packet of biscuits.

*Oh, and it seems I've got a friend called Arnaud and today - big day - he's coming to visit me. I haven't got a clue who the bloke is and can tell you absolutely nothing about him.*

He gave himself a mental slap. The specialist had encouraged Sebastian to focus on what he could discover about himself rather than get frustrated over this lack of recall.

*My favourite nurse is called Gina. My handwriting is pretty dreadful and I don't seem to be much of an artist. I prefer listening to the radio to watching television and I'd really like to get out of this place.*

A rap on the door and Sebastian's least favourite nurse, Ellen, walked into the room, announcing, "Your visitor's going to be arriving soon, let's get you sitting up properly."

Briskly, she hauled Sebastian up in the bed and picked up his dirty cereal bowl, clattering the spoon.

"I gather the specialist mentioned to you yesterday - he doesn't want your visitor to stay too long. You mustn't get too tired."

"Okay," said Sebastian. *I hate this kid gloves thing*, he thought.

"Anything else you need?" She turned and left, not really waiting for a response.

Sebastian looked down at the smart navy blue pyjamas

somebody had provided him with, and brushed a few crumbs off the jacket. A large cloud cut off the sunshine and Sebastian shivered. He reached over and dragged a dressing gown from the chair on his right. Clumsily, he pulled it around his shoulders and tried to ease it further down his back.

There was a soft tap on the door.

"Come in." Sebastian was surprised how shaky his voice came out. He cleared his throat and started again, but the door was already opening. A tall, lean, slightly rough-shaven man with long grey hair tied into a ponytail walked into the room. His pale blue jeans and navy fleece looked clean, but Sebastian could detect a very faint farmyard manure smell.

He was disappointed. He didn't recognise the man at all.

The visitor, however, seemed extraordinarily pleased to see him.

"Sebastian, it's great you're conscious! You've no idea how glad I am. You've given us all quite a fright."

The let down at not recognising his visitor was mitigated by the man's obvious concern. After a few days of friendly but slightly impersonal nursing care, it was surprisingly good to discover that he really mattered to somebody. More than one person from the sounds of it.

"You don't know who I am? No matter Sebastian. It'll come my friend. Years ago, when I lived back in France, an elderly beekeeper happened to be visiting me. I had only just started to keep bees and my two colonies were doing badly. I was so frustrated, you've no idea. His response? 'All in good time, all in good time.' And you know what - there was a good time. But also some bad times as well." Arnaud's eyes twinkled and he sat down in the armchair at the side of Sebastian's bed, laughing at his own comment.

Sebastian smiled. It felt good and he relaxed. Whoever he was, this bloke was pretty chilled and undemanding.

"You know," said Arnaud, a little more seriously, "they gave me a briefing in order to tell me what I should and shouldn't say to you, but actually I can't play along with things like that. Why don't you ask me some questions and I'll do my best to answer them. Are there things you want to know?"

There were lots of things that Sebastian very much wanted to know and the questions came tumbling out. The two were interrupted an hour later by the reappearance of the nurse.

"I'm sorry, your time is up. I understand you're coming back tomorrow Mr…?"

"Just Arnaud. And yes, of course I'm coming back."

As Arnaud stood to leave, Sebastian tried to quell his annoyance at the intrusive hospital system that wanted to regiment his life. He looked up at the tall Frenchman.

"I still don't remember you Arnaud, I'm afraid, but I'm so grateful for your time and pathetically grateful that you're coming back again tomorrow. And you know what, even though I don't remember you, I like you and I'd choose you as a mate again."

"*Merci*," grinned Arnaud. "*A demain.*"

For a weekday morning in late January, the coffee shop in Hay was surprisingly busy. People carrying trays squeezed past the bistro tables and chairs on the upper floor. Some were dressed in walking clothes, huge boots clomping on the bare wooden floorboards. Others had come for the bookshops, and were busy examining their purchases, exclaiming over rare or unusual finds, or nose deep, reading and lost to the world around them.

"Catherine, I'm so sorry I'm late! I've been trying to close the shop but more people kept wandering in. I've never known such a busy day for this time of year."

Eve was dressed in a long flowing floral print skirt and white cambric blouse, with a sheepskin body warmer. Two copper leaf-shaped earrings swung from her ears as she shook her head.

"No worries, it's actually been quite pleasurable to sit and do nothing for a few minutes."

Eve looked at the empty coffee cup on the table in front of Catherine, offering, "Can I get you another drink?"

"Yes, why not. I'll have a latte please."

Eve swished away, neatly weaving her way through the tables.

Snippets of conversation drifted around the room.

"…in quite good condition. I only need the 1984 annual to complete the set…"

"…over the Gospel Pass to Llanthony Abbey this afternoon…"

"…thought it was quite a lot of money for a second hand book…"

"…got to get back, Ewan's getting ready for lambing and he wants…"

"I'm so glad you called me to meet up. I was hoping you would." Eve was back with the drinks. She placed them on the table, and propped the tray against the leg of the table.

Catherine smiled, unsure how to react to this compliment. She turned the attention away from herself.

"It was so kind of you to listen to me the other week.

It struck me after I left that I didn't ask you anything about you. How long have you been running the shop? I loved it by the way, a fantastic selection of books..." She was aware that her words were clumsily running away with her.

"Thank you. To be honest, I felt very self-indulgent talking to you Catherine. It was so fascinating to hear more about the life of one of our popular authors, and I genuinely enjoyed meeting you."

"Thank you," Catherine replied.

"And I'm so glad you liked the bookshop. You've no idea how hard I've worked on it. I've only had *The Well-Thumbed Page* for a couple of years, and we're just about to break even, so I'm due for a little celebration soon."

"Well done, that's fantastic! What made you start the bookshop?"

"That's not so fantastic. My husband, Julian, died of lung cancer. We'd moved to Hay the year before, so I didn't even know that many people - perhaps that's why I really felt for you the other day. The plan was that we were going to retire here and spend our time walking, eating out, enjoying the scenery...that kind of thing. It didn't turn out quite like that."

"I'm so sorry, that's dreadful."

"It was, I feel like I'm only just coming out the other side of a long tunnel. It was the bookshop that rescued me really. I needed a project - something to occupy my time so I wasn't thinking about my own woes. And I needed something to challenge me. Well it certainly did." Eve smiled wryly.

"It can't be easy - there's so much competition around you."

"Yes, as you can see, Hay is positively infested with

second hand bookshops. It's good, in as much as it brings the right audience to you, but the competition is fierce." She ran a hand through her short, neatly cut silver-grey hair, pushing her fringe away from her dark brown eyes.

"Do you have a literary background? You obviously love books." Catherine was curious.

"Not really. I was a human resources manager before I met Julian. After we married, I gave up working to bring up our two girls. Julian was a software designer and he made a reasonable income, so I wasn't under any pressure to work. But I've always adored books - of all kinds. I love being transported into so many different worlds…"

Catherine nodded her head, understanding completely. She relaxed, genuinely enjoying the company of the elegant, kind lady.

"And your daughters?"

"I couldn't ask for better. They are both so talented, so generous. One is working for a conservation charity in France and the other is living with her boyfriend in Australia. I just wish they weren't so far away. What about you Catherine? Do you have children? Or is that a difficult question?"

"No, not at all. I only married five years ago. My husband, Arnaud, had been married before, but his marriage broke up when their little baby died - cot death. We never discussed having children - but somehow, I don't think either of us were that keen. Isn't it funny? It's not something that's really occurred to me. I know that sounds a bit odd. I suppose I'm probably terribly self-absorbed with my writing. And Arnaud is a very contented person. I suppose we've never felt the need to augment our family."

Catherine was surprised at herself. It was rare for her

to give many details away about her own feelings.

She thought a bit more. Eve allowed the natural silence to continue, until Catherine resumed, "In a funny kind of way, I do have a sort of child."

"Oh?"

"Not long before I met Arnaud, I inherited my aunt's house. It's in a remote cove on the Kent coast. There were already several grace-and-favour lodgers in the house when it passed into my hands; people my aunt had taken pity on and allowed to live in the house rent free. She had a very generous heart. Anyhow, two of the lodgers were a father and son - Toby and Noah. Noah was nine when I ended up living in the house too. His mother had abandoned them when he was a toddler. So, I guess, Noah has become a kind of surrogate son. We're very close and fortunately Toby isn't a jealous kind of father. In fact, I think he was only too relieved to have somebody share the burden of parenting."

She smiled softly to herself.

"Catherine, your life sounds like a novel" Eve exclaimed.

"I suppose it's been a little unusual," Catherine admitted.

"You've no idea how unusual," Eve rejoined.

It occurred to Catherine that the other woman might be interested in her latest news. "Actually, I made a discovery the other day. Do you know Johanna? The hermit who lives on the edge of the mountains?"

"No, I've heard of her, but never met her."

"You'll never guess…" Catherine plunged into the details of her recent encounter with Johanna. Eve listened avidly. Then, the conversation ebbed back and forth, touching on elements of the two women's lives.

An hour later, Eve noticed the time. "I'm going to have to go soon. I need to package up some books to send out. But firstly Catherine, this may be a bit presumptuous of me, especially with everything going on in your life, but would you consider doing a book signing for me at some point?"

"A book signing?" Catherine's voice was strained.

"Yes, you must have done plenty in your time."

Catherine played with the empty coffee cup in front of her. "Well, no, not really. In fact, never."

Eve was silent for a few seconds.

"I'm not hugely keen on publicity," Catherine confessed. "I've never really needed to do any. Amazingly, my books seem to sell without a huge amount of effort."

"Don't your publishers put pressure on you?" Eve probed slightly.

"Not really, not any more. They know I'm not into that kind of thing. I guess we've reached a kind of truce. As long as I keep the books coming and they sell enough copies, they don't pester me too much."

Eve gave her an appraising glance. "Well, I'm impressed with you for holding out. Publishers can be quite brutal. And I'm sorry, I wouldn't want to force you to do something you detest."

"No, no it's fine. I really appreciate the offer." Catherine felt churlish. Eve had been so generous with her time and so compassionate.

She made a decision. "I'll tell you what, as soon as I can get this wretched synopsis out of the way, we'll work something out, Eve."

"Is the synopsis for your next book?"

"Yes, but I just can't get my head around it. I've never

had a problem thinking of plots - or writing - before. I feel so overwhelmed with the task in front of us at the farm, I don't seem to be able to concentrate on my book. On reflection, it's not just that. Here I am, in this beautiful part of the world, and I'm wishing I was somewhere else. It makes it worse when I see all these walkers around Hay - some of them have come from the other side of the world to enjoy the scenery - and I'm hankering after flat marshes and pebble beaches. I miss the sea terribly and I can't seem to settle here."

"I can understand that. I grew up on the Dorset coast, but I moved inland to Oxford when I met Julian. It was the sound of the sea that I missed the most I think. You don't realise how much it forms a backdrop of your life until it's gone."

*I'm not stupid after all,* Catherine thought to herself. An immense wave of relief washed over her. "Thank you, Eve, I needed to hear that."

"Hello Eve, good to see you," a short burly man put a hand on Eve's shoulder, as he made his way through the crowded cafe.

"Alun. This is good timing. Here's somebody I'd like you to meet."

"Just a second." He strode over to the one free table in the café and put his tray down on it, then returned to the two women.

"This is Catherine. She and her husband Arnaud are running Kestrel Farm for Sebastian."

The burly man ran his hair through a mop of brown wiry hair, a concerned look on his face.

"Any news? How is he?"

"He's literally just regained conscious, but it looks like he has total amnesia," Catherine explained.

"That doesn't sound at all good." The man looked concerned.

Eve introduced him. "Alun owns the tack shop just outside Hay."

"Oh, I didn't know there was a tack shop here. We were planning on driving over to Hereford at some point," Catherine said.

"Good timing indeed. Please do feel free to pop in. I'm aware things are tight money-wise for all the trekking centres round here. Not an easy way of making a living. We've plenty of second hand stock in good condition. Save you a bit."

"Perfect, we'll come over and take a look. That's good news."

"Great, I'll look out for you. And by the way, we've got an old Kestrel Farm flyer in the shop window - you might like to bring along a new one if you have any. It's got a bit faded."

"Thank you - I'll do that. I've found a box of them, but they really could do with updating." Another thing on her to do list. "You don't happen to know any seasonal staff or cooks, do you? We're trying to find staff for this season."

"Cooks, no. I'll have a think about trekking staff for you and give you a ring at the farm if I come up with anybody."

"That's great, many thanks."

Alun bustled off, anxious not to lose his table to another walking couple who were searching for somewhere to sit.

"Eve, you are my guardian angel!" Catherine laughed.

"My pleasure," Eve smiled. "Now I really do need to go. Let's get a date in the diary to meet up again - if you think you'd like to, that is."

"Absolutely," replied Catherine.

It wasn't until later that afternoon that Catherine managed to catch up with Arnaud. As soon as he'd returned from visiting Sebastian, he'd been busy feeding the livestock and milking the sheep. She was glad of the warmth from the Aga as they sat in the kitchen. A pot of stew was simmering on the hotplate, filling the room with a mouthwatering aroma. Catherine's stomach rumbled and she realised she'd forgotten to eat lunch. That wasn't uncommon nowadays, in their busy schedule, she thought.

After Arnaud had described his visit to Sebastian, Catherine mentioned her encounter with Alun, the tack shop owner in Hay.

"That's good to know. Why don't we sort through the saddles and bridles here tomorrow morning, and then drop by Alun's afterward?"

She felt encouraged by her meeting with Eve, and the discovery of Alun's tack shop. The past week or so had felt like wading through treacle. Every time Catherine had ticked something off their to do list, she'd thought of at least two more things to add to it.

Catherine was determined to be positive, and had convinced herself that Sebastian's memory would return soon, and perhaps then, there may even be a way out of running the farm. Part of her still hoped desperately that something would happen to change Arnaud's mind and cause him to want to leave. She told herself that if she and Arnaud could get the place up and running properly, it would be that much easier for Sebastian to find somebody to fill their shoes. Despite her encounters with Johanna and Eve, Catherine felt awkward and out of place in this farm in the Welsh mountains, like a piece of a jigsaw puzzle that has been put into the wrong box.

Arnaud wasn't so sure about Sebastian's recovery. The one-sided conversation with his old friend had felt very peculiar and he was reluctant to admit to Catherine how much it had shaken him.

"Okay, let's finish working through this list," Catherine pulled the piece of paper towards her, anxious to keep the momentum going. "Ads for staff – booked. I've sent them to all of the magazines we talked about and posted them online. I've also sorted through the kids' bunkhouses and made a list - another one - of a few more repairs we need to do in the building. I'd still like to give the whole inside a lick of paint if we can find the time and money. There seems to be enough bed linen for the bunkhouses, but it's a bit tatty. I guess we'll have to live with that for the time being. I called the farrier - Glen - and he's coming next week. Turns out he's Alun's brother. I guess it makes life easier with so many people being related…"

Arnaud smiled. He'd lived in a small community before and was enjoying the experience again.

"My biggest worry is finding a cook, for the residential groups. I'm sure there are plenty of horsey people willing to come and work as trek leaders, but I know nothing about catering and I'm not exactly the world's best cook." Catherine feared the job would fall to her if they couldn't find anybody soon.

"We may well get a reply to one of the ads. And we can keep asking around locally too." Arnaud was more confident. He continued, "I want to try out a couple more of the trek routes that are in the farm manual. There is a small group of riders booked for Saturday who want to ride to a pub and back. I might drive to a couple of the local pubs sometime this week to check them out and choose a decent one."

"There's a list of pubs in a file on the computer, but I'm not sure how accurate it is. Some of the other stuff hasn't been updated for a good while."

Sebastian had shown them Emily's folders on the farm computer, containing all the information she had used to run the centre. Filing clearly hadn't been her strong point and many of the documents were stored randomly. While Arnaud had busied himself getting to know the horses, Catherine had steadily worked her way through the files and folders, trying to get to grips with the business.

She'd finally managed to make sense of the document listing the school groups booked into the farm for the coming year. It turned out that the groups were booked in from April until October, the majority of them staying for three to four nights. They could expect anything between twenty to forty pupils, accompanied by a handful of teachers.

It looked like at one time the centre had also been used for other residential groups - small parties who stayed in the teachers' accommodation. Catherine assumed they had been self-catering groups who had been given the run of the centre kitchen. It seemed as if that side of the business had tailed off for the last couple of years. It was something they intended to take a look at and possibly revive again.

"Do you want me to help out with the admin for the school groups?" Arnaud asked.

Judging by the records, Emily usually emailed all the school groups early in the year to confirm the bookings for that season. Most of the schools had only paid an initial deposit. Arnaud and Catherine were desperately hoping they wouldn't pull out for any reason.

"No, don't worry. I'm happy to crack on with that," Catherine told him. Inwardly her heart sank, there seemed to many things to do - and still so many gaps in the information they required.

"You know what?" Arnaud slapped his hands on the table. "I think we are looking at this the wrong way. We are trying to run the farm how Emily did. And the problem is, we don't know exactly how she operated. I think we have to change tactic and decide the way we would run this place instead."

Catherine had to admit that approach made far more sense. But at that point in time, she had little enthusiasm for the job in hand. Somehow, she was going to have to drum some up - for the time being, at least.

# 11

## HITTING THE GROUND

### Noah's Diary

*Saturday 10 February*

*Quote of the Day: "And indeed, a horse who bears himself proudly is a thing of such beauty and astonishment that he attracts the eyes of all beholders." – Xenophon of Athens*

*Are all characters a fragment of their author's persona, I wonder? Gosh I'm good #originalthought #theboysgotitinhim #topwriter. If so, I'm not sure I'd have many characters in my book. I think I'm quite one-dimensional myself. It's not like I've done much with my life really. Not like Arnaud. I mean he's gone and upped himself from his native Brittany and moved to a foreign country and now to Wales. Oh yeah, Wales is a foreign country too, I guess. So, if I went to work for Catherine and Arnaud, I'd be living in a foreign country. Hmmmm (strokes chin). Actually, double hmmmm, I have a cunning plan. It involves a lot of deviousness, which I am good at, I confess. I might just pull it off. Watch this space, readers. Need to do some planning and have a chat with my mate, Mac I Avelli.*

It was that time when night and day fuse into one. In the opaqueness of the early morning, she could hear, rather than see, the bodies around her; the click of a hoof

134

hitting a stone, a breath exhaled a few metres away. She picked her way slowly down the steep hillside, her feet slipping every now and then on the wet grass. A horse materialised in front of her. A curious head, neck extended, sniffing her jacket for food. She brushed past, allowing her hand to slide along its rump. It came away glistening with moisture - the horse was wet from the overnight drizzle.

In front of her, a long skid mark where a hoof had exposed the red soil underneath. She walked to one side of it to avoid the slippery earth. Gradually more creatures appeared around her as the night receded. Then a darker line on the horizon, forming the edge of the pine forest. The day was easing into being. Catherine felt as if she had stepped into another world.

A squeal from further down the hillside, followed by a sharp movement. Two ponies fighting. They emerged out of the gloom, jostling one another half-heartedly. One of them nipped the other on the shoulder and it trotted sharply off. For the most part, the ponies were stationary: some nibbling at the dew-laden grass, others dozing, leaning on one hind leg.

A slow drizzle began to ooze from the sky. It dripped from the edges of Catherine's hat onto her jacket. Her hands, outstretched to keep her balance, were raw and chilled. Finally, she reached the trees at the bottom of the meadow. A few ponies, huddled together, were sheltering underneath the branches. One of them was resting its head on its neighbour's back. Inquisitive eyes looked at her. She lost her footing and skidded into the fence, grabbing the wire to steady herself. Then, turning around, she raised her head and looked up the field. Over the lip of the brow, unseen, Arnaud stood waiting for her call.

Catherine cupped her hands around her mouth and took a deep breath.

"Okay!"

Her shout startled the group of ponies. One of them spooked, trotting away for a few paces before coming to a standstill. The others shifted uneasily, ears pricked. She listened for an answering shout and heard nothing.

She tried again.

"Okay!"

This time a whooping cry swept down from the corral, far up at the top of the field. At first nothing happened. Then, slowly, one of the horses higher up the field began to walk stiffly up the hillside. The whooping cry continued. Catherine cleared her throat and shouted at the group by the fence.

"Come on, you lazy lot."

They stared at her.

She walked towards them, her arms wide. A snort, and then finally, thankfully, movement. A chestnut pony disentangled itself from the group and began to pick its way past her. A stocky black pony peeled away to join it. Now she could sense movement all over the paddock. She walked the entire stretch of the lower fence, checking for stragglers. At the far end, a tall dark horse stood underneath a low hanging branch, its back hunched. It was Jester. Catherine walked over to him, trying to keep her movements calm, not wanting to spook him. As she drew nearer, she realised the horse wasn't alone. Just behind him, almost out of sight was a small shaggy grey pony.

"Hey Jester, you've found a friend," she spoke softly to him.

The little grey pony whickered at Catherine and walked

over to her. It put its soft muzzle into her hand, sniffing. She took a few pony nuts out of her pocket and let it nibble them. Jester's nostrils flared. He came nearer, barging the pony out of the way. He nuzzled her coat and Catherine brought out some more pony nuts. The grey pony struck up the hillside, now keen to join the rest of the herd. Jester followed cautiously, with Catherine lagging behind, scrambling awkwardly up the steep terrain, panting with the effort.

On her way back up, she shooed a couple of stragglers who were tearing at a last few mouthfuls of grass. They snorted at her, and moved on up the hillside. By the time she had reached the top of the paddock, almost the entire herd was in the corral, the gate closed. Only Jester remained in the field, tied up at a fence post just outside, standing as far away as his halter rope would allow.

The corral was a seething mass of horses. Catherine spotted the tall figure of Arnaud in the middle of the morass, an armful of headcollars in one hand. Deftly he grabbed a horse, slipped a headcollar on and led it to a nearby fence post. A short loop of red bailing twine had been tied to each post around the corral. Arnaud swiftly pushed the end of the headcollar rope up through a loop of twine, twisted it, tied a slip knot, then moved onto the next horse.

Nervous of the shifting, squealing mass of horses, Catherine walked along the outside edge of the corral fence to the barn door and stepped inside. Her eyes took a few moments to adjust to the gloom. Gradually they focused on rows of green plastic feeding buckets lined up on the floor. She climbed over to the end of the row, measured out a scoop of dry food mix from a wooden bin and threw it into each bucket, before carrying the buckets up to the corral and placing one in front of each pony.

Catherine was still breathing hard from the effort of walking back up the hill. At least her leg muscles were getting used the constant climbing up and down the steep paddocks and no longer ached all night, as they used to do when she and Arnaud had first arrived.

There was little respite. Breakfast - a few slices of toast and a huge mug of tea - hastily consumed - and it was time to remove the empty feed buckets and sort out which of the horses were going to be used for the day's ride. As Catherine rinsed the dirty buckets under the tap outside, her fingers red and hurting with cold, Arnaud moved the day's trek horses into a corner of the corral. Then he slipped the headcollars off the rest of the herd, opened the corral gate and shooed them back into the field.

A couple of the smaller ponies lingered, nibbling at a few spilled patches of feed. Arnaud slapped their rumps to get them moving. They trotted swiftly off to join the rest of the herd, ears back. He closed the corral gate behind them, and walked through the squelching mud to join Catherine at the barn door. The drizzle had eased off and a few rays of sun were fighting to escape through the cloud.

Above them, a car rattled over the cattle grid and crunched to a halt in the small gravel car park opposite the farmhouse. Three car doors opened and slammed shut.

Catherine was exhausted and the day had hardly started. She picked up her riding hat and gloves and straightened up, back aching.

Arnaud had turned to meet the day's riders. His cheery greeting echoed across the corral.

A tall skinny, blonde girl in her early teens dragged a short, slightly plump dark-haired girl over to the trek horses in the corner of the corral. She pointed at them and said in a loud, confident voice, "From left to right we have Prezel," she waved her arm theatrically towards a stocky ginger horse. "Then Tigger," Catherine recognised the pretty bay pony, "Gizmo," a neat dapple grey pony that was stamping its foot impatiently. "He can be a bugger sometimes," the girl said, then turned quickly to check whether the older woman accompanying them was within earshot. She was talking to Arnaud and wasn't listening. "You need a good rider on him, then he's fine. Otherwise he'll take the piss. The dark grey is Mouse."

Catherine looked at her mount for the day. Mouse had an attractive neat muzzle and pretty face.

"I don't know who that horse on the end is, he must be new," was the blonde girl's final comment.

"That's our horse, Baloo, from the Camargue in France. He's quite feisty," Catherine informed them, drawing closer to the pair.

The outspoken girl glanced over at Catherine. "Are you the new managers? Emily's replacements?"

Catherine gritted her teeth. The girl's tone had been condescending.

"Yes, we are. I'm Catherine and that's my husband, Arnaud."

"Arno - what a weird name. Sounds like Arnold Schwarzenegger or something."

"It's a French name. He's from Brittany, on the west coast of France." Catherine forced herself to be cheerful.

"Ooh, does he speak English?"

"Of course he does." Catherine was cross with herself. The words had come out more sharply than she'd intended. She would have to get used to being polite to all sorts of clients. It didn't come naturally.

Arnaud walked over towards them with an older woman. She had short cropped brown curly hair and large, friendly eyes.

"Lucy, this is Catherine," he introduced her to the woman.

"Oh yes, we spoke on the phone," Catherine smiled.

Lucy nodded. "I think I said Samantha and I used to come over here quite a lot to ride. We haven't been for a while. How are you settling in?"

"Fine, yes, very well, thanks. There's a lot to take in though." Catherine wondered how much the other woman knew about Emily and her reasons for leaving the farm.

"I'm sure there is," Lucy was sympathetic. She glanced at the two girls, who were feeding pony nuts to the waiting horses.

"This is Samantha, my daughter," she pointed to the blonde-haired girl, "and Clare, her friend." More softly, she added, "Don't take any rubbish from Samantha. She's at *that* age," and rolled her eyes.

Catherine smiled sympathetically.

Arnaud was keen to get going. "Okay, Lucy as you requested, we've given you Prezel. He turned the girls. "Samantha, your mum said you were a confident rider, so we're putting you on Gizmo. I hope you're happy with that."

Samantha grinned, "Absolutely."

Clare, you can ride Tigger. He's a lovely pony and very calm - you won't have any problems with him."

Catherine walked over to the farmhouse door and locked it, putting the key in her jacket pocket. She envied

Arnaud his easy way with the clients. Everything in her wanted to put the over-confident teenager in her place. She kicked herself mentally. These people were paying towards the farm's running costs and she needed to keep on the right side of them. Dealing with the horses was a piece of cake compared to handling the customers, she decided.

"Okay, everybody ready? Let's get going." Arnaud picked up his hat and pushed it onto his head.

They all moved towards their mount, tightening their girths and looping the ropes from the headcollars around the horses' necks. Arnaud checked the two girls to make sure they were okay.

"I think we can get Gizmo's girth up a bit," he told Samantha. The teenager slid her left leg forward, as Arnaud lifted the saddle flap and pulled Gizmo's girth strap up a notch. The pony put his ears flat and stamped, bouncing his rider in the saddle. Against her will, Catherine admired the young girl's steady seat, unperturbed by the pony's restlessness.

When they were sorted, Arnaud sprang up onto Baloo and squeezed his heels. The grey Camargue horse resisted slightly, shaking its head and then strode out, heading up the track towards the cattle grid at the farm entrance. Lucy followed on Prezel, leaning forwards slightly to straighten her reins. A slight scuffle as Gizmo jostled with Tigger for the next place in the line. Gizmo won, and Samantha turned round to grin at Clare who was looking slightly nervous.

Mouse stirred beneath her and Catherine realised she had been daydreaming. The dark grey pony trotted out of the corral to catch up with the rest of the trek, Catherine bouncing in the saddle, caught off guard.

A few minutes later, Arnaud was opening the gate by the cattle grid. Catherine admired Baloo's practised movements, waiting patiently while Arnaud undid the catch and then backing slowly as his rider swung the gate open. Arnaud held it, allowing the rest of the trek to pass through, the horses' hooves clipping onto the tarmac lane. Baloo stamped impatiently, eager to be back in the lead, but Arnaud kept him at a standstill until all the horses had passed through the gate. Then, he backed Baloo, pushing the gate shut. Baloo lifted his head and trotted smartly past the file of the trek back into the lead.

Ahead of Catherine, Samantha was explaining to Clare. "Some of the horses are natural leaders. They're the ones that are used to head up the treks. The other horses respect that and don't object to them riding past the line. If Gizmo came out of line and tried to overtake the other ponies would get annoyed and there would be a helluva fight…"

*Pony politics*, thought Catherine. *It's a whole new language I've had to learn.*

The watery sun was winning its battle with the clouds. She looked through the bare hedgerows at a field of winter wheat, green spikes sticking up through the red earth. There were precious few signs of spring. Everything felt bleak and dead.

Another gate, this one leading onto the mountain itself. The clopping noise of the hooves changed to a soft thud on the damp grass. Arnaud smiled at Catherine as she rode past him. This one was trickier to close. It needed to be lifted up onto the catch. Baloo was impatient and Arnaud had to pull him around for a second try. It banged shut, spooking Gizmo who pranced out of line. In front of him, Prezel put his ears back and threatened to kick out. Gizmo slid back behind him.

"Okay *chérie*? How's Mouse?" Arnaud drew alongside her.

Catherine could see the enjoyment in his eyes. "He's very sweet thanks, I like him. Baloo looks happy to be out." She reached out and stroked the Camargue horse.

"Poor old chap. He's been a bit confined to barracks lately."

Baloo shook his head, as if he knew they'd been talking about him. Arnaud touched Catherine's hand lightly, then squeezed Baloo into a canter back to the front of the trek.

The group emerged from a narrow track running alongside a stand of trees onto a large common. A breeze whipped across the exposed ground, snapping into them. It was icy, cutting into their cheeks. Ahead, Catherine could see Baloo's magnificent cream-coloured mane and tail rippling in the wind. He stepped forward, dainty black hooves onto the springy turf and sniffed the air. A lone buzzard wheeled over their heads, circling around the common.

Arnaud whispered to Baloo, patting his neck. Behind them, dry stone walls snaked along the edge of the sheep pastures that patchworked along the foothills. In front, clumps of gorse were dotted around the lower edges of the mountain. Dark brown patches of last year's bracken littered the grass. It was the pureness that struck Arnaud, the unsullied air and quietness. Nothing but the odd call from the buzzard and the click of a horse's hoof on a stone. Everything smelled fresh, sharp. Then, more sounds insinuated themselves. The constant whisper of the breeze, sheep calling to each other, a crow cawing in the distance. No human noise at all.

*I've come home.* Arnaud thought. *This is where I belong. Raw nature. Elemental.*

The trek behind him ceased to exist. He rode along the track, suspended in a wilderness, his senses alert. Baloo's ears flicked. A rabbit broke cover and ran across the track. The horse's superior senses hearing, scenting everything before Arnaud. He knew the horse would be his tutor in this new world and he had a sudden aching to discover every inch of these mountains. To walk and ride and submerge himself in this landscape.

*All my life has been leading to this.* Arnaud couldn't imagine tearing himself away from this place. He had to believe that Catherine would come round, would begin to feel as he did.

Catherine shivered. She hadn't appreciated how much colder it was up on the exposed foothills of the mountain. It felt as if the wind was tearing at her, clawing at her flesh. She looked down at her hands in front of her, clutching onto stiff leather reins. In between her riding gloves and thick jacket sleeves, her thin wrists were exposed to the air. She tugged the sleeves down and hunched her shoulders.

Above her, the mountains looked bleak and unfriendly. Dark crags loomed overhead, staring at her as if asking what she was doing in their territory. Hostile whispers of air, hissing through the scattered trees seemed to be repelling her. She longed for the sound and movement of the sea; the unending song that had accompanied her life for the last few years. This wind would have whipped up white horses onto the surface - a yachtsman's gale, Isaac would have called it. The mountains stood silent, upthrust ridges of grey rock, impenetrable, saying nothing.

Resentment bubbled unpleasantly to the surface of her thoughts, like a sulphurous pool. She felt trapped. She could hardly begrudge Arnaud his love of this wild, rugged place, but she could feel resentment at Sebastian, using his friendship with Arnaud to bring them to a complete mess of a situation, and then virtually abandoning them. And then his car crash. Catherine knew the accident wasn't deliberate, but she was angry with him. Illogically. Unreasonably. And for that she disliked herself.

The horses picked their way through a mountain stream. Samantha kicked Gizmo, who leapt the little brook. Tigger followed suit, nearly unseating Clare. Catherine held Mouse back, and the grey horse lifted its feet high, treading delicately through the water, almost on tip toe. The wind strengthened, making talking harder. Samantha's almost ceaseless chatter died, bubbled up and died again. Currents of air, swirled around the riders, drawing each one of them into their own little world.

Catherine became conscious of the living creature beneath her; the muscles of its legs working; the slightly acrid, almost wet-wool smell of horse. She closed her eyes, listening to the jingle of the bit, the hypnotic creak of the saddle. Mouse snatched on her reins and she blinked. The trek was climbing upwards, the red earth of the track cutting through the side of the foothill. She leaned forward, beginning to feel her movements were more in step with Mouse's. As they tracked on, Catherine's dark mood began to slip away. She let her eyelids slide shut again, feeling the countryside around her.

When she opened them, she was lying on the ground. At first, she was aware of nothing. And then a sharp pain in the middle of her back began to register. She rolled over and the pain dulled. She had been lying on a small rock. The other riders wheeled their horses round. Arnaud jumped off Baloo, leaving the him to his own devices. Catherine could hear Samantha's voice. It sounded fuzzy, distant.

"I think something spooked Mouse and she just sort of slid off…"

She forced her hands to push her up to a sitting position. The ground was damp.

Arnaud, anxious, strained eyes, "Are you okay?"

Catherine nodded, unable to find her voice.

Moments later, Lucy appeared in front of her, kneeling on the turf beside her. "I'm a nurse Catherine. Do you mind if I just quickly check you over?"

Catherine did mind, but she had no energy to say so. She sat, feeling sick and limp.

Lucy peered into Catherine's eyes and asked her a few questions. Catherine responded numbly. Gradually the nausea receded and suddenly clarity snapped back.

Lucy's professionalism was discreet and businesslike, putting Catherine at her ease. From the corner of her eye, she could see that Arnaud had tactfully drawn the two girls a slight distance away and was talking to them, holding their attention away from Catherine.

"I'm, okay now. Thank you, Lucy."

"You look a bit brighter. Just a bit shaken up, I think."

Catherine felt stupid, annoyed at herself for not concentrating earlier.

Arnaud reappeared beside Lucy and asked Catherine, "Do you want to get back on? If not, we can walk home and let the others ride on. It's not far to lead the horses back to the farm from here. Or I can ride back and get the car to come and pick you up."

"No, no I'm good. Honestly." Catherine forced a smile.

She pulled herself to her feet, using Arnaud's outstretched arm.

The mountains came back into focus. Catherine glared at them, as if they had somehow engineered this. She gritted her teeth and flung them a challenge, taking hold of Mouse's reins and swinging back up into the saddle.

# 12

## THE BLACKSMITH

### Noah's Diary:

*Thursday 22 February*

*To do or not to do, that is the question. Min emailed back this morning and said I should go for it. I am still undecided, although, O readerly one, I do confess to a serious case of scabrosus pedibus (that's itchy feet). Isaac would know what to do. He's no longer with us, enuff said. Isaac used to ask God, but I'm not sure God listens to me. I don't think I've got enough credits there. Come to think of it, how do you get God credits? Good works? Hmmm don't fancy that. Last time I tried to help an old lady she thought I was trying to mug her. Mind you, Jesus was a friend of sinners apparently. Maybe I need to do a bit more sinning. Been a bit lukewarm on that front recently too. Okay, here's the deal - I sorely confess I am tempted to go to Cambria (that's Latin for Wales) and help Catherine & Arnaud out. But am I up to the task? Am I man enough? Can I handle the horses and the kids? I'd hate to let them down. Think I'll just toss a coin, it's easier than trying to decide. It's doing my head in.*

Inside the barn, a Hobbit-like man was standing over a furnace. Short and stocky, his arms were solid with muscle. A horseshoe, glowing angry red, spat sparks into the air with each blow of his hammer. One final tap, and he turned back towards the dark bay horse tied to a ring in the barn wall. As he bent over to pick up the horse's hind leg, it deliberately shifted its weight onto that foot. The man's language was very unHobbit-like.

His companion's response was sympathetic. "I swear he works out in his mind how to be as awkward as possible," Arnaud's face was buried in Jester's flank, muffling his voice. One hand was braced on the horse's chest, the other holding firmly to its headcollar, to keep Jester from moving.

Glen, the blacksmith, put his shoulder to Jester's flank and pushed hard in one quick motion, throwing the horse off balance. He bent down again and lifted the foot. Jester deliberated, then gave in and stood quietly, head down, nuzzling Arnaud's leg.

Held in the grip of a long pair of tongs, the glowing shoe hissed as it made contact with the bare wall of the hoof. An acrid burning smell filled the barn. Glen inspected the fit, released the hoof and dipped the shoe into the barrel of water. A sizzle and cloud of steam spurted into the elemental atmosphere.

The blacksmith took hold of Jester's leg again, placing the now-cool shoe on the horse's foot. With practised ease, he pulled a nail from his mouth, placed it in the shoe and tapped briskly. His hand slid round, another nail from his mouth and that was tapped in place. Within minutes the job was done. He lowered Jester's foot and the horse tried its weight on the new shoe.

"Just the one shoe on him, was it?"

"Yes, you've got away lightly this time."

Glen straightened up and looked at his watch. He rubbed his hands through his short, dark curly hair.

"I'll just take a breather and then start on the grey." He glanced over at the pony tied up to the wall beyond Jester. "That looks like Willow to me."

"Correct."

"Nice pony that."

Arnaud agreed. Willow had fine features and a bright, intelligent face. He was one of the lead horses and knew the job well. Arnaud untied Jester and led him towards the barn door, pushing it open. A blast of cold air whooshed into the building. He walked the horse out into the yard and across the corral to the paddock. As soon as he removed the headcollar, Jester took off, skittering across the field, his breath coming out in frosty puffs.

Arnaud made his way back to the barn, where Glen was filling up the kettle from a tap in the corner.

"Tea?"

"Rather coffee please. It should be me doing that," Arnaud protested.

"No worries, I probably know my way round here better than you do. How are you finding it Arnaud?"

"It's an amazing life. The location, the horses - what's not to love?" Arnaud grinned.

"It's not everybody's cup of tea here. It's a bit bleak in the winter. Whereabouts in France are you from - not the south, I take it?"

"No, from Brittany, on the west coast, so I'm used to wet weather. I don't mind the outdoors. I'd rather be here than cooped up in an office."

"Me too, I tried it once - for a day," the burly Hobbit grimaced.

Glen was easy company and Arnaud liked the affable Welshman. He had a no-nonsense approach to his work and although he was firm with the horses, Arnaud could sense his innate kindness towards them.

Glen sat on a grain bin and drank his tea in big gulps, seemingly oblivious to its heat.

"Oh, I'd forgotten to ask about Sebastian. I hear he's recovering. Don't know why it slipped my mind."

"No worries. Yes, he's conscious but he still can't remember anything. He's had a few other visitors, apart from me, but doesn't recognise anybody. It's quite strange."

Glen put down his cup, and slid off the bin. "What's going to happen to him? I mean, he's going to have to leave the hospital at some point."

"Yes, although they want to keep him in for a few weeks. His back was quite badly damaged. No question about it, he can come here. After all, it's his place and there's plenty of room. We're happy to help him convalesce. Maybe being back in familiar surroundings will help. Who knows?"

"Good of you, all the same."

"Well, I guess at the very worst, when he recovers physically it's another pair of hands." Arnaud shrugged. He felt strangely bereaved at his friend's memory loss.

He untied the grey pony and led it into the middle of the barn. Willow stood alert, ears pricked, head turning behind him to look at the blacksmith. Glen moved over to a large wooden box and pulled out a small horseshoe. He ran his hand down the front of Willow's leg and picked up his hoof, matching the shoe to his foot.

"That'll do." He picked up an old large-handled pair of pliers and eased the existing worn shoe from Willow's foot.

The barn door opened, and Catherine appeared. Absorbed in their work, the men didn't notice her at first.

She smiled inwardly at the contrast between the tall skinny Frenchman and the short, stocky Welshman. And then a wave of jealousy washed over her. Arnaud seemed so in his element. Everything came naturally to him here. These two men were inhabiting a world that she hadn't yet walked into. The smell of burned hoof caught on the back of her throat and she coughed.

Arnaud looked at her over Willow's back, his grey eyes lighting up at the sight of her.

She spoke, "Alun's just phoned back. He reckons he's got a couple of second hand saddles that might be good for us. Do you want him to hold on to them until one of us can get over to Hay?"

"Yes, please. It would be good to have a few spares."

"Okay, I'll give him a call back. I could even pop over to Hay later. Is there anything else we need?"

"Yes, actually a couple of medium sized headcollars would be good. Two of the ones here are really beyond repair."

"Okay." She left, in a brisk flurry, eager to be gone.

As she walked back across the muddy track to the farmhouse, Catherine's stomach tightened. She had spent a completely fruitless hour that morning, sitting at her computer trying to work on the plot for her next novel. Nothing seemed to be coming together. She'd decided to cut her losses and tackle one of the many jobs on the list. Maybe doing something physical would help. She veered towards the accommodation block, heading for the back entrance to the teachers' wing.

In the passageway, an assortment of paint pots and decorating brushes were standing on a piece of plastic sheeting. She sighed heavily. It was mid-February and they still had five teachers' rooms and the entire bunkhouse left to paint. Not to mention all of the other jobs. The heating was on the minimum setting to save costs and Catherine could almost see her breath in front of her. It was freezing. She forced herself to get moving - that would help warm her up.

She picked up a large tin of white emulsion and a couple of brushes and headed towards the bedroom where she'd made a start the previous day. As she stepped over the threshold, Catherine tripped on a rumpled dustsheet. She fell forward, flinging her hand out to catch herself, dropping the can of paint in the process. Gloopy white paint spilled out over the sheet. By the time Catherine had picked herself up and righted the tin, it was almost empty.

"Damn." She was going to have to clean up the mess. And they could ill-afford to waste the paint. In a fit a rage, she whipped around and marched out of the room. She'd had enough.

Catherine strode across the yard, desperate to get away. Flinging the kitchen door open, she grabbed the Land Rover keys from the hook and swung round, slamming the door shut behind her. In the Land Rover, she struggled to get the key into the ignition. Her hands were shaking with emotion. Tears pricked at the corner of her eyes. She forced herself to breathe slowly, calming herself down. Then she started the engine and pulled up the hill. She would collect the saddles and walk around Hay to give herself some space.

As she neared the end of the drive, a sudden impulse caused Catherine to swing the steering wheel to the right at the cattle grid instead of left. Hay could wait. She needed to talk to somebody.

Ten minutes later, she pulled up in front of Johanna's

tumbled-down cottage. Slamming the car door behind her, she strode briskly up the path and tapped on the side door. Silence. Disappointment welled up in Catherine. She hadn't expected Johanna to be out. Tears welled up again in the corner of her eyes. Catherine quickly wiped them away, annoyed at her own weakness. Reluctantly she turned to leave, and walked back to the waiting Land Rover, feet dragging.

"Catherine! How wonderful to see you again." A voice called out behind her. She turned to see Joanna emerging from a passageway next to the house.

"I was just watering some plants in my greenhouse. That's a rather misleading term for a couple of panes of glass barely held together in a rickety wooden frame." Her words rolled over Catherine, soothing.

"Why don't you go inside, out of the cold and make yourself comfortable. I'll come in and put the kettle on in a minute. I'm nearly done at the back - if I don't finish this off, I'll forget and they'll die on me."

"Okay. Thank you."

Catherine eased the wooden side door open and ducked under the low entrance. She was greeted by the smell of wood smoke and a comforting warmth from the black log burner. Slipping her boots off, she curled up in the old sofa. A feeling of deep tiredness overwhelmed her. It was such a relief to sit and do nothing, with no pressure. Lulled by the heat, Catherine could feel her eyes closing and the room gradually receding from around her.

Johanna peered in through the window. Catherine lay asleep on the sofa, her head tucked into her folded arms.

"Good," barely a whisper from the older lady. She walked back round to the greenhouse, which was far larger than she'd made it out to be, and busied herself repotting a cluster of red geraniums.

Catherine dreamed of a man climbing a dark, craggy mountain. Just as he neared the summit he slipped, grabbed onto a rock and stabilised himself. He relaxed too soon and slipped again, scrabbling in a rockfall of scree, falling out of sight...

When Catherine awoke, she remembered nothing of the dream. She stretched and for a moment wondered where she was. A glimpse of the black wood burner reminded her and she opened her eyes wide. She felt refreshed, brighter than she had done for a long time. Johanna was sitting in the rocking chair opposite her, deep in a book.

"I'm so sorry, I must have drifted off. How long have I been asleep?" Catherine felt guilty.

"A good while. Don't apologise, you needed it. I've never seen anyone looking so pale. Would you like that cup of tea now?"

"Yes please." She was suddenly thirsty and hungry.

Johanna pushed herself off the rocking chair, and left the room, returning a few minutes later with a tray containing two china cups of tea and a plate of biscuits.

"Home made, but that's not saying much. Actually, that's not true, this batch wasn't too bad." She held out the plate.

Catherine took a biscuit, nibbled it tentatively, then took a larger bite. "They're good, what's in them?" she asked.

"A bit of this and that - anything that's in the store cupboard. I think these have got coriander and lemon peel in them. It was one of Min's recipes originally."

"Min from the Wily Wolf?"

"One and the same. Lovely girl. Amazingly creative cook. Needs to spread her wings a bit."

The conversation rambled on easily. Catherine felt utterly comfortable with Johanna, as if she had known her for years. Which in a way, she had.

Johanna gradually led the conversation around to Catherine. Under the woman's gentle probing Catherine opened up, and once she had started to talk, everything came gushing out.

"I know it's beautiful here - but I miss the sea and the marshes so much. And at least I felt I belonged at Gull Cove, where my grandfather's house was. Here I feel like a fish out of water. The trouble is Arnaud - my husband - loves it here. I can't take him away from all this. I feel guilty, and I know I'm being miserable and I must be awful company. What's worse is that I just can't seem to write any more. I sit down and the ideas don't come. That's never happened to me in my life before. I've always been able to write. I guess that's carried me through everything."

Johanna was silent for a while, considering the tangle of threads that Catherine had placed in her lap. Then she drew out one of them.

"Do you have to belong anywhere in particular?"

Catherine's brows furrowed. "I don't understand."

"Well, it's not the place that defines us. You are still Catherine - with all your memories and experiences - just as much here as back in Kent."

Then, Johanna took a risk. "I understand your need to find out about your mother - and your father. You've no idea how much joy it has given me to be able to provide you with some of the information you've wanted to know for years. I can see how you find comfort from connection to your relatives and the security that the family home in Kent has given you, but don't let that stop you from living your own life, Catherine."

Catherine flinched, not sure if she was angry or grateful.

"There I go again," Johanna looked chagrined. "I'm sorry. I'm not good at tact I'm afraid."

Catherine bit her lip. "Perhaps you're right. I'll think about what you said." She glanced at her watch. "Right now, I need to go and pick up those saddles and get on with the painting."

"I do hope you aren't angry with me."

"No, not at all. And I am so deeply grateful that I bumped into you the other day. I'm enjoying getting to know you," Catherine reassured her.

"I'm glad. I'm enjoying your company too. And, if you don't mind Catherine, I will pray for you every now and then."

Catherine wasn't sure if she believed in God, but having somebody tell her they would pray was somehow reassuring. She was touched.

"One more thing," Johanna ventured, "as for your writing - forgive me, I'm going to nag a little - it's my experience that in order to be creative one needs space. Time to think and to breathe. I don't get the impression you've had a lot of that recently."

"You're right - again." Catherine smiled, kissed Johanna lightly on the cheek and swept out of the house.

When Catherine finally arrived back at the farm, Arnaud and Glen were dealing with the last two horses.

Grudgingly, she decided to follow Johanna's advice. Leaving the saddles in the Land Rover, she ducked under the corral fence and climbed down into the lower paddock. The horses were grazing peacefully in the early afternoon sunshine, enjoying the warmth on their backs. Catherine walked over to a boulder and sat down, looking at the view over the pine forest. Steam rose up between the trees, snaking down into the valley below, like a long Chinese dragon, shifting and reforming itself.

A black mare with a white blaze on her nose, wandered past her, nosing the ground for grass. Catherine tried to recall her name. Jade - that was it. She remembered Sebastian pointing her out on their first visit. The mare was thirty-five years old and still actively working. She lost herself in the horses' world, watching their interactions. A couple of smaller ponies were play fighting, nipping one another's necks. Further down, a large dappled grey horse was lying on the grass, feet tucked under its body.

She realised it must be a wonderfully natural way for them to live - here in a herd, rather than cooped up in some stable, separated perhaps from any other horses. Watching their various interactions, she could see how important it was for the horses to be part of a group. She was amazed at how different each horse and pony was. Each had their own personality - their own friends - and enemies. It began to feel something of a privilege to have such an insight into their lives.

Then, a warm breath in her ear. She jumped. Mouse retreated slightly, before returning to nuzzle Catherine's head. She reached out with both hands and stroked the sides of his face, breathing softly into his nose, as Arnaud had taught her. Mouse responded, blowing gently back.

Slowly, so as not to startle him, Catherine stood up and wrapped her arms around his warm neck. She felt privileged that the horse had sought out her company. She stood there, drawing comfort from Mouse's presence.

Arnaud came round the corner of the barn, leading the last pony back to the field, while Glen was packing up his equipment. He spotted Catherine in the field and stopped, watching his wife hug the dark grey pony. From this distance, he couldn't judge if she was happy or sad. Arnaud was all too aware that Catherine was still struggling and that perhaps their time in Wales was limited.

He would respect Catherine's decision if she wanted to leave. He knew what it was like to see a marriage disintegrate and he had promised himself that this time around, he would pay whatever price he needed to keep his marriage going. But it might well be very painful.

# 13

## SNOW

The real snow came in March, tumbling incessantly from dark, brooding skies, until the landscape had been thickly iced, distorting shapes and reducing them to muffled outlines. In the lane by the cattle grid it was waist height, prohibiting travel. For three days, Catherine and Arnaud were marooned in a snow globe of their own. Apart from brief sorties outside, to feed and water the animals, they stayed wrapped in the warmth of the kitchen.

When the hard weather had set in, Arnaud opened the door to the indoor school, providing extra shelter for the herd. It was filled with shuffling, furry bodies, the horses now wearing their thick winter pelts, jostling to reach the hay racks in the corners of the building. The sheep and llamas were huddled in their field shelter, peering out into the unfamiliar white world in front of them.

Within the cocoon of the farmhouse, Catherine and Arnaud talked. About nothing and everything. It was as if Johanna's words had unleashed a dam inside Catherine, and now she had time to properly consider them. Emotions, that had lain buried for years, surged to the surface of her mind. She discovered a deep vein of anger at her mother. Hidden feelings unwrapped themselves inside her, revealing their true intent.

Arnaud listened, watching his wife come alive. As she discarded old thoughts and habits that were of no use to her any longer, Catherine visibly changed; her features became more animated, inflection flowed into her voice. It was like watching a pen and ink drawing being filled with subtle colours.

On the second afternoon, Catherine wandered upstairs and found herself sitting at her laptop, looking out of the window at the white desert that lay in front of her. Gradually her ideas began to frame themselves into something probable. She powered up the computer, and began to write.

Arnaud was sitting in the kitchen, looking at the accounts. He tried doctoring a few figures, but however he juggled them, he couldn't escape the fact that they were running into debt. They owed Rhys money for grain and silage, Glen for two days' worth of shoeing and Alun for various bits of tack. What made it worse was these people were becoming his friends. They were all understanding of the situation. The farm bank account was overdrawn to its limit and with Sebastian's amnesia, Catherine and Arnaud were unable to access any of his other funds. They had used some of their savings, but they had precious little money of their own. It had never seemed important or necessary to them to have much in reserve before.

The only other source of funding was Sebastian's ex-wife, Emily.

It had taken some time for the police to track Emily down and confirm that she still held Sebastian's Power of Attorney. Two weeks ago, she had called Arnaud at the farm. The conversation had been strained. Arnaud hadn't really spoken to Emily since the break-up of his marriage to Estelle. When he had met up with Sebastian during the intervening years, they had done so in London, just the two of them. He was shocked at how brittle Emily's voice sounded. She seemed to have little sympathy with the fact that Arnaud was trying to help Sebastian.

It appeared that it was in her power to transfer funds from Sebastian's personal bank account to the farm, but she was stalling, being unhelpful. Arnaud had tried to stress the urgency of the situation, but Emily seemed unmoved - perhaps unsurprisingly. His biggest hope lay in Sebastian recovering his memory, but when Arnaud had visited him a couple of days previously, Sebastian was still unable to remember a thing. If nothing happened soon, they would be in serious trouble.

Arnaud knew that he needed to let Catherine know about the deepening financial crisis, but he couldn't bring himself to do so. For the last couple of days, she had seemed happier in herself. The snowfall had given them a break in their punishing schedule and he wanted to make the most of it. He resolved to call Emily at the end of the week, to see if he could persuade her into action.

On the third day, the sound of a tractor in the lane drew them from the house. The snow had finally stopped falling and the sunshine was sparkling, scattering shards of light onto the white landscape. A figure in the cab waved to them, as the tractor swung into the farm drive. A snowplough, pushed by the tractor, carved an arc through the snow, flinging white spurts of powder to either side. The driver came into focus. It was Rhys, the neighbouring farmer. He swung the vehicle round in a circle on the parking space near the house, drew to a halt, engine running and opened the tractor door.

"Good to see you're both okay." Rhys's ruddy cheeks were glowing red in the warmth of the tractor cab. "Fancy a lift down to the village? Or is there anything I can bring you?"

Arnaud and Catherine jumped at the chance to get out for a few hours and hitched a ride, squeezing in the cab alongside Rhys. They jolted down the lane, making slow but steady progress.

On the way he was talkative, filling them in with local gossip. Arnaud was annoyed with himself. He'd meant to make time to visit the older man, but they'd been so busy.

Rhys finally exhausted his fund of stories and turned to Arnaud, "How are things at the farm? Not helping you, this weather."

"No, we could do without it. We've had to cancel a couple of bookings and the horses are eating their way through the feed." Arnaud hoped desperately that Rhys wouldn't mention the outstanding food bill. He didn't.

"How about the bookings for the summer?"

Catherine frowned. "I've managed to contact most of the schools and let them know about the change of ownership. So far, the bulk of them have come back to me and said it's not a problem, but two of them have cancelled. Sorry Arnaud, I meant to tell you. I only just saw the emails when I was on my computer upstairs. It looks like the internet is working again."

Arnaud felt his stomach contract. That was a serious blow. "No! Did they say why they cancelled?"

"Well, I don't quite understand it. One of them referred to the 'situation' that we have here at the farm. I mentioned that we were the new managers, but nothing more than that, as you know."

"Maybe it's worth calling them, to try and see if there is anything we can do," Arnaud suggested.

"Yes, I'll definitely give it a go," responded Catherine.

The elderly farmer left them at the Wily Wolf pub, with a promise to pick them up later after he had finished clearing the network of lanes that lay to the south of the village. Behind the bar, a curly haired man with a rough stubbled face was polishing glasses. It was Min's brother Joseph, the owner of the pub.

"Hello strangers. Haven't seen you for a while. What do you think of our Welsh weather now?"

"It's pretty impressive, I've not experienced snow like this before. We've been so busy recently, you're right, we've not been down here for ages. I've just remembered how good your mulled cider is. Nearly as good as our Normandy cider." Arnaud smiled at the Welsh man.

"That's my brother's. He's got a farm just beyond Hereford."

"I'll have one too," Catherine pulled her gloves off and unwound the scarf from her neck.

"Grab a table near the fire. Are you eating?"

"Yes, if you have food available."

"A bit of snow don't stop us. Min's been working on a new foraged menu if you want to try it," Joseph asked.

"Sounds perfect. Catherine?"

"I'm up for it."

They sat down at the round pine table. Arnaud stretched his legs underneath, leaning back in his chair and commented, "This is the first time we have eaten out for ages."

Catherine dragged her eyes away from the menu. "We should make ourselves get out from time to time, you know. Particularly when the farm gets busy. Otherwise we're just not going to have much of a life."

"It's a deal."

She looked back at the menu. "This is amazing! I thought Toby and Noah were good at foraging, but Min's taken it to a whole new level here. What have we been missing out on."

She could almost taste each of the dishes as she read through the menu. It had been handwritten on card with a printed wolf's head:

## *Wily Wolf Foraged Menu*

### *Starters*
*Wild Mushroom Pâté with Welsh Lava Bread*
*Nettle & Potato Soup with Wild Garlic Toasts*
*Comfrey Fritters*

### *Mains*
*Rabbit, Leek & Wild Mushroom Pie*
*Pork Cheeks with Wild Garlic Mashed Potatoes & Seasonal Greens*
*Sea Bream with Scallops & Nettle Sauce*

### *Desserts*
*Blackberry Panna Cotta with Fennel Cookies*
*Hazelnut & Elderflower Ice Cream with Strawberry Fruit Leather*
*Lavender & Blackberry Sorbet*

Joseph came over to the table with their drinks. Arnaud waved the menu at him. "This looks incredible. I can't make up my mind what to choose."

Joseph grinned, "Wait until you've eaten the food. You'll not taste better in those posh London places, I bet you. It's a shame we can't keep Min."

"Is she leaving?" Arnaud asked.

"Sadly, yes. She's been helping us out for a few months as my wife, Steph, broke her ankle. She's pretty much up and about now. It's a shame really, but we can't afford to keep Min on a permanent basis. She was talking about looking for jobs over by the coast near St David's. A friend of hers is working in a nice restaurant there. But to be honest, I think Min would rather stay near here, where all the family are."

"We'll have to make the most of her while she's still around." Catherine had immediately taken to the dimple-cheeked girl they had met over the Christmas period at the pub. She recalled that Noah had also struck up a friendship with her on his visit.

"How are you managing at the farm? I hear Sebastian still hasn't regained his memory. That must be a worry for you." Joseph looked concerned.

"Yes, it is. We're still trying to sort everything out for the new season. We're meant to be interviewing potential staff next Saturday, but that might depend on the weather, I suppose."

"I don't think there's any more snow forecast, so it should clear by the end of the week, I'm guessing. Is Sebastian likely to be discharged soon?"

"I saw him last week. His broken leg is improving but his back is still quite a mess and the hospital say it will be a few weeks before he can be discharged. Of course, he can come and live up at the farm with us. We're hoping it will help his memory. He says there is the odd thing that comes back to him - but totally disjointed. Just flashes and nothing really substantial."

"Do they reckon he'll be okay eventually?"

Arnaud shrugged his shoulders, "Nobody can say. It seems the brain is still a bit of a mystery, even with modern technology. I had no idea about these things."

Joseph noticed Catherine looking hungrily at the menu. "I'm so sorry, you must be wanting to eat."

He took down their orders, and disappeared into the kitchen.

Arnaud saw the fire was getting low, and picked up a couple of logs from the wood basket. They sent sparks flying up the chimney as he dropped them onto the burning embers. Flames licked around the logs and soon they caught, with a whooshing noise. Catherine gazed into the fire, enjoying the peace.

Ten minutes later, Min appeared with their starters, her frizzy brown hair swept up in a spotted scarf.

She slid a bowl in front of Catherine and a square white plate in front of Arnaud. The mushroom pâté was decorated with primrose flowers. Next to it sat a chunk of golden yellow butter in a flower shape, and two slices of dark brown, seaweed-speckled lava bread.

"Min, this looks amazing. Did you forage for the mushrooms too?" Arnaud was impressed.

She grinned, brushing back a curl of hair that had escaped from the scarf. "Yes, I did a couple of courses on mushrooms. Joseph wouldn't forgive me for poisoning his customers. These are velvet shanks. There's not an awful lot of other fungi around at this time of year. It goes a treat with the lava bread."

Catherine was looking appreciatively at her steaming bowl of dark green soup. "I don't want to be disloyal, but this looks more...expert...than Noah and Toby's nettle soup," she had to admit.

"We were talking about foraging when they were down at Christmas. I gave Noah a couple of new recipes to try out. A bit of nutmeg makes all the difference in nettle soup," Min commented. She turned, and hurried back to the kitchen. Despite the weather, the pub was filling up and her foraged menu was proving popular with the customers.

As they were eating, Catherine noticed a woman in the opposite corner of the bar. She was wearing outdoor clothes - muddy jeans, boots and a checked shirt. Her long straight hair was pulled back into a rough pony tail, accentuating the sharpness of her narrow face. Every time Catherine lifted her head, she noticed the woman seemed to be looking over at her and Arnaud. She was puzzled. They didn't usually attract much attention.

Arnaud noticed the frown on her face. "Is there something wrong with the soup?"

"No, no it's excellent. I was just a bit distracted by something." The woman's attention seemed too trivial a thing to comment on.

The main courses were no less delicious. Arnaud waved his fork at Catherine, a lump of pork cheek skewered on the end.

"You English, you don't always like to eat all of the bits of the animal. Some of the best bits are the offal or the brains."

Catherine grimaced. "Toby and Noah introduced me to rabbit, but it was a struggle at first, I have to admit. This, however, is excellent," she spoke through a mouthful of sea bream and scallops.

The taste of the fish suddenly gave Catherine a wave of nostalgia for the coast. When Isaac was alive, he had regularly provided fresh fish for the household, and had taught Catherine to search for shellfish in the cove. She and Noah had spent hours digging for cockles and razor clams in the muddy sand, or picking little black winkles off the breakwaters. She pushed the memories to the back of her mind, determined not to spoil the moment.

It was Arnaud who commented on the woman.

"I feel under scrutiny. The lady at that table over there keeps looking at us. Is it my face? Do I have food everywhere?" His eyes were twinkling.

"It's funny, I noticed her staring at me earlier. I've no idea why." Catherine was perplexed.

"Perhaps we have reached the dizzy heights of fame? Or maybe the local grapevine has some juicy gossip about us," Arnaud wasn't bothered by the attention.

Catherine shrugged her shoulders and turned back to her food.

The desserts were delicate works of art. Catherine had chosen the blackberry panna cotta. The slightly tart flavour of the blackberry was offset by the subtle aniseed of the fennel in the light, crisp cookies. Arnaud opted for the hazelnut and elderflower ice cream. It didn't last long on his plate.

They enjoyed a leisurely coffee after their meal, glad that Rhys hadn't yet returned. After the last customers had been served with their desserts, Min appeared at their table with a plate of chocolates. She'd taken off her scarf and her dark brown curls massed around her face.

"I'd love it if you try these and let me know what you think. It's a new recipe - chocolate mushroom truffles. Joseph wasn't sure if people would go for them."

Catherine took one and ate it, sighing appreciatively.

"It tastes amazing. I don't think you're capable of

169

producing anything that isn't excellent, Min."

"You'd be surprised, I have plenty of failures when I'm testing new stuff."

Arnaud pulled out a chair for Min and encouraged her to have a coffee with them. She agreed easily, happy to take the weight off her feet, now that her work had finished. Joseph came over with a cup for his sister, tousling her hair as he placed it on the table.

"Where did you learn to cook Min?" Catherine was curious.

"I was at catering college in Aberystwyth. Then I did a stint at a posh restaurant in Cardiff. I hated the atmosphere - they were all a bit up themselves, but the emphasis was on foraged food and I learned a lot. I don't regret it, and I enjoyed the course, but I do love the mountains round here. Brilliant for foraging too."

"It's a shame Noah's not around. We were trying to encourage him to come and work here. I'm sure he'd have loved to go foraging with you."

Min opened her mouth and shut it quickly. Noah had asked her to keep things quiet for the moment. She hated secrets.

Arnaud rescued her. "Min, there was a woman sitting over in the far corner, with long hair tied in a ponytail. She was with a man wearing a red shirt. I was wondering who she was. It was funny, she seemed to keep staring at us." He was curious.

Min's face clouded over. "That doesn't surprise me. I'd keep well away from her if I were you. Her name's Laura and she runs a trekking centre the other side of the valley. She was a good friend of Emily's and if you ask me, she's a right cow. I expect she was sizing up the competition."

Arnaud nodded. "Well that makes sense, at least."

The outside door opened in a gust of wind and snow. Rhys strode into the room, stamping his feet. Min bustled off to find him a plate of food and the conversation was dropped.

It was five o'clock by the time Rhys dropped Arnaud and Catherine back at Kestrel Farm. Darkness had fallen, and the moon was shining on the snow, filling the fields with a clear blue light. They went to check on the horses, most of whom were dozing in the indoor school. A few still munched on the remains of the hay that Arnaud had bundled in for them that morning. Arnaud spotted a tall chestnut horse standing in the far corner, next to a couple of smaller ponies. It could only be Jester.

"Look Catherine," he pointed.

She followed his gaze and breathed in. Jester was resting his nose on the edge of the fence, relaxed.

"I never thought I would see him in the herd and happy," said Arnaud.

# 14

## JOB INTERVIEWS

**Noah's Diary:**

*Saturday 17 March*

*Well, I tossed the coin and it came down tails. Seemed like a done deal. Then I thought, not so quick. Once, it could be just chance. So I tossed it again. Tails. Seems pretty clear, but you never know. I chucked it up a third time and...it fell down a crack in the floorboards before I could see. Doh.*

*Anyhow, my mind is made up. Tails for Wales. So...emailed Min and she reckoned it's not too late to ask Arnaud and Catherine. In fact, she said today's a good day as they're interviewing for trek leaders. It's time to swallow my pride me hearties, and take up my courage in both hands. Let's see how Wales turns out. Hope my riding skills are up to it. A new chapter in the Life of Noah begins. A watershed moment (haha). The floodgates open (ha). Joking apart, I heard it's quite wet in Wales. Better get some waterproof stuff. Note to self - check riding gear.*

*I wonder if Dad will even notice I'm gone. He's so busy with exhibitions and London galleries and all that stuff these days. Maybe I'll just go and see how long it takes him to spot I'm missing. Mind you, he always seems to be right on the case when I'm late for work or something.*

Catherine put the file down on the kitchen table. "I'm still worried there's not much margin for error."

Arnaud picked up the blue folder and flicked the front cover open. On the first page was printed a list of names and times, with a short summary of each interviewee next to their name. "How many again? I know we've discussed it, but I've been so busy with the horses, it's escaped my mind."

"We've got six people coming for interview and we need to fill five posts - that's what we reckoned anyhow. It's a bit tight, but I don't think we should be forced into a corner and take anyone we're not happy with. They're going to be looking after schoolchildren after all."

"Yes,' Arnaud agreed. "That's fine by me."

He leafed through the folder. Beyond the interview list was a series of CVs. The third interviewee was a gamble. On paper, the candidate looked good, but his photograph showed a heavily made-up Goth. Catherine had wanted to exclude him on the grounds the teachers might take exception to him. Arnaud was all for giving him a chance. The applicant had teaching experience, good references and excellent riding skills - or so he claimed. Arnaud was intrigued to meet him. Catherine less so.

Four of the candidates had their own transport, so Catherine had arranged with them to come directly to the farm. Two were able to get as far as the Wily Wolf, where the local bus service made an extra stop if requested. Min had offered to run them up to the farm. Catherine's immediate reaction was to decline her offer, but something had overridden it. A growing understanding that the little community they had landed in flourished on interdependence. Instead, she accepted and made a mental note to find a way of reciprocating.

She mentioned to Min, "You might recognise the first person - Caitlin. She worked here last year."

Min did, but was strangely non-committal about her.

Even so, Catherine wasn't prepared for her own instinctive dislike of the girl. Tall, willowy with long white-blonde hair and cheekbones to die for, Caitlin was stunning, but there was a hard edge to her jawline and her eyes were cold. Catherine struggled to overcome her first reactions and remain neutral until she had given the girl a chance. She tried to open the interview in a chatty, conversational tone, but Caitlin seemed distant and aloof. It wasn't long before Catherine was getting the strong impression the girl found her gauche and old-fashioned.

It didn't help that Caitlin was immaculately dressed in a fitted navy quilted jacket, white blouse and fawn coloured trousers, with smart brown boots. Her outfit was beautifully accessorised with jewellery that looked as if it was worth more than Catherine's annual clothes budget. Catherine had struggled to find a clean pair of jeans and semi-decent top.

It seemed to Catherine that Caitlin responded more positively to Arnaud's questions, so she decided to take a back seat and let Arnaud lead the rest of the conversation.

Catherine had briefly explained the current situation at the farm to Caitlin on the phone when they were arranging the interview. Caitlin had made no comment about Emily's departure, although she had seemed shocked to learn of Sebastian's accident. Catherine had been surprised. She was under the impression that Sebastian had had little contact with the everyday life of the farm.

Now, Arnaud briefly updated Caitlin on Sebastian's progress. As he explained about his memory loss, Caitlin's eyes narrowed. "You mean he can't remember anything at all?" Her tone was strangely insistent.

"No nothing. And the doctors have no idea how much - if anything - he will ever remember."

"Never. Never at all?" Caitlin pushed him.

"We honestly don't know," Arnaud shrugged his shoulders. "Personally, I am trying to be positive. I am sure this will change."

Caitlin swallowed. Her self-composure seemed shaken.

Arnaud moved the conversation onto Caitlin's experience at the farm the previous year. She told them she had enjoyed herself and was keen to spend a second season at the farm.

Catherine was puzzled. Caitlin's answers seemed lacking in enthusiasm and she had a sense that something didn't add up.

"…Catherine?"

She gave a start. She realised she hadn't been listening to the interview.

"I'm so sorry, I was nodding off in this warm kitchen. We were up early this morning."

Caitlin wasn't interested in her response. She'd already stood up and was heading for the door. It seemed as if Arnaud had wrapped up the formal part of the interview and they were about to head to the indoor school.

Catherine wouldn't have had the courage to give Caitlin a riding test, but Arnaud wanted to check out everybody's skills for himself. Marley, a showy bay horse, who rather fancied himself, was tied up to the fence near the entrance. Arnaud hadn't saddled him - he was keen to see the candidates' skills with tacking up.

Caitlin changed into the jodhpurs she had brought along with her. She made short work of saddling and bridling Marley and swung herself lightly onto his back. Walking the bay horse around the school once, she then pushed him into a trot, and finally a neat collected canter. It was a polished performance, but, Arnaud noticed, no pat for the horse or stroke of its nose. In fact, very little emotional connection with Marley at all.

After the interview, Catherine tried to rationalise her feelings. Caitlin had all the necessary experience - she and her sister had their own ponies as children, her father owned a stud farm, she'd spent last summer working at Kestrel Farm and the winter helping out at her uncle's polo farm in Australia - but her whole demeanor suggested a studied boredom. There didn't seem to be much enthusiasm for the job in question.

The second candidate was a complete contrast. Lily was medium height, curvy with long, unruly dark - almost black - hair. She wore jeans, an old calfskin jacket, red silk scarf flung casually around her neck and a wide brimmed leather bush hat. Her generous mouth smiled easily and was accompanied by a twinkle in her eyes. Both Arnaud and Catherine instinctively warmed to the friendly, natural girl. Lily was almost apologetic about her previous experience with horses.

"I had my own pony as a child. My mother dragged me around all the local shows and I went to all the Pony Club events, but to be honest, I'm happier just hacking out in the countryside. The bit I enjoyed most at the Pony Club was helping out with the younger children."

Catherine was curious. "What are you doing at the moment? I saw on your CV that you finished a business degree last year."

Lily acknowledged, "Yes, I enjoyed the course, but

I've no idea what to do next. As I mentioned, I've given myself a year out to decide. I spent the last few months helping at a ski chalet in Courchevel. I like the outdoors, so this job looked a great idea. It will give me a deadline too. I'll have to sort something out by the end of the season," she grinned.

Lily's riding skills were exemplary, but where Caitlin merely showed trained expertise, Lily was a natural horsewoman with an empathy for her mount. She laughed at Marley's pompous attitude to himself. "He's a quality horse though. I don't mean to be rude, but not quite what I expected to see at a trekking centre."

Arnaud acknowledged, "We were surprised too. Apparently, the owners have always had an eye for decent horses. I understand a fair proportion of them were bred by the family from local Welsh mountain stock."

Catherine had been dreading the next part of the interview. There had been so many other things to sort out, she and Arnaud hadn't really taken a proper look at the staff accommodation until a few days before the interviews. Sebastian had merely shown them the outside of the little red brick house on their first visit and neglected it completely on his later tour of the premises.

She was apologetic to Lily, "There is just one thing. The staff accommodation isn't to the standard we would like, so please do bear with us."

As the three of them made their way over to the old cottage on the edge of the pine forest, a short distance from the centre, Lily seemed impressed. "Gosh a whole house to ourselves. And tucked away from the guest accommodation."

"Yes, the location is good," Arnaud had to agree.

They were walking along a little track leading from the

far side of the bunkhouses. The path wound through the pine trees, which hid the cottage from sight of the trekking centre.

Lily gasped when she saw the raised wooden decking at the back of the house. A few old chairs were stacked in a corner. Below the decking was a patch of grass and a few bare bushes.

"This looks great," she enthused.

"The garden's the best bit I'm afraid," Catherine was embarrassed.

She had opened the windows the day before to air the house, but as she turned the key in the lock and opened the back door, nothing could hide the overwhelming smell of mould which hit them. They stepped straight into a dingy kitchen, with an old fashioned electric cooker, a few mismatched cupboards, scratched, broken worktops and an old cracked sink. The rest of the house was in a similar state. There was a downstairs lounge with a pair of dingy sofas, sporting a scattering of cigarette burns on the arms. The cheap green carpet was dirty and stained. A tiny room built in underneath the steep stairs was just big enough to house a filthy shower cubicle. Each of the bedrooms had a crude metal bed frame and thin, lumpy mattress.

I'm so sorry," Catherine could only apologise. "Obviously we are intending to sort this out before the season."

Lily was surprisingly blasé. "I've seen worse in my student days - well maybe not worse, just similar," she added with a smile. "A lick of paint and a good clean should sort most of this out."

Catherine was grateful. She had been terrified the accommodation would put Lily off. All bar one of the other candidates were male, and most likely not too fussy about living quarters, she reasoned. Caitlin must have been aware of the conditions in the house and was prepared to put up with them, although Catherine had a struggle to picture the smartly turned out girl living there.

Lily had one more surprise for them up her sleeve. Just before she left, she cleared her throat and looked hesitantly at Catherine and Arnaud.

"I need to tell you this, and you might decide not to take me after all, on the basis of it."

Catherine wondered what was coming next.

"My father is a famous politician." Lily mentioned his name. It was very familiar. Lily's father regularly featured on the news. "There is always the possibility that a journalist might come sniffing around here, trying to dig up some dirt on my father. It's happened before." She continued quickly, "They won't find anything. I would never do anything that might have a negative impact on him - we're really close and I respect what he does. But just in case..." she shrugged her shoulders, uncomfortable.

Arnaud looked at Catherine. It was clear they both held a similar view.

"That's not a problem at all," he told the girl, who sighed with relief.

At the end of the interview, Lilly had earned herself a large tick next to her name on the candidate list.

"My real name's Nigel, but everyone calls me Goff. You can too if you like."

A slightly toned-down version of the young man in the photograph sat at the kitchen table opposite Catherine and Arnaud. Min had dropped him off, with a wink, and headed up the valley to call in on Johanna. The heavy, dark make up of his CV images wasn't in evidence, but Goff was dressed head to toe in black, his large - but not fat - body encased in an ankle length black leather overcoat. His scalp was shaved, apart from a wide strip of long hair in the middle running from back to front. Catherine wondered how he was going to be able to fit it into a riding hat.

His manner, however, was at odds with his appearance and Catherine felt shamed. Arnaud was so much better than her at not judging people. He seemed to view them from the inside out, struggling even sometimes to describe a person's physical appearance. Catherine was aware she had a tendency towards snap judgments which she often later regretted. It was clear this was case with Goff. Mild-mannered and affable, he had them both laughing within minutes. She could see that he would go down well with the schoolchildren. His CV stated that he had worked as a teacher at an inner city school for several years. It occurred to her that Goff could be useful if they had any particularly difficult children.

"So why are you giving up your teaching job?" Arnaud was curious, but not challenging.

"Well, I'm just about at the end of my tether," was Goff's response. "When I started the job, I thought teaching in an inner city junior school was going to be tough, but meaningful if you know what I mean. And it has been both of those. But I'd say more demanding than I realised. I'm not a small bloke, but I've had kids swing punches at me, try to cut me with broken glass, bite my hand, you name it. I'm not saying I wouldn't go back to that kind of thing. My heart's still in it - I just need a bit of a break. When I saw this job, it seemed ideal. Still working with kids, but out in the fresh air. Horses in the mix too. I don't want to sound desperate, but it seems a bit of a godsend."

Catherine hoped that Goff hadn't had some kind of a breakdown. The last thing she wanted was to have to support their staff emotionally. All the same, she had warmed to the young man's honesty and she could see he'd had the same effect on Arnaud.

Goff's riding skills and horsemanship were surprisingly good given that he'd admitted to being a self-taught rider. And he moved with a poise that belied his size. Again, Catherine was impressed by his attitude when they showed him the rather dilapidated cottage.

"If you guys are happy, maybe we could all arrive a day or so early and help decorate it," was his suggestion.

She pounced on the idea. "That's brilliant, Goff - you've got the job." She didn't need to see Arnaud's slight nod of encouragement. She knew what he was thinking.

Catherine made a round of sandwiches for lunch while Arnaud dropped Goff back at the pub. She was interrupted by a phone call and had bad news for Arnaud when he returned, still laughing at Goff's parting joke.

"You'll never believe this. One of the candidates has just pulled out - Rachel."

"No! Wasn't she the other one who worked here last year?"

"Yes, that's so frustrating. She sounded a bit cagey. She's been offered a job at another trekking centre, which she's accepted. For some reason I got the impression it must be in this area," Catherine told him.

"Shame. Oh well, onwards and upwards." Arnaud was a magnet for English phrases.

Candidate number four was the young man every mother would like their daughter to date, Catherine decided. Skinny and tall, with large brown puppy-dog eyes, Justin was softly spoken, but confident. His mousy hair was half-hidden under a navy woollen beany hat.

"I've got to be honest, I really want to make it as an artist - or a musician - or even both. But money doesn't grow on trees and I enjoy working with kids and horses."

"That makes sense," Arnaud sympathised. "I'm sorry, tell me again your experience with horses?"

"I used to help out at our local riding stables. It was a bit of a community project - I learned to ride there, then when I got older, I ended up as one of the helpers in my spare time. That's where I did my British Horse Society exams and got my DBS check. We eventually did a bit of work with disabled riders too. I really enjoyed it."

They talked a bit about Justin's background. Coming from Hastings, he shared a mutual love of the sea with Catherine and she warmed to him further.

When they walked into the indoor school for Justin's riding test, Marley was dozing in the corner. The horse had obviously decided he'd done his bit for the day, and Justin struggled to get Marley to move at any speed. Catherine noticed his riding position was slightly unorthodox - his legs and arms had a tendency to stick out at odd angles, a contrast with the precise, tidy riding that Caitlin had demonstrated. But, she had to concede, he seemed to have a natural empathy with the animal and did finally manage to encourage Marley into a shambling, half-hearted canter.

Justin too seemed unfazed by the accommodation. The fact that the trek leaders had a house all the themselves seemed to be a huge plus point to him. As he drove out of the farm in a little red Fiesta, Catherine and Arnaud debated his future.

On the whole, Catherine felt happy with Justin. She had warmed to the lad.

Arnaud was more reticent. "I wonder if he isn't a bit too laid back. It's a lot of work and the trek leaders will need to be good with timekeeping, and also quite on the ball with the children," were his concerns.

But by the end of the day, Justin gained a tick. The pool of potential trek leaders had narrowed. Their last interviewee, a small freckle-faced Welsh lad called David, clearly had no idea how to tack up a horse, and jabbed at Marley's mouth to the point where an annoyed Arnaud had called a rapid halt to the riding test.

Things were looking up. They only had one more trek leader and a chef to find. Arnaud felt quite satisfied with the day's outcome, as he sat on the sofa in the lounge, his feet propped up on the pine coffee table. Catherine had rung the successful candidates earlier that evening, and thankfully, they were all pleased to accept the job. More importantly, they were able to start in time for the first school group, just three weeks away in the middle of April. And all of them were happy with Goff's suggestion of turning up early and decorating their accommodation.

Even so, Catherine was still panicking, overwhelmed with the enormity of getting everything ready in time. She tried to steady herself. "Worst case scenario, you'll have to take a trek out while I sort out the catering and hold the fort here."

"It's possible," agreed Arnaud, enjoying a well-earned glass of wine. "But I believe things have a way of sorting themselves out. I'm sure something will fall into place."

Arnaud wished he felt so confident about the farm's finances. He'd finally managed to get hold of Emily two days ago and her reaction was far from positive. She had been annoyed with Arnaud for 'hounding her' and was still dragging her feet on the thorny issue of funding for the farm. According to Emily, the place was a dead loss and she was reluctant to release funds from Sebastian's account into a business that was doing so badly. As far as she was concerned, it wasn't in his 'best interests'.

Arnaud explained, as calmly as he could, that a failed business was a far worse asset than a failing one. Emily's only response was to tell Arnaud that he'd always been a soft touch and to hang up. Arnaud had felt alternately sick and furiously angry. He had no idea how he would break the news to Catherine and it was haunting him. He'd never kept anything from her before. His thoughts were interrupted by a call on his mobile. It was Noah.

"Arnaud old man, how are things?" Noah tried to sound casual. Arnaud detected the note of panic in his voice.

"Are you okay Noah?"

"Never better."

A slight pause. Unusual from the garrulous Noah. Arnaud filled in the gap.

"And Toby?"

"Elusive, but still alive the last time I saw him."

Another pause. Then Noah cracked, "Are you…do you think…is it still open? The job offer I mean. Would you have a vacancy for a trek leader? I know it's a bit late in the day…"

"You want to come and work here? We would love you to. In fact Noah, you would be getting us out of a very deep hole. Our first school group is arriving in three weeks' time and we are one trek leader down."

"Well, I did hear a rumour you guys were in the process of hiring staff and, well, I thought perhaps I could help out."

Arnaud wondered who the rumour had originated with.

"That's very kind of you Noah. Are you able to come over soon?"

"Tomorrow? Oh well, perhaps not tomorrow, I just need to sort out a few bits and pieces. The next day?"

"There's no immediate rush. Just whenever you can be ready. Everyone else is starting on 12th April."

Noah felt foolish and decided he needed to be slightly less available.

"We-ell, a couple of weeks' time would be better for me. A few loose ends to wrap up etc."

"Perfect. I'm guessing you'll bring Oscar?"

"Yes of course. That is, if it's okay?"

"It would be great to have him around. And what about your chickens and ducks?"

Noah hadn't even considered his poultry. He couldn't imagine them lasting long under Toby's distracted care.

"Er yes, that would be great too."

"Fine, let us know when you're coming so we can make sure somebody is around for you."

"Will do. Bye."

"Bye Noah. Take care."

Catherine stared at Arnaud. "Did I just hear what I thought I heard?"

"Yes, Noah will be joining us. So now we're sorted on that front."

Catherine smiled. And then frowned.

"I hope he manages okay. He does seem to have a

history of lapses on concentration when it comes to the job front."

"Catherine, I don't believe it! Your problem is solved and you have found a new worry."

She grinned. "Okay, promise I'll chill. In fact, if you can sort me out a chef, I'll superchill."

Arnaud looked rather pleased with himself. "As it happens, I have an idea…"

He told Catherine.

# 15

## SEBASTIAN

Sebastian stood at the window, looking out over the courtyard. Two men, one with a leg in plaster, were standing under the shelter of an awning, smoking. Heads bent together, shoulders hunched against the wind which was buffeting their dressing gowns, they looked like a couple of oddly-dressed conspirators. Sebastian had got to know them from his trips to physiotherapy. Eric, the older man, with yellowish grey hair and rough sandpaper skin, was recovering from a mild stroke. Andy, a cheerful farmworker, who'd broken his leg when he'd slipped off a trailer hauling manure, was an eternal optimist. He maintained he was glad to have the break from his three teenage kids, but Sebastian suspected Andy was relieved to be going home in a few days' time.

Going home. That was happening to him today. Whatever 'home' was. It looked like a beautiful place. Arnaud had brought in his iPad and shown Sebastian a series of pictures of Kestrel Farm. As usual, he had drawn a big blank, recognising nothing. He was trying hard to take a leaf out of Andy The Optimist's book. At least he had somewhere to go to and people who took an interest in his welfare. Things could be a lot worse.

For the last weeks, as his body had begun to mend, Sebastian had been increasingly desperate to leave the confines of the hospital. He was bored, frustrated and tired of the limited views from the hospital windows. Watching television only made him more anxious to get out and see new, different scenery.

But now the time had come, he was anxious. It was only during the last few days, when he'd taken to wandering clumsily around the building on his crutches, that he'd discovered just how little energy he possessed. It didn't take much effort before he was beset by a thumping headache and started to feel dizzy.

He was unconfident around people too. A few kind souls had popped in and visited him; Joseph - a man in his mid-thirties who apparently ran a pub in the village near Sebastian's farm, Rhys - an old, grey-haired farmer who declared himself Sebastian's neighbour and family friend, plus one or two others. All of them had been pleasant enough, but clearly unsure of how to deal with a Sebastian who had no idea who they were. Conversation had been stilted at best, and they'd all seemed relieved when the time came to leave. Apart from Arnaud, of course.

Sebastian had rapidly come to look forward to the regular visits from the Frenchman. If he thought about it, which he wasn't about to, Arnaud was main thing that really kept him going. He had an instinctive feel for when Sebastian was thirsty for information, and when he just wanted to clam up and listen to amusing, mundane things. Most importantly, Arnaud had a knack of not making him feel stupid.

A week ago, Arnaud's wife, Catherine, had visited with him. At first, Sebastian was dismissive of the softly-spoken, pale woman with mousy hair. It didn't take him long to revise his opinion. Her unprepossessing exterior hid a sharp wit and kind, undemanding but perceptive personality. She'd had the foresight to bring things that Arnaud hadn't thought of. Some more clothes, books, a food parcel containing homemade cake, biscuits, chocolates and a small bottle of whisky.

His injured leg and back started to ache and he eased himself into the armchair. At first, the consultant had been nervous of discharging him directly to the farm, worried about uneven surfaces and steep gradients. Arnaud's gentle persuasion had won over.

A spattering on the window caught Sebastian's attention. Rain. He glanced over at his possessions lying on the bed. Amongst the clothes that Catherine had brought was a winter jacket. He'd be glad of it now. He stood up again and moved restlessly to the window. Rivulets of rain ran down the glass. He followed them with his gaze as they merged into one another, then splashed onto the windowsill.

A knock at the door. He turned his head to see Arnaud.

"Come on Sebastian, let's get going. I feel like I'm busting you out of jail. That nurse Ellen gave me a really filthy look just now."

Sebastian grimaced, "I've never seen her smile once in all the time I've been here."

"Just as well there are some cheerful faces around as well. I think that one would have me jumping out of the window in no time."

"Well, I did consider it once or twice," Sebastian was only half-joking. He looked at his possessions on the bed.

"Not much to show for three and a half months'

occupation is it really."

Arnaud ran his eyes over the pile of things; a laptop, a tan leather suitcase Catherine had found in a cupboard at the farm, a couple of plastic bags containing assorted junk and Sebastian's crutches, propped up by the door. That was it.

"Well, it's about time you sampled the fine living we have at Kestrel Farm my friend. Home cooked food, a comfortable bed, beautiful views. You're not going to know what's hit you."

Sebastian limped over to the bed and put the jacket on awkwardly, immediately feeling stifled in the heat of the hospital. Still, he'd only have to endure it for a few minutes and he didn't want to wrestle with the jacket and his crutches when they got outside. Arnaud picked up the crutches and handed them to him. Then Arnaud slung the strap of the laptop case over his shoulder, took the suitcase and grasped the plastic bags with his other hand. Sebastian followed him out of the room.

Five minutes later, they were in the open air. Sebastian stood at the hospital entrance, shivering in the cold despite his warm jacket, while Arnaud went to fetch the car. He looked behind him, into the busy corridor, with the day's visitors just arriving, and breathed deeply, wondering what awaited him next.

Citroën 2CVs, Noah reflected, were definitely not built for motorways. Or strong winds. A combination of both was proving quite a challenge. Even with all of his gear weighing the car down, it still needed a very firm pair of hands on the wheel to stop the vehicle swerving sideways every time there was a heavy gust of wind. Ditto the passing lorries. Oscar didn't seem happy at all, and was crouched down on the front passenger seat, bracing himself. In the boot, the chickens were rustling around in their cardboard boxes. Now and then, a muted squawk reached Noah's ears. By the time they reached the Chieveley Services, Noah's arms were shaking and he decided a pit stop was in order. At a standstill in the car park, the Citroën still shuddered in the feisty April wind. Cold air breezed through the cracks around the flimsy doors and Noah shivered, despite having the heating on full blast.

He left an anxious Oscar in the car and dashed out into the elements, running towards the services building. At that moment, the rain, which had been brooding overhead with black clouds all day, decided to let rip, and in the short distance from the car to the building, Noah was drenched by the downpour.

By the time he made it back with a Coke, burger and chips, his clothes were sodden. Noah placed the food and drink on the driver's seat and ran around to the other side to let Oscar out for a walk. He clipped the lead onto Oscar's collar. The black dog sat on the seat, looking at him.

"Come on, come and have a pee."

Oscar dug his paws into the seat as Noah gently tugged on the lead. He wasn't going anywhere.

Noah gave up and returned to the driver's side. He picked up his food and drink and slid into the seat, glancing around for somewhere to put it. The only free space was next to Oscar. He wedged the Coke in between Oscar and the seatbelt and put the chips next to him. As Oscar's nose headed towards the chips and burger, Noah pointed a finger at the dog and uttered a stern, "No!"

Oscar's shiny black eyes looked mutely back at Noah.

His nose remained two inches away from the burger.

Noah stripped off his sweatshirt and rummaged around in a bag on the back seat for a replacement. He towelled his wet hair with the sweatshirt then pulled a dry one over his head, battling with the sleeves in the confined space of the car. As he started on the burger, his phone pinged. He wiped his greasy hands on the discarded sweatshirt and checked. A message from Catherine.

*'How are you? Driving must be hideous. Take your time and be careful.'*

Of course, Catherine would know what her old car would be like in this weather. Another ping.

*'Forgot to say, Sebastian's arriving from hospital today as well.'*

He texted back a smiley face and *'Doing ok'*, gave the last two chips to Oscar as a reward for good behaviour, finished off his burger and turned the key in the ignition.

After what felt like a lifetime of battling the elements, the 2CV drew into the little village of Llaneilar. Noah breathed a sigh of relief. Almost there. His stomach lurched, struggling to digest the additional three burgers he had purchased from various services along the way. Oscar had steadfastly refused to leave the car for a pee, even though he now was shifting in his seat and looking uncomfortable. The rain was coming down in sheets. The windscreen wipers were doing a valiant job of keeping a field of vision for Noah, but the windscreen was pretty blurry and Noah's eyes were tired and fuzzy. He spotted the Wily Wolf at the last minute and swung the car sharply to the left, skidding slightly as he did so, just as a small figure with frizzy hair emerged from the side door. He swerved to avoid Min, screeching to a halt a few metres away. Min jumped away from the car, and dropped the box she was holding. As he emerged, red-faced from the car, Min's face turned into a grin. Noah breathed a sigh of relief. He'd been expecting a mouthful.

"That's twice now Noah. Let's hope it's not third time lucky," she quipped and gave him a quick hug.

"I'm so sorry, the rain and all that. Long journey. Can hardly see," Noah stuttered.

"Good you got here in one piece. Have you got time for a coffee? I've just finished clearing up after lunch."

"Fantastic idea."

A whining noise came from the car behind him.

"Cripes Oscar, I forgot him. Is he allowed...?"

Min's face lit up. "Ah, the famous - or should I say infamous - Oscar. Of course, he's allowed in the pub. The farmers bring their sheepdogs in all the time."

Noah opened the car door and Oscar flew out, ran towards Min and then past her.

"Huh...?" came from Noah, until he saw the desperate dog was relieving itself on the side of Min's dropped box. "No, Oscar...!"

"It's okay, I was just about to throw it away. And obviously Oscar's tank's a bit full," Min laughed.

Noah was shamefaced. This wasn't the entrance he'd been planning.

Oscar wagged his tail and jumped up at Min to greet her properly. She made a fuss of the little dog and Noah felt slightly better.

"Come on, let's get out of this rain," Min ran to the pub door and opened it, Oscar slipping between her legs and leading the way inside. Noah followed, relieved his long journey was behind him.

A few minutes later he was sitting next to a roaring fire

with a pint of Joseph's best. Oscar was sprawled out on the carpet in front of him. It was a relief to have the journey behind him.

"Have you heard the news about Sebastian?" Min eased back in her chair, stretching out her stiff legs in front of her. She'd been on her feet since early that morning and was glad of an excuse to sit down for a few minutes.

"Yeah, Catherine texted and said he was coming back today. Great eh?"

"Yes, I'm sure he'll be much happier at the farm than stuck in the hospital. I can't imagine Sebastian has enjoyed being cooped up inside for weeks," Min said, knowingly.

"But somehow weird too. It sounds like he still can't remember anything. What's going to happen to him?"

"Maybe coming back to the farm will jog his mind, who knows?"

"What if he never remembers anything?" Noah asked.

"Well, between you and me, that might not be such a bad thing," Min said, then clammed up and quickly changed the subject. "Noah, I'm glad I saw you when I did. I wanted to sound you out about something."

"Ask away," Noah took a long sip of beer and relaxed deeper into the stuffed armchair.

"You know I said that I'd be finishing up here soon?" She looked slightly awkward.

"Yes, how's your job search coming along?"

"Well it's not. I mean it is and it isn't. I have been offered a couple of positions."

Noah was confused. "That sounds good to me."

"Well, it is, I guess. They're both in west Wales, by the coast. Both good restaurants too."

"So, what's the problem?"

"I don't really want to leave this area. The thing is, Joseph was trying to encourage me to spread my wings a bit, and I guess I listened to him. But now I'm faced with the chance of moving, it doesn't feel right. Do you think I'm just being stupid?"

"No, not at all," Noah leaned forwards, concerned. Min looked stressed and worried.

"A good friend of mine once told me that you should listen to your gut feelings. He'd been around a bit, had Isaac, and he wasn't often wrong."

"So you don't think I'd be mad to throw up the chance to work in an up and coming restaurant?"

"Not necessarily."

Min's face softened, and Noah realised just how taut and anxious she'd been.

"You need a plan B if you want to get Joseph off your back though. Had you thought what you might do?"

"As it happens, I have," replied Min, smiling. "Arnaud and Catherine have just made me an offer, and I'm thinking of accepting it."

Noah settled back into his chair. "I'm all ears," he said.


Sebastian climbed awkwardly into the front passenger seat of the Land Rover. Arnaud had the foresight to move the seat back as far as it would go, to give Sebastian as much space as possible, but it was still an effort to swing his leg into the footwell. Arnaud threw the crutches onto the back seat. He ran around the car, head ducked against the rain, which was now driving down, bouncing back off the tarmac.

Then, he swung himself into the car, and took off his dripping coat, slinging it behind him onto the seat.

"You certainly picked a good day to come out. It's raining cats and dogs. What a funny expression. In French, we say *il pleut des cordes* - it's raining ropes. See how the rain looks like strands of rope," he pointed out of the windscreen. "I don't know what cats and dogs have to do with it. Rather frogs and fishes or something like that."

On the way to the farm, Sebastian gazed at the scenery - what he could see of it through the driving rain. The outskirts of Hereford were unremarkable. A succession of blurry houses, for the most part uniform and uninteresting. Once they cleared the city, the countryside began to come into its own and as the rain eased slightly, Sebastian was given a glimpse of a river winding its way through the valley to their left.

"That's the river Wye," Arnaud informed him. "We're driving along the Wye valley. Shame about the weather, it's beautiful in the sunshine."

"Looks great to me," muttered the ex-hospital inmate.

The trees on either side of the road were covered with a soft green haze, the first flush of leaf growth. Along the banks, drifts of yellow daffodils bobbed their heads in the wind. The verge was green and lush with the spring rain. The undulating road twisted and turned. Sebastian studied the names on the road signs; Sugwas, Bishopstone, Bridge Sollars... Flat, deep green fields of winter wheat stretched out to the right of them, interrupted only by a deep red-brown ploughed swathe of ground and a bare-branched orchard. They passed an attractive red brick farmhouse with green timber and lattice windows, as the arable crops gave way to pastures full of sheep. The lambs were huddled together, standing underneath a tree for shelter. The ewes seemed unconcerned, grazing hungrily despite the weather. Another village signpost, Weobley. Sebastian sighed inwardly. Nothing was registering with him, but it was good to be out and looking at the scenery. Then the landscape began to subtly change, as the fields on the right-hand side began to slope upwards and on the left, a view of the valley opened up beyond the river.

Arnaud broke into his thoughts. "I'm going to swing through Hay. I just need to stop at the supermarket and get some milk. We've nearly run out and with Noah arriving too... Oh I'm so stupid," he slapped his forehead theatrically. "I forgot to tell you. We have another arrival today. Noah called late yesterday evening to let us know he'll be turning up this afternoon. Typical young lad, they don't give much notice. I hope it's not too much for you."

"No, no bother." Secretly Sebastian was relieved. Another person would hopefully take the attention away from him. "And Noah is…"

"I'm sorry. Catherine used to live in the same house as Noah and his father."

Sebastian glanced quizzically at Arnaud, who grinned. "It's not like that at all. It's a long story and really the tale belongs to Catherine and Noah, so I'll let them tell it to you. Suffice to say he's eighteen and a good friend and he's arriving to help us out with the trekking. I hope he makes it okay in this weather. He's driving Catherine's old 2CV which isn't brilliant in these conditions."

Arnaud indicated right and swung the car into the supermarket car park.

"Are you okay in the car for a couple of minutes? I won't be long."

"I'm fine."

Sebastian sat back in the seat and closed his eyes. He

felt exhausted and on sensory overload. The half hour drive from Hereford had tired him out. His head throbbed.

He woke up with a start when Arnaud opened the car door. He'd dozed off. Arnaud looked at Sebastian, taking in his grey face and the dark rings underneath his eyes. "Let's get going, not much further now," he said, encouragingly.

The Land Rover wound up through the narrow Hay streets, and out the other side of the little border town. Then Arnaud turned right, off the main road into a narrow country lane. Sebastian was aware of tall hedges and little else. He closed his eyes again and dozed, waking up when the car drew to a halt. He blinked, rubbing his eyes with his hand. The car was surrounded by sheep, jostling and jumping to get past the vehicle. They were spattered with mud and scruffy, one or two with almost bare patches where their fleece had caught on something.

He cracked open the window slightly and the air was filled with bleating and the clatter of feet on the road. A rank animal smell assaulted his nostrils. Behind them, somebody was shouting and whistling. As the last of the sheep skittered past, a black and white sheepdog ran behind them, its long pink tongue lolling out of one side of its mouth. It was followed by a red-haired man on a quad bike. He was clothed in navy waterproof trousers and a dark green waxed jacket, the collar pulled up against the rain. He waved at the car as he passed.

Further along the lane, a dark-haired man on a battered looking red quad bike was blocking the road, directing the sheep into a field. A stray sheep with a black spotted head slipped past him and was quickly retrieved by the dog. The whole operation was over in a remarkably short space of time. Arnaud eased the clutch and drove off.

"Llaneilar's just ahead now," he informed Sebastian.

They came into the village and turned left past the pub. Arnaud spotted a familiar pale blue 2CV parked outside the Wily Wolf.

"That's Noah's car. Great stuff. He's made it."

Shortly after, they took the left-hand fork and drove up the steep incline through the pine forest. The Land Rover handled the gradient with ease. As the trees thinned out, the farm came into view on the right. Arnaud was silent, wondering if anything would register with Sebastian. He glanced at his friend's face. It was blank. Nothing. Arnaud felt a surge of disappointment. He was hoping against hope that the return to a familiar environment would be enough to jog Sebastian's memory. *Patience my friend*, Arnaud told himself, not wanting to contemplate the future if it didn't come back soon.

# 16

## EARLY DAYS

Suddenly, the farm came to life. Accustomed to the solitary existence of the past few months, interrupted by the occasional visitor and weekend trekkers, Catherine found herself constantly tripping into people. The first afternoon, when the trek leaders were arriving and settling in, they fanned out, exploring every last inch of the farm. She caught sight of Lily and Justin sitting in the large paddock, surrounded by a circle of inquisitive ponies, Noah introducing Goff to the llamas and Caitlin lounging in a chair outside the barn, making the most of the sunshine, lazily chatting on her mobile.

Noah's chickens and ducks had taken up residence in the farmhouse garden. They were enjoying their spacious second hand chicken house, courtesy of Min's brother Joseph, who'd given up keeping poultry a couple of years previously. The two Indian Runner ducks were having to make do with a small washing up bowl until a suitable pond could be constructed for them. At first, Noah had been worried about the farm cat, who was showing a stealthy interest in the new arrivals, slinking along the side of the dry stone wall near their home. The Indian Runners put paid to that, charging at the cat, quacking loudly. She turned tail and fled to the top of a low wood shed, swishing her tail angrily.

Oscar was loving his new life. He had scoured every inch of the farmyard, and the arrival of the new trek leaders was proving a rich source of back rubs and treats. Catherine was concerned about what they would do with the little dog when Noah was out on trek. She didn't want him trying to follow the horses, or wandering off unsupervised. She added the thought to her list of things to tackle.

In the evening, a trek leaders' visit to the Wily Wolf was followed by the sound of Justin's guitar, drifting over to the farmhouse in the stillness of the night, and a girl's voice singing. Catherine was unsure whose, but it was very good.

Surprisingly, Min seemed shy, reluctant to join the group. Catherine was bemused. This was a different Min from the confident girl serving behind the bar or cooking up amazing creations at the Wily Wolf. She also seemed ill at ease around Caitlin – even though the two must have encountered each other on any number of occasions the previous season. Catherine noticed how Min quietly avoided Caitlin. And if Caitlin was aware of Min's behaviour, it certainly didn't seem to bother her.

Mainly, Min was preoccupied, anxious to get preparations for the school group underway. She had moved into the staff house the same day the others arrived, and plunged into the job of planning menus, sorting out food suppliers and stocking up the kitchen larders. Together, she and Catherine checked out the equipment in the kitchens. It was a relief to discover that in this area at least, they had all they needed and more, and everything was in good condition.

Even so, Catherine was nervous at the size of the shopping list for the forthcoming school group. Arnaud had warned her that they were running short of funds and the school would only be settling the bill at the end of the week. Hopefully her credit card would tide them over, although it had taken quite a battering recently and Catherine had a feeling she was uncomfortably close to her credit limit.

The next morning, while Min was deep cleaning the kitchen, Catherine stationed herself in the laundry, sorting out bed linen for forty people.

"Hi there, do you need any help?" Lily's head appeared around the laundry door. Her long dark hair had been loosely tied into a knot at the back of her head. It accentuated her large green eyes, and neatly plucked eyebrows, Catherine noticed.

"That's sweet of you, but you really don't have to."

They had agreed in the end to get the trek leaders briefed and up to speed as soon as possible, and let them spend the weekend painting the house.

"To be honest, I'd rather have something to do, and we've got an hour before Arnaud starts our briefing."

"Well, it would be fantastic if you don't mind." Catherine was grateful for the extra pair of hands. "If you could sort the sheets and pillowcases into bundles of eight, we can start making up the bunkhouse beds."

Lily took a pile of pillowcases from Catherine's outstretched arms and placed them on one of the large industrial washing machines, commenting, "Isn't this place beautiful? I love it. So peaceful."

"You wait until we're descended on by a hoard of over-excited children."

"Yes, I guess we should make the most of the quiet,"

Lily grinned. "I love the design of this," she pointed outside at the buildings that wrapped around the central courtyard. How many people will the centre take?"

"Well, the maximum capacity is sixty, but fortunately our first group is relatively small. We've got thirty-five children and five teachers, so hopefully we'll all get broken in gently."

Catherine and Arnaud had been completely honest with the trek leaders about the state of affairs at Kestrel Farm when they were conducting the interviews, and Arnaud gave them a brief update about Sebastian as soon as they'd arrived the previous afternoon. More than anything, it seemed to have engendered a team spirit amongst the staff. When Arnaud had mentioned Sebastian's return to the farm, Caitlin had let out a small gasp, which she quickly stifled. Arnaud picked up on it and approached her after the talk.

"I'm guessing you met Sebastian last season. He's not very mobile at the moment, but I'm sure he'd appreciate visitors if you want to pop over to the farmhouse some time," he'd suggested.

Caitlin had coloured slightly and muttered a non-committal answer. Arnaud, distracted by a call from Catherine, had thought no more about her reaction.

With the bed linen sorted, Catherine and Lily walked across the courtyard to the bunkhouses, their arms full. Lily tripped on a stone and only just managed to save her load from falling onto the dusty earth.

"This is high on my list of priorities - getting this quadrangle sorted out," Catherine muttered. "I know there's a path that goes around the edge, but as you can see, it's quicker to walk across the middle. If it rains, the kids are going to tramp dirt into the buildings. It's going to be a nightmare to keep clean."

"Mind you, most kids seem oblivious to a bit of dirt," was Lily's sage rejoinder.

"True, I hadn't thought of that. But it would be good to get the surface evened out. I don't want to have to deal with sprained ankles. I'm sure we'll have enough incidents with the kids getting trodden on by horses and things like that. By the way, did Arnaud tell you there's a first aid course for you all tomorrow morning?"

"Yes, he did."

Health and safety. Another of the things Catherine had been forced to study lately. She knew it was crucial to have everything up to date, but the sheer boredom of grinding her way through endless reams of red tape made her want to scream.

Catherine balanced her pile of sheets in one arm and pushed open the door to the first bunkhouse room. Lily followed behind, with a gasp, "Wow, I love the bunks!"

"They're clever aren't they.'"

On either side of the room were two sets of bunk beds housed in a pine box surround. At the front, cheery blue and cream striped curtains could be pulled across to give the occupant a little privacy. At the base of each bottom bunk, a set of drawers had been built into the box surround. The effect was neat and homely. Right at the far end of the room, a pine wardrobe stood next to a large window, which overlooked the upper tip of the large paddock. The walls were bare, honey-coloured stone.

"Gosh, this is a cut above your usual bunkhouse accommodation, isn't it." Lily was impressed.

"Yes, it's a real selling point for us." Catherine cast a fresh eye over the room. Arnaud had repaired and revarnished the bunks, and with the newly washed and mended curtains, the room looked vastly improved from its condition a few weeks previously. She was encouraged by Lily's reaction. Their arduous work over the winter months had paid off.

They made up the bunks and returned to the laundry for the next set of bed linen. On the back wall, the two large tumble dryers were churning, finishing off the last of the sheets.

"We'll do a proper tour of the farm for you all a bit later on, but you guys can use these machines for your bed linen - and take fresh stuff from here. There's a couple of standard size washing machines in your cottage for your clothes - I'm sure you've seen them already."

When the bunkhouse was sorted, Catherine led Lily into the teacher's accommodation. The fragrant scent of pine from the cladding on the walls and ceilings filled the air. As they went along, they opened the windows and doors, allowing the soft April breeze to air the rooms. For the first time, Catherine felt a sense of pride in the farm. It was looking good.

In the farmhouse kitchen, Arnaud was checking the final list of ponies for the first school group. They had sent him a summary of all the pupils and teachers, with an indication of weight, height and riding ability next to each name. He looked up as Catherine came into the kitchen.

"I'm trying to match the school group members to the horses and ponies. We seem to have a lot of novice riders in this group. I only hope we've got enough bomb proof ponies for them all."

"Have you told the trek leaders which horses they'll be riding?" Each trek leader would have their 'own' horse for the season.

"I'll do that this afternoon, after we do the tour."

Catherine sat down heavily in the chair opposite Arnaud. The thought of no longer having the farm to themselves was draining.

"Okay?" Arnaud was concerned.

"Yes. Just a bit tired. There's a lot to think about and do in the next few days."

"We'll get there," he took hold of her hand across the table.

"How's Sebastian?' Her eyes flicked up to the room above the kitchen, which Sebastian was currently occupying.

"Frustrated he can't help. Relieved at least he's out of hospital and able to move around a little. Tired. Annoyed that he still can't remember anything. I'm just glad that he's here. It makes life easier, not having to drive to Hereford to visit him, and it's also good he's in his own place, even if he doesn't recognise anything. I can't believe his memory won't start to come back soon."

"You said you thought he'd changed a bit?"

"Yes, it's funny. He's not quite the old Sebastian I knew. He seems a bit more…mellow, somehow. Less frenetic."

"Perhaps he's more chilled without the pressure of his job," Catherine hazarded a guess.

"Maybe," Arnaud wasn't totally convinced, "it feels a bit deeper than that. We'll see. I'm intrigued."

Caitlin smiled in a self-satisfied way when Arnaud brought Calico in from the paddock after lunch. She had asked if she could ride the palomino as her lead horse for the season and Catherine could see why. The showy mare had tossed her head, flicking her long, fine cream-coloured mane. The horse and rider made an impressive pair.

*That girl likes getting her own way. We need to watch her.* Catherine was surprised at the negativity of her thoughts. *I need to give Caitlin a chance*, she told herself.

Six horses were tied up in the corral. The plan was to familiarise the leaders with two trek routes that afternoon and another three on Friday, the next day. There was no margin for error. Unfortunately, the weather didn't realise that. Rain was forecast for Friday, with unsettled conditions stretching into the weekend. They could plan for everything but the weather.

"Justin, you've got Willow," Arnaud announced.

Justin, now dressed in an old pair of jodhpurs and a worn white T-shirt, looked even skinnier than he had done at his interview. He appraised the pale grey horse appreciatively, admiring his fine lines.

"Lily, do you want to try Barnum?" Arnaud pointed to a glossy black horse with a white diamond on its face and long, flowing main and tail.

"Yes, he's beautiful," Lily enthused and walked over to Barnum, hugging his neck, her dark hair perfectly blending in with his mane. The horse turned its head to nuzzle her, sniffing for treats.

"Noah, I've put you with Mouse for now." It was a safe option and Noah knew it. Arnaud was concerned at Noah's comparative lack of experience and decided to match him up with an old timer that knew the ropes.

"Cool," Noah tried to sound positive.

"And Goff, you've got Jester. He's a bit wary of the other horses, so you'll need to give yourself a bit of space." A gamble. Catherine was initially doubtful about using the nervous outsider in trek so soon, but Arnaud had a sense that Goff would enjoy the challenge. And the leggy bay horse had been settling down more every day.

"We can change things around if you have any problems, but let's start off like this and see how we get on."

Goff nodded slowly, appreciating the trust that had been placed in him.

Twenty minutes later, the little group had made friends with their new lead horse, tacked them up and were riding off with Arnaud, the sound of hoofbeats receding along the lane towards the mountains. Catherine knew there were a thousand jobs that needed doing, but she could barely keep her eyes open. The night before, short bouts of sleep had been punctuated by lengthy periods of wakefulness, worrying about their first school group and imagining all the things that could go wrong. She decided to take a quick catnap on the sofa in the farmhouse, before she had another look at her to do list.

Sebastian was sitting in the kitchen, his broken leg propped up on a stool.

"Hey, you're up," Catherine greeted him.

"Yes, I'm bored of bedrooms. I wanted to see a different view." He sounded frustrated.

"I don't blame you. At least you've got some decent scenery to look at now and not just a hospital courtyard."

"Tell me about it. Do you know what Catherine, this place does feel a bit familiar, but in a strange kind of a way. As if I had a dream about the farm."

"That sounds like a good sign." Catherine felt a surge of hope.

"I've given up with 'good' or 'bad' signs," Sebastian said, philosophically. "I've decided to just take one day at a time. If I never remember anything much, then I guess I just start my whole life again. There must be people who would give a lot to do that." His smile was crooked.

Catherine had a sudden thought. "Arnaud said you were feeling a bit frustrated, about not being able to help out." Even as the words left her mouth she cringed, hoping she hadn't been too blunt.

"Don't even get me started," Sebastian sighed.

"Actually, there is something you can do if you'd like."

Sebastian's eyes lit up. "Oh?"

"We need to somehow get Noah's dog Oscar trained to stay here at the farm when the treks go out. They'll be away for most of the day which is too long to shut him up inside, and Arnaud and I have got too many things to do, without having to keep an eye on him. I'm sure he'll get used to the routine eventually, but would you mind keeping him with you for the first week or so? We're worried he's going to try and follow Noah's trek."

"Not a problem at all," Sebastian was only too glad to be of some use, and he liked the cheeky little dog.

In the saddle, Noah was enjoying the ride. He remembered some of the landmarks from the two treks he did with Arnaud over Christmas. The surroundings looked so different now from the barren December landscape. The hills had burst into life; gorse bushes were smothered with bright orange-yellow flowers and everywhere, little soft green sprouts of bracken pushed their way up from the red earth. Birds, no doubt feeding a nest of chicks, fluttered purposefully in and out of the scraggy trees.

In front of him, Goff expertly negotiated Jester through a narrow gateway. Noah kept Mouse at a slight distance from the bay horse, although Jester seemed comfortable in trek. Noah wouldn't have recognised him from the nervy, hesitant animal he rode at Christmas. Part of him was disappointed that he hadn't been given Jester to ride. Clearly Arnaud thought he wasn't up to the job. But another, wiser, side of Noah, was relieved to have an easier horse to ride. He was going to have enough on his plate, learning all the routes and handling a trek of seven kids.

*Concentrate Noah, concentrate,* he told himself, and forced himself to look around, taking in landmarks to help him remember the trail. He turned in the saddle. Behind him, Caitlin was looking relaxed and expert on Calico. She held her reins in one hand, the other playing with the mare's soft mane.

"There's a lot to remember," Noah tried to be chilled and chatty, though he was slightly in awe of the self-possessed girl.

"It's pretty straightforward. You just need to remember that most of the routes we ride are parallel to the mountains. We don't usually climb up over them, so you can take your bearings from the range."

Of course, Noah had forgotten, Caitlin had done it all before. He felt stupid.

"Are you some sort of relative of Catherine's?" Her question sounded more of a polite formality than genuine interest.

Noah forced jollity into his voice. "Not really. My dad and I lived in the same house as her for a few years."

"Oh," Caitlin raised an eyebrow.

"Not like that. There was a whole bunch of us. We all had separate rooms," Noah was gabbling, flustered. He felt like a gawky child beside the sophisticated girl.

"So how long have she and Arnaud been married?"

Noah wasn't sure he liked the way the questions were heading.

"Ages," he bluffed.

"Oh, I thought Min said they'd not been together that long. He's quite good looking isn't he, in a rugged kind of way."

"I guess so," Noah had never thought about the way Arnaud looked and he felt uneasy with Caitlin's comments. The last thing Catherine and Arnaud needed was hassle from flirtatious trek leaders.

Caitlin looked away, and studied her fingernails, which had been painted white with gold flecks that caught the light. Noah got the message loud and clear. He was boring.


The next day, Arnaud took the trek leaders out early, aware they had a lot of ground to cover that day.

"It's going to be quite a fast ride. We'll be stopping off to have lunch at the Green Dragon in Traneffwy. Sorry about the weather guys."

The rain, which had begun as drizzle, was now coming down steadily and the wind began to pick up. As the group cleared a bank of trees and turned right at the edge of the mountain, an icy blast struck their backs. Noah was not looking forward to the return journey, when it would be in their faces. The horses were unhappy, and walked with heads down, ears back.

Arnaud nudged Baloo into a canter and the others followed suit, careful to keep in line. At the back, Noah's face was soon covered with mud flicked from the hooves in front of him. The old, worn leather reins were slippery in his bare hands He realized he'd need to invest in a decent pair of riding gloves as soon as possible, to give his fingers a bit more grip in this kind of weather. Soon, the rain began trickling down his neck, then further down his back. His feet started to grow numb, and one slipped out of the stirrup.

Thank goodness he wasn't riding next to Caitlin today. As they slowed, and pulled back to a walk, Lily, just in front of him, looked back and grimaced.

"I'm freezing. I should have put an extra jumper on." Her dimpled, round cheeks were white with cold.

"Yes, I forgot how exposed it is up here," Noah agreed.

Lily noticed Noah's fingers slipping on his reins. "I've got another pair of gloves back at the farm. You can borrow them if you like."

"Cheers, thanks Lily. I'll have to buy some when I get a chance. I'm not used to these conditions."

"I've just spent the winter in Austria, but it was sunshine and snow rather than freezing wind and rain." She turned round to concentrate. The track dipped sharply down a gully. The horses felt their way slowly downwards, balancing against the steep gradient, then once at the bottom, picked up speed and cantered up the other side. Lily almost fell out of her saddle. She turned back laughing.

Noah warmed to her. He was relieved that not everybody was like the 'ice queen' as he'd mentally christened Caitlin. They all seemed very confident in the saddle though. He hoped he didn't look as amateurish as he felt. He transferred his reins to one hand, in imitation to the others, realising he'd have to get used to riding one handed to negotiate all the gates on the treks. Another gust of wind picked up a stray plastic bag that had caught in a bush and rustled it. Mouse, surprised, shied slightly and Noah slipped sideways, only just managing to save himself from falling by grabbing the horse's mane. He was glad he was at the back of the trek and nobody had spotted him.

*Concentrate, Noah, concentrate*, was rapidly becoming his new mantra.

# 17

## THE FIRST TREK

Noah couldn't sleep. His head was buzzing with a thousand and one things. Monday was the big day - his first trek on his own. *Please don't let there be any accidents*, he prayed to whatever god was listening.

*Man up Noah*, he told himself. *But am I man enough for the job?* came the faltering reply.

As the early morning light chased away the shadows, Noah's eyes opened. He must have finally fallen asleep. His eyes felt gritty and sore. He rubbed them and sat up in bed, noticing the growing pile of dirty clothes in the corner of the room. He'd only been at the farm a few days, and already virtually every item of clothing he possessed was filthy. A trip to the washing machine was going to be in order pretty soon.

Oscar lay in his basket by the window, still asleep. As Noah rustled the bedclothes, the dog lifted his head up and looked over at him, tail thumping lazily. Noah's heart lurched as he remembered what lay in store for them today. The first school group. If only the weekend hadn't slipped by so quickly.

On Saturday, Arnaud had appeared at the cottage in

the Land Rover with a car boot full of paint, brushes and other equipment. Lily and Caitlin chose pots of green and blue paint, while the boys had been content with plain white, disinterested in fancy colour schemes. When they'd finished their own bedrooms, Goff had organised them into two groups; one tackling the lounge and stairs, while the other did the kitchen and bathrooms. The girls had insisted on a few touches of colour in the main living areas - a pale terracotta accent wall in the lounge and vivid yellow door frames and windowsills in the kitchen. Noah had to admit, it did brighten the place up. As they'd painted, the group had begun to bond. Hesitant, slightly unsure conversations turned to more fluid, jokey chatter as each got the measure of the others. Only Min still seemed more of an outsider. She'd spent most of the weekend in the catering kitchen and on a food shopping trip to Hereford.

With the exception of Caitlin, Noah found it easy to like the other trek leaders. Goff, slightly older than the others, gradually slipped into the role of unofficial leader of the little group. Nobody seemed to resent this at all. He led by example and was the least bossy person Noah had ever encountered. Even so, Noah felt slightly in awe of him. Lily was cheerful and laid back, only grudgingly revealing that she'd got a first class business degree the previous year. It was clear that she came from a pretty privileged background, although she seemed a little cagey about it, but she was unpretentious and Noah felt completely relaxed in her company.

He only wished he could feel the same about Caitlin. When she was around, Noah felt clumsy and tongue-tied. Every now and then, he could feel her gaze on him and he was sure she was unimpressed and critical of him. He hoped she would keep her thoughts to herself and not try and belittle him in front of the others.

Justin was easy to like. He and Noah found a mutual love of the sea and discovered they had both spent a large part of their respective childhoods looking for shellfish in rock pools and lying reading on the beach in the summer. Noah wished he could be as naturally cool as Justin. He was fashionable without being over the top, and his guitar playing was sensational. The two girls loved it, and were constantly asking Justin to play for them in the evenings, while Goff kept them amused with anecdotes from his teaching days.

Monday morning passed in a flurry of activity, until at almost exactly midday, a coach arrived and halted outside the farmhouse, disgorging hundreds of screaming, giggling children. At least that was how it felt to the waiting trek leaders, Min, Catherine and Arnaud. The air was full of high pitched squeals.

"Hi, I'm Simon." A tall, middle aged man with thinning brown curly hair, emerged from the mob.

"Hello, we've spoken on the phone - I'm Catherine. And this is Arnaud, my husband."

Simon shook their hands, then turned and shouted, "That's enough! Hush up now."

The screaming subsided. Noah was impressed.

While the children were shown their sleeping accommodation and fed lunch by the waiting Min, Arnaud gave the trek leaders a final briefing. "Just to remind you again, this bunch of kids are quite young - between eleven and thirteen - so you need to take extra care with them. I'll chat through my list with the teachers, then I'll split up the treks and let you know which riders and ponies you've got. You're all happy with where you're going this afternoon?"

Noah's stomach was a mass of butterflies. He'd managed to force breakfast down, but he'd not really felt hungry. *It's just a short half day's ride around an easy route*, he told himself. *What could go wrong?*

As it happened, several things.

He was impressed at how smoothly tacking up went. Arnaud had given him a group of the older, more experienced riders, and most of them were able to sort out their own ponies, with a little assistance from Noah and the teacher who was accompanying his group ("Clare to you - Mrs Norman to the kids.").

His riding demo - including instructions for tackling steep hills - was slickly given to a reasonably attentive audience. He even managed to not be the last trek out of the yard. That honour went to Justin, who was still checking girths when Noah led his group along the track to the forest.

Fortunately, Clare/Mrs Norman didn't notice what happened soon after the trek started off. Luckily, she'd been fiddling with her own girth and hadn't seen one of her pupils nearly come flying off Pepper. The girl, the least experienced rider in the group, wasn't holding Pepper's reins tightly enough and as the trek walked next to a grassy verge, the little roan pony had put its head down and begun to eat the grass, seizing great mouthfuls as if its last meal had been a week ago. Noah, eyes fixed hawk-like on his little group, had quickly spotted the incident and as Pepper was just behind him, he'd reached out with his riding stick and given the pony a smart tap on its rump.

*Cripes I didn't anticipate that one*, thought Noah when Pepper bucked. The girl managed to hold on, and giggled, finding the experience funny. Noah was relieved. *One tale for the pub this evening*, he thought.

The second incident didn't go unnoticed however. Impressed with his group, who for the most part were doing well with their ponies and concentrating hard on their riding, Noah decided to allow them a short canter. He had his little speech prepared, and stopped the trek first, as Arnaud had instructed.

"Right guys - are you all up for a little canter?"

Seven nods and a thumbs up from the teacher.

"Okay then, keep in line or the ponies could end up racing each other. Try not to squeal or anything as you'll spook them. If you've got a problem, just shout 'stop'. Got that?"

Eight nods.

"Right, off we go." Noah had never cantered while half-turned in the saddle, keeping an eye on riders behind him. He was quite pleased with his performance. So much so that he forgot to look in front of him properly, and as they came around a corner, his group cannoned into the back of the trek in front. Which just happened to be Caitlin's.

*Of course, it would be*, thought Noah, trying to placate her as she gave him a withering glance and regrouped her scattered trek.

"Perhaps you'd better take your group in front of mine Noah. You've got the better riders. Then you won't run the risk of any further disturbance," she told him icily.

Noah felt like a five-year-old caught doing something he shouldn't.

As luck would have it, Arnaud appeared around the

corner at just that moment. He was riding Baloo, checking on each of the treks, to make sure things were under control.

He pulled the horse up, concerned, "Is everything okay guys?"

Caitlin smiled sweetly at him, flicking her hair off her shoulder. "Yes, Noah's trek just came round the corner a little too smartly. I'm letting him go ahead as his riders are faster than mine."

Noah gritted his teeth. Why did Caitlin have to land him in it?

"That's a good move," replied Arnaud, nodding at her. Then, looking at the kids, "Are you all enjoying yourselves?"

A chorus of 'yes' came from the two groups.

"Great. I need to get on and see how the others are doing." He pushed his heels into Baloo's flanks and the horse trotted off, then eased into a graceful canter.

As Noah started his trek moving, he could hear Caitlin behind him, replying to her kids.

"...it's a Camargue horse, isn't it beautiful. Arnaud's French and such a natural rider..."

Arnaud was frowning slightly as he pulled Baloo back into a walk. He was unimpressed with Caitlin landing the blame on Noah just now, but on the other hand, it was good to know who had been responsible for the little incident. *It was just a minor thing*, he told himself. *It's early days*. Even so, he felt tense.

Ahead of him, at the other side of the common, Goff's group was tracking alongside a dry stone wall, punctuated with small trees. Arnaud rode towards them, trotting beside the wall. The May blossom was just coming out, dotting the green foliage with myriad white stars. Every now and then, as he drew past a clump, his nostrils were assailed by the strong, sickly-sweet smell of the little flowers. Baloo tossed his head, glad to be out. Arnaud too was relishing the freedom, enjoying being in the saddle, out on the hills.

The dark green, fresh spring grass, stimulated by the recent rain, was replacing the sparse winter grazing, and a flock of mountain sheep, accompanied by their fat lambs, were spread out over the common, greedily chewing great mouthfuls. Every now and then, a lamb would approach its mother, bending down to butt its head against her stomach, reaching for her teats. The ewes would be weaning them off their milk soon, Arnaud thought. Even now, they seemed reluctant to allow the lambs to feed for long, walking forwards impatiently after a few minutes. He squeezed Baloo on, and cantered over to Goff's trek. Everything seemed to be going smoothly with them, which was no less than Arnaud had expected.

The third incident could have happened to anybody, Noah told himself later. He'd been so careful to check the girths on the saddles of all the children, he'd managed to forget his own. As he led his trek up a steep incline, reminding his riders to lean forwards in their saddles to ease the strain on the ponies, his saddle slipped backwards. There was nothing for it but to halt the trek, undo the girth and reposition his saddle. In the meantime, the ponies put their heads down and began to eat the lush grass. When it came to set off again, it took a while to get them back in line. Behind him, Noah could sense another trek approaching. Caitlin again.

"Got a problem?"

Noah ignored her acid tones, kicked Mouse forwards and just hoped that his riders would manage to sort themselves out and follow him. They did, and he breathed a sigh of relief.

Back at the farm, Noah supervised the children untacking and feeding their ponies. Once the horses had been turned out into the field, he started to make his way back to the cottage. His mouth was dry and he was desperate for a cup of tea.

"Noah, just a word." It was Clare, the teacher.

His heart sank and he blew his cheeks out. "Sorry, sorry I'm new to this. Stupid of me to..." he mumbled, his voice dying away.

"I know this is your first time as a trek leader. Arnaud did tell me. That's why he put me with your group - I've been coming to Kestrel Farm with the school for years now. I just wanted to say, I was really impressed with how you handled the trek this afternoon. I know there's a lot to take in and I thought you dealt really well with the children. And Noah," he was in a dream, hardly believing his ears, "don't worry about Caitlin. I was with her trek last year. She's a little madam. Don't let her get to you. And forget I said that."

Noah wandered to the cottage in a daze. *Blow me down*, he thought.

Sebastian's day had so far been uneventful. By the time he'd managed to hobble down the stairs for breakfast that morning, Catherine and Arnaud were long gone, busy with preparations for the school group. Oscar was dozing on an old blanket in the corner near the Aga. Sebastian spent the morning in the garden behind the farmhouse, sitting in a faded green and white striped deckchair, bundled up in his waxed jacket. Oscar took up residence at his feet. At first, they had been surrounded by curious chickens, but they'd soon spread out across the garden again, in search of worms and insects. The weather was sunny, but fresh. Despite the slight chill, Sebastian was desperate to be outside, sick of being cooped up for so many months. The small patch of lawn was enclosed by a low, dry stone wall that separated the garden from a huge field beyond. Up above it, to his left was the smaller paddock with the llamas and sheep. At the furthest edge of the field was a small stand of native woodland. Some of the trees were already in leaf, others still bare.

He lifted his eyes up to the mountain range, above the tree line. The early morning cloud had lifted and the mountains were silhouetted sharply against the clear blue April sky, a dark purple ridge.

His frustration at not being able to help the others, was mitigated in a small way by what was happening to his mind. Sebastian hadn't said much to Catherine and Arnaud, in an almost superstitious fear of hindering his mental progress, but he'd been getting a number of flashes of memory. He'd somehow known where to find the old deckchair that he had dragged out of the shed to sit in. And he knew that once there had been a flower border at the end of the lawn. Now, there were a few weeds and a straggle of long grass, but in his mind, he could *see* crimson dahlias, spiky red-hot pokers and sunflowers, waving in the breeze.

He woke up, an hour later, with a start. He must have dozed off again. It was amazing how he seemed to sleep for huge chunks of the time. The doctor said it was normal, a part of the healing process, but Sebastian found it extraordinary how great snatches of his day seemed to be stolen from him.

At some point Catherine found a few minutes to track him down and ask if he wanted any lunch. Min had made sandwiches for the schoolchildren and there were a few left over. Catherine left him with a couple of cheese and pickle rolls and a bag of salt and vinegar crisps. As he ate, Sebastian watched a buzzard wheeling above the copse of trees, looking for its own midday meal. It drifted on the thermals, hardly beating its wings at all. *I must get the binoculars from the living room sideboard.* Sebastian didn't realise he'd remembered something else, he was drifting off to sleep again.

When he woke again, he was cold. The sun was battling with a steadily advancing bank of clouds - and losing. He limped awkwardly into the house, had a pee and, on a whim, decided to take a recce around the farm, leaving Oscar in the kitchen. The place seemed deserted, apart from the tabby cat who was slinking out of the barn with a mouse hanging from her mouth.

He pushed his crutches under his arms and decided to do a tour of the farm buildings while things were quiet. His progress was painfully slow. It was hard work negotiating the uneven surfaces and steep gradient. He made it as far as the courtyard, when his strength suddenly deserted him. A clattering came from the kitchen and he decided to investigate. Inside, Min was beginning preparations for the evening meal.

"Mind if I come in a second?"

She turned round, startled, "You made me jump! No, of course not, grab a chair. Do you want a coffee? I was just about to put the kettle on."

"Yes, yes please." Sebastian was suddenly thirsty. "I'd do it myself, but crutches and boiling water are proving a dangerous combination for me."

Min was sympathetic. "It must be so frustrating."

"It's annoying seeing you all so busy and not being able to help."

"Actually, there is something you can do Sebastian. Would you be up for chopping up some onions and garlic? That would really make a difference. Catherine's had to rush over to Hay to pick up some light bulbs."

"Of course."

Min made the coffee, then brought over a large chopping board, a small knife and a huge string bag full of onions. "It's not the nicest job," she apologised.

Sebastian began to make inroads into the onions. *I'm good at this*, he thought, and added another skill to his mental list. Every little thing added to his sense of purpose.

Min was relaxing company. They had been introduced when Min had arrived at the farm the previous week and it was evident from her easy way with him that she'd known him for some time and was comfortable in his presence. She worked fast, but her movements were deft and there was no sense of panic about her, more a calm busyness. They chatted idly about the menu Min had planned for the school group.

Sebastian found himself opening up. "You know Min, I can't help wondering why on earth I was working in the City when I could have been here, helping run the farm. It's such a beautiful location. Arnaud says the farm needed the money I earned, but I'm sure there could have been another way of helping the finances. London seems such a long way away."

Min glanced at him sharply, wondering how to answer him. "I'm not sure you would have been happy spending all your time here Sebastian. You seemed to enjoy life in London. It's quite sleepy around here. It didn't really suit you. Not then anyhow."

"That's odd," Sebastian mused. "I'm loving the peace here - and being surrounded by nature. Maybe once my memory comes back I'll see things differently."

Min turned away, lifting a heavy saucepan of water onto the stove. She lit the gas and put the lid on the pan, waiting for it to come to the boil.

Sebastian started on another onion, unaware of her scrutiny as she swung back to face him.

Min hesitated and then plunged in, "There was another reason why you wanted to stay away last summer. One you should perhaps know about sooner rather than later." She swallowed, hating this conversation.

"Go on...."

She sighed heavily, feeling awkward, trapped into divulging something she knew would open up a can of worms. "I'm afraid there's no easy way of saying this Sebastian." Min stopped, unsure of herself. Sebastian was fragile at the moment. She was scared of upsetting his mental balance.

"Come on Min, you're going to have to tell me. It sounds like there's something unpleasant in the offing. If so, I'd rather know as soon as possible."

She pursed her lips. "Yes, I guess it's only fair to let you know about this. Last season, you had a fling with one of the trek leaders. I think your marriage with Emily was pretty much on the rocks by that stage. She'd been messing around with other men for ages, and you finally snapped. I don't think you were very proud of yourself though and you tried to end things before it went on too long."

She had a mental image of a very drunk Sebastian, slurring a confession over the bar in the Wily Wolf, just after the pub had closed. He'd spent the night crashed out on the long sofa in the saloon.

Sebastian was shocked. He blanched. "I did? How do you know this? Is it common knowledge?"

"I'm not sure. You told me and Joseph about it at the pub one evening. I can't remember why, but all three of us were drowning our sorrows for some reason. There was a lot of cider sloshing around."

He groaned, "Judging by the age of this current lot, she must have been just a kid." He thought for an instant. "Was she hurt? Did I upset her."

Min winced, "I'm afraid she was pretty gutted. I think she'd fallen for you quite badly. Anyhow, you thought it was wise to keep out of the way a bit and you hot-tailed off back to London as soon as you could."

"Poor girl," Sebastian grimaced.

"Well, she probably had it coming," Min had less sympathy.

She steeled herself for her next revelation. "There's another thing you need to know Sebastian."

"Oh yes?"

"She's back at the farm this year. Her name's Caitlin."

# 18

# FROM BAD TO WORSE

Noah was sitting on a raft, rocking on the waves in the middle of a huge expanse of blue-green sea. He scanned the horizon: no land on any side as far as his eye could see. The sun, sole occupant of the unclouded sky, hammered down, sucking the moisture from his body. He swallowed. The movement hurt his parched, scratchy throat. He looked down at the raft to see if he could spot anything to drink. There was nothing on the makeshift vessel, which was little more than a few logs tied together with old, frayed rope.

A wave sloshed over the far edge of the craft, which seemed rather low in the water. As Noah leaned forwards, the raft tipped over, flinging him into the sea. He choked, struggling to breathe, his mouth full of salt water, just as a ringing noise sounded somewhere in the background. He fought with the waves, his clothes impeding his movements.

The ringing grew more insistent, hurting his ears, and now something slimy was attacking his face. He opened his eyes and woke up, to be greeted by another lick from Oscar, who had jumped onto his bed. The old-fashioned twin bell alarm clock Toby had given him as a leaving present (with a huge hint about getting up on time) was ringing right next to his head. Noah tried to reach out to stop it and discovered he was trapped, wrapped up in his duvet. He untangled a hand and batted at the clock repeatedly, fumbling for the off switch. After what seemed like ages, the ringing stopped. He looked at the clock face. Seven fifteen.

A thump from the next-door room brought him back to his senses. He heard its occupant, Justin, leave the room and head into the shower. Noah sat up, heart hammering. It was the first full day of the school group. He decided against having a shower - there was no point when he'd only get filthy the minute he stepped into the paddock, and he'd showered the evening before.

Instead, he pulled on his clothes; his 'lucky' horseshoe print boxers, an old grey T-shirt, an even greyer pair of once-white walking socks and his faded black jodhpurs. He yawned and glanced through the bedroom window which overlooked the forest. Thin wisps of mist swirled around the deep green pine trees. Shafts of sunlight were just breaking through in places, illuminating the undergrowth. *Cue Hansel and Gretel*, thought Noah.

Downstairs in the hallway, the back door was open. Through it, Noah could see Goff trying to locate his riding boots from a knobbly pyramid of footwear on the covered decking just outside. His head was still shaved on both sides, although the centre strip of black hair had been cut short to fit underneath his riding hat better. Lily had wielded a pair of scissors for him a few nights back. He'd toned down his piercings to just one ear stud and a nose ring. Nothing could hide the tattoos on his arms, exposed by his black T-shirt. The overall effect was more subdued but most definitely still Goth.

He joined Goff on the patio and rummaged through the heap of footwear for his own riding boots. They were caked with dried red mud. The cloying soil got everywhere. Worse, his boots seemed to have grown two sizes smaller overnight. Noah hopped on one foot, trying to squeeze the other one into his boot. Oscar thought it was a game, and joined in, grabbing Noah's shoelace and tugging on it. He nearly fell backwards, steadying himself just in time on the wooden verandah rail. Lily and Caitlin emerged, yawning, from the farmhouse and began to search through the pile of footwear. Oscar took hold of a brown jodhpur boot and jumped down the steps onto the lawn, tail wagging, eager to be chased.

"Give that back, stupid dog," Caitlin snapped, bleary-eyed and irritated.

Laughing, Goff went to rescue the boot, while Noah finished tying his laces. He looked up at the girls. Lily wore a bright pink top and purple jodhpurs. Caitlin was immaculately turned out in clean beige jodhpurs and a pale green polo shirt.

"We'll be able to spot you a mile off," Goff teased Lily.

"Likewise," she retorted and punched him in a friendly way.

"Where's Justin?" Goff peered into the house.

"He was in the shower," Noah informed him.

"Oh yeah, I forgot, he's Mr Clean."

"Better than smelling like a dung heap," was Lily's rejoinder and ducked Goff's return punch.

The four walked along the track and climbed over the fence into the lower paddock. Noah, Lily and Caitlin headed for the bottom, followed by Oscar, while Goff peeled off and marched over to the corral. He unlatched the huge wooden gate and swung it back, leaving the entrance free.

All of them begin shouting down into the valley, "In you come!"

The grazing horses shifted and looked at the trek leaders, reluctant to move.

Noah headed off towards the right hand bottom edge of the paddock followed by Lily. Oscar jumped into the undergrowth, diverted by a particularly interesting smell. Caitlin picked her way down the steep slope to the left. As they went, they slapped rumps, shouting at the horses in an effort to start the herd moving. The first few began to pick their way slowly up the paddock. More and more joined them, until the field was filled with snaking lines of horses moving their way up towards the corral. Noah ran down the hill to check for stragglers at the bottom. Sure enough, the usual suspects were hanging out by the trees, reluctant to move.

"Come on you lazy lot," he shouted at a group of three chestnut ponies. They stared him out, unmoving. He ran towards them, flapping his arms and suddenly they sprang into life, cantering up the hillside, before dropping back to a trot and then a walk.

Noah zigzagged his way back up the steep slope, watching Lily and Caitlin above him, almost at the gate. He paused for a few seconds to get his breath back. His calves ached from the effort. *Next time out I'm gonna hitch a lift back up on one of the horses*, he told himself.

As he climbed, panting, round the bottom corner of the barn, Noah could see Justin standing at the corral entrance making sure the horses who had entered the enclosure didn't come rushing back out. That had happened to them a few days ago and they'd spent a further hour trying to round them up again. Goff was standing in the middle of the herd of ponies, a bundle of brightly-coloured headcollars slung over his shoulder. In his hand was a paper list. Noah felt in his back pocket and drew his own list out. On it were written the horses in his trek and alongside them the names of his riders.

*Mouse - Noah*
*Jade - Clare (teacher)*
*Jewel - John*
*Koko - Jasmine*
*Pepper - Charlotte*
*Milo - Michael*
*Dudley - Sarah*
*Duster - Anita (nervous rider)*

His next job was to locate his trek ponies in the corral, catch them and tie them up next to each other along the fence post. He swallowed hard and plunged into the midst of hooves, bodies and heads. Goff had hooked the headcollars over some of the corral fence posts. Noah eased his way around the edge of the enclosure and picked up a handful of headcollars, looping them over his shoulder.

He peered into the teeming mass of ponies and spotted Mouse. That was an easy one. He wove in and out of the ponies and went up to the dark grey horse, seizing a piece of his mane. Then he slipped the halter rope around Mouse's neck, holding both ends so he couldn't get away. Mouse stood calmly and allowed Noah to pull the headcollar up over his face.

"Good boy," Noah patted the old timer and led him through the throng to a clear patch of railing, tying him up to a piece of baling twine. He glanced around. Further along the fence, Lily already had three ponies tied up next to each other. She waved at Noah, smiling and headed towards a dark bay pony.

Noah cast his eye over the herd, trying to spot another one of his trek ponies. There were so many horses milling around, it was difficult to pick out the ones in his group. Aha, there was Jewel. The slender blue-grey roan mare was the matriarch of the herd. She was standing near to Noah, resting her head on a corral post. Noah pushed his way over to her and slipped the rope around her neck, before putting her headcollar on and leading her over to a spot next to Mouse.

Two down, six to go.

He heard chattering from the other side of the fence. Some of the schoolchildren were grouped in an excited huddle, watching the trek leaders. It almost felt like hero worship. Noah puffed out his chest and looked around for his next pony.

Ten minutes later, his trek was complete. He threw a glance at the other leaders. They were all pretty much there too, but Caitlin was looking at her list and frowning. She glared over at Noah's trek, then strode over to him, and began untying one of his horses.

"Noah, that's Hobo and he's in my trek. Who did you think he was?"

Noah felt stupid. He examined his list. "Er, Dudley."

Caitlin sighed theatrically and cast an eye over the rest of the herd. Her eyes fixed on a black and white pony the other side of the corral. "He's over there. He's much chunkier than Hobo."

*Of course, I can totally see the difference now*, Noah thought, annoyed with himself. "Thanks Caitlin," the words came out sounding rather strangled.

He could hear giggling from a couple of schoolgirls the other side of the corral. He ignored them and aimed for Dudley, brushing past Justin, who was leading a tall chestnut horse over to his trek. It must be for the teacher, Noah thought. It was way too big for the kids. What was its name? Doh, Adagio, of course. She was a bit flighty. Justin's teacher must be a good rider, he mused.

"Okay Noah?" Justin asked, sensing Noah's frustration.

"Yeah, stupid me, picked the wrong pony."

"I did that yesterday," Justin confessed. "Could have ended in tears if Lily hadn't spotted my mistake. The pony would have been way too difficult for the kid riding it. I guess it takes a while to get used to things."

Noah breathed a sigh of relief. He wasn't the only one. He could have kissed Justin. If he hadn't been a bloke, that was.

There was no time to breathe. As soon as all the trek ponies were tied up, the rest of the herd needed to be shooed out of the corral. Easier said than done, Noah discovered, when they found one or two lurking next to their equine best friends after they'd closed the corral gate. He grabbed a little chestnut pony by its mane, and walked it sharply over to the gate, ejecting it from the compound. Noah dimly recalled hearing the breakfast bell ring a while ago.

By the time the leaders made it up to the refectory, the children and teachers had nearly finished eating. The noise was overwhelming. The trek leaders moved as a group to the counter where Min was waiting with scrambled egg, toast and bacon for them. As Goff reached for his plate, a flying lump of bread hit him on the side of the head. He looked around at thirty pairs of innocent eyes. None of the teachers had spotted the incident. Then, another piece went soaring past the teachers' table and Clare, Noah's teacher, stood up.

"THAT'S ENOUGH. ANY MORE BEHAVIOUR LIKE THAT AND NOBODY GETS TO RIDE THIS MORNING."

She didn't shout, but she certainly knew how to project her voice. Noah was impressed. He'd have to ask her for voice coaching lessons during the week.

The children disappeared to get ready for the day's ride, granting the trek leaders a few blessed moments of silence. They ate quickly, hungry after their early morning exertions.

Noah scarcely had time to get his own things together before it was time to tack up the ponies with the children. It was a punishing schedule, he reflected. Fortunately, there was no riding demo to give today.

His group was waiting with Clare just outside the corral.

"Morning guys," Noah tried to be Mr Cool.

"Did you get the wrong pony for Sarah?" a short, dark-haired girl asked. Noah racked his brain to try and remember her name. Charlotte, that's right, Charlotte. He'd play it smooth and straight.

"Yes, I did actually Charlotte. It's an easy mistake with so many ponies. There are over eighty in the herd."

"I'm Anita," said Anita. "That's Charlotte," she pointed to a girl with long blonde hair.

Noah retreated into action. "Right follow me then, down to the barn and we'll get your tack."

The group trailed at his heels. At the barn, it was

chaos. Thirty children were milling around, pushing each other to get to the tack room.

Caitlin appeared behind Noah and took over, undaunted by the shambles. She spoke with authority. "Okay, everyone out of the barn. Wait at the door in your trek group and we'll bring your tack out to you."

Noah was grudgingly impressed with her control of the children. They all fell silent and immediately shuffled to the door. Once he'd given out his trek's tack, Noah slipped Mouse's saddle and bridle off the rack and strode out of the barn to the corral.

His little group had already started tacking up, under Clare's supervision, with mixed results today. Charlotte was struggling to get Pepper's bridle on. The roan pony kept throwing up its head every time she tried. Noah saw the chance to redeem himself and hefted Mouse's saddle onto the corral fence before moving over to her.

"Right Charlotte, is Pepper playing up?"

Charlotte was close to tears.

"It's not your fault, it's tricky to put the bridle on over the headcollar and Pepper can be quite stroppy too." Noah had no idea if that was the case, but he hoped it might help ease the tension. "It's good you've got the reins over his head, well done for that. Now, put your right arm under his face and pull his nose down, then slip his brow band over like this. After that, hold the bit just in front of Pepper's mouth and..."

Pepper, recognising a firm hand, gave in gracefully and opened his mouth for the bit.

"I'll leave you to do the buckles up," he told the girl, and walked off to check on the other ponies in his trek, feeling relieved something had gone right that day.

It took an unbelievable amount of time for the group

to get ready, even with Noah and Clare's help. Noah looked at his watch. They should be leaving the yard any time now. He checked Mouse's girth and turned to Clare, saying, "We're gonna need to get off."

"I'll just make sure they have a final pee before we head out."

None of them needed the toilet. *Good*, thought Noah, *a bit of time saved*. He started helping the children up onto their ponies, tightening up their girths for them once they were in the saddle. They were still tied up, as he didn't want them to get mixed up with the other treks.

Arnaud appeared in the yard just as the groups were ready to leave. He cast an appraising glance over the ponies, then walked over to Noah.

"You've forgotten your saddlebag," he commented quietly.

"Darn it," Noah went tearing back to the tack room, nearly slipping down the slope in his haste. He'd managed to forget the most important piece of equipment. Arnaud had spent time drumming into them how vital it was to have a saddlebag on each leader's pony. They had all been allocated one, containing a first aid kit, mobile phone, hoof pick and other emergency supplies. He snatched it from a rusty hook in the tack room, ran back up to the corral and spent precious time untying Mouse's girth so that he could loop the straps of the saddle bag around it to keep it secure.

He could see Lily's pink T-shirt disappearing down the lane. The other treks had all left. He unknotted Mouse's headcollar rope, tied it around the pony's neck and swung himself up into the saddle, forgetting to untie the rest of his group.

Arnaud was on the case. "Don't worry Noah, I'll take care of these. If you start walking on, they can follow as they're untied."

"Okay," Noah was shamefaced. He gritted his teeth and squeezed Mouse's sides.

Mouse paced up the farm track, followed by the other ponies, all eager to get going. At the lane, Noah turned right, towards the mountain. He glanced back to check his trek. All present and correct.

"Everyone up for a trot?"

Everyone was, and they clipped smartly up the narrow country lane. Noah was determined to forget the shaky start and enjoy the morning. It was a relief after the wet weekend to see a blue sky, dotted with small puffy white clouds, which hid the sunshine every now and then, sending shadows racing across the fields and hedgerows. The weekend's rainfall had given everything a new flush of life. Long tufts of grass, dotted with delicate white flowers, hung onto the steep banks at the foot of the hedges on either side of the lane. The tiny flowers, on long, thin stalks, bobbed at them as the rode past.

The smell was intense; fresh grass, intermingled with sharp blossom and the pervasive smell of horse, that seemed to follow Noah everywhere he went. Mouse tossed his head, sniffing the breeze.

As they neared the gate onto the mountain, Noah's heart sank at the sight of a small herd of ragged sheep grazing just by the entrance onto the hillside. He rode Mouse into the middle of them, shouting in an effort to move them out of the way. They stubbornly stood their ground, milling around Mouse's legs and baaing at Noah. He was annoyed. He'd have to get off Mouse and sort them out. Behind him, the ponies were putting their heads down to eat or wandering off down the lane. Some of the children were pulling ineffectually at the reins, battling with their strong-necked mounts.

Noah climbed off, holding onto Mouse with one hand, as he tried to push the sheep away from the gate. They wouldn't budge. Frustrated, he kicked one with his foot. The ewe twisted round and tried to head butt him. He'd never come across sheep like this before. The ones grazing on the mountains were nervous and flighty. These were a different kind altogether. Behind him, he heard the roar of a vehicle coming up the steep gradient. He looked up. It was Catherine in the farm Land Rover. She stopped and got out.

"I'm just popping over Johanna's. Are the sheep giving you a hard time?"

Noah was red faced and annoyed. He tried to smile, but the tension must have showed. "I've never known them like this before," he muttered.

"I reckon they must have got out of the field just back down there. I noticed the gate was hanging open," Catherine commented.

She seized one, grabbing hold of the fleece on its hindquarters and trotted it smartly back down the lane. The others followed and soon the way forward was clear. Noah sprung back up onto Mouse, opened the gate and his trek walked smartly through, the ponies now eager to be on their way. All apart from Milo, a shaggy black pony, who was still tearing great mouthfuls of grass from the verge. Michael, his rider, was pulling at Milo's head to no avail. Noah grabbed Milo's reins and yanked the pony's head up. Noticing the other ponies were already through the gate, Milo dashed to join them, nearly throwing Michael off. Noah followed them through, closed the gate behind him and cantered up to the head of the trek, trying to restore order.

The rest of the morning's ride went reasonably smoothly. Once they were on the mountain, away from the lush hedgerows, the ponies forgot about grass snacks. The only annoying thing was the number of pit stops they had to make for the children to pee. Noah decided that in future, he would force them all to go to the toilet before they left the farm. It was a learning curve. He looked ahead of him, as the trail they'd been following turned away from the edge of a field and cut across a swathe of boggy grass. Noah let Mouse pick his way carefully though the ground, avoiding the worst of the sucking mud.

In the distance, he could spot Lily's pink shirt, standing out against the green and brown of the hillside. Up to his right, he caught a glimpse of Goff, riding on a track higher up the mountain. They were all heading for the lunch venue, a picnic site near Hay Bluff that they'd christened the waterslide due to the stream running across the road at that point. Noah slipped his feet out of his stirrups and flexed his ankles. His legs were stiff after spending a couple of hours in the saddle. He was glad when they rounded the final bend fifteen minutes later, and spotted three other treks tied up to a long fence near a little used stretch of road. The hill banked quite steeply to one side, sheltering the clearing from the chilly breeze that had begun to blow across the mountainside.

Noah twisted back in his saddle and commanded his trek, "Right guys, take your feet out of your stirrups, and swing your right leg over the back of the saddle. Bend your knees when you land. Then run the stirrup irons up their leathers and loosen the girth a couple of holes. You can tie the ponies up by their headcollar ropes to a piece of string. He pointed at the bright blue bits of baling twine that were fluttering from the fence in the breeze. Arnaud had driven up to tie them onto the fence a few days previously.

Once he'd got the ponies sorted, Noah staggered over to join the other trek leaders. He'd used up so much energy getting on and off Mouse all morning to hold ponies for the kids who needed to pee, his legs felt like jelly. Goff, Justin and Lily were sitting on a grassy bank, a short distance away from the children, comparing notes about the morning's ride. Caitlin and her group hadn't arrived yet.

"I saw her loop round the top of the road, so I'm guessing she's going to swing back and join us from the other side. She got off fairly quickly and she was making good time this morning," remarked Goff.

Noah spotted the Land Rover parked a little further up the lane, just as Catherine appeared from the other side, walking towards them with an armful of lunch boxes. He looked inside his pack - ham sandwiches, a bag of crisps, an apple and a Mars Bar. He'd make short work of that, he thought. Hunger was stabbing at his belly.

The sound of hooves clopping along the lane announced the arrival of Caitlin. She came into view, followed by her trek, all in perfect order, walking at a steady pace along the road. They pulled up together and dismounted correctly, without needing any advice. Smooth operation, Noah had to admit. He wondered if anything ever went wrong for Caitlin.

The plan was to spend an hour at the picnic spot to rest the ponies (and the trek leaders, Noah decided) before returning to the farm. The mid-April sunshine was surprisingly strong, and having finished his lunch, Noah lay back on the bank, smelling the fresh green grass all around him. The sound of birdsong drifted through the trees, interspersed with the occasional baa from the sheep that dotted the mountainside and the shouts of the children chasing each other around the trees. It felt good.

The afternoon's ride went smoothly. The sun was shining out of a now-cloudless sky, illuminating the mountains in their spring colours. Everywhere, tiny whorls of pale green bracken were unfurling, crows wheeled overhead and young rabbits hopped around the edges of the dry stone walls, nibbling at fresh shoots of grass. If things had only continued that way, Noah would have been in heaven.

Sadly, by the end of the week, he'd managed to notch up a whole series of unfortunate incidents.

As he sat in the Wily Wolf on Friday night with the other trek leaders, enjoying the prospect of a well-earned day off over the weekend, Noah felt a sinking feeling in his stomach. He forced himself to be cheerful, but he was all too aware that nobody else had experienced anything like the same number of issues with their treks as he had that week. He swilled the last dregs of beer in his glass, and swerved unsteadily over to the bar, intent on blotting out his misgivings with another pint of Joseph's finest.

Arnaud and Catherine were sprawled on the sofa in the farmhouse lounge, a bottle of wine in front of them. Sebastian sat in the armchair, his leg propped up on a footstool.

He picked up his glass and smiled at them. "I think a toast is in order. Well done - the first school group out of the way, and judging by what you've said, a bunch of happy teachers - and children."

Catherine felt mentally and physically drained. She leaned forward to take hold of her glass from the coffee table in front of her. It seemed to require an awful lot of effort.

"Well, no fatalities anyhow," she commented, and drank a generous mouthful of wine. It felt good to be able to relax, not on duty.

"So how have things gone? I've hardly seen you both all week." Sebastian was curious.

"Okay, okay. We've had a few small incidents, but I'm sure you would expect those anyway with mainly new trek leaders. There's a lot for them to take on board," Arnaud sounded cautious.

"How are they doing?" Sebastian wanted all the details. Catherine sighed and Arnaud glanced over at her.

Sebastian looked at them both quizzically. "What's the matter?"

"It's Noah," Catherine said heavily.

"Noah?"

"Yes. He's brilliant with the children but he just hasn't had a lot of experience with horses and he can be pretty dippy. Taking him on was a bit of a gamble, and we're a bit - well more than a bit - concerned it's too much for him."

"He's not coping?"

"You could say that," Arnaud chipped in. "Most of the incidents we've had this week happened with Noah's trek. For example, on Wednesday he missed a turning and took his group miles down the wrong road. By the time he'd realised the mistake, I was out in the Land Rover frantically looking for them, they were so late back."

"One of his riders managed to get bitten on the stomach by a pony and he didn't believe them at first. Why he didn't just ask the child to show him the bite I don't know. In the end, the boy reported the incident to a teacher and then it looked really bad for us." Catherine added. She felt disloyal to Noah even talking about it.

"He's also had several riders fall off this week. Once because he let his Mouse - his horse - jump a stream and of course all the ponies in his trek followed suit. Most of the children in his group had never jumped before and one of them went flying off. Fortunately, the child was okay, but even so..." Arnaud continued.

"It's things that he could deal with if he concentrated more," Catherine defended him.

Sebastian shifted the conversation, aware she felt uncomfortable. "The other trek leaders? How are they doing?"

"Mostly okay," Arnaud responded. "A few bits and pieces, but nothing serious. Justin can be rather dreamy and he's often running a bit late. As for Caitlin, well, I don't know exactly, I don't feel totally comfortable with her behaviour."

A strange look passed over Sebastian's face. "Why not?"

"Well, Catherine wasn't hugely keen to take her on in the first place."

"Oh?"

"To be fair, for no real reason," Catherine added quickly, "I just didn't really take to her. And I still feel the same way. She has a way of introducing Noah's faults into a conversation. I almost get the feeling she seems to have it in for him. Why on earth that would be the case, I've no idea. Noah doesn't have a mean bone in his body."

"There's nothing you can really put your finger on. She's competent, good with the kids, but she seems to act a bit superior and she's very flirty with the male teachers. It's good that the other trek leaders seem to get on okay with her. I guess we'll just have to keep her under observation." Arnaud said.

Sebastian didn't want to comment about Caitlin. Not yet. He changed topic quickly. "What will you do about Noah?"

Arnaud spoke tightly, "We're not sure. We'll have to see if things improve or not. I suppose we could always try and transfer him to kitchen duties if he doesn't settle down. He gets on well with Min, but he'd be humiliated by the move. And then we would be a trek leader short as well." He sighed. "Let's just hope that Noah can raise his game."

# 19

## MEMORY

*Monday 30th May. I'm living on the side of a mountain. I still can't quite believe it.* Noah scrawled in his brown leather notebook. The huge boulder he was sitting on was becoming uncomfortable, digging into him, so he pulled off his sweatshirt and sat on it. He had found a spot at the far end of the lower paddock that was hidden from view.

Inspiration seemed to come flying at him, as he sat surrounded by splendour of the mountains to one side, and the river valley below. In fact, Noah wished he wasn't having quite so much inspiration. He'd already thought of ideas for three separate novels and a fourth one seemed to be hovering just at the edge of his mind. He'd made separate sections in his notebook to jot down the ideas for each of the three books, but he kept writing things in the wrong place. He was now wondering if he should try a stream of consciousness novel instead, and see where it took him.

As he turned over a page, Noah dropped the notebook, which fell onto the grass below. A small black and white pony, who had been grazing nearby, shambled over and began sniffing the notepad to see if it was edible.

Deciding it was, the pony began to chew it.

Noah jumped off the boulder, shouting, "No, give that back Hobo!"

He tussled with the pony, nearly getting a nipped finger into the bargain. He finally managed to retrieve his notepad, minus a page which the piebald was now grinding with its huge molars. Deciding it wasn't that interesting after all, Hobo let the soggy paper drop and moved off, sniffing the grass. Noah picked up the wad and tried to uncrumple it. His last page of writing was illegible.

"Darn it," he climbed back onto the boulder and sat down quickly, picked up his pen and tried to retrieve the ideas before they disappeared.

"How's the writing going Noah?"

He looked up. Min was standing on the slope just above him, a basket in her hand, on her way back from an early morning foraging trip.

"Look what Hobo just did." Noah held up the soggy page and Min laughed. Then her face changed to annoyance, as Hobo reappeared and started trying to help himself to the contents of her foraging basket. It was Noah's turn to laugh.

"Did you find much?" he asked.

"Yes," Min pushed Hobo away and turned back to Noah. "Hop shoots, dandelion leaves for salads, sweet violet, herb bennet, and some ground elder. It's all starting to appear now."

Noah admired her hoard. In between school groups, Min was cooking for the centre staff. Nearly all of them were very enthusiastic about her foraged food. Caitlin had been reluctant at first, but gradually Min had won her over.

"Catherine's keen for me to include some foraged food for the school groups - well at least for the teachers anyhow. She thinks it will give us a difference over the other trekking centres," Min commented, one eye on Hobo who was still eyeing up her basket.

"That's a great idea."

"Yes, but it's quite labour intensive, and once we start to get really busy, I'm not going to have much time for foraging trips. Catherine was talking about seeing if we could get some help with cleaning at the changeovers, but I'm not sure there's really the money for another member of staff. She's trying to give me as much help as she can, but she's got all the admin and other stuff to do."

"We could all pitch in and help you Min. There's usually a day or two between groups. Why don't we get all the other trek leaders to do a Friday evening forage or something?"

"That would be a laugh. I reckon Justin, Goff and Lily would be up for it. But Caitlin? She's bound to look down her nose at something like that."

"She doesn't have to come along if she doesn't want to."

"How are things with her?" Min was concerned.

"Honestly Min, I can't understand why she seems to have it in for me. I'm falling over myself trying not to get in her way or wind her up, but somehow, she always has some sarky comment waiting for me. And she's crafty - more often than not, she does it when no-one else is around, so they can't see how unpleasant she is."

Min bit her tongue. She had her own reasons for not liking Caitlin, but she was keeping them to herself. She thought for a moment. "My brother Joseph always says, 'truth will out,' and he isn't often wrong. People like her end up showing their true colours at some point. Just don't let her bait you and keep the moral high ground."

"Easier said than done," Noah muttered.

He slid off the boulder and they began to walk up the hillside towards the farmhouse. Noah's stomach rumbled. He was ready for food.

While Noah helped Min get the breakfast ready in the kitchen, the other trek leaders gradually appeared in the dining hall. They'd been given a lie in that morning, as their next trek wasn't due in until the following day and they'd been working hard all weekend with casual riders. Justin, Goff and Caitlin had taken advantage of the late start with a session in the Wily Wolf the night before and both boys were looking red-eyed. Caitlin was nowhere to be seen.

Noah looked around the dining hall. It was his favourite room in the whole complex. He loved the huge oak crossbeams which spanned the room. The ceiling had been left open under the roof, exposing the wooden roof struts and creating a huge airy space above them. Whitewashed walls and cream stone flooring added to the lightness of the space.

Lily walked in through the door and greeted everybody with a cheery, "Morning!" She went to join Justin and Goff at one of the long bleached wooden tables, pulling out a chair and sitting down. Justin winced as the chair legs scraped on the stone floor.

"Feeling a bit worse the wear, are you?" Lily asked loudly. Justin groaned and said nothing.

Behind the counter, Min was cracking eggs into a huge stainless steel frying pan. Piles of bacon and sausages were warming in the oven. "Could you just pop some bread in the toaster for me Noah?" she asked.

He turned round and picked up a handful of bread slices, slotting them deftly into the catering toasters.

Arnaud appeared just as the food was ready, briefing notes in hand. Goff and Justin were already standing at the counter, jostling each other for first place. Min crammed their plates with sausages, bacon, eggs, mushrooms and fried tomatoes. Both topped their meals off with a generous squish of ketchup. Appetites were running wild with all the fresh air and physical exercise. She served the others, made up a plate for the missing Caitlin, covered it with foil, put it in the still-warm oven and came to join them all at the table.

Arnaud waited until the end of breakfast before he began the briefing. Just as he was picking up his notes, Caitlin burst through the door. Her hair was mussed up and her crumpled clothes looked as if she hadn't changed them from the night before. Min realised she hadn't heard Caitlin come back from the pub the previous evening. The two girls had been allocated the bedrooms at the top of the house, underneath the eaves, and Min, a light sleeper, was usually aware of Caitlin's comings and goings.

Arnaud brushed Caitlin's apology aside, while Min fetched her plate of food from the warm oven. To her surprise, Caitlin threw her a thankful glance.

Arnaud cleared this throat and began, "Okay everyone, thanks for all your hard work over the weekend. I just got a letter this morning from our first school group and I thought you'd like to know that the teachers were glowing in their praise of you all. Well done guys."

He took a sip of black coffee and plunged into the details of the forthcoming group - the second school of the season.

"I don't want you to stress at all, but it's only fair to tell you that the teacher in charge of this group has been giving Catherine a bit of a hard time," he sighed, running his hand through his hair. "I want to be up front with you. We don't quite understand it, but it seems as if somebody has been in contact with the schools, saying that we are not at all geared up for the season and as new managers, we're not quite together with things."

"Who would have done that?" Goff was curious.

"The teachers we have spoken to seem a little reluctant to give away too much information, but we get the impression another trekking centre has been contacting them - trying to get our business," Arnaud replied.

Min frowned, "Do you know which one?"

"No, they don't want to give any names, and I don't want to push them."

She looked annoyed. "I might have an idea what's going on there. Perhaps we can have a chat a bit later, Arnaud?"

"Of course. When we're all done here. I need to sort out a couple of things at the farmhouse, then I'll come back and give you hand with the washing up. We can talk at the same time."

"Thanks, that would be great."

Arnaud turned back to the trek leaders. "Anyhow, Catherine managed to talk the teacher round, and now we have the positive feedback from the first group, that should help too. But we really need to make sure that everything goes smoothly this week. Not to put any pressure on you all," he grinned at them, to lighten the atmosphere.

Inside, his heart was heavy. Arnaud didn't tell the group that two of the other booked schools had pulled out. Catherine was hard at work trying to find new clients to fill the gaps, but most schools and activity groups had already committed themselves for the year. It was a blow that would cost them.

Instead, he got down to business. "Okay, there's a few areas we can all tighten up on. Riding demos - don't cut these short, particularly the bits about leaning forwards and backwards when riding up and downhill. Also - it's important to check all of your ponies before you leave to make sure they're tacked up properly. We don't want any saddle sores developing. Once we've got a few bigger groups, we won't have many ponies spare and I want to keep injuries to a minimum. Any shoes that come loose on trek - let me know as soon as you get back. If we can take them off and reuse them, so much the better."

Noah felt his head expanding. There seemed to be so many things to remember, as well as dealing with all the unexpected things that cropped up during a ride out. He thought back to his first week's trek, reliving some of his less successful moments.

"...and Noah will be tack cleaning with Caitlin. Everyone got that?"

Noah heard his name being mentioned and snapped back from his thoughts. "Sorry, could you repeat that Arnaud?"

"You're on tack cleaning with Caitlin. Okay, when you're done, you can have the rest of the day off, but no rushing through your jobs please. The group will be arriving at lunchtime tomorrow, so you'll be kicking off with a short trek in the afternoon. Goff, I've given you the beginners this week. They are complete novices, so you might want to take them into the indoor school and give them a basic lesson instead of riding out."

"Fine," Goff nodded.

Noah's heart sank. Why did he have to work with Caitlin? He was hoping for a chilled day before the next school group came in.

Arnaud left the refectory, and Min put on another pot of coffee before they started their tasks. The atmosphere was relaxed. Goff and Justin were carrying on a joke from the evening before.

"What's everyone else doing? I was miles away." Noah asked Lily.

She grinned at him. "I'm poo picking the field with Justin and Goff's helping Min sort the store room out and get the new food order sorted.

Noah saw his chance, and said to Lily, "If you don't want to spend the morning picking up dung, I'm happy to swap..." That might get him away from Caitlin.

"No worries Noah. I'm quite happy being out in the field. Thanks for offering though."

Noah felt guilty. He hadn't wanted to deceive Lily into thinking he was doing something kind when he was being totally selfish. Served him right that she declined his offer. He gulped his coffee down and headed over to the barn to begin the day.

Catherine was in the laundry room, sorting sheets for the new group when Arnaud bustled in.

"Have you seen Sebastian? He's not in the farmhouse, and I can't find him around. He mentioned something about getting a lift into Hay when somebody next went. Min and Goff will be going to the supermarket in a bit."

"No - not since before breakfast. He can't be far away," Catherine responded.

Arnaud frowned. "I've looked in most places. Oh, and

by the way, Min thinks she might know something about this mysterious person who has been contacting the schools. I'll let you know what she says," and Arnaud was gone.

Catherine finished stacking the sheets and walked over to the barn with a pile of clean saddle cloths. Picking her way carefully down the steep slope, she noticed the old farm truck wasn't in its usual place by the side of the barn. Occasionally the trek leaders borrowed the vehicle for an evening trip to the Wily Wolf. She frowned and made a mental note to ask one of them if something had happened to the van.

At that precise moment in time, the ancient truck was parked outside Johanna's cottage. Its ex-occupant was cautiously making his way along the footpath to the side door. One of his crutches sank into the soft turf at the edge of the footpath and Sebastian nearly overbalanced. *Damn*, he swore mentally. He would be glad to get rid of the wretched things.

At the door, he lifted a hand to knock and hesitated, peering in the small glass window instead. Through the thick, swirled pane he could see Johanna kneeling in front of the cross at the far end of the room. She was praying. *Damn*, Sebastian thought again, loathe to interrupt her. He stood for a few seconds deliberating. He was saved by a black and white cat which appeared at his feet, slinking around them, mewing. Johanna's head turned at the sound and she caught sight of Sebastian's face in the window. She eased herself up stiffly and walked towards the door.

"Sebastian! What a lovely surprise! Come in."

He stomped into the cottage.

"Sit in the rocking chair, it's probably easiest to manoeuvre yourself into that."

*Typical Johanna*, Sebastian thought, *always practical*. He lowered himself carefully into the rocking chair.

"How did you get here? Did someone give you a lift?" Johanna was curious.

Sebastian grunted. He didn't want to recount his jerky, almost out of control trip to her cottage. Driving with an injured leg had proved far harder than he'd anticipated.

Johanna scrutinised him, eyes piercing his soul. "You've no idea how thankful I am to see you safe and sound. You had us all so worried for you." And then it registered with her. "You know who I am. Your memory has come back," she said.

"Yes."

"Let me put the kettle on and we can talk more comfortably."

"Actually, you don't have a drop of Scotch do you?"

Johanna's mouth twitched. "Yes I do. Wait a minute."

She disappeared into the kitchen. Sebastian eased back in the rocking chair and looked around the room. Nothing had changed. It was reassuringly the same as the last time he visited, apart from the cat, which was now preparing to jump onto his knee. Sebastian pushed it away. He was more of a dog person. The cat gave him a narrow-eyed look and sprang onto the sofa opposite, where it began kneading a cushion with its claws.

Johanna materialised carrying a tray. On it was a glass of whisky, two mugs of coffee and a plate of biscuits. She put the tray on a wooden crate that served as a coffee table and sat down next to the cat. She noticed Sebastian stare at the whisky. "Go ahead."

He rocked forward in the chair, picked up the glass

and drained it, eyes closed. It felt good. A shaft of sunlight came into the room, warming him. The silence of the cottage was peaceful, therapeutic. When he opened his eyes again, Johanna was calmly drinking her coffee. The cat stared at him, eyes unblinking.

Sebastian felt the frazzled feelings inside him dissipating. The stillness of Johanna and her house had a way of absorbing tension.

"Take a biscuit Sebastian. They're quite good, though I say it myself. Chocolate and hazelnut."

Sebastian did as he was instructed, and had a sip of coffee to go with it. Johanna had made it strong with a dash of milk, exactly how he liked it.

"How much do you remember Sebastian?"

"My whole life. Well, up until the accident - those details are a bit hazy. But apart from that, everything."

"Is that a relief?"

"Yes…and no," he admitted.

"I can understand that."


Noah hadn't been on tack cleaning duty before and wasn't entirely sure what it involved. Whenever he had ridden one of Arnaud's horses back in Kent, the saddles and bridles were always scrupulously clean. He carried a couple of old wooden chairs from the barn into the farmyard - it was a beautiful day and he'd much rather be working outside than in the gloom. As he filled a black plastic bucket with hot water, he looked around the farmyard. Caitlin was nowhere to be seen.

Noah recalled seeing a long saddle horse in the barn and wandered back in to take a look. Sure enough, the wooden frame was in the far corner, draped with rugs. It would be perfect to put the saddles on for cleaning. He threw the rugs off and dragged the frame out of the barn, pulling it in front of the chairs, then went to find a couple of old sponges. Still no sign of Caitlin.

Lily and Justin appeared around the corner of the building, pushing two old wheelbarrows. A couple of spades rattled in Justin's barrow.

"No Caitlin yet?" was Justin's comment.

"Haven't seen her since breakfast mate," Noah retorted.

"She was looking a bit out of it at breakfast," Justin commented.

"I don't think she came back to the cottage last night," Lily explained, raising an eyebrow.

"That would explain it. She was getting quite cosy with some bloke and didn't want a lift back up the hill with us." Justin said, frowning. After a pause, he and Lily picked up the handles of the barrows and trundled off towards the field.

Noah walked into the barn and headed for the tack room at the far end. Inside the room, his eyes ranged over the saddles and bridles neatly arranged around the wall in alphabetical order. He wasn't sure if he was meant to be cleaning all the tack or just the gear that had been recently used and was dirty. He decided to go for the lot and slid the first saddle - Acorn's - off a black metal saddle tree that had been screwed into the wall. The bridle was hanging over the back of the saddle. Noah slung the bridle over his shoulder and hooked the saddle over the crook of his arm.

He decided to take out a second set and save a walk, so he slipped a hand underneath Adagio's tack too. He still hadn't quite got the knack of carrying a saddle on each arm. They were surprisingly heavy and awkward. He came out blinking into the sunshine, and stumbled on a stray brush lying in the yard, dropping one of the saddles onto the stony ground, just as Caitlin arrived. She gave him a disparaging look and disappeared into the barn. Noah placed Adagio's saddle and bridle on the wooden rack in front of him and retrieved the fallen tack. He sighed, moved one of the chairs in front of the saddle rack and sat down heavily. Then he picked up a sponge, soaked it in the bowl of hot water and began washing the saddle down.

A few seconds later, Caitlin emerged from the barn, expertly carrying two saddles as if it were no effort at all. She slid them onto the saddle rack, not bothering to thank Noah for getting the set up ready. Pulling a small metal tin out of her pocket, she sat down and looked over at Noah, who was busily slopping water all over Adagio's saddle, rubbing at a stubborn patch of mud.

Out of the corner of his eye, Noah could see Caitlin running the stirrups of her saddle down the leathers and unbuckling the straps. She was taking the whole thing to pieces. Noah's heart sank. He was obviously doing it the wrong way. Caitlin spotted him looking at her.

"Have you ever cleaned tack before Noah?" Her tone was scathing.

"Er, no not that I remember."

"It doesn't look like it. You're going to ruin that saddle if you're not careful. You're using far too much water and you'll never get it properly clean unless you take it apart." She sighed theatrically.

Noah swallowed hard and remembered Min's comment about keeping the moral high ground. "Thanks Caitlin. Arnaud always kept his tack immaculate back in Kent. I was quite lucky, I never needed to clean anything.

I appreciate the advice."

"Watch what I do. You just need a sponge with a tiny bit of water to dampen the tack, then get some saddle soap - there are some pieces in this tin - rub the sponge onto it and work it into the leather. You don't want too much."

"Okay, cheers."

"You're going to have to learn quickly. When we get really busy, we won't be able to carry any freeloaders."

Noah seethed inwardly. That was rich, coming from somebody who'd been late to breakfast and tardy in turning up for the day's task. He wished he could think of some clever retort, but nothing came to mind. So much for his skill with words. He glanced over at Caitlin, watching as she moistened a piece of sponge, rubbed it into the saddle soap and began expertly applying it to the saddle. Then he spotted the name tag on the saddle. Badger. She'd missed out a couple of ponies.

"I haven't done Alfie or Arnie's saddles yet," he informed her. "I was working through in alphabetical order."

"I had a quick check and they look fine. There's no point in doing more work than we need to," came the retort.

Just then Arnaud walked past and asked, "Hi guys, everything okay?"

Caitlin smiled sweetly at him. Noah could swear he saw her eyelashes fluttering.

"I'm just showing Noah the ropes."

"Thanks Caitlin, that's good of you. Do we need anything from the tack shop? I'm making a list for Goff and Min. They can swing by when they go to the supermarket."

"I noticed we're a bit low on saddle soap and we could do with a few more sponges."

"Well spotted. Noah?"

"Er no, I think we're fine for everything else," Noah mumbled.

Sebastian was sitting at the table shelling walnuts. He wasn't quite sure how Johanna had managed it, but at some point in their conversation they'd gravitated to the kitchen.

"I desperately need to use up last autumn's nuts before they dry out too much and I've promised Min to try out a recipe for her," had been Johanna's excuse. She knew Sebastian felt most comfortable when he was doing something.

"...so that's where things stand. I don't know which way to turn, Johanna. Arnaud has already confided in me that he hasn't told Catherine the whole truth about the centre's finances and now I'm going to have to drop this bombshell on them."

Johanna looked worried. "Let me get this straight - I'm sorry Sebastian, I'm not good at finances, as you well know. At some point shortly before your accident, you invested most of your savings on the stock market."

Sebastian suddenly felt the need to unburden himself completely. He hadn't been quite honest with Johanna the first time around. "I was acting on a tip off from a friend. Actually, it was a dodgy tip off - an insider job."

Johanna looked puzzled.

"He gave me information he wasn't supposed to," Sebastian explained. "If anyone found out we would have been in trouble. I guess, as things have turned out, it doesn't matter."

Johanna kept her face blank. It wasn't her place to judge. "So…as I understand it, this tip off proved to be unhelpful."

"Yes, I won't bore you with the details, but let's just say, when I went online this morning, with my newly acquired memory, I discovered the shares have crashed. I've pretty much lost all of my savings."

Johanna began to grasp things more clearly, "And worse - your company has dropped your salary to statutory sick pay - I'm guessing that is a fraction of your normal monthly income. So, the money you were using to pay off the loan for the accommodation refurbishment at the centre is pretty well non-existent."

Sebastian nodded, "Yes."

"And you're not even sure you have much of a job to go back to."

Sebastian put his head in his hands.

Johanna paused for a few moments, then continued, "I'm not sure I understand this part. I thought companies were legally obliged to keep a job open."

Sebastian looked up. "I'd need to talk to somebody in human resources to get my head round it completely. But basically, while I've been…out of it, my boss has been replaced. My new boss is somebody I've never got on well with - a rival I guess you could say. This has played nicely into his hands. The entire department has been restructured and my old job doesn't exist anymore. In theory, I do have a post to go back to, but with this guy as my boss, I'm pretty sure he'll find a way to get rid of me as soon as he can. He's starting by offering me a job that isn't a patch on my old position. I've been shafted."

"What are the hard facts Sebastian?"

"Well - for the centre. I could get a very temporary

break for the loan repayments. There's a little money coming in, but we're dependent on the school groups to really cover the costs, and for some reason a couple of them have pulled out. I guess we could, at the best, stagger through this season, but we'll not have any meaningful income once the winter sets in. Unless I can get back to work soon and keep my head down, realistically the farm isn't going to make it beyond the year. If I can manage to work at all that is."

"You don't look fit for an office, I must say."

"You're right. I'm still getting bad headaches and struggling with energy levels. My back and leg are still healing. Realistically I can't see myself functioning in a high pressure environment for a few weeks at the very least."

Johanna made herself breathe in and out slowly. She needed to be calm, to reassure Sebastian. She prayed as she did so. Sebastian stared out of the window, watching a robin sitting in a nearby tree. A few minutes elapsed. Finally Johanna spoke, "There's something that strikes me about this situation. It seems to me as if you're taking all the burden on your own shoulders."

"It's my mess," Sebastian acknowledged.

"I understand what you're saying. But from my perspective, I can see that both Arnaud and Catherine have invested considerable amounts of effort and emotion into the farm."

Sebastian thought. "Well Arnaud certainly. Catherine - yes, she's put the time and effort in, but I'm pretty sure she'd rather be back in Kent right now. This could be a way out for her. Who knows, at least one of us might end up happier."

Johanna put a hand on his arm. "I'm not so sure. Yes,

I know Catherine is struggling with her writing, and she's not comfortable being surrounded by so many people, but, I think this place is having more of positive impact on her than she realises…" she glanced down at the table, then looked at Sebastian.

"It may be the solution lies with all of you. I would just be open to other possibilities. New ways of going forward. See what the others have to say."

Sebastian nodded, "Well, I'm not sure what anyone else can do, but I promise you I will discuss things with them. Keep the future open ended - for the time being, anyhow."

He paused, then remembered the other reason for his visit to Johanna.

"There is one final thing Johanna…"

"Caitlin."

"Yes," Sebastian looked surprised. Then, despite himself, he laughed. "I should have known you'd be on the ball. You don't miss much, do you."

"I heard she was back at the farm. And after what you told me about last year…"

Sebastian's face clouded, "What on earth possessed the girl to come back here this year? It's beyond me."

"Aren't you being a little harsh on her? As I understand it, Arnaud and Catherine contacted all of last year's trek leaders and made it clear that Emily had left and you were out of the picture, for the time being at least."

"I think you're being too generous Johanna."

"So, what are you going to do?"

"I'll have to speak with her I guess. So far, I've not had much contact with any of the other staff at the centre, apart from Min that is. I've pretty much been keeping to the farmhouse. Who knows, perhaps Caitlin's got over me and I'm worrying about nothing."

"Perhaps," said Johanna, but she didn't sound very certain.


It was mid-morning by the time Arnaud left the kitchen, his face grim. His conversation with Min had been enlightening and worrying. He crossed the farmyard, pausing by the saddle horse, where Noah and Caitlin were still busy cleaning tack.

"I forgot to check, you are cleaning all of the saddles aren't you - even the ones that weren't used for the last trek? They could all do with a bit of attention."

"Yes, of course," Caitlin was quick to respond, her eyes holding his for a second or two longer than necessary.

Noah's mouth opened and then shut. He looked flustered and unhappy.

Arnaud sighed inwardly. Catherine was right. That girl was trouble and from the looks of it, Noah was suffering. The sound of a vehicle coming down the farm track distracted him. Noah, Arnaud and Caitlin turned to look. It was the farm van, being driven very badly. The gears crunched and the van slewed sideways, narrowly missing a fence post. It straightened up and came to a halt just outside the farmhouse.

Noah and Arnaud watched, open-mouthed as Sebastian emerged awkwardly. Neither noticed Caitlin's expression. She sat rigid in her chair.

"Sebastian, what on earth…?" Arnaud was astonished. He ran over to the van as Sebastian turned to pull his crutches out of the vehicle.

Noah could hear every word - Sebastian's voice carried

across the farmyard.

"We need to speak Arnaud. I've got my memory back."

Arnaud's face lit up, "Sebastian, that's wonderful!"

"I wouldn't put it that way," Sebastian replied grimly and swung himself on his crutches towards the farmhouse. The two went inside and the door shut behind them.

Noah sensed, rather than saw, Caitlin become very still. He turned to look at her. She was pale, staring at the farmhouse.

"Are you okay?" he ventured.

She stood up and dropped the sponge she had been gripping in her fingers.

"I don't know," Caitlin answered and walked off swiftly towards the trek leaders' cottage.

# 20

## STORMY WEATHER

### Noah's Diary:

*Friday 4th May*

*That's it. I can't take much more of this. I am a totally useless trek leader. Another disastrous week: three kids fell off, Mouse lost a shoe and I didn't even notice until Caitlin (of course it had to be her) pointed it out to me, one of my trek ponies escaped at lunch time onto the mountain and we had to spend an hour catching it. I told all my kids the weather would be fine and they didn't need to bring waterproofs and guess what - it poured down. What else? Of course - how could I forget - I took a route that led past a field of pigs, even though Arnaud had warned us to avoid it as horses are scared of pigs, and the ponies bolted. That took ages to sort out and get all the ponies back in trek again. How nobody fell off that time is beyond my comprehension. I am the last thing Arnaud and Catherine need right now, I'm sure. I think they must have had more bad news about the farm too - Catherine has been avoiding everybody and Arnaud looks pretty unhappy, even though he's clearly trying to be positive. Anyhow, I've decided to tell Catherine I'll leave if they want. I can't be a millstone around their necks.*

Catherine bent down and eased under the fence railing. It was early evening and the ponies were spread out across the steep paddock, grazing in the sunshine or lying down, relaxing. She pulled the crumpled note out of her back pocket. Noah must have pushed it through the farmhouse letterbox just after supper. A single word, 'Catherine', had been written on the envelope and a torn off sheet of paper inside bore the words:

*Please can you meet me by the big boulder at the bottom of the lower paddock around 7ish if possible? Cheers, Noah xx*

The heavy feeling of guilt washed over her again. She knew Noah was struggling with his treks and from Caitlin's unaccountable animosity, and she should have made time to talk to him and offer her support. It felt as if she was constantly fire-fighting - rushing from one task to another, without really planning her time properly. Noah must have been getting desperate to resort to writing her a note. She was dreading this encounter with him, on top of everything else. It didn't take much insight to see what was coming. She steeled herself and walked down the hill.

"Noah!"

Noah looked up from his diary and turned his head. Catherine was picking her way down the paddock towards him, followed by an inquisitive pony. The palomino mare was too chubby to be Calico - Caitlin's mount - this had to be...Saffron - that's right, it was Saffron. At least he was getting better at identifying the ponies, if nothing else.

"Yo, Catherine," Noah's voice was flat.

As she approached, Noah could see dark circles underneath her eyes, which looked a bit red, as if she had been crying at some point, and washed her face to try and hide the fact. Noah was shocked at Catherine's overwrought appearance.

"Sorry I'm a bit late, the phone rang just as I was leaving the farmhouse. It was a new booking for tomorrow, so I'm glad I caught it."

She came alongside the boulder and climbed up next to Noah and Oscar, who was sprawled out on the rock. She stroked Oscar's head. There was an unease in the atmosphere that Noah had never felt with Catherine before.

Then they both spoke together,

"Catherine, I just wanted to…"

"I'm so sorry Noah, I haven't made the time…"

Catherine gestured, a quick nervous flick of the hand. "You go ahead, you wanted to talk."

Noah didn't know where to begin. Then, a completely different set of words to the ones he had been rehearsing for the past twenty-four hours came out, "Catherine, are you okay? You look terrible."

Tears welled up at the corners of her eyes. She brushed them away with her sleeve, but once they'd started coming, Catherine couldn't stop the flow. She began to cry, heavy, hiccupping sobs. Shocked, Noah put an arm around her and hugged her as she wept. Oscar got up and padded to the other side of Catherine, licking her hand in reassurance. Noah felt odd, shaky.

Eventually, Catherine's sobs died away. She gave her nose a final wipe and rubbed her eyes, saying, "I didn't mean this to happen. Sorry Noah."

"Don't be. Can you tell me what's wrong?"

"Only if you promise not to say anything to the other trek leaders." She shrugged, "Oh, this is useless Noah. I feel such a stranger to you nowadays. I used to be able to talk to you about anything, and now you're working for us, I feel like our whole friendship has changed. It's like I've lost you somehow."

Noah understood. He felt the same. "What if I left? Would that help?"

Catherine's head jerked up. She looked at him, shocked. "No way! Oh Noah, it's all such a mess. What are we doing here? Maybe Arnaud and I should never have come. Then you wouldn't have got caught up in this either…"

"What's kicked off now?"

Catherine stared out over the valley below them. "In no particular order…" she breathed in deeply, "…Sebastian has got his memory back, as you know. What you don't know is that he's discovered he doesn't have any money any more - it's a bit complicated to explain, but to cut a long story short, he's lost most of his savings in an investment that didn't work out, and his old job is looking shaky. We need Sebastian's income to help meet the farm's financial commitments. Arnaud - in his infinite wisdom - chose not to tell me just how desperate a financial situation this place is in. If we're lucky we might scrape through until the end of the year. After that, well, Sebastian is seriously considering selling Kestrel Farm."

"No!" Noah was shocked. "I didn't realise it was that bad!"

"Neither did I Noah, or I would never have agreed to come here. It gets worse," she paused to blow her nose, and continued, "as if that wasn't enough, it turns out that one of the other local trekking centres is run by a close friend of Sebastian's ex-wife. She's been contacting most of our customers - presumably Emily has given her their details - and has been telling them that Kestrel Farm is in trouble and the new managers don't know what they are doing. So far, two school groups have pulled out and another two are hesitating. It seems as if Emily's friend - Laura - is offering discounts to them if they book at her centre instead. We couldn't work out what was happening, and why the schools were being so funny, but Min has put two and two together, and one of the schools has just confirmed it."

"Can this woman Laura do that? Isn't that kind of behaviour illegal?" Noah was horrified.

"I don't know, I just don't know," Catherine shook her head.

"How does Arnaud feel about it all?"

She gulped and her voice sounded shaky, "I don't know that either Noah. I was so angry with him when I discovered he hadn't been upfront about the finances. I haven't spoken to him properly since Monday." She looked at Noah. "Arnaud's never hidden anything from me before. And we've never argued like this. I don't know what to do or who to go to. I've tried to call in on Johanna, but she's not been around. And Eve is so busy with her shop at the moment, I don't want to burden her with anything."

Noah felt slightly sick. Catherine and Arnaud were two of the anchors that held his world together. He dreaded to contemplate anything happening to their marriage. He tried to think what Isaac, his old friend and mentor would have said. But nothing came to him.

"I can't believe I've just dumped all this on you Noah. And it was you that wanted to talk to me. What kind of a friend am I?"

"One that's always, always been there for me through

thick and thin," said Noah firmly.

She shrugged off her problems and focused on him. "I'm guessing you're struggling too. Is it Caitlin? Or the work?"

Noah swallowed hard. "Well, both. Mainly I feel totally useless. I don't think I'm cut out for this trekking stuff, but I hate the thought of letting you and Arnaud down. And I don't want to do anything to bring the centre into disrepute. I'd feel terrible. I don't know what to do. I keep expecting Arnaud to sack me…"

Catherine sighed. She needed to be as honest as she could with the boy. She turned to face him. "It's true that we are both worried about you Noah. But there's a lot to take on board. You've never done this kind of thing before. All the other trek leaders have far more experience. And you know, the teachers in the treks you have taken out, have said how brilliant you are with the kids and what a great person you are."

"Really?" Noah scrutinised her face, looking for lies.

"That's the truth. You're a bit scatty and inexperienced, that's all. But Arnaud and I both knew that when we took you on. If anything, we are guilty of putting you in a difficult position. Perhaps if we'd had more resources, we could have let you go out in another leader's trek for a couple of weeks, to learn the ropes better. That hasn't happened."

The lump that had been living in Noah's stomach seemed to grow smaller. "So I'm not useless?"

"Not at all."

"But what if I don't get any better Catherine? What if I can't learn the ropes?"

"Well, I can always take some treks out and you could cover for me - helping Min out and other stuff. Arnaud could do the rest."

"No, that wouldn't work, you couldn't do that. You need to be doing your writing Catherine, not taking on yet another job."

She looked away. "You're right Noah. I'm not getting enough writing done as it is. I think that's half the reason I'm feeling so out of sorts. But honestly, we'll work something out, I promise. And please, please feel free to talk to me. I know it's hard and I guess you don't want the other trek leaders to think we're favouring you, but I can always meet you secretly for coffee in Hay or something."

They both smiled. Catherine knew the clandestine suggestion would appeal to Noah's sense of drama.

"Okay, I agree to see how it goes. But you and Arnaud must be honest with me. If I can't crack this thing in the next couple of weeks…truly I don't want to be a burden to you."

Catherine smiled tightly. "Arnaud always says things have a habit of working out. I'm going to believe him in this case."

"And what about Kestrel Farm?"

"That's a tougher one. We've agreed with Sebastian that we won't say anything to the other trek leaders or Min, so I really need you to keep this to yourself. It won't affect any of them, as we'll keep going for the rest of this season. After that, who knows? All we can do is give it our best shot and see what happens."

"And," said Noah, with a sinking feeling in his stomach, "what about you and Arnaud?"

"I don't know Noah, I really don't know," replied Catherine.

Friday night was Wily Wolf night. Live music, good beer, decent company. None of the trek leaders cared that they had to get up the next day for the weekend casual riders. It had become a ritual. Joseph had even invited Justin to play a set at the pub in a few weeks' time. The trek leaders were becoming part of village life. But that Friday evening, the Wily Wolf had lost its appeal for Noah. He watched Catherine climb back up the hill, wondering if things would ever be the same again. He'd declined the offer to accompany her back to the farmhouse. Noah needed time to think. Oscar had followed Catherine partway up the steep slope and then returned, curling up at the base of the boulder.

Noah sat in a daze, listening to the splash of the stream further down the hillside. Birdsong drifted over from the forest, along with a faint tang of pine. Around him, the ponies grazed contentedly, or dozed. He sat back, leaning on his hands, letting the peace of the evening wash over him, thinking of everything and nothing.

Suddenly Oscar whined and sprang up, running around the other side of the boulder. Noah turned to see Min coming down the hill towards him.

"Hey, Noah! Catherine said you were here," she waved at him. Her frizzy black hair had grown longer, and for once Min had left it untied. It looked good like that, Noah decided.

Oscar ran up to her and was licking her hand as if he hadn't seen her for days. Min was a firm favourite of his, particularly as there were usually plenty of scraps to be had in her kitchen. She was wearing an old pair of denim dungarees which were ripped at the knees, with a faded red shirt underneath. She stood just above Noah on the slope, hand shielding her eyes from the glare of the low evening sun.

"Are you not going down to the Wolf?"

"Actually no. Not this evening. I don't really feel like it."

"What's up Noah?" Min was concerned. "Is Catherine okay too? She looked like she'd been crying," then, noticing the wariness on Noah's face, "Oh I'm sorry, I didn't mean to pry. It's just that she's been very quiet all week and I can see something's upsetting her. I really like Catherine, and I wish I could do something to help."

Noah thought for a moment, wondering how to phrase an answer without giving Catherine's confidential information away. "I think it's tough on her Min. Trying to find the space to write - she's got her publisher breathing down her neck, and Catherine's usually well in time with her work. She doesn't like being under pressure. And I guess, the worry of trying to pull everything together here at the farm..."

Min didn't look convinced that was the whole story, but she didn't push Noah further.

He changed the subject. "You don't look like you're going out either, I mean, sorry that sounds bad, as if you look a mess, you don't at all, your hair looks really good like that..."

He stopped in confusion. Min laughed, her eyes crinkling. "No, you're right. To be honest, I'm knackered. It's been such a busy week with the school group and I've been on my feet all day, every day. Sorry, it sounds like I'm moaning. I know it's pretty full on for you guys too."

Noah nodded, then replied, "But the horses are doing the hard work when we're riding. And it's nice to get out of the centre, onto the mountains."

Min shrugged her shoulders. "I enjoy the cooking. And Arnaud's promised I can come out for a ride with one of the treks on a Saturday or Sunday. I'd like that."

The thought had never occurred to Noah. "Can you ride?"

Min smiled. "I'm okay. I'm not nearly as proficient as you guys though."

"I'm not sure I'm that good at it."

She looked at Noah. "I thought that was getting to you. I've heard the others talking."

"What do you mean?" Noah's heart sank. "Are they saying how rubbish I am?" He felt the stab of treachery.

Min was quick to reassure him. "Not at all Noah. They know you're new to this game. If anything, I think they'd like to help you out more. But you seem so determined to get everything right first time. No-one wants to make you feel stupid. Well, no-one apart from Caitlin that is, and she doesn't count for anything."

Noah detected steel in her voice. "What is it with Caitlin? You never say, but I know you don't like her. Was it something that happened last year?"

Min clammed up. "I can't say Noah, I'm sorry."

He felt disappointed, shut out.

"That's okay," he said, lying.

Min glanced down at the notebook in his hands. "Okay if I sit on the boulder for a while? I'd love to see some of your writing. Or even better, you could read me something? Would you mind?"

"Be my guest," Noah swept his arm expansively over the space next to him and Min climbed up. Oscar sat at the bottom, whining. She scrambled down, picked up the little black dog and tucked him under her arm, before climbing back up again. Oscar padded behind Noah and lay down, stretching out again on the rock that had been warmed by the sunshine.

Noah hadn't shared his writing with anybody for a long time. He felt unsure.

"I mean it Noah, I'd really love to hear something you've written."

He flicked through the pages of his notebook, and came across a few paragraphs he'd jotted down when he'd first arrived in Wales. It was a description of the mountains. Noah had read somewhere that it only takes a few weeks to become accustomed to an environment and to stop seeing it with fresh eyes. He had been determined to capture the spirit of the mountains as soon as possible, before that happened to him. Although, as it had turned out, the scenery changed almost daily with the passage of time. New growth, spring morphing into summer. Every day, there was something new to see and Noah was constantly entranced by his new life in the natural world.

"Okay, listen up then. This is called, unimaginatively, 'Arrival'," and he began to read.

Min lay back on the rock and closed her eyes, concentrating. As Noah spoke, she could see the landscape unrolling in front of her. Noah recreated the sights, sounds and smells with lilting, twisting, musical words. He captured the mystery, the timelessness and tiny details perfectly.

Min was entranced. "That's amazing Noah. I had no idea you were that good."

"Thanks, I think," replied Noah, teasingly.

"But it's really professional. What does Catherine say? About your writing I mean. She must know how good it is."

Noah closed his notebook and shifted slightly on the

rock. "I haven't shown anything to her for ages. I used to, years ago when I was younger. But now, I suppose I'd feel a bit stupid."

"No!" Min's eyes were wide. "Don't you ever say that Noah Foster. You've got real talent there. You need to nurture it."

"Yeah, right," Noah mumbled, feeling suddenly shy.

"If I were you, I'd be picking Catherine's brains, getting her to look at my stuff and comment on it."

"I guess, but she's so busy now. She doesn't even have time for herself."

"True," Min acknowledged. And then, suddenly, "I know what you can do though. Catherine was telling me she's promised Eve from the bookshop to do a talk for Eve's writers' group. Why don't you go along? And, why don't you join Eve's group? I'm sure she'd be happy to have you."

Noah tapped his chin with his pencil. "Maybe I will, maybe I will," he reflected.

Later that night, Catherine was standing by the window, her bare feet chilly on the wooden floorboards. In the distance, a huge white moon hung over the mountain range, washing everything in silver. It was so bright, when she looked down, she could see detailing on the flowers in the garden below her.

Even while she gazed on the beauty, Catherine felt torn inside. All week she had wanted to scream at Arnaud, but she knew that he had kept the true nature of the farm's finances from her in order not to distress her. There wasn't a deceitful bone in his body. She was aware of that. She also knew how much he was loving this new existence in Wales. Part of her felt anguished for him at the possibility of having to give it all up.

"Catherine," Arnaud's voice was low.

"I didn't want to wake you, I'm sorry," unable to sleep, Catherine had crept over to the window, lost in contemplation.

"No worries. Actually, it's me that is sorry."

Catherine was silent. The bedclothes rustled as Arnaud sat up. "I've not known what to say to you all week. I know you're angry with me," Arnaud's voice sounded hoarse. She stood, frozen to the floor, unable to pull her eyes away from the view.

He continued, "We agreed to give it a few months here, and, well, things seem to be going from bad to worse. But most importantly, I feel I've lost your trust in me. I'm sorry. All I can do is promise that I will never hold anything back from you again. I can't stand the fact that we are hardly talking...strangers to each other..."

Catherine felt tears welling up in her eyes. She broke into Arnaud's words, "That's all I needed. Just to hear the word 'sorry'."

He climbed out of the bed and came to stand next to her at the window. She heard his soft intake of breath, as he saw the moon illuminating the view with its intense, white light. He stood, hesitantly beside her.

Catherine turned to look at him, "I felt so hurt. And then, tonight, I couldn't sleep. As I was standing here, looking at the view, the feelings just melted away. I hate to admit it, but there is something about this place...I can understand why you're so drawn to it. I'm not sure I feel the same way - I still miss the sea. And I'm desperately struggling to find time to write." She hesitated, seeing the guilt surge into Arnaud's eyes.

He spoke, "My first priority is you, Catherine, and our

marriage. If necessary, we will hand our notice in to Sebastian and leave as soon as we can."

She opened her mouth to object, but Arnaud continued, "Sebastian is well able to get through the rest of the season. Now he's got his memory back. He has friends locally, who would be willing to help. I am sure. I'm serious."

Catherine was silent, thinking. "I can't leave now. That goes against the grain. It would feel like we're letting everyone down; Sebastian, Noah and the other trek leaders. But...I don't know how to go on here either. I'm desperately worried about my writing. I'm late with the first draft - that's never happened to me before."

She hesitated, then plunged in. "I was thinking, just now...what if I went back to Kent - to the white house - for a week or two, just to give myself some space to write. Sebastian could cover off the admin stuff for me here. I know he's still struggling with his health, but he should be able to manage. Min's pretty well up to speed with the catering."

Arnaud felt uneasy. They had never spent time apart since they had been married. But he owed it to Catherine. She had made so many sacrifices for him. "Yes, why not. I know Sebastian has been feeling guilty about the situation. He'd be glad of a chance to help you out."

Catherine felt a sense of release, as if a weight had been lifted from her. The thought of spending time at Gull Cove lifted her spirits.

She smiled at Arnaud and said, "Thank you."

"It's the least I can do," he responded. But his heart was heavy. He hoped that she would come back. He wasn't sure. Not any more.

# 21

## THE SAVING OF NOAH FOSTER

On Sunday evening, the trek leaders were grouped on the decking, overlooking the forest. On his last visit, Glen the blacksmith had left them an old metal container, which Goff and Noah had turned it into a fire pit. The smell of burning pine wood filled the air.

Noah stared into the flames, thinking about Catherine's departure that afternoon. She'd told him that she and Arnaud had made things up, and that she was going to spend a couple of weeks at the white house to finish her manuscript first draft. Noah wasn't so sure things were back to normal. There was a tightness about her mouth and she'd seemed on edge. As Catherine had driven off, Noah's heart sank. He remembered the vulnerable, withdrawn woman who had come into his life years ago, and he was terrified that Catherine was drifting back into her old self.

Next to him, Justin was strumming on his guitar, humming along. The music drew Noah out of his gloomy thoughts.

"Nice song mate. I've not heard it before - who's it by?"

Justin strummed a few more bars, and stopped. "It's

just something I made up. I'm still tinkering with it."

"It's great. Are you going to play it down at the Wolf?"

"Might do, if I can make it work."

Justin looked back at his guitar, then said, "Hey, that reminds me Noah. I meant to say, I had no idea who your dad was. You kept that quiet."

"My dad?"

"Yeah, Toby Foster, the artist."

"How did you find out?" Noah had made a point of leaving his famous father out of any conversations.

"I was talking to Min. Telling her about who my favourite painters were. I mentioned your dad - and she told me the connection. Said he was up here last Christmas with you."

"Yeah, that's him," Noah acknowledged. "How did you hear about him?"

"I did a project about marine paintings when I was at art college and we went to one of your dad's exhibitions on a field trip. He was there and he was kind enough to talk to me for a bit. I guess his paintings really resonated with me. I love the sea. I'd never be able to capture stuff the way he can though. Somehow he just gets motion and feeling into his art."

"I know what you mean. I've no idea how he does it. He doesn't really say much about his work. I'm useless with drawing and stuff, so I guess he never bothers to discuss things like that with me." Noah suddenly remembered, "Hey Justin, you were going to take some of your paintings into Hay, weren't you? Did you find a shop for them?"

Justin coloured slightly, "Yeah, a couple of them actually. One of them suggested I get some greetings cards printed up with a few of the designs too. It seems that can be quite a good little earner."

"Fantastic," Noah was genuinely pleased. "What are you working on at the moment?"

"I'll show you," said Justin. He got up, handed his guitar to Noah and went inside the house. Noah tried out a few chords that Justin had taught him. It sounded terrible and he winced. He clearly wasn't cut out to be a famous musician any time soon.

Justin emerged from the house with a large sketchpad, and flipped through it, looking for a page. Then he handed the open pad to Noah. Min stared back at him from the page. Drawn in charcoal, with a few, precise strokes. Justin had captured her slightly turned-up mouth and lively eyes perfectly.

"It's good isn't it," Noah turned around to see Min standing behind him, leaning over his shoulder. She'd just returned from babysitting Joseph's children.

"Er, yes, yeah," Noah was taken aback. "Brilliant actually."

"It'll be a birthday present for my mam when Justin's finished it and I've got it framed. I wanted to find her something a bit different, and Justin had the idea of drawing me. I'll pay him, of course."

Inside, Noah felt the stirrings of something unfamiliar and not particularly pleasant. He didn't want to think about it just then, so he pushed the feelings down.

"We should show my dad some of your work Justin. That is, if you're interested. I mean, you never know, he might be able to help with introductions to galleries and things..." Noah offered.

Justin's face lit up, "I'd like that Noah. I'd like that very much indeed."

"Any more ginger wine?" Min asked, a note of

desperation in her voice. "I need something to soothe my nerves. The kids kept getting out of bed the whole evening. They only just got to sleep before Joseph and Stef arrived back home. No wonder they look so frazzled half the time. Give me a dog rather than children any day." She bent down to stroke Oscar, who wagged his tail appreciatively.

Justin picked up the bottle and handed it to Min, saying, "There's a glass on the table over there."

She reached behind her and picked up a glass, pouring herself a generous dose.

"I'd never tried ginger wine before I came here," Justin commented. "Top stuff."

"Joseph tried making some, but it wasn't as good as Stones Ginger Wine," she pointed to the green-labelled bottle. "Any more you two?"

They both nodded and Min gave them a top up. The drink slipped down very nicely indeed, thought Noah hazily, leaning back on the step behind him.

The only light came from the fire pit, flickering on their faces and bodies. It had the impression of making them appear as if they were in an old cine film with stilted, jumpy movements. From the other side of the decking, Lily got up and walked down to the metal container. She put another few logs from the nearby pile onto the fire and the flames leapt up, golden sparks spitting into the black velvet sky.

*If only there wasn't another trek to face tomorrow*, thought Noah. *If only Sebastian could keep Kestrel Farm and Catherine could get her manuscript finished...* There were an awful lot of if only's knocking around, he decided.

The next morning, Noah regretted the camaraderie of

the evening before. A late night and several glasses of ginger wine weren't conducive to an early start. This new school group was fairly local and would be arriving at nine thirty am, which meant pretty much a whole day's ride. He rubbed his blurry eyes with his hands, and plunged into the mass of ponies in the corral, list in hand.

Over breakfast, Noah reviewed his list again, trying to memorise each rider's name and which pony they were on. He'd discovered things went much more smoothly the sooner he could get their names off pat. All boys in this trek. He didn't think anything of it, distracted by the effort of getting as much food into himself as possible before it was time to tack up the ponies. Two bowls of cereal, three slices of toast, seven sausages and a double portion of baked beans were washed down by three cups of tea.

Just as he was debating whether to have another sausage, the sound of the arriving coach could be heard in the yard outside. Noah wiped his mouth on his sleeve and headed outside with the other trek leaders. Arnaud liked them all to be around to welcome the new arrivals. As Noah watched the over-excited kids plunging off the bus, he gritted his teeth. He had to make this week go smoothly.

While the other groups began tacking up, Noah looked around for his trek. They were nowhere to be seen. Usually the teachers were helpful at chivvying the children along, but Noah couldn't spot any of them either. The last time he saw them, they were sitting in the sun outside the teachers' wing, looking very chilled. Unusually, none of them were accompanying the groups out riding this week.

That left the trek leaders on their own with no adult back up. To save time, Noah decided to start tacking up the ponies himself.

By the time his group of boys appeared, sauntering over from the bunkhouse, he'd finished saddling up all the ponies. By now, most of the other treks were mounted and ready to go. Noah had a bad feeling in the pit of his stomach. Halfway through his riding demo, he was conscious that none of his boys were paying attention. Instead, they were jostling each other and pointing at Barnum, who'd just done a steaming poo.

"Yeah, yeah it happens," Noah was trying to play it cool.

He finally managed to get the boys up on their ponies and sorted out. He untied Mouse, flung the halter rope around his neck, checked his girth for the umpteenth time and jumped up into the saddle. Glancing at his watch, Noah noticed they were twenty minutes behind schedule. Thankfully Arnaud had gone to take a phone call and wasn't around to notice.

"Okay lads, remember single file behind me. No overtaking."

Noah rode along the track to the pine forest, looking behind him every few seconds. So far so good. No stragglers. Maybe things were going to be all right after all.

Ten minutes into the trek, the boys began singing. Noah grinned. They sounded happy at least.

"To the left boom boom, to the right boom boom."

The words floated towards him. He put his hand on the back of his saddle and turned to look over his shoulder. His grin faded. The trek was in disarray. The words 'to the left' were being accompanied by a sharp pull of the left-hand rein. 'To the right' was accompanied by an equally enthusiastic tug in the other direction. The ponies were beginning to look disgruntled and a couple of them were already jostling for position, out of line.

"Hey stop that!"

Six pairs of eyes bored into him.

"You're jabbing their mouths - that really hurts them," Noah tried to be reasonable and explain.

He turned his head and rode on. A few minutes later, the same song started up. He looked back. A couple of the boys had started the actions again. They stopped when Noah glared at them, but he felt his tenuous control of the group slipping through his fingers.

The only respite of the day was out on the mountainside, when one of the riders wanted to stop for a pee. Noah got off Mouse and held Buzz, a dun coloured pony, for the boy, while he disappeared into a nearby clump of trees. For once, he didn't tell the rest of the trek to pull their ponies' heads up when they started to graze the sparse mountain grass. At least it stopped them from wandering off.

The chatter was interrupted by a loud shout, from above Noah's head.

"Help! Get me down!"

He looked up and had to bite his lip to keep from laughing. Neil, the most irritating boy in the trek, was clinging to the neck of a black pony with a long, shaggy mane. Pixie, the pony, had managed to scramble up the steep side of a bank and was standing at the top, squashing his rider against the edge of the rock face. Noah was impressed that Neil had managed to stay on. It was doubtful whether he'd do so for much longer.

"Hang on a sec. Don't move," he commanded the boy.

The little pony seemed to have a conspiratorial glint in its eye. Noah remembered Goff commenting about Pixie's antics on his trek last week. It seemed that the pony usually got bored at forced stops and tended to wander off, invariably choosing the highest ground possible.

Noah handed Mouse's reins to the boy who had returned from his pee, and clambered up the bank to rescue Neil. There was no room on the narrow ledge to get Neil off Pixie, so Noah was forced to take the pony's head and lead it in a zig zag down the bank, with Neil clinging white-faced on top. When they reached the bottom, the boy seemed genuinely grateful.

"Thanks mate," he grunted.

In an ideal world, the incident would have changed Neil's behaviour, but within a few minutes of the trek starting off, the singing had begun again. By the time they returned to Kestrel Farm at the end of the day, Noah was at his wits' end.

The next morning, the other trek leaders were all in a good mood. They were riding to the pub at Traneffwy that day, which meant chicken and chips for lunch and possibly even a half pint of beer. Any more than a half, and it was hard to stay awake on the return journey to the farm, Noah had discovered. He wished he could have shared everyone else's enthusiasm, but it was difficult to see how he was going to prevent his day from becoming an annoying repetition of the previous one. Even before they'd started out, the boys were already up to mischief. Red and blue plastic curry combs - which should have been used for grooming the ponies' manes and tails - were flying through the air.

"Hey, stop that at once, you're spooking the ponies," Caitlin's icy tones brought the boys to a standstill. "Pick them up and use them properly."

The boys did exactly as they were told and ten minutes later, Noah had the neatest trek in the yard. For once he was grateful for Caitlin's intervention, and by a stroke of luck, Arnaud seemed to have missed the curry comb incident. He appeared in time to see Noah's trek departing.

"Looking good Noah," was his approving comment. Noah didn't feel good at all.

Once they were up on the mountainside, the song started again. But today the boys were sneakier, and every time Noah turned around to try and see what was going on behind him, they stopped misbehaving and looked back at him as if butter wouldn't melt in their mouths. Then, things began to take on a whole new dimension. As they rounded the far edge of the common, and began winding their way down a little valley, a ruckus kicked off at the back of the trek. Noah twisted round in his saddle to see one of the ponies darting out of the trek to one side. Midge came to a halt a few yards later, scratching his protesting rider on a huge gorse bush.

Noah stopped the trek, asking, "What was that all about?"

Silence. Then he noticed one of the boys sneakily drop a long stick onto the ground. Noah guessed he'd hit or poked Midge with it, precipitating the dash. "Right, Paul, bring Haribo out of the trek and up here behind me."

"What? Why me? I haven't done anything…" Paul acted the innocent.

"Just do as I say," Noah was firm.

Paul made a half-hearted effort to pull at Haribo's

reins. The chestnut pony stayed where it was. Eventually, Noah had to ride Mouse back down the trek and drag Haribo and his protesting rider to the front of the group. The boy on Midge had managed to pull his head up and get him back into line, but now they were in front of Saffron, a chubby palomino pony who didn't like Midge. She bared her teeth and nipped Midge on the rump. Midge squealed and jumped out of line again. This time, his rider did fall off. Noah sighed, slid off Mouse and walked back to sort out the chaos. Luckily, the boy wasn't hurt, but they were under strict instructions to notify Arnaud any time a rider fell off and Noah didn't trust the boys to keep this quiet. His spirits sank even further.

That night, Noah tossed and turned, trying to get to sleep. In his mind, he kept replaying the last couple of days. He couldn't think how he was going to impose some kind of discipline on the boys in his trek. And things were getting worse by the day. He eventually drifted off, only to be woken up an hour later by a low, throaty growl from Oscar. For a minute he lay still, staring into the inky blackness, wondering where he was. Suddenly, the silence of the night was pierced by a loud screech followed by a high-pitched squealing. A predator was on a killing spree in the forest. So much for the tranquil rural life, he thought.

Just as he began to doze off, a gentle hooting started in the far side of the valley. It echoed softly. Then, it was answered by a raucous hooting from nearby, making Noah jump. He pulled the covers over his head and turned over. But sleep eluded him, so he got out of bed, opened the window and let the night air drift over him. As he stood, his elbows resting on the windowsill, face splashed by the coolness, a thought occurred to him. He mulled it over for a while. *It might just work* he said to himself. He walked back to bed, lay down and fell asleep.

The next day started with bad news. Lily had picked up a stomach bug and was in bed, sick.

"Sorry, I'm going to have to add a couple more riders to each of your treks," Arnaud informed the leaders at breakfast.

Noah looked at his revised list, which now included...Gavin and John. He'd hoped for a couple of girls to water down the testosterone and distract the boys. No such luck.

Once again, his trek was slow off the block. By the time they appeared after breakfast, Noah had finished picking the dirt out most of the ponies' hooves. Just as he was doing Alfie's back hoof, the black pony let out a slow juicy fart in Noah's face. Raucous laughter. His group had timed their arrival perfectly.

*I could write a book about all of this and earn some money*, Noah thought, trying to keep positive.

Things improved when they were fifteen minutes into the trek. At the end of the road, a herd of sheep had gathered by the field gate that led onto the mountain. He glanced around, but there was no help in sight. No Catherine behind him in the Land Rover this time. He gritted his teeth and met the challenge head on.

Flinging Mouse at the gate, Noah whooped noisily and waved his arm in the air. This time, the sheep decided to co-operate and scattered, running away from him. Noah opened it one-handed, swung Mouse round, chased off the few stragglers that remained, then turned and held the gate for the trek to come through. The boys were impressed. A couple of them began to imitate Noah's one hand on the reins technique, their ponies swerving as a result.

Noah nipped it in the bud. "Do that again and the whole trek is returning to the farm."

Surprised, the boys immediately obeyed him.

He waited until the last pony was through the gate, clanged it shut deftly and turned Mouse on his heels, cantering past the riders to take his place at the front. Noah turned in his saddle and yelled, "Right, listen up. I'm operating a system of Monkey Points for the rest of this week. I don't do it with every trek, just a privileged few."

The chatter faded. For the first time, that week, Noah commanded their undivided attention.

"This is how it works. If you do something helpful you get a Monkey Point. If you spot something of interest, like a buzzard or a kite, you get a Monkey Point. If your riding improves, you get a Monkey Point. Three Monkey Points gets you five pick-and-mix sweets from the tuck shop. And…if you go above and beyond the call of duty, you could earn yourself a Golden Monkey Point. That's worth a Mars Bar. Starts now."

He turned back towards the trail, looked between Mouse's ears and headed off. Then he thought again, and turned back, "Oh, and anyone caught singing the 'To The Right' song gets a minus Monkey Point."

*I'm giving it my best shot*, thought Noah. *If this doesn't work, I'm screwed.*

When they got to the foothills, Noah tracked right, heading towards the Brecon Beacons, destination the Smoky Inn Pub at Porth Mynydd. He kept the pace slow as they splashed through the mountain streams, then led the trek in a well organised trot across the edge of the common. He noticed Neil, who had been bouncing about in the saddle the previous day, had managed to conquer rising trot.

"Monkey Point for Neil. Nice trot."

Suddenly, the rest of the boys were working hard at their rising trot too. Noah nearly whistled in surprise. At the far end of the common, he slowed the group, and let Mouse pick his way downhill, towards the stream. The rest of the ponies followed, snaking down the winding path. A voice piped up.

"Does spotting a sheep count?"

"No, too many of them," Noah replied.

Another voice, "What about a sheep with a black bird on its back?"

Noah looked back and then followed the boy's pointing hand. Sure enough, a large crow was sitting on the back of a sheep, picking at the ticks in its fleece. "Yep, Monkey Point for you, Gavin my man."

Noah hardly dared believe it. Who'd have thought they would have fallen for such a shallow ploy?

By the end of the day, he'd dealt out another twelve Monkey Points and a Golden Monkey Point. The latter was earned by John who managed to stay in the saddle when his pony, Duster, was spooked by something and cannoned into a gorse bush. Noah figured it was well worth the small outlay on sweets.

*Well I'm blowed*, he thought, and for the first time in ages, he began to enjoy himself.


Sebastian re-read the email in the farm's inbox and breathed a sigh of relief. One of the schools which had been considering cancelling, had decided to stick with

Kestrel Farm. But only after Sebastian had offered them a generous discount. He was going to have to tackle the issue of Emily's friend, but he had no idea how. He only had a vague recollection of Laura. He'd met her on a couple of occasions, not long after she'd started up her trekking centre across the valley, but he hadn't really paid much interest in her. At the time, Emily was well in control of Kestrel Farm and he'd not considered Laura as a threat to them.

He was impressed with Min, who'd come up with the identity of the mystery person calling the schools and criticising Kestrel Farm. She'd discovered that over the winter, Laura had taken to hanging out occasionally in the local pubs, asking people questions about the new management at Kestrel Farm. Laura's approach had been far from subtle, but a few of the locals were happy to offer embellished stories of Sebastian's accident and Arnaud's relative inexperience.

Sebastian bent down to scratch his leg - the plaster was off now and the peeling skin itched like fury. He looked back at the screen, willing himself to concentrate on the work in hand. Catherine had done a good job of tidying up the computer files and putting things in order. Even so, Sebastian's brain still felt scrambled after a couple of hours' work.

A few minutes later, Arnaud's face appeared at the front window. The door opened and he walked into the kitchen, his head brushing against a bundle of herbs hanging from a rack. It released a musty scent of lavender and rosemary into the room.

"Arnaud, you look tired."

"I've got a bit of a breather before the treks get back. I'm just going to grab a mug of tea and sit in the sun for a few minutes. I haven't stopped all day."

Sebastian felt guilty. It was a relief to be able to lift some the admin burden from Catherine, but he was still acutely aware how much physical work Arnaud had to do.

"You sit down. I'll put the kettle on." Sebastian jumped up and limped over to the Aga. "Have you eaten lunch today?"

"Yes, no. Actually, I can't even remember. I think I had some chips at the pub when I met the guys for lunch. I'm not really hungry, just thirsty."

"How did the morning go?"

Arnaud sighed heavily, "Willow lost a shoe. He'll be okay for Justin to ride this afternoon, but the horse will be out of action for tomorrow. Glen is due at the end of the week to do a few shoeing jobs for us. At least we've got a spare lead horse for Justin as the teachers aren't riding. I'll give him Prezel I think."

"And Noah?" Sebastian hesitated to ask. Arnaud's face clouded over.

"Another rider off this morning. He's not saying, but I think his trek is a bit out of control. I overheard Goff and Caitlin talking about it. I could swap trek leaders and give one of them Noah's trek - they are the two most competent leaders - but it's not going to look good and it will really demoralise Noah."

Sebastian grimaced in sympathy. "Well, I've got a bit of good news to cheer you up. I've managed to keep the Norton school group from cancelling. I had to give them a discount, but we should still make a profit out of the week."

Arnaud's face lightened. He sat down at the table, and took a sip from the cup of tea that Sebastian had just put in front of him. "That's great news, well done. And I've just remembered, talking of groups, I've had an idea of where we might get some new business from." He leaned forward, elbows on the table and explained.

Half an hour later, the sound of hooves in the yard signalled the return of the treks. Arnaud got up and wandered over to the window. He stretched lazily, pulled on his boots and went out into the yard to meet them. Sebastian listened to the familiar noises; trek leaders shouting orders, horses snorting, feet scrambling on the stony track to the barn. He smiled. The farm was alive and breathing. Perhaps, by some miracle, they might be able to turn the situation around. Without thinking, he got up from the table, slung his jacket on and hobbled outside to take a look. He emerged from the farmhouse just as Caitlin was walking down the slope past the front door. She spotted him and stopped dead in her tracks, paused and then walked towards him.

Sebastian's mouth went dry. There was nowhere to run. He was cornered.

# 22

## CAITLIN

Noah was ebullient, sending soap suds flying all over the kitchen each time he pulled his hands out of the washing up water and waved them around. Oscar spotted the bubbles, and pounced on them as they drifted down to the floor. He snorted when a group of bubbles went up his nose, causing Min to laugh at his antics.

Noah was in full flow, "Honestly Min, I nearly died. Who'd have thought something so simple as a bribe would work with the boys?"

Min looked over at Noah. She wasn't surprised at all. She had three older brothers and knew just how well bribery and ego-boosting worked with them.

"I told you Noah, you do have it in you. There's a lot to pick up with trek leading and you've had waaay less experience with horses than the others. I still think you're doing a really good job. You just need to not be too ditsy every now and then."

He admitted, "I do get carried away sometimes. I'm riding along and I get a great idea for my book, so my mind goes into creative overdrive and then before I know it, something's kicked off in my trek."

"Why don't you take a little notepad with you and jot

stuff down as you go along? You could get one of those weeny ones that could fit in your pocket," Min suggested.

"Good thinking. I'll do that."

Min wondered if she'd been too harsh with Noah. "All the same," she added, "I think you've done brilliantly with that group of boys. I overheard one of the teachers today saying what a pain they were."

She gave the counter a last wipe and went into the storeroom, reappearing with a huge bag of flour.

"Are you up for helping me bake a few cakes?" she asked Noah. "I'm a bit behind and I need to get some done for the lunch packs tomorrow."

"Yeah, no worries. What are you going to make?"

"Sweet cicely cake, black bean chocolate loaf and, if I have time, a batch of lavender biscuits for the teachers."

"Nice one." Noah hoped there would be plenty left over for the weekend.

Min brushed a stray wisp of hair from her face, tucking it back into the green headscarf, which was keeping her curls in order. "I'm quite excited. This batch of teachers seem really interested in our foraged food and a lot of it is healthier too, which is a real selling point when they're encouraging the parents to send their kids on a trip."

Min assigned Noah the black bean chocolate cake. He stood at the pine worktop, weighing ingredients. A ray of light shone through the stained glass suncatcher that Min had hung in the kitchen window, sending a shower of green and blue sparkling dots tumbling onto the light stone floor. Oscar noticed, and jumped from one patch of light to the other, trying to catch it between his paws.

"That's one crazy dog you've got there," Min commented. "I can't believe he's eleven years old. Half the time he acts like a puppy."

"You should have seen him when he was younger," Noah replied, opening a parcel of butter. It felt good to be baking again. He had always helped Toby with foraging and cooking, ever since he was a child, and, nice as it was to have all his meals cooked for him, there was something satisfying about getting hands on in the kitchen.

Min started chopping a batch of sweet cicely leaves, with fast, precise movements. Noah watched in admiration at her dexterity.

"You're wasted here, honestly Min." He ventured onto dangerous ground, aware that Min was a bit prickly about her decision not to take either of the two jobs she'd been offered in restaurants on the Welsh coast.

"I'm enjoying the challenge here, really I am. It's the first time I've been in charge of my own kitchen."

Noah hadn't seen it that way. It made sense. "In an ideal world Min, what would you really want to do?"

"This," she stopped chopping for a few seconds, "I mean, I didn't realise how much I would enjoy the autonomy here. Catherine and Arnaud are really great about letting me try things out and they hardly ever change anything I want to do. I suppose if wishes were horses, I'd love my own little place. Like a small restaurant or tea room. Nothing huge. Just a handful of covers, where I could experiment and do foraged recipes. But that's not going to happen any time soon."

She sighed, and rubbed her nose with a flour-covered hand, leaving a white dusting behind.

Noah thought it looked cute, and refrained from telling her about it.

"You're the one always telling me to go for my dreams." He pushed her a bit further, "I think you should look into it Min. You never know what you might find. I've seen one or two shops to let in Hay." He wrapped the leftover butter back in its waxed paper and walked over to the fridge.

"I don't have any capital though Noah. You need something to get going. The banks aren't going to lend with no collateral."

Noah persisted, "Don't give up on your dream Min. Everyone has to start somewhere."

She pursed her lips and chopped more furiously. Noah dropped the subject.

An hour and a half later, the kitchen worktop was full of cooling bakes standing on metal racks. Under Min's supervision, Noah was pressing fern-like sweet cicely leaves onto the top of the cakes. A delicate aniseed smell from the leaves scented the air. Min set a few lavender heads to one side, to put on a plate with the biscuits when she served them up for the teachers. Noah admired the way she always added little extra touches to her baking.

Suddenly, Oscar jumped up and ran over to the dining room door, wagging his tail. A few seconds later, Justin and Lily barged through the entrance, laughing.

"Hey guys, we wondered where you were," Justin bent down to stroke the dog.

"Cakes, oh that smell…" Lily sniffed appreciatively.

"Have you got any spare? I'm starving," Justin walked over to the counter. "Wow, these look amazing. You're such a genius, Min."

"It's just a few cakes," she was modest.

"No way, you're brilliant," he insisted.

"Best cake maker I've ever come across, and I'm not just saying that because I want to eat one now," Lily agreed, hovering over the rack of cooling lavender biscuits."

Min was uncomfortable with the attention. "If anyone round here's got talent it's you, Justin. I popped over to my mum's this afternoon and gave her that picture you did of me. She was totally over the moon. Joseph was there too, and he wants to know if you can do one of his kids."

Justin glowed, "Really? Of course, no worries."

"You've got a day off on Sunday, haven't you? Why don't you come down to the Wolf with me then and you can chat it over with Joseph?" Min was enthusiastic.

Noah felt a lurch in his stomach. Min seemed to be constantly singing Justin's praises nowadays. The two went head to head, discussing whether Justin should use watercolour or pen and ink to paint the children. Lily's mobile rang. She sat down at one of the dining room tables, trying to talk through a mouthful of cake. Noah felt surplus to requirements. He got up, clicking his fingers for Oscar to follow.

"Just taking the dog for a walk," he threw over his shoulder and headed for the door. Nobody replied and it stung.

Outside, Noah could hear the chatter coming from the bunkhouses. On the verandah opposite, several teachers were sitting outside with a few bottles of wine. They waved at Noah as he crossed the courtyard and headed for the paddock. He waved back, but decided not to go over and chat. He needed space. Oscar followed at his own pace, quartering the ground in search of dropped sweets and other bits of food.

As Noah moved away from the accommodation, the deepening dusk of the late May evening wrapped around him. The air was filled with a rich combination of scents; honeysuckle, may blossom, spring grass, pine. He ducked under the corral fence, not noticing Caitlin, leaning on the rail overlooking the paddock, until he was almost upon her. It was too late to swerve away and take another direction, so Noah decided a polite 'good evening', casually thrown over his shoulder in passing, was in order. But as he took a couple of steps nearer, he noticed something was wrong. She was hunched over the rail, crying, her shoulders shaking.

Noah couldn't just ignore her. He asked, "Are you okay?"

Silence for a moment as Caitlin realised who it was asking the question. Then she turned. Her face was blotched. "As if you didn't know," she spat at him.

Something inside Noah snapped. There was only so much he could take.

"Huh? How should I know what's upset you? I don't get it. I was just trying to help and you jump down my throat."

She stared at him. This was a Noah she hadn't come across before.

Noah saw that Caitlin hadn't changed from the day's riding. She was still wearing her dusty jodhpurs and top. It was unlike her.

"Are you really telling me you have no idea?" Her tone was sarcastic.

Noah held out his hands. "Honestly Caitlin, I'm not a mind reader."

She sniffed and wiped her nose with her hand in a childish gesture. It occurred to Noah that Caitlin wasn't as adult as she appeared.

"You mean to say that Catherine and Arnaud haven't

talked about me and Sebastian to you? I can't believe that."

Noah was totally confused. Women were like that sometimes, he knew from bitter experience. They assumed you knew exactly what was going on. Noah was generally the last person to pick up on things. So much for his writer's antennae.

Something in his expression seemed to convince Caitlin.

"Well if you must know, Noah I'm-so-in-with-all-the-trekking-centre-managers Foster, Sebastian has banged the final nail in the coffin."

Noah's brain was working overtime, trying to understand what Caitlin was talking about.

"You and Sebastian…?"

"No," Caitlin hissed back. "Not me and Sebastian. Not ever. Just me."

The penny finally dropped. "Caitlin, I'm sorry."

"So, they did tell you. I knew it. I bet you've all been having a fine old time laughing at me behind my back."

"No, no you've got it all wrong. It was something I heard down at the Wolf one night. Nobody's said anything to me at all. Some bloke I was chatting to commented about Sebastian and a trek leader getting together last summer. I didn't think much about it at the time as he didn't mention you by name."

Caitlin was scathing. "You expect me to believe that?"

"It's the truth."

She recovered herself a little. "Oh of course, I should know, Mr Goody Two-shoes doesn't ever lie, does he."

Noah had had enough. "Look Caitlin. I don't know any details, but you're obviously really upset and I'm sorry to see that. But don't take it out on me. If things ended badly with Sebastian last year, which I guess they did, why on earth did you come back here?"

Caitlin swallowed and pulled out a tissue from her pocket, blowing her nose noisily. Black streaks of mascara had run down her cheeks. She looked like a character from a Halloween horror movie.

"I knew it was a stupid idea to come back here this season. I just couldn't help myself. When Catherine and Arnaud contacted me, asking if I was interested in working here again, they mentioned that Emily had left. I thought if there was a chance of meeting Sebastian here, there might be something between us again. And when I discovered he'd lost his memory..." she shrugged, "I don't know, I thought that maybe he'd change. That when he got his memory back he'd see things differently. Well, now I know. He doesn't."

Her voice was flat, lifeless.

"How do you know that?" Noah asked.

"I bumped into Sebastian earlier this evening. I was walking past the farmhouse after we got back from the trek, just as he was coming out of the door. Nobody else was around and he couldn't avoid me. I suppose...I suppose I hinted that I would be open to being more than just friends with him again. He told me straight. He didn't even smile," fresh tears welled up in her eyes. She sniffed and continued, "As far as Sebastian is concerned, there is no future for us. Last year was, in his words, 'a few days of madness'. That's all I was to him. I knew that really, but it still hurts to hear it."

Noah was taken aback. "But Caitlin, you could have any man you wanted. You're so good looking. All the guys fancy you. Why are you still bothering with Sebastian? After all, he's years older than you."

"Because Noah, for once in my life, I really fell for somebody. Perhaps because it was me who had to do the chasing. Sebastian didn't run after me like all the other men." She heaved a shuddering sigh, "I'm going to have to find another job now. I can't stay here."

"No!" Noah was forceful. "You can't just walk away Caitlin. You're bigger than that. As far as I know, none of the other trek leaders have any idea about you and Sebastian, and if Min knows anything, she's certainly never breathed a word to me. Neither have Catherine or Arnaud - if they even know. Why should you go now? I'm sure you'll get over Sebastian. And what's more, you're a brilliant trek leader. We need you here."

Caitlin was surprised. "If I'm any good, it's only because I was here last year and I know the ropes."

"That's not true. You're so good at dealing with the kids - you get them eating out of your hand in minutes. And you're brilliant with the ponies too. I don't think things would run nearly as smoothly without you."

She considered. "And Min's really said nothing to you? That girl really hates me you know, Noah."

"I can't believe that. I can't imagine Min hating anybody. I do know that something you said or did has upset her, but she refuses to speak about it. And to be fair to her, I've given her every opportunity. I've been griping about your attitude towards me for ages." He paused, then plunged in, "While we're at it Caitlin, what have I done to you? You just seem to have it in for me. I can't get my head round it."

Caitlin winced. "I'm sorry Noah. I'm sorry about my...my behaviour towards you. I guess I had you all wrong. When we arrived...I don't know...I was feeling like I shouldn't have come back. Then when I spotted

Min here at the farm - and saw that you two were such good friends it threw me even more. She gave me a piece of her mind last year when I was down the pub one night, and we didn't end on a good note. She thought I'd taken advantage of Sebastian when he was vulnerable. Arnaud and Catherine didn't say anything about her working up here this season, or I might have thought twice about coming."

"It was a last minute thing," Noah explained. "They hadn't spoken to Min about the catering when they did the job interviews."

Caitlin nodded, then continued, "And you were so in with Arnaud and Catherine. I guess I just felt off balance - I was sure you all knew about me and Sebastian and thought I was just some stupid idiot. And," with a weak grin, "you did make it easy for me to target you."

Noah was gracious, "I'm sure I did."

A pause.

Then Noah ventured, "So you're gonna stay?"

"I've got nowhere else to go," Caitlin was subdued again. "I was meant to be working at my dad's stud farm this year, but I fell out with my parents at Christmas and haven't spoken to them since. I don't know what else I would do. I don't even know where I'm going to go at the end of this season. Back to Australia for the winter I guess."

"If it's any help, I don't think many of us trek leaders are totally sure about what we'll do next. I guess there's still time to make plans. I think we should enjoy the summer first," Noah was philosophical.

"What about Sebastian?"

"What about him? You've got that first encounter out of the way. And he probably won't be around that much when he's well enough to work in London," Noah reassured her.

Caitlin managed a weak grin.

"Who knows, if you can manage to put the whole thing behind you, maybe the universe won't stop after all. And we really do need you here Caitlin. I'm not trying to blackmail you or anything…"

Her shoulders lifted slightly.

In the twilight, a movement came from the paddock in front of them. A palomino pony slowly meandered over to where Noah and Caitlin were standing. It was Calico. The mare stretched out her neck and sniffed at Caitlin's pocket for a treat. Caitlin found a couple of pony nuts, and extended her hand. Calico nibbled Caitlin's palm, delicately taking the treats. Then she stood for a few minutes before wandering off into the gloom, leaving Noah and Caitlin wrapped in silence.

# 23

## CATHERINE

Catherine stood on the shingle, gazing at the incoming waves, which were weaving patterns of lacy froth at her feet. The rattle of tiny pebbles dragged back by the retreating water was interrupted by the swoosh of a new wave. Suddenly a large one rushed towards her, washing over her bare feet. It was cold, but she didn't mind. The water seemed to have a life of its own, tickling her toes with grains of sand. She breathed in, dragging the sea air into her lungs like a desperate smoker enjoying a forbidden cigarette.

On the nearby barnacle-encrusted breakwater, a gull sat looking at her. Then, for no apparent reason, it flew up and swooped at another bird bobbing on the sea nearby. The ensuing squawking pulled Catherine out of her reverie. She looked at her watch. Time to get back to work.

She turned and crunched up the beach toward the white house, her feet sinking into the shingle with each step. It was hard work and she was out of breath by the time she reached the front door, hot from the surprisingly strong May sunshine. Inside, the circular entrance hall was cool, welcoming. Her damp shoes slapped across the floorboards, leaving a trail of wet footprints behind her. Climbing the staircase, Catherine took each step deliberately, savouring the view over the bay. As she swung round and came up to the huge first floor room, she spotted Toby standing at the kitchen counter.

He glanced at her, saying, "I'm just about to put the kettle on. Do you fancy a tea?"

"Yes, but if you don't mind, I'll take it up with me. I promised myself I'd finish the next section this morning and it's nearly twelve already."

Toby grinned, and brushed a lock of hair away from his face. The smile, and hair were so like Noah's, only Toby's hair was greying now, with strands of white scattered through his black curls.

"How's it going?" he asked, then immediately added, "No, no don't worry. I hate it when people ask me that. Don't even bother to answer."

Catherine laughed. It felt good to be in an environment where people understood the pressures and pleasures of creativity.

She perched on one of the driftwood chairs, waiting for the kettle to boil and asked, "Have you heard from Noah?"

"Yes, I had a phone call from him this morning. Apparently one of his friends at the farm is quite a good artist. He wants me to see what I think of his work."

"Oh, that would be Justin, I expect. I've spotted him sitting around the place sketching, but I've not seen any of his stuff. The others seem to think it's pretty decent artwork."

"I'll take a look. No harm done," Toby said, pouring the water into two turquoise pottery mugs. He jabbed at a floating teabag, "He seems a lot happier. Noah, I mean,"

Toby sounded slightly awkward.

"That's good news," Catherine was encouraged. "He sent me an email yesterday and it sounds like he's having a better week. Learning how to manage the kids."

"Yes, he muttered something about monkey points, but I didn't quite get it," Toby confessed.

Catherine smiled, "Who knows what Noah's imagination is conjuring up for the children." She was pleased. If Noah was getting to grips with the job, that was one less thing to worry about.

Toby placed a mug of tea in front of her. Catherine was anxious to end the conversation, not wanting to talk about Wales any longer.

"Thank you," she picked up the mug and turned to leave.

"Catherine…" Toby hesitated, unsure.

She looked at him, and felt the scrutiny behind his dark brown eyes.

"If you fancy supper tonight, I'm cooking rabbit casserole."

She breathed in, relieved. "Yes, that would be great. Thank you."

Once, Catherine would have walked up to the third floor studios and sat in her cubicle, overlooking the beach. But her old space was currently in use. Noah had kindly volunteered his bedroom for this visit and Catherine had readily accepted.

She climbed the flight of stairs from the first floor space towards Noah and Toby's rooms on the second floor. With every step upwards, the view from the front window expanded, encompassing more of the bay. The tide was on its way out, and the seagulls were waddling along the water line, searching for stranded shellfish and other detritus. She strode along the gloomy corridor, past Toby's room until she reached Noah's bedroom door. An old driftwood sign, written in childish scrawl, still hung there.

## Keep out! Danger!

It was typical of Noah to have left the sign hanging on his door for years, almost as if he hadn't quite left his childhood behind. She stepped into the room, still feeling a little nervous about entering his private space.

Inside, the room was in chaos, every scattered object telling the story of Noah's life - a few driftwood mobiles he had made to sell when she first came to the house; a broken lead of Oscar's hanging from a peg; a battered copy of Shakespeare's complete works - a legacy from Milly. And more recent things - scattered CDs of bands Catherine had never heard of, a broken iPhone and a stack of textbooks.

At the far side by the window overlooking the marshes, was Noah's wooden desk. On the floor next to it were piles of books, papers and a jumble of writing materials that had been scattered over the table when Catherine had arrived. Now it was clear of everything apart from her laptop, a small notepad and a pencil.

As she sat down, Catherine's gaze flicked involuntarily over the marshes, towards the cottage where she and Arnaud had lived. Every time she looked in that direction, she still half-expected to see the llamas and sheep grazing in the field outside the house. But the paddock was empty. Already the grass was growing back, unevenly. The new occupants had painted the exterior an attractive pale yellow and fixed a long washing line between the building and the shed. A row of clothes hung flapping in the breeze.

Memories of her time there with Arnaud wormed themselves into her consciousness. Of candlelit evenings, snug inside the tiny dwelling when the winter wind raged outside; milking the sheep in the winter mornings, her breath frosty, and sitting cooped up in the little attic bedroom, in a world of her own, writing.

Catherine shook her head and stood up. She shuffled around the desk and pulled an old dusty blue and green striped curtain across the window, shutting out the view, then sat back at her laptop, staring at the words in front of her.

An hour later, the document was another five pages longer. The room was stuffy, and in the gloom with the curtains drawn, Catherine could feel her eyes closing. She fought to keep them open. Her whole body felt so heavy.

*A five-minute sleep can't do any harm*, she told herself. She pushed herself up from the desk, almost stumbling as she walked over to Noah's bed and lay down. Her eyes closed and she was asleep within minutes.

The sky was a pure, unbroken pale blue, stretching for miles. No clouds anywhere, not even a wisp. Mouse picked his way along a stony track at the bottom edge of the mountain, sure-footed as always. On Noah's left, an old dry stone wall with a rusty strip of barbed wire running along the top enclosed a small group of mountain sheep. The lambs were large and fat now, nibbling the grass alongside their mothers, long tails twitching.

Noah could hear the occasional burst of chatter from his trek behind him. Mostly they were quiet, lulled by the rhythm of the ponies' hooves and the warm sunshine. Noah glanced up at the mountain ridge to his right. A solitary buzzard wheeled high, riding on the thermal. As it came down closer, swooping along the side of the ridge, Noah could see the mottled brown and beige markings on the underside of its huge wings. He turned back to his trek.

"Monkey Point if anyone can tell me what that big bird is," he waved his arm in the direction of the buzzard.

"Eagle?" came a guess from the far end of the trek.

"Nope," Noah shouted back.

"Buzzard?" a small boy just behind Noah ventured.

"Monkey Point for you, Harry," he responded with a thumbs-up. The other children began to scour the hillside, looking for unusual things to gain them favour in Noah's eyes.

Just then, a strange smell hit Noah's nostrils. It was cloying and unpleasant, a bit like sewage, but much stronger. As they rounded a tree Noah discovered the cause. A dead sheep lay at the edge of a mountain stream, its eyeballs already picked out by the crows. Chunks of ragged fleece were snagged on rocks, floating in the water. Noah changed course and circled away from the carcass, but not before his group had seen it. A chorus of groans and cries of 'yuk' echoed down the line behind him.

"Sir?" called out Nigel, an annoying freckle-faced boy with a high-pitched, whining voice, "Does dead sheep get a Monkey Point?"

"No it doesn't," shouted back Noah, his arm over his nose to block the smell.

Further along the path, a movement above his head caught Noah's attention. The buzzard was flying over a tall tree, swooping to avoid a flock of crows darting angrily at its tail. As they rode underneath the fighting birds, Noah and the group of children gazed up, mesmerised. Noah pulled a little notebook out of his jodhpur pocket, unhooked the pencil stump he'd tied to it and jotted down a few words, his pencil jerking on the page as Mouse strode along the uneven ground.

Noah sighed contentedly, eyes sweeping across the hillside covered in its new growth of soft green bracken, contrasting with the wizened, weather-beaten old trees.

A gentle tapping at the door woke Catherine. She felt disorientated, dragged out of a deep slumber. The door opened slightly.

"Sleeping on the job?" It was Toby.

She sat up, blinking. "What's the time?"

"Going on six o'clock. I wanted to let you know food will be ready in half an hour."

Catherine drew a deep breath. "I must have been asleep for hours."

"I'm not surprised," Toby retorted. "You've been looking exhausted ever since you turned up."

"It has been a bit full on," Catherine admitted, rubbing her eyes. But Toby had already left.

She sat still for a few minutes, trying to gather her scrambled thoughts. Her eyes felt gritty. A shower would help, she decided, but when she came out of Noah's room, Catherine found her feet leading her upwards, past the artists' studios, to the roof of the white house. As she came up the steps, she shivered. The sun had lost its strength and the early evening was chilly. Catherine wrapped her arms around herself for warmth and looked across the roof. In one corner stood an old wooden hammock stand. The varnish was peeling off the wood and the hammock fabric was tattered, strands of cloth flapping in the breeze. The roof used to be Noah's domain. He would spend hours up here, reading books or scribbling in his diary. Catherine used to join him sometimes, when he was younger. They hadn't spent time here together for a couple of years at least, she realised with a painful stab. The chill bite in the air drove her back into the warmth of the house.

On the next floor down, Catherine pushed opened the door to the art studios. The occupants had all gone home for the day and the room was quiet. Stepping over to her old writing space, she looked at the sketch book and a plastic tray of watercolour inks lying on the battered old table that had once held her laptop and notepad. Two glass jam jars sported an assortment of brushes and pens. Next to the window stood an old blue and white striped jug with a posy of flowers.

As she walked down the stairs to the first floor room, the smell of cooking floated up towards her. The slightly pungent scent of bay leaves formed the top note of a hearty stew aroma. Her mouth watered, she was hungry, having missed lunch. On the table stood an open bottle of white wine. Toby was at the stove, surrounded by steam and bubbling pots. A half empty glass was on the counter next to him.

"That smells good," Catherine sniffed appreciatively.

He swung round. "I didn't hear you arrive. You're like a cat Catherine, you hardly ever make any noise."

"A bit of a contrast to Noah and Oscar then," she grinned.

Toby raised his eyebrows.

"It must be strange without having them here," Catherine added.

Toby picked up a pan, walked over to the sink and began to drain the contents through a colander.

"Yes and no. I mean, I do miss having Noah around, that's true. But honestly, it was time he spread his wings a bit. He'd been driving me mad hanging around here and moping."

"The house always seems pretty full of people nowadays too."

"Yes, it's not lonely. Far from it."

Toby placed the pan on the table. "Broad beans from the garden. We've got rabbit stew. I thought you'd enjoy a trip down memory lane."

Catherine laughed. When she first moved to the white house, Toby's rabbit stew was one of the first foraged meals she'd ever encountered. It had been quite an adjustment moving in with the motley assortment of occupants in the house, their semi-bohemian lifestyle a contrast with her former rigid, narrow existence. Now Toby was the only one left at the house from that group of people. It felt strange.

She bent down to retrieve a couple of plates from the cupboard and placed them on the table, asking, "Is it just us?"

"Yes. I invited Sarah too, but she had to leave early for an appointment at the dentist."

"Shame, it would have been lovely to catch up with her properly. I've only seen her in passing this week." Catherine was fond of the quirky, diminutive artist.

Toby put on a pair of red-trimmed oven gloves and swung open the oven door, removing two foil-wrapped baked potatoes. He put one on each plate, while Catherine poured herself a glass of wine. She sat down, and spooned a helping of beans onto each plate. Toby picked up the casserole and placed it on a wooden mat in the centre of the table.

He served the stew, and then refilled his now empty glass.

"Cheers. Here's to your next book Catherine."

"Cheers, and thank you."

They ate in silence for a few minutes. Catherine savoured the earthiness of the stew. Carrots, large chunks of rabbit meat, parsnips and apple were flavoured with a rich stock, garlic, rosemary and bay leaves. It was delicious.

Toby broke the silence, "So, how is the draft going? I've hardly seen you since you've been here."

"Sorry, I have shut myself away rather. Needs must. I've never been under such pressure before."

"Yes, you said," Toby looked at her with that penetrating gaze again. "Was that the real reason for coming here, Catherine?"

She hesitated, thinking. What was the truth? Catherine wasn't even sure she knew herself.

"If I'm honest, I think I just felt on total overload. So many things have happened since we moved to Wales. Meeting Johanna - my mother's friend - was such a fantastic coincidence. It was amazing to bump into somebody who knew my father and could describe the time when my parents met each other."

Toby listened, focused on her words.

She continued, "But the whole saga of the farm - Sebastian's accident, the finances - we just seem to lurch from one crisis to another. And not being able to get time to write properly. It's...it's impossible really."

Toby chewed reflectively. Then he waved his fork in the air at Catherine. "I can understand that. But now

Sebastian is up and running - well, walking anyway from what I hear - surely he can take some of the pressure off you?"

"For the moment, but he's still hoping to get back to London to work. He needs to earn money desperately. I don't know," she shook her head. "If I'm honest, I'm not sure how he's going to get on there. It sounds as if he'll be facing quite a difficult work situation and..." she paused, "...he's not the same person as he was. Somehow, he seems softer. Not quite so cut and thrust, if you know what I mean. I'm not sure he'd do well in the kind of pressured environment he used to work in."

"And Arnaud, how's he?"

It felt like a blackbird stabbing at a worm on the lawn. Catherine couldn't lie. "I don't honestly know Toby. We've not really been speaking for a while. Not properly."

"I thought as much. What's happened?"

Catherine looked down at the table, heavy hearted. "I was annoyed - he didn't tell me just how bad the finances were. It felt as if he was treating me like a child. Maybe - I'm sure actually - I overreacted. It's more than that, though. Arnaud has settled so quickly into life in Wales. I still feel an outsider."

"And you think coming back here is the answer?"

"You mean both of us returning here? Or me now?"

"You choose."

Catherine swallowed, "I can't see Arnaud here. Not now he's lived in Wales. I mean, I could drag him back here with me. I know he would come. But I'd feel dreadful. I couldn't do that to him." She paused, scratching at a blob of wax on the table that had fallen from a candle. Then she looked up at Toby.

"And me. If I'm honest, part of me was glad of the

excuse to get away from Wales. To run back to Gull Cove. I was even mulling over the idea of staying here for good - I have to admit. Of cutting Arnaud loose somehow and moving back here on my own. But, in a weird kind of way, it feels as if this house has cut me loose. It doesn't feel like home here anymore."

A faint smile crept to the corner of Toby's mouth. This was what he'd hoped for.

Arnaud watched as the last of the ponies was turned out into the paddock. Mouse walked into the field, sank to his knees, and rolled over. The pony squirmed, kicking its legs in the air and rubbing its back on the grass. Then it rolled back, stood up jerkily, and cantered off down the slope, whinnying.

Noah closed the paddock gate and turned towards the farm, holding a blue headcollar in his hand. He spotted Arnaud at the far end of the corral and waved. Arnaud walked towards him across the dusty earth.

"Hey Noah, good day?"

"The best ever," Noah was glowing.

"I was just talking to the teachers before they headed off. They were very impressed with you Noah." Arnaud could feel the pride in his own chest. Noah visibly grew taller. "Well done," Arnaud clapped him on the shoulder.

They looked below them at the herd of horses, grazing peacefully.

"I wish I could give them the weekend off, but we've got quite a few riders out, and we need the money."

"That's good," Noah was positive.

"Yes, yes it is Noah, you're right."

"When's Catherine arriving?"

Noah felt Arnaud tense up beside him.

"She said sometime early evening. But you know the traffic. It's impossible to say really," he replied.

"Yeah," Noah felt useless. He wished there was something helpful to say to Arnaud. He hoped desperately that Catherine was coming back for good, and not just to tell Arnaud she'd had enough. She'd emailed Noah a couple of times from the white house, but he'd not really been able to gauge her state of mind from the brief messages she'd sent.

Arnaud sighed, and then turned towards the farm. "I'd better get the house tidied up before she arrives. It's a complete tip. Sebastian and I have been living like two bachelors. At the very least I need to get rid of the beer bottles…"

Noah grinned and walked back across the corral with Arnaud.

Catherine drummed her fingers on the steering wheel. The queue by the Air Balloon pub roundabout at Birdlip was horrendous, as usual on a Friday evening. She was impatient to get back to Wales - and Arnaud. Alongside her, on the front passenger seat was a brown envelope containing a printout of her completed first draft. She wasn't taking any chances with technology and preferred to have a hard copy as well as the files on her laptop.

She thought back to her morning walk along the beach at Gull Cove, before she'd begun her return journey to Wales. The weather had been beautiful, sunshine glinting off a deep blue-black sea. Out in the bay, a dinghy had been tacking along the coastline, heading for Whitstable, its white sail glistening in the light.

As she'd walked across a patch of sand, Catherine had spotted the washed out remains of a sandcastle two children had been building the day before. She'd noticed the family on the beach, the father labouring on a monster construction, the excited children squealing as the tide came in, trying to rescue their castle from the onslaught of the waves by building a long wall of sand. All that remained the next day was a slightly rounded mound, and a scooped-out channel in the sand.

*I'm like that sandcastle*, Catherine thought. *My existence here in Gull Cove has almost been completely obliterated.*

Sitting in the queue of traffic, she recalled that moment. But rather than sadness, she felt relief, as if her past had gently disengaged her, pushing her towards the present.

On the seat next to her, underneath the manuscript, were two bubble-wrapped packages. One of them was a photograph of her mother and her aunt Ozzie. Her mother must have been about fifteen at the time, Ozzie a couple of years younger. They were sitting on the steps of the white house, both clasping their arms around their feet. They looked so young and fresh-faced. It was a present for Johanna.

Underneath it was an oil painting of a woman sitting in the same place, on the steps outside the house. This time the woman was Catherine. It had been a parting gift from Toby. Catherine knew she would treasure it always, take it with her wherever she went.

Arnaud was walking across the farmyard when he heard the sound of the car, turning down the farm track from the lane. His heart leapt, and then sank. For him too, as well as Noah, Catherine's state of mind had been unclear from their conversations. She was always remote when she was in the thick of writing, Arnaud knew that.

But the distance from Kent to Wales had seemed to stretch the now-fragile thread that bound them almost to breaking point. He waved an arm at the hazy figure behind the car window. He couldn't see her features clearly.

As Catherine opened the door, Arnaud hesitated, unsure.

She climbed out and turned towards him, a smile lighting up her whole face.

# 24

# THOSE WERE THE DAYS

"Noah, are you coming?"

For a few seconds, Noah couldn't think who was calling him and where they wanted him to go.

"Noah!"

The voice got louder. He blinked his eyes open. He had fallen asleep on the couch in the living room.

"Noah? There you are! Are you coming?"

It all came back to him - Friday forage. He stretched his arms and a pungent waft of sweat mingled with horse smell reached his nostrils. He'd meant to have a shower, but never made it that far.

"Yes, hang on a sec." He reached down to put his boots on and realised they were still on his feet. He must have crashed out the minute he sat down. No surprise, the farm had been running at full tilt for days now, and he was pretty bushed.

From the doorway, Justin grinned at him, saying, "You look like I feel mate."

Noah noticed that Justin was still wearing his riding clothes too; faded green jodhpurs, an old cropped turquoise T-shirt and dusty boots.

Groaning, he dragged himself off the sofa and

followed Justin through the hall and into the kitchen. Min was standing talking to Goff and Caitlin. On the old kitchen table was a pile of plastic bags and a few pairs of scissors.

Min was organised. "We're just waiting for Lily - here she is."

Lily, still rubbing at her wet hair with a towel, emerged from the stairwell. The smell of coconut invaded the room with her entrance. At least somebody had made it to the shower, thought Noah. It wasn't quite enough to cover the ripe aroma coming from the other trek leaders in the kitchen.

"What are we foraging for this evening Min?" Goff had at least slung some clean clothes on, and by the smell of it, a generous spray of deodorant. His T-shirt sported a purple and yellow dragon flying past a creepy old house. Noah never ceased to marvel at his endless supply of clothing featuring dragons, skulls, the grim reaper…you name it. Nearly all of them seemed incongruous with the mild-mannered, jovial trek leader.

"Elderflowers."

"Elderflowers. And they would be what…?"

"You'll see," Min told Goff.

She handed out the bags and scissors and opened the back door of the kitchen, onto the decking. The intoxicating evening scents of June hit them. Noah followed her out and breathed in wild marjoram and lily of the valley mingled with the sweet undertones of the wild honeysuckle rambling over the hedge beyond the decking. Insects buzzed lazily in the balmy early evening air, which was still as warm as the day.

Lily gave her long black hair a final rub and tossed the towel onto a patio chair as she trotted down the steps behind Noah. Still struggling to wake up properly, he was amazed by her energy. He followed the others taking the path at the bottom of their garden that wound into the woodland. A few clumps of foxgloves were starting to flower on the edge of the track, a tiny scattering of pink dots on each stem. As they moved deeper into the forest, the stillness grew, interrupted occasionally by the rustling of a bird, searching for grubs in the dead pine needles. The group walked in silence, as if overcome by some deep enchantment. Somewhere above, a kite began peeping.

The track wound through a patch of brambles, where hard green blackberries were already appearing on the spiky undergrowth. Then, turning a corner, the path spilled them out onto the edge of a field. In the far corner, a herd of black and white Friesian cows drowsed, lazily chewing and flicking their tails. They couldn't be bothered to come over and investigate the cluster of humans walking along the far hawthorn hedge.

Min stopped. Behind her, Goff came to a halt, towering over her tiny figure.

"This, Goff, is an elderflower." She pointed to a creamy lace blossom, which on closer inspection was made up of a profusion of miniscule flowers on a delicate green stalk that spread out like a spider's web. She pulled out her scissors and cut the flower off the stem, releasing a shower of yellow pollen into the air. The potent scent drifted over the group, causing Justin to sneeze as the fine powder wafted up his nose.

"You can either use the flowers to make a cordial or coat them in batter and deep fry them," Min explained.

Lily rolled her eyes. "I looooove elderflower cordial. I'd never seen what it was made from before."

"How do you deep fry them?" Noah was curious.

"I pinched this idea from Nigel Slater," Min admitted. "You make a batter with flour, oil, fizzy water and an egg white. His recipe suggested eating them with gooseberry fool, so I tried it out and it tasted gorgeous."

It sounded good to Noah.

They spread out along the hedgerow, which at this point was composed almost entirely of elder trees. At Min's instructions, they snipped off the fully formed, pollen-covered blossoms, leaving the less mature flowers.

"We can come back and pick the elderberries in a couple of months," Min commented. "Joseph makes a pretty decent elderberry wine. I'm sure he'll be happy to exchange a pint of beer for a bag of elderberries."

Noah spotted a low tree, heaving with the creamy white blossoms. He kicked a few nettles out of his way and snipped off the flower heads, dropped them into the plastic bag at his feet. Soon his scissors, hand and arm were covered with a dusting of yellow.

"Alright mate?" Justin appeared next to him.

"Cool," Noah responded. He was in his element.

"Not really my kind of thing, this flower picking stuff," Justin confided in a low voice. "All the same, we need to keep the chief cake baker onside, don't we?"

*Do we?* Noah thought. *You don't have to mate, honestly you don't,* he wanted to say. He just grunted instead.

Laughter rose into the air. Noah looked up. Goff was shaking an elderflower over Caitlin's head. She was giggling and trying to bat him off, but Goff persisted until Caitlin's hair looked more yellow than white.

It was good to see Caitlin looking more relaxed. For days after her encounter with Sebastian, she'd worn a tense, unhappy expression and her eyes were often red, from crying. He smiled, watching the two play-fighting.

Next to him, Justin was staring at them and frowning. Noah wondered why. Something touched his shoulder and made him jump. He turned. Min had come up behind the two lads and placed a hand on each of their shoulders.

"Come on, get picking or we're be here all night." A bulging plastic bag was slung over her arm, snowy white flower heads peeping out of the top.

Noah looked at his - only half full.

The three of them picked flowers together, Min now on her second bag. Noah and Justin raced to fill theirs. It became a frantic competition and soon Lily had come over and joined in.

Laughing Min declared Justin the winner, by a tiny margin.

*Of course, it would be Justin*, Noah found himself thinking, put out. Then, annoyed at himself, he determined to enjoy the moment and not let stupid negative feelings bring him down.


Pollen-dusted, light-headed from the pervasive scent, they laughed away the early summer evening, until finally the growing dusk made it harder to pick out the flowers. They made their way back through the forest, now gloomy and taking on a slightly eerie quality.

"What do you do with them next?" Lily was curious.

"Make some sugar water, add a sliced orange and a lemon plus some citric acid and soak the flowers in it for a day or so. Then you just strain and bottle the juice - it's that easy. I want to make gallons of the stuff - it freezes really well."

Noah followed at the tail end of the group, his fatigue returning with a vengeance. He stumbled over a stump and nearly fell. His bed was calling him. Again.

The days seemed to blur into each other. An endless succession of waking, rounding up horses, tacking up, riding out, returning and falling back into bed. The children's names all merged into one in Noah's head: LucyElizabethJuliaMalcolmJohnSarahPeterDavid…

*My life is like one of those old fashioned moving picture lanterns that goes round and round and projects a film onto the wall*, wrote Noah in his diary. *It's the little things that give pleasure, the moments of beauty that enhance our days*, he scribbled on another page. *A purple-topped thistle, batted by the breeze, the scent of wild garlic from the roadside, a wild foal, scrabbling after its mother on the mountain top.*

Noah found himself surrounded by inspiration. Every day there were a thousand new things to look at in the hedgerows, the fields, on the mountains. Each morning, the canvas was repainted with subtle differences. And riding through the countryside on horseback, he had the leisure to see them.

He felt like a sponge, absorbing so many sights, sounds and smells. He never wanted it to come to an end, marvelling at how much of his life he had spent walking past things and not really seeing them.

*Wherever I go in life, I will remember this time as a gift*, he thought.

In the evenings, the day's experiences were revisited around the fire pit, embellished with the retelling, stories floating into the air, mingling with the crackling sparks from the pine logs. Arnaud came upon them one evening, finding a glow of disembodied faces, highlighted by the flames. It struck him how each person had changed. All of them had grown in confidence, sitting easily in the saddle, at one with their horses. Each one of them had faced challenges and grown as a result. But more than that, they seemed brighter, fuller people. Arnaud believed it was the way of life at the farm that was behind the changes. The fresh air, natural rhythm of existence, hard manual work and the proximity to the horses and the natural world.

*This is how we were meant to live*, Arnaud believed it at his very core. *If there was an Eden, it must have been something like this.*

The warm, sunny days rolled on until one day, it occurred to Noah that it hadn't rained for an awfully long time. Some of the mountain streams that splashed their way down to the pastures below, were now just a shallow trickle. The rust-coloured earth was baked hard and everybody returned from a trek coated in red dust. It got into their nostrils, their ears, their hair. In the shower, the water ran red.

The dark green bracken began to brown and shrivel and the grass in the horses' field was short and dry - no longer able to support the herd. One day, Rhys's tractor appeared in the yard, towing a trailer full of huge black plastic covered balls of silage. Noah re-learned the skill he had acquired in winter of balancing on the jolting trailer as it tracked downhill, tearing off chunks of the sickly-sweet smelling fermented hay to feed the hungry ponies.

Lulled into a hazy dream by the weather, the fog caught them completely by surprise. In hindsight, Arnaud kicked himself for not looking at the Met Office forecast properly. As the endless days of sunshine marched on, he'd given the detailed daily report less and less scrutiny.

For once, Noah had left the farm first. He'd been assigned a trek of experienced riders and they'd managed to tack up their horses in record time. When he walked over to his group of ponies after breakfast he was astonished. Seven riders stood next to their immaculately turned-out mounts. Noah's trek was away before most of the other groups were even halfway through tacking up. Once past the cattle grid and onto the mountain, he decided to let the ponies have a run while they were still fresh.

He turned in his saddle. "Everyone okay for a canter?"

The ponies jiggled and tossed their heads. They knew what that meant. Mouse was wound up like a spring and Noah could barely restrain him. His hands were white where they gripped the reins. Then, Noah released the dark grey pony and he was off, hooves drumming on the turf. After a few hundred metres or so, Noah gently pulled him back, slowing him so that the rest of the trek could keep up. Mouse responded, and lifting his legs higher, danced along the rest of the path.

Noah slackened the pace still further, then drew Mouse to a halt as the track reached the foot of the mountain and branched to either side. He glanced back onto the common stretching out behind them. The other treks hadn't even made it onto the mountain yet. He looked at his watch. He had plenty of time to kill before they were due at the waterslide picnic spot for lunch, so he decided to take his group up onto a higher mountain path.

He wouldn't have risked this route with a less experienced trek, as the pathway was narrow and at some points there was quite a steep drop off to their left down the mountainside. This was day four of this particular school and, he noted with satisfaction, the children were confident and competent, familiar with their ponies and their surroundings.

What Noah failed to notice were the brooding grey clouds above them, already covering the tip of the mountain ridge.

The fun started when Badger's rider, Ella, needed a pit stop.

"Do we need to halt right now?" Noah shouted back, trying to phrase his words tactfully.

Helen, the teacher, consulted with Ella, and shouted back an emphatic, "Yes we do".

Noah examined the ground on his left, which shelved away steeply. To his right, the rock face was sheer. No room for manoeuvre. He thought for a moment, then got off Mouse and looped his reins over a small bush sticking out of the rock face. Then, scrambling downhill off the track, he worked his way past the ponies towards the back of the trek. The black and white pony's rider was wriggling nervously, looking anxious.

Noah approached her, his best calming expression on his face. "Okay, here's what we're gonna do Ella. I'll get you off Badger, and you can make your way right to the back behind Helen - Mrs Scott. Okay?"

The girl nodded.

"Swing your leg over his back, and I'll stand here to make sure you don't fall down the slope."

She did so, nearly kicking Noah in the face. He blocked her bodily as she slid off the horse, preventing her from any further downward movement. She was small and athletic, with a shock of brown curly hair and a face red with embarrassment. Noah shouted to the rest of the trek.

"Right, I want everyone looking forwards please. Any backward glances and Mrs Scott will deal with you."

And then, more softly to Ella, "Slip past Mrs Scott.

You'll have to pee in the track, behind that boulder. At least nobody downhill of us will be able to see you. I'll make sure no-one in our trek looks back."

The girl nodded and clambered round Prezel, the teacher's mount. Helen smiled encouragingly at her and reiterated Noah's warning of no looking back to the other children in the trek. Five minutes later, Ella and Noah were back in the saddle with no incidents. Noah breathed a sigh of relief and started off. Ahead of him, he could now see a large dense cloud rolling down the side of the mountain.

"Cripes," he spoke aloud. He'd never seen anything like it on the mountains before. A glance in front of the trek showed him that there was no easy way down to the left. They would have to keep going forwards for the time being until he could find a track leading them back down.

"Have you seen that cloud Noah?" Helen shouted anxiously from the back of the trek.

"Yes, there's not much I can do at the moment. We can't turn around and it's too steep to walk the ponies straight down from here. We'll have to go forward for a while and stick to the track. As soon as I can come down, I will do."

"Okay Noah." Helen sounded confident in him. Just as well somebody was, Noah thought, his own confidence in himself was sadly lacking.

The air grew chilly and Noah started shivering. He wasn't sure if it was from the lack of sunshine or anxiety. A huge flock of butterflies had taken up residence in his stomach. Noah bit his lip and gave himself a stern talking to. He kicked Mouse into a brisk walk. Impossible to go any faster as the track was narrow and tricky for the horses to negotiate. As they moved off, the cloud swirled around them and the whole trek was plunged into the mist. Droplets of moisture began forming on Noah's face, dripping from his nose.

He turned to the rider behind him.

"Make sure you keep in sight of the horse in front of you. If you can't see them, shout so we can wait for you. Pass it back."

The boy twisted in his saddle and repeated the message, more or less accurately, to the rider behind. Noah hoped it didn't get too garbled on its way to the back of the trek. He wiped his face and peered through the mist. He could just about see the path in front of him. Mouse moved forward confidently, picking his way delicately along. The pony seemed completely unfazed.

By the time he saw the first downhill fork, the fog had dampened his light summer clothes and Noah was really cold. He hoped the kids were okay. None of them had brought any waterproof coats.

Noah turned Mouse's head to the left, squeezed his right leg and the grey pony began to walk down the track. He turned in his saddle and repeated his earlier warning to keep together.

It felt eerie, riding along with absolutely no idea of where they were. Noah's only point of reference was the slope of the mountain, but even that could be deceptive, as there were so many gullies and banks around. At one point, the path they were following veered to the right and started to climb the mountain again. Noah was aware he had to be careful not to end up taking the route which led into an area of swampy ground, where a spring bubbled up and created a marshland. He'd almost got stuck there once before. Mouse snorted and shook his head, droplets of water flying from his mane. The horse was still striding forward confidently. Noah remembered something Caitlin had told them - how the older lead horses knew the mountains far better than the trek leaders. An idea came to him. It was a long shot, but hopefully worth it.

"Come on old boy," he reached forward and patted Mouse's neck. "Take us home."

Then Noah loosened his reins, while keeping his feet squeezed on Mouse's sides. He hoped Mouse would interpret the command as 'keep moving forwards but you decide where to go.' Mouse hesitated, then continued on. Soon, another track to the left veered out of the mist and Mouse stepped onto it. Noah turned round, and made the riders in his trek count themselves behind him, so he could make sure everyone was together. The kids were quiet, scared.

A gorse bush suddenly loomed out of the mist, and Noah caught his leg on it, losing his stirrup. It scratched his leg through his jodphurs. He managed to slip his foot back into his stirrup just as the track forked in front of him. Again, Mouse took the left hand fork and soon the track began to steepen downhill.

"Lean back kids," he shouted, feeling more confident.

As they splashed through a stream, Mouse lifted his head again and whinnied. An answering whinny from downhill. Mouse gathered speed.

"Whoa boy, not too fast," Noah checked him. And then, just like that, they emerged from the mist into daylight. Noah looked around to get his bearings. To the left, the mountain road snaked around a field of sheep. It was a familiar sight to Noah. The waterslide was about half a mile in front of them. Behind him, the riders emerged from the mist one by one. Finally, Helen at the back appeared, shouting forwards, "Well done Noah!"

To their right, the cloud hung onto the edge of the mountain. Noah oriented the trek further downwards, heading for the road.

A whinny from behind. He turned and saw Goff on Jester leading his trek along the lowest track, next to the dry stone wall that marked the boundary of the mountain common land. Noah's group was parallel with his, twenty metres higher up the slope.

"Are you guys okay?" Goff shouted, anxious.

"Yeah, Mouse got us down through the mist. I gave him his head and he knew where to go."

Goff whistled. "Clever horse."

"Is everyone else okay? No-one else went higher?"

"No, I was the next trek out, but we were ages behind you and by the time we got to the common we could see the mist coming down, so we stuck to the track here. I could see the fog dropping down onto your trek. Flipping heck Noah, no-one expected that."

"As you always say Goff, the horses know best," Noah gave him a thumbs-up.

He put a hand on the back of his saddle and faced the trek behind him.

"Okay guys, well done for keeping up with each other and communicating. Golden Monkey points all round. Okay, let's go and get some lunch." He set off for the waterslide and food.

## 25

## NOAH SAVES THE DAY

Noah pulled the last of the spare headcollars off the corral post and looked at his watch. Eight o'clock. They'd done well. All the ponies were caught and tied up. Time for a well-earned breakfast. Across the farmyard, Justin and Goff were rinsing off the last couple of feed buckets. Noah was starving and decided to head straight for the dining hall and put the headcollars away after he'd eaten. From the corral, it was quicker to take the side door into the games room and then through the arched doorway into the refectory. Noah tested the door. It was unlocked so he pushed it open.

Voices drifted to him from the far end of the dining hall. Caitlin and Min. Noah had been glad to see the two girls getting on better. Caitlin had made a determined effort to win Min over, and the Welsh girl had responded to her overtures of friendship. As he walked towards the archway into the refectory, Noah caught a snatch of conversation.

"...glad to see you've put Sebastian behind you."

"I can't believe I was so stupid about him. I don't know, I guess he was different from the other guys I'd met. Anyhow..."

Noah hesitated. He didn't want to walk in on the middle of a girls' heart to heart. He wondered about retracing his steps and then decided against it. He was desperate for food. As he walked through the archway, the words hit him like bullets.

"So, when are you two going to get together? You've been dancing around each other for ages." It was Caitlin, asking Min.

Flustered, Noah dropped the headcollars with a crash. His stomach lurched. Min and Justin. It was going to happen.

Min reddened as she saw Noah, and Caitlin laughed, saying, "Talk of the devil, Noah."

Just then, Goff and Lily barged into the dining room.

"Food, food, food, need food!" Lily shouted.

"I'm first in line." Caitlin threw back, her conversation with Min forgotten.

Noah picked up the headcollars and shuffled forwards, eyes down. *Just act normal*, he told himself. *Don't let it get to you. Easier said than done. Justin and Min, Justin and Min...* The words drummed around his head.

He slung the headcollars over the back of a chair and grabbed a plate of food from the counter, eyes averted, not wanting to look up at Min. The forkful of bacon tasted like cardboard in his mouth. He forced himself to chew. The others were immersed in discussions about the day ahead, not noticing his silence. Only Min gave him a worried look from behind the counter where she was dishing out the last of the scrambled egg onto her own plate. She sighed and wondered if all men were so obtuse when it came to matters of the heart.

In the farmhouse kitchen, Sebastian was immersed in a

pile of paperwork, and didn't hear his mobile at first. It was Catherine who prompted him to answer it. She listened to the one-sided conversation.

"Hello, yes, yes, it is…. oh…sorry to hear that…that's no problem, we'll just readjust the schedule a bit…okay see you then…goodbye."

He hung up, grimacing. "Hmm, not a very auspicious start. That was Carol calling about the Bedenham Lodge group. There was a 'slight incident' with one of the children and they're going to be a couple of hours late." He added, "It might be worth getting the guys to give the ponies some water - it's quite hot already and they're going to be standing around for another hour or so."

"Good thinking. I'll go and tell them while you finish that off." Catherine stood up. She and Sebastian had been sitting at the kitchen table, sorting out insurance renewal documents for the farm. Sebastian was due to begin work in London the next week and he was anxious to help out as much as possible before he left.

She scratched an angry red horsefly bite on her arm, hesitating.

"I'm still not sure about this week…" her voice trailed away.

"I think it will be just fine. We've got all the bases covered. I'm quite excited about it."

"Yes, and I know Arnaud is too. I can't help thinking of all the things that can go wrong."

"And some of them might happen, Catherine. But we'll get through."

She wrinkled her nose, commenting, "Well, there's no going back now."

The sun-drenched yard was already hot, even though it

was only eight thirty. Catherine looked around and seeing nobody, decided the trek leaders must all be in the dining room. By the time she had crossed the baked earth quadrangle, she was glad of the cool shade in the dining hall. Arnaud was sitting with the leaders, giving them a final briefing. She stood in the doorway, waiting until he'd finished.

"Okay, I'll just run through things one last time. Today, we'll all be in the indoor school. You'll be in pairs all week - Noah and Lily, Caitlin and Goff and I'll take a trek with Justin - six children each."

"What's exactly wrong with the kids?"

"*Wrong* isn't really the word, Lily." Arnaud was warm, despite his clear correction of Lily, who blushed.

"That's okay Lily, my first reaction was just the same," he reassured her. "I guess that's what these kids must come up against all the time. As far as we understand, they're mainly hyperactive, low attention span. They're all physically capable, but everything is going to have to be explained carefully to them and we'll take as much time as possible getting them used to the ponies. This week is about the kids enjoying themselves and gaining confidence and if that means we don't get onto the mountains until day three, that's fine."

"It's something a bit different for us, it should be interesting," Goff commented.

Catherine was relieved to see that the trek leaders were viewing the week positively. She walked over to the table and everybody turned towards her.

"Sebastian's just heard from Carol - the supervisor - they're running a couple of hours late. He thought the ponies might want water if they're going to be standing around in the heat," she told them.

"Yes, more than that, they might want some shade too. Just as well we hadn't tacked them up yet," said Lily.

"We could put them in the indoor school - it might mean a bit of poo picking just before the kids get here, but there's quite a nice breeze through there if you open the doors either end," Goff suggested.

"Good thinking. Better than turning them back out in the field and recatching them," Arnaud answered. "Okay, if you all can take them over to the school and give them water that would be great. Then you may as well take an hour off, but hang around in case the group makes up some time on the road."

The trek leaders made their way out of the dining hall, at a leisurely walk. Catherine sat down in the seat vacated by Caitlin. "So, you're all ready?" she asked Arnaud.

"Bring it on."

Catherine was encouraged by Arnaud's enthusiasm for the project. If it worked, it would take the farm in a whole new direction. It was a risk, but by now everybody had settled into life at the farm and things were running smoothly. More than smoothly, they'd developed into a slick team. And Catherine was amazed at the change in the leaders. They'd all matured somehow. Noah had gradually eased into the job, making fewer and fewer mistakes and Justin's timekeeping was getting better. The group dynamics were excellent - and to Catherine's surprise, even Caitlin seemed a changed person, joking with Noah and somehow less edgy. They were a different set of people from the ones she and Arnaud had interviewed four months previously.

It was Glen the blacksmith who had first proposed the idea to Arnaud. He knew how much they were struggling financially. "My cousin works for Hereford council. I don't know exactly what her job title is, but she's responsible for sourcing activities for specialist care groups - special needs kids, PTSD military groups and so on. She's been let down by an activity centre and asked me if I knew if any of the local pony trekking centres would be willing to help out."

To Arnaud, it had seemed like an answer from heaven. Catherine had been frantically trying to fill their empty time slots for the year with no success. They'd managed to counteract most the cruel rumours that Emily's friend, Laura, had been putting around, aided by a few excellent reviews from their first few schools, but her actions had left them with a few gaps in their calendar.

Arnaud was convinced this was the perfect opportunity to extend the farm's activity range into other areas. He wasn't sure how Sebastian would react, but his suggestion had been met with enthusiasm.

"It will give us the income boost we need and to be honest Arnaud, having just spent a few weeks recuperating here, it would be great to see more people really benefit from this place."

Glen's cousin, Carol, had arranged the first group. If the week went well, the council would look at scheduling in others.

By the time Arnaud and Catherine wandered out into the sunshine, the trek leaders had moved the ponies and were lazing on a stack of hay bales in the corner of the yard. Catherine spotted Sebastian limping towards the top paddock with a pail of kitchen scraps for the sheep and llamas. His leg had mended well and he he'd gratefully cast off his crutches a couple of weeks previously. He'd got to know the occupants of the top paddock well during his convalescence and had even become quite proficient at milking the sheep. Arnaud had been amused to see the change in his friend. He could never have imagined the pre-accident Sebastian ever offering to milk the little herd. With any luck, Arnaud thought, the other farm animals could also play a role in the development of the centre. In his mind, he was already increasing the livestock and planning how they could be used for the special needs groups. Then he reined himself in. *First things first*, he thought. *Let's get through today...*

Noah hadn't really considered what to expect from the new group. If pushed, he'd have said he was looking forward to a change of routine. The first day would be spent in the indoor school, getting the children used to the ponies and teaching them the first steps of riding. It was a long way from their usual short demo for experienced riders and one- or two-hour session in the school for non-riders. Arnaud had asked the trek leaders to come up with a plan for the day, to make it more interesting for the group.

They'd decided to spend the morning concentrating on the basics - mounting, dismounting, how to sit in the saddle, walk and various exercises such as 'round the world'. Lily had explained that was an exercise used for teaching younger kids which involved getting them to sit in the saddle and move their body around to sit sideways, backwards, sideways on the other side and then back to the front again.

For the afternoon, assuming the pupils had mastered the basics, they'd move on to a few team games - a running race leading their pony, riding the ponies in and out of a line of cones and a few others. On paper, it had looked good. But it quickly became apparent they wouldn't be moving onto the team games any time soon.

As soon as the coach had discharged the group of children, the trek leaders sprang into action with practised smoothness. Arnaud did the general introduction, double checked the children's riding abilities and then, while they all had a quick tea break, scanned his original trek and pony list to make sure he'd paired the right rider with the right pony. They'd selected their quietest ponies for the week, but Arnaud was aware that if they continued down the route of special needs groups, they'd need to invest in a few more bomb-proof ponies. Two or three of the current mounts might prove a bit lively. He hadn't mentioned that to Catherine.

Arnaud handed out his revised lists to the trek leaders, who shunted a few of the ponies around - they were tied up in their groups in the four corners of the indoor school. Goff and Justin grabbed a barrow and two spades and swiftly dispatched the mounds of dung that had appeared in the school. Noah and Lily led their group to the far corner.

The children were excited, looking all around the building, chattering and pointing wildly. Noah hadn't anticipated the amount of questions that would come flying at them. He tried to begin their planned talk, only to be constantly thwarted by interruptions.

"Sir, what's that pony's name?"

"Noah, I'm Noah. You don't have to call me sir."

"Sir, which one am I riding?"

"Noah, I'm Noah. We'll get to that in a minute."

"Sir - Noah" (the kids all laughed at that and from that moment on he was Sir Noah).

"I need the loo."

"Okay, that's fine, there's a toilet outside by the barn."

"Where's that?"

"Just outside that door," Noah pointed.

"I'm not sure…"

"I'll take you," Lily said hurriedly to the lanky girl with blonde frizzy hair, seeing Noah's patience already wearing thin. She disappeared off, leaving him with five restless souls. One of them, a short boy with freckles and carroty red hair, started wandering off towards Goff's group.

"Come back here, what are you doing?" Noah tried to keep his cool.

"My friend's over there. I want to swap groups."

"Well you can't, they're all sorted."

The boy looked like he was going to cry.

Glancing around the barn, Noah could see the other trek leaders facing a similar battle. Even Caitlin and Goff seemed to be struggling. The children were far more interested in Goff's tattoos and haircut than listening to Caitlin.

Lily reappeared without the frizzy-haired girl. She walked up to Noah and whispered, "She's scared and doesn't want to ride. I left her helping Min in the kitchen."

*Oh well*, thought Noah, *one less to worry about.*

Then he had an idea. He hadn't needed to pull this one out of the hat for a week or so.

"Right, listen up guys. I'm operating a system of Monkey Points with this trek. I don't do it with every trek, just a privileged few. This is how it works…"

By lunchtime, the other leaders and Arnaud were at their wits' end. They'd all managed to get their pupils mounted and going through some exercises, but the ponies were being pulled around and one or two of them had begun nipping at each other in annoyance. Only Noah and Lily seemed to be making progress. Their group was noticeably quieter than the others and by the end of the session, they were even walking round in a little circle on their ponies, even if it was a bit stop-start.

Arnaud sat with the trek leaders as they ate their sandwiches. For once, he wasn't his usual calm, positive self. He spoke quietly to them. "I'm really am sorry for landing you with this. I'm not sure how we're going to get through the week. I think we're just going to have to grit our teeth and take it slowly. I wasn't expecting it to be this challenging."

Then he turned to Noah and Lily, saying, "I don't know what magic you two have, but you seemed to have cracked it. Do you mind giving us a heads up?"

Lily looked at Noah. He didn't want to appear cocky and nodded at her to let her do the talking.

"It's Noah's Monkey Points system, it's brilliant."

"Monkey Points...?"

Noah explained, recounting how the Monkey Point system had saved the day with his all-boy trek. Arnaud was chagrined. He'd had no inkling that he'd given Noah such a difficult week. He was impressed with the boy's resourcefulness.

"It's worth a go," Arnaud nodded. "But I don't want you guys to be out of pocket, the farm will fund the rewards."

The trek leaders were silently relieved. It could have proved an expensive week.

Armed and dangerous, the leaders went out to meet their treks in the afternoon with renewed vigour. By the end of the afternoon, Noah was a hero in everybody's eyes. His Monkey Point system was working brilliantly.

Catherine was upstairs doing the edits to her first draft when she heard the crunch of tyres on the gravel outside the farmhouse. She looked out of the window and spotted Sebastian, dressed in a smart business suit, climbing out of his Subaru. She hadn't even noticed him leave the farm. Curious - and thankful for the excuse of a break - she came downstairs and walked into the kitchen as he opened the front door.

"Sebastian, fancy a tea? I was just going to put the kettle on."

She noticed that he looked rather pleased with himself. At first glance, she wondered if he'd sneaked out for a difficult meeting with the bank manager. She wouldn't have put it past Sebastian to have tried to take the flack himself, rather than let it fall on her or Arnaud. His demeanor suggested otherwise.

"That would be great, thanks. I'll just go upstairs and change." He was giving away nothing. By the time Sebastian had reappeared, Catherine was intensely curious.

"Been on a hot date, have you?" Even as the words were out of her mouth, she remembered the Caitlin scenario. Sebastian had told Arnaud and Catherine about his brief conversation with the girl. All three of them had expected fireworks, or the hurried exit of Caitlin. True, she hadn't gone out of her way to speak to Sebastian since the exchange, but she hadn't disappeared from the farm either.

"You could say that," Sebastian's words jerked her out of her reverie. Fortunately, he hadn't taken her comment awry. In fact, he seemed to be enjoying keeping her in suspense. Catherine resorted to plain talking.

"Come on, out with it. What have you been up to?"

"I have just landed myself a job." He said the words with pride.

"A new job? What about London?"

"I called my old office half an hour ago and told them I wouldn't be coming back after all. I don't know who was more glad - my boss - or me."

"What are you going to be doing?"

Sebastian sat down, grinning broadly. He leaned back in the kitchen chair, arms behind his head.

"It's consultancy work, in Hereford. When Glen's cousin Carol was talking to us about the special needs work, she mentioned a local company that was in need of a financial director and wondered if I'd be interested. I popped over to see them and I start next week."

"That's fantastic news! And I'm so glad it's local. If I'm honest, I was dreading the thought of you returning to London - for you as much as for us. It didn't seem to be right somehow."

"The best news," Sebastian added, "is that it's four days a week, and I can work from home for a couple of those. Plus...it's pretty decent money. More than I was expecting, I have to admit."

Catherine's face lit up.

"We're not out of the woods yet," Sebastian cautioned. "There's a hell of a big hole in our finances to plug. But at least it's progress."

"We should celebrate, open a bottle of wine this evening. Actually, Arnaud might appreciate the wine, I think they've had a pretty hideous morning. This special needs lark is proving quite a challenge," she told him.

But when Arnaud turned up at the farmhouse at the

end of the afternoon he was jubilant and explained how Noah had saved the day.

By the afternoon of day two, they'd managed a short trek onto the mountains, even though another girl had refused to ride that morning. Min found herself with two helpers in the kitchen, and both girls seemed to be enjoying themselves enormously. She was even planning to take them on a foraging trip that afternoon with Catherine as back up in case of trouble. If only the rest of the week had continued in the same way, they would have been celebrating big time in the Wily Wolf on Friday evening. But no-one could have anticipated what happened next.

As Noah headed the trek onto the common on the Wednesday afternoon, he spotted a glider wheeling backwards and forwards over the mountain range above, using the thermals for lift. They could stay up there for hours, Noah knew. He'd watched them often enough as he rode along the foothills. Lily was bringing up the rear. Noah decided the kids were doing so well, they could even venture a trot. After a quick consultation with Lily and the group, to check everyone was happy, he quickened the pace, heading for the top corner of the common and the trail leading to the waterslide.

Noah, who was focused on keeping the trek in line and making sure everybody was comfortable with the trot, didn't notice the glider take a sudden dip downwards. He eased Mouse back to a walk at the end of the common, and prepared to turn left alongside a line of hawthorn trees. In front of him a little mountain stream flowed down across the track. He kept Mouse's pace slow, so that none of the ponies would be tempted to jump it. He was determined to have a zero fall rate this week. Behind the trek, the glider turned and made a return sweep, sinking lower all the time.

It was Caitlin who spotted the red and white aircraft, lurching unsteadily in the sky. Her ponies were snaking their way across the middle of the common, following a well-trodden path.

"Goff, look!" She pointed at the glider as it sank rapidly and veered down towards them.

There was nothing anybody could do. The glider made a sudden turn and came into land on the common, alongside the trek, causing the ponies to scatter in all directions in sheer panic. After a short tussle, Goff managed to get Jester under control and looked around him. The ponies were gradually slowing to a halt and amazingly, it looked like none of the children was hurt. A couple had slipped off their ponies, but they were standing upright with no sign of injury. Goff breathed a sigh of relief and prepared to regroup them. Then he heard Caitlin's scream.

"Okay, if you're still on your pony, get off, stand still and hold it tight," he yelled at the kids. Without checking to see if they'd obeyed his instructions, he kicked Jester into a canter and then a gallop. Caitlin's cry had come from in front of him, but he couldn't see her. Suddenly the ground fell away from him and he wrenched Jester's head around, just preventing the horse from crashing into a huge ditch. A clump of bracken had obscured it from view.

At the bottom of the ditch, Caitlin was crouched next to Calico's head. The beautiful, cream-coloured palomino was lying on the ground, with its legs at an impossible angle, horribly still. Its eyes were open, staring at nothing.

The horse was dead. Caitlin shaking uncontrollably. Goff jumped off Jester and dropped the horse's reins. He slid down the bank to join Caitlin.

"Caitlin. Are you okay? Have you hurt yourself?"

She was shivering, her gaze fixed on the horse. It was as if Goff didn't exist. He took hold of her shoulders.

"Caitlin, Caitlin listen to me. Are you all right?"

"I'm okay, I think," she managed to stutter. "It's Calico, she's dead, isn't she?"

Goff stood cradling the shaking girl in his arms, shocked at the sight of the palomino mare in the ditch next to them.

He stood there for a few minutes, holding Caitlin.

Then he spoke, "I'm going to need you to be brave for a short while Caitlin. I'm going to go back up and keep the kids away. Can you manage to stay here for a few minutes? I'll phone Arnaud and see if Noah and Lily can take over our trek - they were just across the common from us. They must have seen what happened."

He wasn't sure how much Caitlin took in, but she nodded and slumped down in the bracken, hands over her face.

Goff climbed back out of the ditch and scanned the common. His riders were all standing by their ponies as they had been told to do, and Noah was cantering over toward them, having left Lily in charge of their trek.

Goff walked unsteadily back to Jester and reached in the saddlebag for his mobile. He tried hard to stop his hands shaking, as he dialled Arnaud's number.

# 26

## A TIME TO MOURN

Catherine walked along the farm track towards the trek leaders' cottage. On her left, a wave of chatter and clattering of plates came from the dining hall. The excited babble contrasted strongly with the dull silence in her head. Her feet felt heavy, dragging in the dust of the track. The trees and foliage around her looked dried out and wrinkled, aged before their time by the relentless sun.

She followed the little path to the rear of the cottage. It had been a while since she'd been over here and she was amazed at the changes. On the verandah, a silver wind chime tinkled in the faint breeze. The decking had been painted white and chairs made from pallets and other bits of wood were scattered around, covered with brightly-coloured crochet blankets. She climbed up the verandah steps towards the back door. Inside the cottage, the heat was stifling. She trod softly along the corridor and began walking up the stairs, holding onto the banister for support. On the top floor, she stopped and listened before gently tapping on the left-hand door. A pause and then a faint response, hardly audible.

"Come in."

She turned the wooden handle and eased the door

open. Inside Caitlin's room, the floor was a jumble of clothes. The immaculately turned out Caitlin wasn't so neat when it came to her room it seemed. On the bed, Caitlin was sitting hunched up, leaning against the wall. Her red eyes contrasted with the pallor of her face.

She looked up at Catherine. "I'm so sorry," her eyes filled with tears, which began to run down her cheeks. She didn't bother to wipe them away.

"Caitlin, *I'm* sorry. What an awful thing to happen."

She noticed a chair next to the bed. It was covered with clothes.

"May I?" she gestured towards the chair.

"Yes."

Catherine moved the clothes off, placing them carefully on the floor and sat down. She said nothing for a few minutes.

"How are all the kids?" Caitlin ventured.

"They're fine Caitlin. Right now, I'm concerned about you."

"But isn't the group going to leave? The kids must have been so upset? I've just messed up everything."

"Not at all. Unbelievably, none of the children saw what happened to Calico. You were hidden in the ditch and they were all too concerned with trying to stay on their ponies when the accident happened. Once Arnaud arrived, he asked them all if they wanted to continue and they said yes. He told them that Calico had been a bit hurt and you were staying with him. I know that wasn't true but we needed to keep them calm. Noah and Lily merged your trek with theirs. The other trek leaders and staff have all agreed to try and act as normal as possible. I think it's fine. The children are now telling the others about their brush with the glider. They have absolutely no idea what really happened."

"I think Arnaud did try and say something to me when we were on the common."

"You were in shock Caitlin. Of course you couldn't take anything in. To see Calico lying there must have been absolutely hideous."

Catherine could feel her eyes pricking with tears as well. Calico was a beautiful, gentle-natured horse. She hadn't deserved to end her life like that.

"The only saving grace is that Calico would have hardly felt anything," she reassured Caitlin. "She must have died almost instantly."

Caitlin was sobbing now. This was what Catherine wanted. According to Arnaud, Caitlin had been in shock when he had arrived at the scene. Arnaud had stayed with the corpse, waiting for Sebastian to arrive with the horsebox. Min had driven over in the Land Rover to pick up Caitlin and bring her back to the centre. Caitlin hadn't wanted to leave Calico, but Arnaud and Goff had insisted. They didn't want her to see the corpse being manhandled into the horsebox. After handing over his trek to Noah and Lily, Goff had ridden back to the farm, and spent some time with Caitlin. Catherine had been shopping in Hay when the incident happened.

"Where...where is she now? The body I mean." Caitlin's voice was hoarse.

"They took her to the far paddock. Rhys came over with his digger and they buried her immediately. I can show you where, if you want."

"Thank you. Maybe tomorrow..."

Caitlin was silent a while. Then she looked up at Catherine, a stricken expression on her face, "When should I leave? Can I stay until the weekend?"

"What do you mean?"

"You can't want me to stay after this."

Catherine was horrified that Caitlin would even think that way. "Caitlin, none of this was your fault. You couldn't have known what was going to happen. There's no way you could have stopped her from going in the ditch. Goff said he nearly ended up in it too. The whole thing was just a freak accident."

"I loved Calico, Catherine, I would never have done anything to hurt her."

"Of course, I understand. You can't blame yourself. Caitlin, everybody knows you're the best trek leader we have. You're a brilliant rider and you're great at keeping the kids in order. Don't beat yourself up."

"What will happen now?"

"Well for a start, you're having the rest of the week off. I'm happy to work with Goff for a couple of days in your place. I haven't been out riding for ages and actually I'd quite enjoy the chance to join a trek."

She looked at Caitlin's anxious face and said, "It's not a punishment Caitlin. I want you to have a chance to get over this. You need to be kind to yourself."

"That's so good of you. I can't believe…"

"It's what anyone would do Caitlin."

"I'm not so sure. At the polo stables I last worked at, I would have been out on my ear."

"Well we're not like that here. But the point is, are you still happy to continue? We don't want to force you to stay either."

"Yes, yes please."

"See how you go. Arnaud has an offer for you. He's been worried that Baloo isn't getting enough exercise. Would you like to use him as your new lead horse?"

"Baloo? I can't believe it."

Catherine wondered at the life Caitlin must have led, if a simple act of kindness surprised her so much. She chided herself for having judged Caitlin so harshly.

"Thank you, thank you so much," Caitlin reached out her arms to hug the older woman.

In the dining hall, Noah and the other trek leaders were subdued. After the evening meal, the children dispersed, most of them into the games room. A few hung around in the dorms or in the courtyard. The trek leaders stayed at the table in the dining hall, feeling numb. Min appeared with a tray full of mugs of freshly brewed coffee.

Arnaud came into the hall just as she was putting them down. He pulled out a chair and sat at the end of the table.

"I want to tell you how impressed I am. You've all managed amazingly today. I can't believe it, but the children all seem fine and the teachers are happy to continue here for the rest of the week. They understand accidents like that happen and they were really impressed with how you all handled the incident. I know you'd normally do some activities with the group this evening, but the teachers have offered to step in and give you all the evening off."

"How's Caitlin now?" Goff was anxious.

"Catherine has just seen her. I think she's going to be okay. Obviously, she's shaken up. We've given her the rest of this week off, but she wants to ride out again next week."

The trek leaders looked at each other, relieved.

"I don't know about the others, but I'm happy to carry

on and entertain the children this evening. I think we should do things as normally as possible." Lily spoke into the silence.

"I'm up for it too," Noah volunteered.

"Count me in," Justin chipped in.

"I'm thinking somebody ought to stay with Caitlin if she wants company," Goff ventured.

Min gave him a knowing look and said, "Why don't you pop up there Goff? You were there when the accident happened, so you know best what she's going through. I'm happy to help with the kids in your place."

Goff looked relieved, "Thanks Min."

Arnaud smiled at the group, immensely proud of them. "You don't know how grateful I am, guys."

It was late in the evening by the time Arnaud made it back to the farmhouse. He had stayed with the trek leaders to make sure the evening went off well and there were no residual worries amongst the children. They had arranged a game of tag in the upper field. Arnaud marvelled how they and the schoolchildren had so much energy. He was relieved to walk into the kitchen and pour himself a glass of Sebastian's blackberry wine.

He glanced through into the lounge, where Catherine was curled up on the old blue leather sofa, reading a book.

"Arnaud, you're exhausted. Come and sit down."

He almost staggered into the room, his legs were so tired and his head was spinning. It was a relief to flop into the armchair.

"The end of this week can't come soon enough," he groaned.

"Well, here's something to cheer you up. Sebastian's

had some good news. He's got a new job - and it's local."

Arnaud brightened immediately, and stared at her, eyes glowing.

"Tell all," he said.

# 27

# THE GREEN-EYED MONSTER

As June slipped into July, the scorching hot weather continued. On the mountains, the bracken had frizzled to a crumpled brown mess and there was talk of cutting the treks shorter by half an hour, to help the ponies and schoolchildren, struggling with the heat. They were trying to keep to the cooler rides - through the pine forest and at the lower edge of the mountain, on the tree-lined tracks.

The one word on everybody's lips was 'fire'. All of the activity centres in the area had been briefed not to let their staff use any kind of match or lighter near the mountains, and to keep their eyes peeled for the first signs of smoke. The local fire brigade had been putting up posters in Hay and the other tourist spots, warning people. The dead bracken would catch in seconds, and with the hillside covered in it, a fire could get out of control and spread over the mountains in minutes.

Noah tossed and turned all night, struggling to sleep. He'd left his bedroom window wide open, but the air was completely still and the night was barely cooler than the day. It didn't help that when he did finally drop off, he woke half an hour later, sweating, to find Oscar had climbed onto his bed and was providing an unwelcome hot water bottle service. Noah pushed the dog off, grumbling.

At six o'clock, he gave up and went down to the kitchen for a glass of water. It seemed he wasn't the only one who couldn't sleep. Min was rummaging in the freezer in an attempt to find some ice cubes.

"This is crazy, it's six am and I'm sweltering," she commented, pushing her hair off her face.

Oscar, struggling in the heat with his thick curly black coat, tried to push his face into the freezer. Laughing, Min pulled him away and dug deeper into the drawer. "Aha," she commented, and pulled out a blue plastic tray in triumph.

Noah filled a couple of glasses with water, and Min dropped some ice cubes in each. Then she bent down and popped the rest into Oscar's drinking water. Curious, he nosed the ice cubes around the bowl, caught one in his mouth and crunched on it, a look of surprise on his face.

"That dog," Min said affectionately, rubbing Oscar's head.

The atmosphere between them was slightly awkward. Noah fished for something to say, but Min beat him to it.

"I haven't seen you properly for a while Noah, it's been so busy."

"Yeah crazy," Noah replied.

"How's your writing going?"

"It's good. I finished the short story I was working on. I thought I'd send it off to that competition you told me about."

"That's great," Min looked pleased.

"I was thinking about what you said a while ago..."

Min started a little and coloured. Noah wondered why.

"...you know, about taking my writing more seriously. If that's what I really want to do."

"Oh," she looked slightly taken aback, as if she'd expected to hear something different altogether.

"I'm gonna change my university course - I checked and I've still got time. I've decided to opt for a creative writing degree, instead of just English."

"Fantastic!" Min was thrilled. "Where would you go?"

"Well..." Noah hesitated. "There are a couple of courses I really like. One's up north, but there's another one at Aberystwyth. It's not too far...I mean, I guess I quite like Wales. It would be nice to be near...well, you know, Catherine and Arnaud for one. Well two."

Min seemed pleased, but a little hesitant. Noah couldn't shake off the feeling she was expecting him to say something more. Confused, he babbled on.

"Oh, and I'm going to go to Catherine's talk tonight. The one she's doing for Eve. You know, the one about how to be a writer. Well, tonight she's just going to do a brief introduction, but then she's doing another two more in-depth ones."

"Good, good," Min looked as if she was about to say something else, when a thumping noise broke into the peace of the morning. It was Justin coming down the stairs.

"Morning. Anyone like a cuppa?"

Noah could have groaned with frustration. Why did Justin always have to turn up and spoil the party?

As Arnaud walked into the farmhouse kitchen, Catherine was talking to somebody on her mobile. She turned and pointed at the kettle, which had just boiled, listening intently to the caller, and then responding, "No, no, as I said, I'd been thinking the same thing myself. How funny. Well, okay, I'll let you know. Yes, I'll tell him about Justin - he's hopeless about keeping his phone charged. Okay, bye."

She hung up and studied the phone for a couple of seconds.

Arnaud looked at her, quizzically.

"That was Toby. He's really impressed with Justin's artwork. He wants to come over and see some more. He also said it was about time he visited Noah - and us."

"That's great. He won't believe the change here."

"No, that's for sure." Catherine smiled, confident.

"When's he planning on coming?"

"In the next few days I think. He's been trying to get hold of Noah for a while. To be fair, we've been so busy, I expect Noah has hardly had any time for anything other than eating, sleeping and working."

She picked up the mug of tea that Arnaud had placed on the table. There was plenty of time to let Arnaud know the other reason for Toby's call. She needed to think a while before she broached the subject with him.

Noah's ride wasn't going too well that morning. It all started with a sheep. Trekking would be a whole lot less hassle without the wretched beasts on the mountains, Noah decided. They were always clustering around gates, getting their heads stuck through the square wire fencing that surrounded many of the hillside fields, or dying right in the middle of the tracks. There was also an unwritten code that if you saw a sheep in distress, you did what you could and called the farmer if necessary.

Half an hour into the trek, Noah spotted a good clear

spot on the track for a canter ahead, but the sun was already burning down on them and the ponies were sweating from the steep climb up to the mountainside. He decided to give it a miss for once.

Just then, his attention was caught by movement in the field on his left. A sheep was lying on its back, struggling frantically to get upright. Noah called a halt and jumped off Mouse, asking the teacher, Ray, to keep an eye on the trek. He ran over to the dry stone wall, and climbed over it, snagging his jodhpurs on a strand of barbed wire as he did so. He dashed over to the animal, which was struggling feebly.

Rhys, the neighbouring farmer, had told him, one evening at the pub, that if a sheep rolled over onto its back and couldn't get up again, its digestive process began to create gas which expanded the body cavity and eventually squeezed the life out of the animal. Somehow, the ewe in front of Noah had become wedged between two rocks and couldn't extricate itself. Noah seized the sheep and tried to pull it forward, away from the rocks. The animal's coat was filthy and his hands were soon slippery with sweat. He managed to slide the sheep forwards slightly, but as soon as he let go, it rolled back again. He tried a couple more times, with no success. It was surprisingly heavy.

Ray climbed over and offered to help. Between them, they managed to get the creature out and tried to help it stand up, but every time they released it, the animal collapsed. It was no good. The sheep had lost all strength and they were forced to abandon the mission. Noah and Ray walked back to the trek. Noah pulled the phone out of his saddle bag and called Kestrel Farm, explaining what had happened. Min, who'd answered the phone, agreed to give the farmer a call.

Frustrated, Noah got back on Mouse, regrouped his trek and set off for the waterslide.

As a result of his sheep experience, Noah's trek was the last to arrive and the other leaders were already laughing at some ongoing joke that had obviously been diverting them since they'd arrived. Noah felt slightly out of things. Justin and his teacher Katy, began regaling the other trek leaders with stories of their morning. At Katy's instigation, they'd been teaching the kids a song and, according to Goff, the noise could be heard halfway across the mountain.

Noah didn't feel much like telling everybody about his, potentially now dead, sheep. He felt hot and disgruntled.

On the return journey, his group of riders seemed unusually subdued. Noah decided to take a leaf out of Justin and Katy's book and liven them up with a song.

He twisted round in his saddle, and shouted back, "Okay, listen up, we're gonna do a song. I'll sing a line, then you repeat it, then I sing the next line and so on."

The children looked back at him, saying nothing.

"Here we go, everyone ready?"

Nothing.

"I had a dog called Bingo, Bingo was his name."

Noah tried to make his voice carry, more shouting than singing. The kids made a half-hearted attempt to repeat the line.

"B-I-N-G-O, Bingo was his name."

The attempt was even more pathetic this time.

After a few more tries, Noah gave up. This was the most apathetic bunch of riders he'd ever taken out. Usually the children loved singing and it was a good way of helping the more nervous riders to relax.

Down on the lower path, he could hear Justin's trek making a huge racket, singing and laughing. They all seemed to be having the time of their lives. Noah had got a trek of zombies, it seemed. Could Justin do no wrong, ever, Noah wondered.

By the time Noah got his trek back to the farm, all he wanted to do was wash the grit from his mouth and face and put his feet up. The mountain tracks were dusty and the ponies' hooves seemed to kick up great clouds of dirt wherever they went. It got into everything - eyes, ears, nose, mouth and clothes. He longed for a good rainstorm to clear everything up.

In the barn, he checked Arnaud's duty roster. Typical - his trek was on feed duty that evening. That meant sorting out fifty buckets of food, feeding the ponies, then collecting and washing the buckets up. No respite.

Justin came strolling over to him and clapped him on the back, grinning, "How are you doing Noah, my man? You look tired mate."

"Yeah, it's been a long day." Noah was ashamed of his growing resentment of Justin. The boy had done nothing wrong, he told himself. At least not deliberately.

"Do you want a hand with the feeds?" Justin offered.

Noah swallowed his pride. "That would be brilliant, cheers." He felt even worse.

Justin helped dish out the feeds into the buckets, while Noah supervised the children carrying them up to the waiting ponies. They'd just finished, in record time, and were stacking the now clean bowls when Arnaud materialised into the gloom of the barn.

"Noah, there you are, Catherine's been looking for you. Your dad's been trying to get hold of you. He wants to come up and visit. Oh, and Justin, Toby said how much he liked your artwork."

"Really?" Justin glowed.

"Yes, that's what he told Catherine. I'm sure he's got more to say to you, Noah."

Noah swallowed hard again. He had difficulty getting the words out, "That's great. I'll give him a buzz after supper - I'll let you know what he says as soon as I can."

Jaunty, Justin went off to have a shower.

Arnaud looked at Noah. "Are you okay Noah? You look a bit down?"

"I'm just hot," Noah lied.


After the evening meal, Noah dashed off to phone Toby. As he was nearing the cottage, he realised he'd left his mobile in the dining hall. He swung round and walked back. Approaching the refectory, he heard laughter floating out of the open door. He stopped in his tracks. Then he heard his name.

"Bless him, he looked so funny Min. It was clear the sheep had had it, but he wasn't having any of it."

It was Justin. And by the sounds of it, he'd spotted Noah's episode with the sheep. Clearly, Justin thought the whole episode hilarious.

Min looked stern. "At least Noah tried, Justin. You've got to credit him. I think that was noble."

Noah had already turned in his tracks and didn't hear Min's response. He strode back to the cottage, cheeks burning.

After his shower, Noah made his way to the dining hall to pick up his phone. Nobody was around, apart from a few boys playing pool in the games room. He spotted his mobile on the shelf in the kitchen, where he'd left it earlier when he was helping with the washing up. Toby answered at the first ring and spent the next ten minutes telling Noah what a promising artist Justin was. The usually restrained Toby was enthusiastic. Noah had hardly ever heard him so animated. It wasn't until the end of the call, almost as an aside, that Toby mentioned visiting.

"Yeah dad, that would be great." Noah struggled to sound enthusiastic.

Toby picked up on Noah's tone of voice and misread it completely.

"Well, only if you want me to Noah. I don't want to get in your way."

"No, no Dad it would be really good to see you, honest."

Noah kicked himself. Now he'd managed to offend his dad.

The next morning at breakfast, Noah was feeling decidedly out of sorts. The previous evening, the other trek leaders had decided to pop down to the Wily Wolf for a quick pint. Justin was buzzing with the news that *the* Toby Foster wanted to talk more about *his* artwork when he visited next week. Lily had banged on Noah's door, but he'd pleaded a headache and stayed in. He just hadn't felt like socialising.

Over breakfast, Lily was teasing Justin about his inability to cope with Joseph's cider.

"I tell you, alcohol is my undoing. One pint of that stuff and I'm anybody's," lamented the bleary-eyed Justin.

"You could say that again," Min commented, passing by the table.

The others laughed. Noah wondered what that was all about. He didn't want to ask and nobody seemed forthcoming with any details.

Arnaud approached the leaders at the end of breakfast to give them a final briefing for the day.

"I think we'll do a loop ride this morning and come back here for lunch. It's so hot just now, I want the children and the ponies to get a good rest at midday. One or two of the kids were feeling a bit dizzy when they got back yesterday afternoon, and want to have a day off, so I'd like to check the others are all okay to go back out in the afternoon."

He turned to Noah and Justin. "I've combined your treks. Katy is going to stay behind with the non-riders and Ray wanted to ride with another group. As you're both a couple of people down, we may as well put you both together.

Noah wondered what was behind Ray's decision to join a different group. Perhaps he didn't want to be involved in any more sheep raising episodes. Or maybe he just wanted to be with a trek leader who had a better rapport with the kids.

That afternoon, Noah and Justin opted to ride through the forest. It was one of Noah's favourite routes and slowly his good humour returned. The sunlight pierced through the foliage, illuminating the young pine trees that were growing alongside the track. This would be a great place to live around Christmas time, Noah decided, thinking how easy it would be to pop into the forest and pick his own tree. The scent of pine filled the air, dulling Noah's senses. He was lulled by the clopping of the ponies' hooves on the track.

"Hey Noah, still awake?" Justin had come to the front of the trek to ride beside him.

"Cor, I'd nearly nodded off," Noah confessed.

"We missed you last night, it was hilarious."

"Yeah, I had a headache."

Justin looked concerned. "Sorry to hear that man. By the way, I was chatting to Min last night. I told her she ought to get her own little restaurant. She'd be great at it, wouldn't she? She's so organised and stuff."

Noah's throat tightened. He muttered, "I'm not sure about the finances though. It would be a lot of money. She wasn't so keen when I spoke to her."

"Oh, that's funny. Min seemed to think she knew somebody who might help her out. She seemed quite up for finding somewhere."

Noah felt like putting his head in his hands. He wondered what had gone wrong with his life. Just when everything seemed so good.

By the time the trek had returned, Noah felt like punching Justin in the face. He hated the unpleasant feelings that were churning in his stomach. He genuinely liked Justin and the two of them had got on well for the first few months at the farm. Now, everything seemed to be unravelling. His first port in a storm nowadays, Noah realised, was Min. Her common sense and steadfast support of Noah had been a huge encouragement in his early days at the centre. But this wasn't something he could talk to Min about. Not when it involved her. Noah thought about chatting to Catherine, and dismissed the idea. He would only sound stupid, jealous and pathetic. Then he had an idea.

After supper, he slipped off alone to his room and picked up the keys to the 2CV. It was sitting in the yard next to the Land Rover, covered in a thick coating of dust. Noah wiped the windscreen with his elbow. It just smeared the grime and made it worse. He opened the door and got inside, turning the key in the engine. It whined into life and he pressed the windscreen squirter. A tiny sputter of water and foam came out and then nothing. It had run out.

Noah got out of the car and went into the kitchen to find a jug. Inside, Justin and Lily were sitting on the counter chatting to Min. Noah gritted his teeth and muttered some pleasantry before grabbing a jug and making his escape. He filled it from an outside tap. He just didn't want to be in the same room as Justin and Min.

He sorted out the windscreen water, wrenched the gearstick into reverse and screeched backwards on the gravel, then crunched forwards, nearly running over a squawking chicken.

"Serve it right," thought Noah the monster.

The car rattled down the lane, leaning over sharply as Noah took the corners at full pelt. Fortunately, there was nothing coming along the road in the other direction. Five minutes later he screeched to a stop and sat in the car, breathing heavily. Then, he swallowed his pride and climbed out, striding down the broken flagstone footpath to the tumbledown cottage entrance. He rapped tentatively on the window. A narrow, friendly face, framed with thick grey curly hair appeared in the window and the door opened.

"Hello." The greeting was friendly.

"Er, hi, I wondered whether…I'm Noah, a friend of Catherine's, and I wondered if I might…"

"Noah, come in, I've heard all about you. I'd be delighted to make your acquaintance. I was just about to make myself a coffee. Would you like one too?" asked Johanna.

# 28

## FIRE

The atmosphere in the cellar was stuffy, which was hardly surprising. Thirty people were crammed into the low-ceilinged room, and the fans that Eve had placed strategically around the space were merely recirculating stale air.

Catherine was regretting her decision. She hadn't anticipated such a big audience.

"I thought you said you normally get about five or six people to these events," she growled to Eve, who was looking delighted at the turn out.

"We do," rejoined the unruffled older woman. "But it's not every day we get to pick the brains of such a famous author."

Eve, as usual, was beautifully turned out. This evening, she was wearing a moss green Indian style skirt and blouse, which she had accessorised with an oversize wooden bead necklace and matching earrings.

It felt strange hearing herself talked about in those terms, but, Catherine grudgingly admitted to herself, ten successful novels did at least give her the right to the title of author. She wasn't sure about the 'famous' bit. The group was meeting in the basement of the bookshop, which had been turned into a miniature café, with a cluster of small tables made from old barrels and an assortment of second hand wooden chairs. An antique sideboard held a selection of drinks and nibbles. Each table boasted a huge beeswax candle, the honey-scented aroma of the burning wax disguising the faint mustiness of the underground room.

The audience was squeezed around the tables, chattering noisily, many of them with notebooks in front of them. Just as Eve was clapping her hands to get everyone quiet, signalling the start of the event, a figure slipped down the stairs and slid along the wall, coming to rest in a chair at the far end of the room. Catherine blinked in the dim light, peering at the newcomer. It was Noah.

Suddenly all eyes in the room were turned on her.

"Okay, let's get cracking. Who's got the first question? Michelle." Eve pointed to a large woman wearing a bright orange smock dress with a chunky silver pendant dangling around her neck.

"What made you start writing in the first place?"

Catherine hesitated, uncomfortable at having to reveal so much of herself. She took a deep breath and plunged in.

"Well, to tell you the truth, my first book was totally fraudulent. It was started by my mother, Amelia Dewar, but never finished. She died in an accident before she had completed the manuscript. Without really thinking about what I was doing, I finished it off and sent it to her publishers. It took a while for the truth to come out, and by that time the novel was in print."

Sitting at the back, Noah could see the frisson that went through the audience. Catherine continued with her story. They lapped up every word. Noah imagined himself in the spotlight, in Catherine's place, at his first 'meet the author' evening. He had a fairly off the wall family background himself, and pictured himself recounting it to his audience, throwing in the odd enhancement or two. Then he noticed that the questions were getting more technical. Catherine was describing tips to keep motivated as a writer. He opened his notepad and began scribbling furiously. This was what he had come for.

Afterwards, when Eve had wrapped up the evening and the visitors had left, just Noah, Eve and Catherine remained. They toasted Catherine's success with the last of the Prosecco. Catherine had resisted a drink beforehand, wanting her wits about her.

"Noah, you little rat. You didn't say you were coming," she said, mussing his hair.

"I didn't want to put you off your stride. I hoped you wouldn't notice me, but I was late. Catherine, you were brilliant."

"She was, wasn't she." Eve was enthusiastic, feeling satisfied that her gamble had paid off.

"Thanks for supporting me Noah." Catherine said.

Noah blushed. "To be honest, I was thinking of me. I realised that all the time I've known you, I've not really picked your brains much about writing. Min said I should come along. She told me if I was really serious about being a writer, I should seize any opportunity to learn more about my craft."

She raised an eyebrow. "Good for Min."

As Catherine drove back to the farm, a huge orange moon was brooding in the velvet sky above the newly-harvested hay fields. Through the open window, she could smell the freshly cut grass, permeating the evening air. Sinister, lumpy shapes in a field turned into cows as she drew nearer. She inhaled deeply and came to a decision.

At the farmhouse, Arnaud was sitting on a wooden bench in the back garden, a glass of brandy in his hand. A faint shuffling noise came from the llamas and sheep in the top paddock. He motioned to Catherine to join him on the bench, putting his arm around her.

"How did it go?"

"Much better than I expected. In fact, I think I even enjoyed it."

Arnaud grinned. "I never thought I would hear you say something like that. My little hermit, happy in such a public situation? How things change."

"Yes," Catherine smiled, and leaned back, relishing the stillness.

Arnaud took a sip of brandy, rolling the liquid around his mouth, savouring it.

"I'm sorry Catherine, I'm rude. Do you want a drink?"

"No, I had a large glass of Prosecco after the talk. I'm quite fizzed up thanks."

She paused, forming the words in her mind, and then ventured, "You were right, Arnaud."

"About what in particular?"

"This place. Coming to Wales."

A slow warmth spread through Arnaud, "You really think so?" He spoke softly.

"Yes. I feel as if I've changed. I'm more myself. At peace. That would never have happened if we hadn't come here."

Arnaud was overjoyed. "That's so good to hear."

"I was thinking too," Catherine paused, "it's not just

me. Look at Noah - he's...he's grown up somehow. He's not a boy any more. Caitlin is more relaxed, even happy. Min's really come into her own with managing the catering. This place seems to have an amazing effect on people."

"Yes," Arnaud agreed. "That's one reason I'm so glad things are moving forward with all the special needs groups. I really think we have something profound to offer them here. I'm excited Catherine. We just need to find a way of making things work financially."

"I've found one," Catherine announced. "How would you like to be co-owner of Kestrel Farm?"

Arnaud sat forward, looking at her.

"What do you mean?"

"Just that. If you could own this place together with Sebastian, would that make you happy?"

Arnaud breathed in. "Of course."

"Well consider it done."

He looked at Catherine quizzically, "I don't understand."

She smiled, enjoying the moment. "Toby has offered to buy the white house. That's one of the reasons he wanted to come over and visit - to talk through the proposal. And unless you have any objections, I intend to accept him."

Arnaud gasped, "No Catherine, that isn't the way to do things! You can't just sell your inheritance for me. I won't let you do that."

She put her hand on his arm, reassuringly, "I'm sorry to say I'm not that generous, Arnaud. I'm doing it for me too. I've been thinking about it ever since I came back from Gull Cove. This is our future now. Here."

Noah heard shouting in the distance, tugging him out of his sleep. He lay still for a few seconds, then sat up and stared at his alarm clock. Seven thirty - he'd overslept. He jumped out of bed, momentarily dizzy and looked around for his riding clothes. A pair of grimy jodhpurs lay on the floor next to a crumpled red T-shirt. He could smell them from where he was standing. Not good.

He glanced over at the wardrobe where a second pair of riding trousers lay on top of a bundle of assorted clothes. They looked marginally cleaner. He padded over to the wardrobe, grabbed a pair of navy boxers and pulled them on, followed by the jodhpurs and two mismatched socks. A faded brown T-shirt completed the ensemble.

Rubbing his eyes, he scrambled down the stairs, crossed the kitchen in three strides and dashed out of the open back door. Outside on the verandah, the boot pile had already been raided. Still half asleep, he pulled on his riding boots and staggered along the little track to the accommodation blocks. Everything was eerily quiet. Noah wondered where all the kids were.

Still not thinking clearly, he crossed the courtyard and emerged opposite the corral. Lily was standing in the far corner, looping headcollars over the fence posts in anticipation of the ponies' arrival up from the lower paddock.

"Hi Lily," Noah called, husky-voiced from sleep.

"Hey Noah, you're up early!"

"Early? I've overslept."

Then it struck him. It was Saturday. He'd got the day off. Doh.

Lily laughed at Noah as he realised what he'd done.

"Oh well, seeing as I'm up, I'll give you guys a hand getting the ponies in," Noah offered. He crossed the corral, ducked under the fence and walked into the field where Goff and Justin were herding the ponies.

Over breakfast, Noah asked about their day.

"I've got a group of adults out this morning," Justin told him. "Then I've got a family this afternoon."

"Goff and I are taking out a group of walkers who are camping the other side of Hay. They've booked in for a day trek, so we thought we'd go to the Black Sheep pub, towards Tregaron." Lily commented.

Justin put his knife and fork down on his plate with a clatter. He'd been frantically scooping sausage, hash browns and beans into his mouth.

"It's going to be a hot one again. I wonder when the weather's going to break," he mused.

"Not anytime soon I hope," Min commented from the kitchen area. "I'm enjoying the change from our usual summer downpours."

"Well I'm off back to bed," Noah said, rising from the table. He'd forced himself to sit down and eat breakfast with Justin. It was an effort, but he'd promised Johanna he would try and man things out.

"Have a good one guys," he offered and walked back to the cottage.

He slumped onto his bed, still fully clothed, and within a few seconds he was out for the count, only waking to hear the faint clop of hooves along the road as the treks left the farm. He turned over and fell into a restless sleep.

Johanna awoke to sunshine streaming into her bedroom. Her head was pounding and her neck ached. She opened her eyes and light danced in front of her pupils. She groaned. A migraine. Opening the drawer of her bedside cabinet, she felt for a packet of painkillers, then looked for her glass of water. It was empty. Loathe to move, she swallowed two pills, gagging slightly at the bitter taste. Then she lay back on the rumpled pillows and closed her eyes.

Half an hour later, she woke again. The thumping seemed louder. It took a couple of moments before she realised the noise was external. Somebody was knocking on her door. She blinked, sat up and cautiously lowered herself off the bed, pulling on her dressing gown. The knocking persisted. By the time she made it to the front door and opened it, the visitor was walking back down the path. He heard the door open and turned back.

"Excuse me - oh sorry to bother you," the delivery driver took in Johanna's dressing gown. "I've got a parcel for Yew Tree Farm. Is that you?"

"No, I'm Yew Tree Farm Cottage. If you go back down the lane - to the left - the turning is about half a mile on your right. Keep following the track - it's quite a way along it.

"Cheers love." The courier turned on his heels and disappeared. Johanna watched him leave, then felt a stinging in her left arm, as if somebody had pricked a needle in it. She looked down and spotted a long-bodied grey horsefly latched on to her forearm.

"Drat," she mouthed and swiped the insect off. She was allergic to horsefly bites and hoped she'd managed catch it in time. Johanna headed for the kitchen to take a couple of precautionary antihistamines. With any luck, they might help her sleep off the migraine too.

In his van, the courier lit up a cigarette and sat for a couple of minutes, giving himself a breather. He'd been on the go since early that morning and was already sweltering in the heat. He started the engine and headed back down the lane, tossing the glowing butt out of the window without a thought.

It landed on a patch of bracken and smouldered for a while. The bracken began to glow red, and soon tiny wisps of smoke curled into the air.

On the edge of the common, the riders in Lily and Goff's trek were getting into their stride. Goff was at the back, chatting to the man in front of him who just happened to be a special needs teacher. They were discussing the challenges of working with that type of pupil. Goff had enjoyed the week with the Bedenham Lodge group and wondered if that was where his future lay. He was aware that time was creeping on and he needed to make a swift decision about what to do next.

Behind them, Justin's trek was a short distance away. He'd opted to take the road past Johanna's cottage, looping round by the waterslide and back through the forest. In the distance, Lily noticed a thin coil of smoke drifting towards edge of the mountain. Before she had time to think about it, she was distracted by somebody in the trek who needed a pit stop. *There's always one*, Lily thought, and looked around for a convenient gorse bush for them to go behind.

A slight breeze fanned the smouldering bracken near Johanna's cottage and it whooshed into flames. They licked along the edge of the dry growth, hungrily consuming the patch of bracken before moving onto some dry twigs and sticks beneath a nearby tree. The flames quickly spread out, fuelled by the bone-dry undergrowth.

Back at the farm, Noah had just finished his second breakfast of the day. In the kitchen, Min was in the process of giving Caitlin a cake making lesson, with Noah lending assistance by licking out the dirty mixing bowls.

"So, the fig, hazelnut and ale cake is a new recipe. I'm not quite sure how it's going to turn out."

"I can't believe I've never done much baking before, it's really good fun," Caitlin was slicing strawberries for a red berry and elderflower praline sponge.

"I suppose you had a cook to do all that kind of stuff for you," said Noah, flippantly.

"Yes, we did actually," replied Caitlin, smiling good-naturedly at Noah's discomfiture.

The outside telephone bell rang, echoing around the yard.

"I'd better get that," Noah commented. "Catherine and Arnaud popped to over Hay. They asked me to keep an ear out."

He gave the cake mixture-covered spoon one final lick and ran out into the yard and over to the farmhouse. Luckily, whoever was calling was patient. He rushed into the kitchen and picked up the receiver. It was Rhys.

"Noah, I've been trying to get Catherine and Arnaud on their mobiles, but there's no answer. Have you got any treks out this morning? There's a fire on the mountain."

Noah muttered an expletive. "Yes we've got two out. Where's the fire?"

"Well the fire service reckon it's over in the direction of Yew Tree Farm, but it's spreading quickly. They've got a number of appliances on their way, but they wanted to alert all the trekking and activity centres as soon as possible."

"No man! That was Justin's route. Lily and Goff were

going to take the other direction, towards Tregaron."

Noah quickly pulled his mobile out of his pocket. No missed calls.

"I've not got any messages from any of the trek leaders on my phone."

"If you run down to the end of the farm track Noah, I'll come and pick you up in the Land Rover. Maybe we can spot Justin's trek if we drive up there. I'm worried about Johanna too. Her cottage is just beyond Yew Tree Farm."

"Of course," Noah hadn't thought about Johanna. "I'll just brief the others and meet you by the lane."

Noah slammed the receiver down, skidded across the farmhouse kitchen floor and out of the door, heart thumping. As he ran, he tried calling Justin's mobile. No answer. In the refectory, they agreed that the girls would stay close to the farm telephone and try to get hold of Arnaud and Catherine. Sebastian was at a hospital appointment in Hereford, uncontactable.

Noah hurtled along the farm track to Rhys's waiting Land Rover, kicking up puffs of dust as he went. In his head, he could see vivid images of panicked ponies, scattering across the mountain. What if their riders fell and couldn't get away from the flames? What if they got cut off and couldn't escape the fire? Was Johanna okay? He felt sick.

Rhys's face was grim. He gave Noah enough time to leap into the Land Rover before they squealed off, the tyres leaving rubber marks on the road. He took the corners at breakneck speed. Somewhere in the distance, Noah could hear the wail of sirens. Ahead, plumes of smoke were spiralling along the bottom edge of the mountain and a pungent, burning smell laced the air.

Noah prayed. Johanna believed in God. Maybe He would help her out and extend the courtesy to Justin and the others as well.

The Land Rover shuddered over the cattle grid and lurched around the bend by the waterslide, nearly skidding on the stream where it crossed the road. Rhys wrenched the wheel back just in time. Then they juddered to a halt, faced with a wall of smoke. Coughing, Noah hurriedly wound up the window next to him. Smoke began to trickle through the edges of the door.

"I'm going to try and get as near to Johanna's cottage as possible. Are you up for that?" Rhys sputtered.

"Yeah, go for it."

The elderly farmer rammed the Land Rover violently into first gear and drove forwards. To their right, they could see the first licks of flame.

Noah muttered another expletive. *Justin - Johanna - Justin - Johanna - Justin - Johanna -* their names whirled around his head like a mantra.

The Land Rover swung round the corner. The smoke was really dense now. It was getting harder to breathe. Rhys suddenly braked and swung the wheel hard around. In front of them was a wall of fire, heading their way. Now they were in danger. He did a quick three-point turn and drove back the way they came, foot on the floor. Noah twisted in his seat to look behind. He could see the flames licking the edges of the trees, darting towards them. Rhys kept his foot hard on the accelerator as they splashed through the waterslide and back along the lane. Half a mile further on, beyond the line of smoke, he came to a halt, wheezing from the fumes.

"There's nothing we can do from this direction. I can't get the Land Rover up onto the mountainside from here either - it's too steep. We'd never make it. The only way to Johanna's cottage is from the other side. We can only hope it's accessible from there." He was panting heavily, and could barely get the words out.

A wailing noise sounded in front of them. Two huge fire engines drove into view, almost taking the gate post with them as they tore over the cattle grid. They stopped next to the Land Rover. Rhys ran out and briefed them. The appliances moved off forwards, towards the fire. Rhys came back to the Land Rover.

"They asked us to keep out of the way for now. We might be needed later if they want beaters. The best thing we can do is get back to the farm and wait. There's other fire engines coming from the other side. They're trying and get to Johanna's cottage and Yew Tree Farm from both directions."

Noah tried for the umpteenth time to reach Justin on his mobile. Nothing. He swallowed.

Rhys headed for the farm. He had to give way to another two fire appliances and a police car en route. Nobody had any news about victims or survivors. The policeman mentioned some horses had been spotted galloping across Hay Bluff, but it wasn't yet clear if they were wild ponies or a trek.

Noah eyes were streaming. He wasn't sure if it was smoke or tears.

He tried a different kind of prayer tack. *God if you let Justin live he can have Min. I won't stand in his way. Just let him live…* He felt guilty that his stupid jealousy had begun to affect their friendship.

Back at Kestrel Farm, Catherine and Arnaud were standing with Min and Caitlin in the yard when Rhys drew to a halt in front of them.

Catherine ran towards the vehicle.

"Are you okay? Your faces!"

She hugged Noah, crying with relief. "Thank God you're safe. I was so worried about you."

Noah couldn't speak. He pulled back and wiped his smarting eyes, noticing for the first time that his clothes and body were covered in black soot from the fire.

"We're fine, but we've no idea about Johanna and the treks," Rhys's voice was hoarse.

Min ran to get them a drink of water.

"We were on our way back from Hay. I picked up your messages as we were coming through Llaneilar," Catherine was telling Rhys.

Noah felt strange. As if everything was happening at a distance.

Arnaud's mobile rang. He answered it immediately.

"Goff," he listened intently.

"All of you? Amazing, thank God. Yes, stay there for now. We'll try and work out how to pick you all up. Well done." He listened some more and then hung up.

"Goff and Lily are okay. They came off the mountainside when they saw the smoke and they're at a farm near Pencader. I'll take the big horsebox and pick them up. Are you all okay to stay here and wait for news of Justin? I'm going to have to do two trips."

"That's fine," Catherine replied. "Do they know anything about Justin's trek?"

Arnaud looked grim. "Only that he stuck to his plan and headed off for the waterslide. That would have taken him right in the path of the fire."

For a few seconds, they were all still, contemplating the thought of what might have happened to Justin and his group. Then Arnaud swung round, "I've got to get going. I want to get Goff and Lily's group back here as soon as possible." He walked swiftly over to the house to pick up the horsebox keys.

Min was tense. "We've still no idea of what's happened to Johanna either. Or anyone at Yew Tree Farm. Dear God…" Noah instinctively put an arm around her shoulders and held her for a few seconds.

It was Caitlin who swung into action, saying, "Noah and Rhys - you need to get plenty of water down you. You've both inhaled a lot of smoke. I'll get my iPad so we can check the regional news and see if there's any more information. Oh and, we need to look at the weather report for the wind direction. We're not massively far away from the fire here. Has anyone thought about what might happen if it comes over this way?"

Nobody had. They all glanced over at the mountains. The entire range in front of them was obscured by smoke. The air smelt sour. Catherine looked at the lower paddock, where the ponies were standing, heads up, sniffing the air. They were restless, shifting.

In the distance, the sound of a siren was coming closer. Caitlin reappeared and opened her iPad. She tried to type in the security code, her fingers shaking. She managed it at the third attempt.

"Go to the weather page first," Rhys prompted, looking over her shoulder anxiously.

And then, "Damn, the wind is in this direction." He glanced across at his farm, just as a huge fire engine stopped outside the gate. A fireman got out and began running down the track towards them.

They rushed to meet him. He looked disheveled.

"We're trying to contain it and make a fire break, but you're going to have to be prepared to evacuate in a hurry if we need you to. Forget about the horses. Just get your cars ready and some bottles of water to hand.

*Forget about the horses.* Catherine's heart sank.

Rhys was on the ball. "If we have to leave, let the horses out of the bottom of the paddock by the stream. It's running low at the moment. They can make their way down there towards the village."

It made sense. There was an old gate they could open at the foot of the slope. If they had time.

"I'm going to have to get back to my own stock," Rhys turned to go. Catherine hated the thought of him heading off on his own.

"Stay safe," she shouted after him and looked up at the mountain. She checked her phone and thought of Johanna, Justin and his trek.

*Please God…* she prayed, echoing Noah's plea.

# 29

# JUSTIN

Murphy snorted and flared his nostrils. Justin didn't usually ride the large black cob, but Willow, his lead pony, had thrown a shoe the day before. Unfamiliar with the horse as he was, he could still see something was bothering the animal. Then Justin smelled smoke. He scanned the mountainside, trying to spot where it was coming from, but a line of trees to his left was obscuring the view. Behind him, his group of riders began muttering. They'd been walking on the mountains the past few days and were familiar with the fire warnings put out by the authorities. Justin halted Murphy and peered through the trees in front of him. He turned in the saddle, facing the trek.

"I don't like this," he called back, wondering whether they should turn and head back to Kestrel Farm straight away.

A cry from the man at the back of the trek. "It's behind us, look!"

Now they could all see wisps of smoke snaking towards them through the trees.

Several of the ponies were tossing their heads, uneasy.

"Right, I'm going to need you all to stay calm." Justin

had a lump in his throat and the words sounded a bit hoarse. He swallowed hard and spoke again.

"I'm going to continue on at a steady trot. The last thing we want to do is spook the ponies and have them bolting. Keep in line please."

He turned to face the front and squeezed Murphy's flanks. The big horse needed no encouragement. He surged forwards and Justin had to pull hard to keep him steady. This wasn't looking good.

Johanna woke coughing. She had been dreaming she was suffocating. Her breath was raspy in her throat. The smell of smoke filled the cottage. She blinked, trying to clear her head and then it dawned on her. Fire.

She rushed to the front door of the cottage and saw flames licking the undergrowth at the end of the pathway. Smoke filled the lane. There was no exit that way. Johanna grabbed a T-shirt from a chair and hurried to the kitchen, soaking it under the tap. Wrapping it around her face, she opened the front door and ran towards the back of the cottage.

A steep bank, topped by a wire fence, enclosed the short rear garden. She was going to have to climb up. Her legs already felt like jelly. A waft of hot air came from behind her, giving her impetus. She ran for the bank and started climbing, feet slipping on the rocks that littered the earth. There were enough exposed roots to help and she began to pull herself up, slowly.

*Don't look down, don't look back, just keep going,* she told herself.

The air was heavy with smoke now, and the riders were struggling to keep the horses under control. Justin was tempted to let them make a run for it, but the terrain was uneven, broken with steep gullies that had to be carefully navigated.

A crackle to their left caused Justin to glance round to see a spurt of orange flames. He swore. This was bad. His mind was racing, trying to think strategically. His only hope was to keep going forwards, around the track and head for Hay Bluff and open ground. If they climbed upwards, the flames would follow, too fast for escape.

Then, one of the riders shouted at him.

Justin turned and saw a woman the other side of a wire fence, clinging to it. Smoke was rolling behind her. She seemed stuck, shouting at them. Justin kicked Murphy, hard. The horse resisted, then moved to the left, towards the woman. She leaned onto the fence and threw herself over the top, staggering. Murphy started, surprised. The woman had wrapped a T-shirt around her face to help against the smoke. She looked strange and it occurred to Justin that she was scaring the horse.

"Unwrap your face. Walk slowly over towards me," he shouted.

She nodded and peeled off the green shirt, revealing a wrinkled face and damp, grey hair. Justin slid off Murphy. The smoke was curling up towards them.

"You're going to have to get up with me," he thanked heaven he'd ended up riding Murphy today. The big horse was strong enough to carry two riders. The elderly woman, dressed in leggings and an old shirt, came alongside Justin.

"Put your foot in the stirrup," he commanded, holding it for her, reins looped over his arm. Murphy was shifting, not making it any easier for them, "then jump, and I'll push you."

The woman nodded, seemingly unable to speak. She coughed hoarsely and raised her foot, barely able to reach the stirrup. Justin grabbed her and virtually slung her onto the horse. Her body was skinny and light.

"Sit forwards," he pulled her foot out of the stirrup and placed his own boot there. Holding the back of the saddle, he swung himself up behind the old lady.

Murphy moved forward a pace, nearly unbalancing Justin. The horses were snorting, close to panic.

*Come on, come on*, Justin told himself. He glanced at the rest of the riders and kicked the big horse forwards, aiming to ride a loop around the smoke to their left. The group was quiet, trusting Justin to get them out of the situation.

If only the ground was flatter, they could make better speed. Justin cursed the gullies in their way, peering past the woman in front of him. She rasped a thank you, as Murphy picked his way down a steep slope, and then ran up the other side. Justin could barely bring him back to an even pace as they reached the top of the gully. Behind him, Duster cannoned into the back of Murphy. Now Justin had a better view. Smoke was pouring onto the bottom of the hillside in front of them. He turned and gasped in shock. The bracken on the foothills was catching. They were going to have to up their speed or they'd never make it.

He shouted back at the white-faced riders behind him.

"Sorry guys, if we don't make a dash for it, we'll be stuck. Sit up straight, give your horses a loose rein, hold the saddle in front of you and grab a chunk of mane. If you come off, yell, and I'll try and swing back to help.

"Okay, let's go," Tony, the group organiser shouted back.

"Follow me, as much as you can," Justin shouted and kicked Murphy.

The big horse rolled into a canter. There was just one more gully, and then the ground levelled out. Justin prayed they would make it. Prayed that nobody would fall off.

Murphy skidded down the incline at a much faster pace than Justin would have liked, but it was their only hope. The horse clambered up the other side, and notched up a gear. Justin allowed himself a swift glance back. The horses behind had all cleared the gully with their riders onboard. Then he turned and clung on.

There was nothing he could do now. Murphy had taken the bit and was racing, eating up the ground. Justin couldn't have stopped him if he'd tried. He focused on balancing, trying to stay on. It wasn't easy with the woman in front of him. His arms were wrapped around her sides, hands grabbed onto Murphy's reins and a handful of mane. He could feel himself slipping to one side and he shifted position, trying to right himself. Behind, he could hear the thud of hooves on the turf.

A movement to his right caught his eye. Duster was drawing level with the now panting Murphy. The big horse was tiring under the strain of two riders.

Justin squinted ahead of him, eyes watering. The common stretched out in front. A clear patch of green, with no bracken. The smoke was now behind them. If they could just make it a bit further, hopefully they could put enough distance between them and the fire to sort themselves out.

Justin pointed in front of him, waving at the common. The rider nodded, bouncing in the saddle. He managed to aim Duster in the right direction.

Over the noise of hooves and the horses' rasping breaths, Justin could hear the wail of sirens. Then he spotted the fire engine, screaming along the edge of the common. He hoped desperately the sight of it wouldn't spook the horses further up the hillside. He swung Murphy's head down to the left more, and prayed the horses behind would follow.

In front, he could see sheep scudding across the mountainside, panicking. A herd of wild horses was standing near the top of Hay Bluff, whinnying and wheeling around.

Underneath him, Murphy stumbled slightly. The horse was breathing heavily. Justin eased back on the reins, and glanced over his shoulder. There was now some distance between them and the fire, although he could see it was gaining in intensity, flames licking up the bottom slopes of the hillside behind the cottage where he had picked up the woman.

A final push and they'd reached the road intersecting the middle of the common. It seemed as good a place as any to stop. Two more huge red fire engines came tearing up the road from Hay. Murphy started, and began to race again, away from the fire engines, but he was too exhausted to keep up the pace, dropping to a trot and then a walk.

Justin could sense another horse just behind him. He looked around. It was Saffron, the chubby palomino mare. Her rider was barely in the saddle. As the horses drew to a halt, the man slid off Saffron and sat on the ground. The palomino mare stood, flanks heaving.

Justin swung his leg over Murphy's back and slipped off the tall horse, landing heavily on the ground, knees jarring. He turned to help the woman, but she was already slithering down. He meant to ask her if she was okay, but his voice sounded distant over the ringing in his ears. The ground seemed to be spinning in front of him.

Then, shouting and a strong arm grabbed hold of him. A man in uniform was asking him something. He couldn't focus and slid to the ground, propping his head up in his hands.

A jolt, as somebody shook him roughly.

"How many riders?" The voice seemed distant. Justin rubbed his eyes, and the world came back into focus.

A fireman was bending down on one knee in front of him, asking, "How many riders in the group? Do you know?"

Justin tried to assemble his muzzy thoughts. "Er, six, well seven with me. And eight with the woman."

The fireman shouted something back over his shoulder.

Then he grinned at Justin. "We've got you all. Now let's get you out of here."

Justin breathed a raspy sigh of relief.


It was Noah who answered the phone. He could barely understand Justin's hoarse voice.

"Speak up mate, I can't hear you. Are you okay?" His heart thudded in his chest.

"Yeah, yeah, we're all okay. And the horses. They're a bit knackered and I think Murphy's strained something. Sorry."

"Thank God. Where are you?"

"At some farm. We came down off the mountain. I'll let the farmer explain where." A rustling noise, then a loud voice with a broad Welsh accent came on the line.

"Lucky to be alive they are. Amazing. It's David

Morgan here."

"Are they all okay?" Noah needed to be sure.

"They're fine. A few bruises, and the old lady's a bit shaken up, but they're okay. Now let me explain where we are, it's a bit remote…"

"Hang on," Noah interrupted, "old lady?" There had been no women in the trek at all. Let alone an old lady.

He could hear a muffled noise in the background. Then the farmer's voice again, "Apparently she's called Johanna."

Noah's shout brought the others running. "They're fine, and it sounds like Johanna's with them!"

He turned back to the phone, trying to make sense of the farmer's directions.

Noah didn't notice, but he was crying again by the time he'd finished the conversation with Justin. He looked at Catherine, Min and Caitlin, babbling, "They're okay, they're okay."

The three women were in tears too.

Noah looked up at the mountain in front of him. The wind had changed direction, away from the farm, and now the flames were being fanned up the mountainside. He could see the glowing red fire, nibbling away at the brown patches. There were huge swathes of black as well, where chunks of the hillside had been consumed by the flames.

Catherine's mobile rang. She picked it up, quickly and listened.

"That's great, thank you. Okay."

She wiped her eyes, and turned the group.

"That was the fire brigade. They think they've managed to establish a fire break at the bottom of the hillside. We should be okay, even if the wind changes direction back again. But we're still on standby, just in case.

She breathed heavily.

"I'm going to put the kettle on." Caitlin announced. Noah looked at his watch. It was only midday. It felt like days had passed.

"Tea and food. I'm starving," he said and followed Caitlin to the kitchen, with Min and Catherine hard on their heels.


Noah drove behind the Land Rover in his 2CV, hoping Catherine was able to make sense of the farmer's directions. The car whined as the gradient grew steeper and Noah slipped down a gear.

Catherine was anxious to get all the riders from Justin's group back to the centre as soon as possible and Noah had agreed to help. The farmer had offered to keep the ponies in his field overnight to let them recover from their ordeal.

A twist to the left and a black metal sign came into view. Hillside Farm. Not original, but apt, Noah thought.

Catherine swung through the gates over the cattle grid and Noah followed, his teeth chattering as the Citroën rumbled over the metal bars.

Outside the farmhouse, a group of people were sitting on the ground talking. Noah glanced at them. No Johanna. Maybe, she was inside. Then he spotted Justin. He opened the car door and ran, enveloping him in a bear hug.

"Justin! Flipping heck man, I thought you were a gonner…"

"Cheers mate," came the reply.

Noah could tell Justin appreciated the hug. He looked

pale and his eyes were red.

"It was a bit touch and go," Justin admitted. "I'm just amazed nobody fell off."

"We were so worried about you. We didn't know if you were all dead or not. Somebody had spotted some horses bolting across the mountain and we didn't know if it was you or a wild herd. I thought you'd all been burned to a crisp," Noah was aware he was jabbering on, but he couldn't stop. "Rhys and I nearly got caught in it too. It was terrifying. I'm sorry I've been so distant recently. I've just been a jealous pig but it's okay. You can have Min. I promised God if you survive you can have Min. She's yours mate."

Justin frowned, trying to follow what Noah was saying. "Huh?"

"Min. I did a deal with God. I said I wouldn't try and stand in your way if He would save you and He did."

"Noah what are you talking about? Min? Why would I want Min and what would I do with her?"

Noah began to feel ever so slightly stupid. "You mean you don't fancy her?"

"Of course not. Why would I? I don't mean that rudely, but she's not my type. I...I liked Caitlin, but I think Goff's stolen a march on me there." Justin shrugged and added, "Anyway, everybody knows Min's got the hots for you Noah. We're all just wondering when you're going to do something about it. The poor girl's been hanging on..."

Noah was breathless.

"Me? You mean...?"

"Yes," replied Justin, sighing and rolling his eyes heavenwards, "you, Noah."

# 30

## THAT'S IT FOR NOW

Noah sat in the cottage garden, watching sparks dancing in the air above the fire pit. The smell of smoke in his nostrils brought back a sudden rush of memories of the fire on the mountain. Had it only been a few weeks ago? It felt like years. Already, new green shoots were pushing their way up through the scorched patches on the foothills. And now, as they rode out, the whole countryside had a softer, sleepy feel as if anticipating the long winter ahead. The hum of tractors and combines could be heard until late into the night, bringing in the harvest and even in early September, there was a slight bite to the evening air.

He took a long sip of beer from the can in his right hand. His left arm was wrapped around Min, who was sitting next to him. It felt good.

The crackling, contorting flames lit up ten pairs of eyes, shining in the reflected glow. Noah couldn't believe it would all be coming to an end soon. It had been an enchanted summer, Noah reflected. Outdoors every single day, senses attuned to the wealth of life around him, learning how to read the subtle signs from his pony that told him something was coming around the next corner. His face was weathered, his hands rough and his body felt good - fitter than he could ever have imagined. But more than that, he felt a peace in his soul. 'Living in Eden' was how Johanna had put it. 'We were created in a garden and we find ourselves best in nature,' was her theory and Noah thought it made sense. There was a rightness about the existence they had been leading.

Catherine looked at the trek leaders, gathered around the fire; Caitlin and Lily were discussing the merits of bitless bridles; Justin was trying out a new song on his guitar; Goff, Sebastian and Arnaud were deep in conversation over the other side of the fire pit and Noah and Min were both looking abstractedly into the flames. It had been a year of so many surprises, trials and joys. And new people in her life.

She smiled when she thought of bumping into Johanna. How amazing that she should come to Wales and meet somebody who had known her parents. And how truly incredible that she had been able to put the ghosts of her past to rest. She made a mental note to visit Johanna again soon. The fire seemed to have left her a bit older, frailer. Johanna's cottage was nothing more than a heap of charred timber and bare, fire-scorched brick walls. All her possessions had been destroyed. Typical of Johanna, Catherine thought, to see the positive in the situation.

"It's about time I came in from the cold. This was the nudge I needed," had been the older woman's comment to Catherine.

She was now living in a little Christian community in the middle of Hay, and helping Eve out in the bookshop. Catherine thought the word 'nudge' was a bit of an understatement, grateful that Johanna had suffered no lasting ill-effects from the fire.

Goff stood up unsteadily, weaving gently in a vague imitation of the flames. The local cider did that to you, Noah reflected. Goff's eyes travelled around the fire pit, drawing everybody's attention.

"I'd like to propose a toast," he proclaimed. "To Arnaud, Catherine and Sebastian, for giving us the best summer of our lives."

Noah heard Catherine's indrawn breath.

"Absolutely!"

"Hear! Hear"

"Well wicked!"

The comments from the other trek leaders echoed around the garden as glasses were raised.

Arnaud pushed himself up stiffly from where he had been sitting on the ground and put his arm around Goff's shoulders. Arnaud was pretty unsteady too, Noah noticed.

"And a toast to you guys for being the most amazing bunch of trek leaders. We could not have done this summer without you. And truly, you are our family now. All of you."

Reminiscences were bandied around the group; the time Goff had ridden for half the morning facing backwards in the saddle for a dare; Caitlin and Lily's race across the common on Willow and Gizmo, ending in a neck and neck draw; the rainstorm after the big fire that had left the hillside a blackened, steaming swathe; the made-up stories they had told to fool the kids...

Noah turned to Min.

"Are you excited about your tea room?"

"You bet. And even more excited that I'll be running it with Lily."

"Have you thought of a name yet?"

"We're just mulling over a few ideas. Goff suggested 'Curiositea' or 'Infinitea'..."

Noah groaned. Life, he thought, was full of unexpected surprises. He'd never have guessed that Lily would have ended up going into business with Min. She was really excited about putting her business education into practice, in, as she'd said, "a far more interesting environment than spending my day with a bunch of farts in the City." It turned out her father was something high up in the government and had offered to put some money into the venture. Noah thought it was a pretty safe investment. There was no doubt the two girls would make a success of the venture. He guessed it wouldn't be long before they expanded into a full-blown restaurant.

Catherine was now chatting to Lily and Caitlin. Lily was enthusiastically outlining the plans for the new venture.

"Where's the tea shop going to be?" Caitlin asked.

"In that run-down old building near Eve's bookshop on the market square. Arnaud, Sebastian and Noah are going to give us a hand to refurbish it - when the season's finally finished. We're aiming to be up and running by the end of October. I know Hay will be quieter in the winter, but it will give us a chance to get bedded in for when the tourist season starts next spring."

Min already had ideas for a dozen new cake recipes she wanted to try. She couldn't wait to get started, and Justin was helping them to design a logo and business stationery.

"How about you Caitlin? What are you doing next?" Catherine felt bad that she hadn't asked her before now.

Caitlin swallowed. "I was talking to my father yesterday. I...I kind of made it up with him and he's asked again if I want to go and help out with the stud farm. A few months ago, it was the last thing I wanted to do. But, well, I thought I'd give it a go. Who knows, I might even enjoy it. I need to try and patch up things with my parents if I can. And anyway," she blushed slightly, "Goff said he'll come and drag me away if I'm really unhappy."

Catherine smiled to herself. She'd never have put Goff and Caitlin together, but they made a good couple. Goff was a strong enough character to handle Caitlin and she seemed genuinely happy to be with him.

"Has he heard about his college place yet?" she asked Caitlin.

"No, he should find out in the next couple of days."

Goff had applied for a last minute placement to do special needs training.

"Well, do remind him he's welcome to come back here and help out here with our new activities, when he's finished. Glen's cousin Carol called me yesterday. They want to place a whole lot more groups with us next season and we're applying for a grant to develop the farm in that direction. All being well, we'll need extra staff who have that kind of skill set."

"Will do," Caitlin promised her. "And I gather that you and Arnaud are now part owners of Kestrel Farm. Congratulations."

Catherine smiled, "Yes, Sebastian very kindly accepted our offer."

Caitlin glanced at her and said wryly, "I bet he was only too pleased to do so. I know he's enjoying the rural life nowadays, but I can't see Sebastian wanting to work at the farm full-time. I'm sure he's happier with a job in Hereford and letting you guys have free rein, if you pardon the pun."

Catherine admitted, "You're right. I think he needs the stimulation of an office environment, and that's fine by us."

Then, more softly, "Are you happy now Caitlin?" She kept the phrase deliberately ambiguous.

"Yes," Caitlin grinned, "I realised I was just chasing a fantasy. Goff's much more fun that Sebastian ever was."

Justin played a final riff on his guitar and put it down. Noah leaned across Min towards him. "Oh, I meant to say Justin, you can have my old room when you move into the white house if you like. Catherine and Arnaud have said I can base myself here during the uni holidays."

"I couldn't do that," Justin protested.

"Course you can, it's going begging and you don't have to pay my dad rent. Well, not until you're a famous artist."

"I owe you one mate," Justin's eyes were shining. He couldn't believe how things had worked out. Toby had plans to develop the white house into an art centre. As part of the project, he was looking for a talented young artist to sponsor and Justin fitted the bill. At the end of the trekking season, in a couple of weeks' time, Justin was going to move into the white house and work alongside Toby.

"Good news about your course mate, by the way."

"Yeah, I can't wait to get started. Noah's career as an author stretched in front of him. He'd been accepted onto the Aberystwyth creative writing course.

"Easy for visits back here," he commented.

Min smiled.

From his position, curled up on an old blanket behind Noah, Oscar listened to the banter and yawned loudly. It was long past his food time and everybody seemed to have forgotten him. Then, he spotted a sausage that had fallen off the grill. It was a bit burned, but Oscar wasn't fussy.

# ABOUT THE AUTHOR

Ellie Philpott grew up near the East Kent coast. Some of her earliest memories are of digging for shellfish along the shoreline and sailing with her father in his small dinghy. She has always been passionate about horses, and has owned and worked with them at various times.

Her career began at the BBC's Foreign Affairs Unit, followed by a spell at Hodder & Stoughton publishers. She then went on to edit and write for an interior design magazine, before taking up the role of communications manager for an international human rights agency. She now works as a freelance writer. Her 'leisure' hours are spent growing vegetables, keeping bees and ducks, and making cosmetics from her own beeswax and honey.

Made in the USA
Columbia, SC
26 February 2018